AF481314

PROPHECIES OF THE BIBLE

UNDERSTANDING THE SINGS OF THE LAST TIMES

"I saw, but not understanding I asked: My Lord, how will be the end of these things? And, He replied: Go Daniel, that these things are closed and sealed until the time of the end. The wicked do not understand but those who have understanding will understand" (Daniel 12, 8).

Carlos Quevedo G.

PROPHECIES OF THE BIBLE

Understanding the signs of the last times

Dedicated to:
All those who with reverent fear wait
 eagerly for the return of our Lord Jesus Christ.

Note.
This work was written more than 30 years ago; but for some reason it was never published openly to the public, until now it is spreading through social networks

Email: misionescatolicas@gmail.com

INDEX

CHAPTER V.
POSSIBLE POLITICAL AND PROPHETIC EVENTS.

CHAPTER VI
ERRORS OF THE END OF TIMES AND OTHER EXTRA-BIBLE PROPHECIES

INTRODUCTION

Finally, **"the history of salvation"** of humanity, is about to come to an end. From the fall of man to its restoration through the redemptive work of Jesus and his next and announced second coming several thousand years have passed; during which humanity has expected the definitive restoration of the state of corruption and death to its original state of communion and life with God its Creator.

Never before have the signs of recent times been more precise and clear; however, as in the first coming of Jesus, few were and currently few are those who will realize the imminent arrival of the Son of Man.

Much has to do with this carelessness of the people, the very well planned and subtle work of the enemy of God, who for some time was sending to many sects; so that they announced their second coming falsely and in advance, so this announcement is currently totally discredited and few believe that this is true.

This has resulted in the majority of members of the Catholic Church; especially the clergy, in an effort to differentiate and contradict the thousands of sects (whom they consider ignorant, apocalyptic and liars); have taken an attitude of total indifference about the second coming of Jesus.

Apart from this, there is the attitude of the modern man, very much given to pride, who has put all his trust and his heart in science, technology, fashion, the media, sex and sensuality; This lack of Christian values in modern life has led humanity to move away from God; therefore, there is a great indifference to the sacred and spiritual realities and it seems that no one cares about Jesus' next return.

But, even with all this confusion and indifference that Satan has created, the prophecies that once were dark and diffuse have become clear and transparent to the understanding of those who love God. As time goes by, the advancement of technology and the fulfillment of many signs has put us in a position to deduce what will happen to humanity in a few more years and so in that way, what God told him to the prophet Daniel comes true:

"Go Daniel, that these things are closed and sealed until the time of the end ..." (Dan. 12, 8).

With what makes us understand that at the time of the end, these prophecies will open for understanding and salvation of those who love God and seek the truth.

According to the Holy Scriptures, shortly before the second coming of Christ there will be several signs both in heaven and on earth and there will be (apparently normal) events in the political, economic, social and religious life of men, aimed at achieving the wellness of the people; but this is just a costume that the Antichrist presented by Satan will wear as a great and charismatic leader politician; who in a short time will manage to dominate humanity and finally proclaim himself God.

Most nations of the earth will participate in these events. Israel, Egypt, the Arab nations, the United States of America, The European Union, Russia, will be the main protagonists, including in the end the Asian giant of China. When all the nations that are still standing meet to make war on Christ, accused of being an extra-terrestrial intruder who has dared to come to earth announcing himself with great majesty and glory and with a great sign in the sky.

This event of the end of time written in the Bible and explained in this work: **"Prophecies of the Bible," Understanding the Signs of the End Times "** is also supported by the analysis of historical and political events past and present, as also in prophecies and predictions of other holy men and especially of the messages of the Virgin Mary that have been continuously appearing and who mentions that the end of this political, social, economic and religious system is coming to an end; To begin a new one under the direction and reign of Christ Jesus, who will not only reign justly, but humanity will recover its lost conditions and attributes as a consequence of sin.

In short, humanity is running towards its destruction and condemnation, so I sincerely believe that it is an obligation, to warn to the people of the latest events that will happen next to the coming of the **King of kings** and **Lord of lords**. Otherwise, it would be to hide the truth selfishly and we would not have a clear conscience; It is therefore more than a duty to give humanity warning of the pains to which it will be subjected for its terrible sins and the great change that is coming, with the hope that many will reflect, change their attitude, repent and be saved.

These books are the studies of the prophecies of the second coming of our Lord Jesus Christ, and remember what the Holy Mother Catholic Church had been saying since centuries ago.

We believe that it is the Will of the Lord Jesus: to remind humanity, that it is time to change course; As the night progresses, the day is near (Romans, 13, 11-14) and that after all, these sufferings and catastrophes will purify humanity for its sake and for the implantation of a new social, political and economic order, under the reign of Christ Jesus, our King and Lord.

The first part of this book is a brief explanation of why we live in a world full of evil, suffering, injustice, disease, and death; followed by the plan of redemption that God has prepared; in order to better understand the following chapters, whose topics have more to do with the current and future events predicted by Jesus and his prophets. May God allow that this humble work, wake up from lethargy, indifference and deception in which many find themselves and instill encouragement and joy; because although there are going to be very terrible events that will cause fright and terror, the Lord Jesus will soon be here on Earth to change this oppressive and painful life, full of miseries and sufferings; freeing us from all evil influence; For only when He will be here, the Beatitudes will come true, the meek will possess the Earth, the afflicted will be comforted; Those who were hungry and thirsty for justice, the clean in heart will see God... (Mt. 5, 1-12).

It is important to mention that to write this book, we have asked for the light of the Holy Spirit to guide us towards the truth.

I hope, in the name of Jesus our Lord, that this book fulfills the purpose imposed and open the eyes of the people to the great events of the last times; but above all, fulfill its main mission, to achieve sincere conversion and total surrender to Jesus and work to spread his Holy Gospel for the salvation of souls.

The Author

CHAPTER I.

WHY DO WE LIVE IN A WORLD OF INJUSTICE AND EVIL?

GENERAL VIEW OF THE BIBLE

Before beginning the study of the prophecies of the Bible, I thought it convenient to make a very brief account of what this holy book is; because without it, it is possible that many readers will not understand everything that is going to be treated.

One of the most widely read books in the world is the Bible; However, the vast majority of people do not give it the importance and seriousness it deserves. They think that the Holy Scriptures are simply stories that were part of Jewish folklore. Even the same ecclesiastical authorities of different Christian Protestant denominations were the first to doubt that the Bible is truly the Word of God.

By the 1800s, from the Protestant theological seminars in Germany, a group of liberal biblical schoolchildren, called the "High Critical School," began to doubt the historical facts of the Bible. Using literary methods of analysis (without relying on the science of archaeology), they rejected most of the biblical books, especially those of Moses, discarding supernatural facts and attributing these books to different unknown authors.

All these protestants flatly denied any supernatural manifestation, simply giving it the category of Jewish mythology. This type of thinking spread throughout Europe and America, so now it is no longer rare to find professors, priests and pastors in most universities or colleges who teach biblical and theological courses simply as literature, or political and social postulates. Many of these even show hostility towards the acceptance of Christian doctrine, and especially of any subject that speaks of something supernatural and miraculous.

What began with the High Critical School of Germany and with the different currents of thought that followed immediately, and lately with the theology of liberation within the Catholic Church; They have led humanity almost to the total rejection of the Bible as a historically true document and even worse as a source of prophecy or prediction of the future. Ironically, the Bible has been discredited and discarded because of the non-acceptance of the supernatural; However, by the 60s of the 20th century, a new stream of esoteric thinking and beliefs began to grow and now enjoy a considerable boom. Most people accept and believe in extrasensory perception, spiritualism, witchcraft, astrology, Asian philosophies and religions and an endless number of rare phenomena. Universities and colleges, especially in the United States and Europe, have their own witches, as satanic churches have also become popular. The majority of modern music groups, especially the so-called heavy metal or heavy rock, are faithful devotees of Satan and in their music they send hidden messages to the naive receptive public, encouraging the follow-up of these abominable practices.

"What is happening with the continuous development of these aberrations, evils and beliefs, both inside and outside the same religious institutions, is not a mere coincidence; Behind all this, there is a mysterious character who works hard to discredit what does not suit him; but at the same time it keeps afloat beliefs that are going to serve its future purposes (which we have already begun to witness). This being does not want a world that rejects the supernatural, he wants a religious, credulous and superstitious world, because that way he can lay the groundwork for later worshiping as a god in the person of the future world leader better known as the Antichrist." (Lindsey Hall)

One of his first steps has been to discredit the Bible so that his plans remain hidden and not discovered, he wants a religious world but one that rejects the personal relationship that God offers to humanity through Jesus Christ.

This character of darkness, to a certain extent has achieved its mission, of making most people reject or not give the necessary importance to the Holy Book inspired by God; because it is right there, where the plans that this being plans to carry out are revealed.

But it has also caused that many who do believe in the Bible be fanaticized so much, that they have become biblical idolaters, considering the Bible as a magical oracle, draw their own generally wrong conclusions and create their own churches separate from the true Church; which constitutes an even greater evil with respect to those who do not believe. Currently there are more than 21,000 sects that swarm the world, all claiming to be the true ones; but in reality they do nothing but confuse and divide humanity, which is a great achievement in favor of God's enemy. We know that God is almighty and will not leave humanity helpless. At the end of time the Holy Spirit will pour out his wisdom on many so that all the

People of goodwill will be saved. But, we must be very careful, because from these same biblical promises the false prophets sent by Satan take advantage of, to confuse and turn people away from God.

"Be careful that nobody cheats you. Because many will come posing as me, and they will deceive many people. You will hear that there are wars here and there; but don't be scared, because that's how it has to happen". (Matthew 24.5)

Also, there are many people who believe that the Bible is the compilation of past events, which can serve as fantastic comics to tell children; others find it boring and even meaningless; But these people do not see the truth, for they look in the opposite direction than they should; they look from the perspective of a historian who only directs his gaze to the past; but the Bible is not past, it is future, and that is why the vast majority of people do not realize the message contained in the Holy Book. On the other hand, the Bible is "Mystery", although it presents a message, not everyone can understand it, so it is necessary the assistance of the Magisterium of the Church, without being confused with the teachings of some infiltrated theologians, who act as teachers but in the end they deny fundamental truths that confuse and lose many.

"Beware of false prophets, who come to you in sheep's clothing, but inside they are rapacious wolves" (Mt. 7:15)

Likewise, before so many manifestations and warnings of the end of this system made by the Virgin Mary and by many saints and prophets, all believing Christians should be changing lives, approaching God and reading the Holy Scriptures, to at least try to understand what the prophecies say about the end, which by the way will not be the end of the Earth in physical form, but will be the end of the world system in which we live, related to the spiritual, social and economic aspect; producing a total change in the way of living, thinking, acting and even nature itself will change from the current, inhospitable, unhealthy state of suffering and destruction, to its original state of harmony, justice, love and beauty; because we will be under the command and direction of the Messiah himself, and of course we will no longer have the evil influence of the enemy. Only then will we experience the true liberation of evil that many today confuse with a political, superficial and misunderstood liberation.

However, few are those who feel that mood and joy mixed with some fear for the events that will happen.

Few read the Bible out of curiosity, curiosity that we could even call it holy, because if we wanted to know the truth through the Holy Scriptures source of divine inspiration, many would be saved.

Unfortunately, those who seek to know the future, do so by other means, on the side of darkness, through horoscopes, witches, fortune tellers and sorcerers, who cannot tell the truth because they cannot inhabit the light in them, and in Consequently they spread confusion and evil among the inhabitants of this world.

"The Bible has many writers, but only one is its Author. At the time of its formation, this Book had very little of the past, some of the present, but almost everything of the future." (Armageddon, Arthur E. Bloomfield)

If we want to understand the Bible it is necessary to realize that its Author has a plan for humanity, which begins with Genesis and ends with the book of Revelation.

The purpose of the Bible is equal to that of a map that tells us the way and the end of our destiny. If we are lost in the desert where there is nothing but sand or in a forest where everything is confusing through the weeds and trees, we will leave there, as long as there is something to guide us with, the Bible is our map and our compass, with it we will go out of the woods, out of the deserts we have in life, out of the stormy oceans of our existence.

The Bible is prophecy and its message focuses on the restoration of humanity to its original state, such as when it was created and enjoyed direct communication with its Creator. Restoration that is done through the envoy of God, Jesus the Messiah. All the prophets speak of Him, of the time he came and was born among men, of his life as a teacher and of his death for the sins of mankind and his resurrection, hope of the righteous. But, he also speaks of his second coming; He no longer comes as the lamb humiliated and slaughtered; but as the "triumphant and glorious King" who returns to take possession of his kingdom forever. It also tells us about the purest "Woman", that God prepared and destined as his daughter, wife of the Holy Spirit and mother of the incarnate Son; whom all generations will call her Blessed, for her leading role in the redemption of humanity (Lk. 1, 48)

When we read the Bible, let's try to put ourselves in the time and place in which the prophets lived; because to explain the visions they saw; events that would take place hundreds and hundreds of years ahead of their time, with different civilizations than they knew, with very changed ways of life, and with a technology of hundreds of years more advanced; from which perhaps nothing understood. They had to adapt their language and explanations to the times and environment in which they lived and met.

Thus, when the apostle John says, that the sun was darkened and that the moon was dyed with blood; Their explanations agree exactly with the consequences and results of a nuclear war.

"... And the sun turned black like sackcloth and the moon became all like blood" (Rev. 6,12)

Recently, The Academy of Sciences of the United States; one of the most prestigious in the world, in its 190-page study, called: "The Nuclear Winter" and the commission of the Department of Defense of that same country; reaffirmed the theory of nuclear winter already announced in 1983. Where it is found that atomic explosions pollute the environment and raise such an amount of radioactive dust, that sunlight would be very dim or void (the sun went black) and the moon would look red (the moon was dyed with blood). Vision Magazine, Special Report. 1-85

"And was thrown into the sea like a great mountain, burning ..."

"And a great star fell from the sky, burning like a torch ..."

"And the third part of the sun and the third part of the moon were wounded ... so that it became dark ... the day lost its brightness." (Revelation 8, 8-12)

Could be these mountains and stars, rockets or intercontinental missiles? in the distance one of these will look like a meteor (mountain of fire) but closer is exactly like a great torch.

When we read the Bible, we also don't expect to understand everything, because only when those days come is when the prophecies will be clarified to the understanding of those who seek the truth from the heart. **"And He said to me: Daniel, close the book and put a seal on it until the end of time ..."**

"You must leave Daniel because these things must be kept secret and hidden until the time comes..."

"The wicked will follow evil and none of the wicked will understand, but those who have understanding will understand." (Daniel 12, 4-9-10)

A few years ago, many of the prophecies we would not have understood, because many things of which the Bible mentions, still did not happen; However, time is passing, science is advancing and the Bible is clearly opening as if we read a newspaper of the day with the latest news of the moment.

The most obvious example of this, to mention one is: the return of the Jews to Palestine from where they were dispersed 2000 years ago; A few years before the proclamation of the State of Israel, no one believed that Israel would be reborn again and those who wrote on these issues thought that when the prophets spoke of Israel, they referred to the Church of Christ. Now we see that it is not so. The Prophecy in this regard has been fulfilled exactly and to everyone's amazement.

"Yahweh answered me by saying: write the vision and record it on tablets, so that it can be read in a row. Because the vision is for a certain time ... "

"Wait it will certainly come, it will not be missing. Behold, he who does not have a straight soul succumbs; but the righteous shall live by his faithfulness. " (Habakkuk 2,2-4)

Last but not least, when we read the Bible, we have to ask God for the grace of understanding and assistance of the Sacred Magisterium of the Church, (although in these times of apostasy it is very difficult to know who tells you the truth and who no) But then if you really love God and want to know his truth, you will see with the eyes of faith that He himself will open them to you.

In the Bible there is a figurative and mysterious language in which, usually there is a relationship between the physical and historical and the symbolic or spiritual, (just to cite an example, that there are many, but we will see them in due time). When Juan tells us about the falling stars, they are not stars we know from astronomy or physics; but spiritual beings belonging to the legions of Satan. In Rev 12, 4. We read: "And his tail dragged the third part of the stars of the sky and threw them on the earth ..." And when he says:

"And there was a great earthquake" he is talking about a great moral and spiritual commotion, a removal of moral and spiritual values as a chaos as earthquakes occur when after them there is desolation and destruction. But this does not mean that the physical earthquake could not occur as we know it and possibly occur.

Then he says: "the sun went black ..." (Rev. 6,12), what is the sun in this regard? It is the light, the heat, which produces life, joy, it is the perfect symbol of Christ, of God our Father who gives us, warmth, joy, light, love. When the sun does not give its light, it means that this light of God will no longer exist; because humanity has rejected it and has been removed from the earth. Man will live in the most horrible confusion, error and moral, intellectual and spiritual darkness, as never before. The third picture of the vision derives from this desperate situation: "And the moon was dyed with blood" (Rev. 6, 12) Why the moon? Is it not at night where crime and evil increase? as a consequence of the lack of the Light of Christ, violence, prey, evil will increase, so much so that violence and blood will be the norm of life in those terrible days. Another quotation that comes to reinforce everything I said is in **Rev. 9, 1-2.**

"... And I saw a star that fell from heaven to earth and was given the key to the pit of the abyss. And he opened the pit of the abyss and smoke rose from the pit, like smoke from a great furnace and the sun and air were darkened by the smoke of the pit."

As you will see, it is the infernal forces that come out of hell that will obscure the understanding of the inhabitants of the earth.

BEGINNING OF EVIL

To understand the content of this book, it is necessary that we go back to the beginning of time, or at least until those distant times of which we have little data, but yes, very revealing and valuable to be convinced that by those past events it is that we live with endless difficulties and sufferings, beset by diseases, imperfections, countless evils and finally attacked by death; consequence of the mistakes of our ancestors.

Some believe that God created the world in six parts, separated by long periods of time; others believe that God simply separated different states of evolution until they made the world we know today. (Which is not denied or affirmed that God created the universe in stages) Whatever the order and form of creation; the truth is that, evil began when the universe was already created and possibly when God had just in mind to create man and make him his masterpiece.

In Job 38.4 it seems to indicate that God created the current universe before the angelic uprising; but before man was created.

"Where were you when I founded the earth?" Are the words that Yahweh tells Job for having dared to judge the Lord in his terrible despair? Just like telling him: were there men when I made the land? Then continue describing the magnificent and portentous facts of creation. While Yahweh did all these wonders; the angels, archangels and powers that were in heaven cheered, applauded, sang and rejoiced at such portents, wonders and demonstrations of Divine Power. This indicates that by that time when God created the universe, there was total harmony between them.

"Tell me if you know so much, who determined its dimensions...? Who laid the cornerstone...? Between the cheers of the morning stars and the applause of all the children of God? (Job-38.7).

Here too, the writer of this book talks about morning stars referring to angelic beings.

Given this situation of harmony in which the universe was, it is worth asking: What happened to start a revolution? What was the cause for the rebellion of probably millions of angelic beings, commanded by the most perfect of them all, Lucifer?

Wouldn't it be that God had in mind to create a being (man) that would have power over the angelic beings? hence, many of these angels did not like such an idea, perhaps they considered it inferior to them, for being less ethereal or having a material part, equal to the lower world and therefore unworthy of having dominion over them.

St. Paul in 1 Corinthians 6.3 says:

"Do you know that we will judge angels?"

In the Letter to the Hebrews it teaches us that man will be the one who has dominion in the new world and then adds some stanzas of the psalmist:

"What is man so that you remember him, or the son of man so that You visit him? ... crown him with glory and honor, you put everything under his feet".

"Well, by saying that he submitted everything, he left nothing that did not submit" (Hebrews 2,6).

Can you imagine at what high levels God had set man?

The apostle John also tells us that when he was receiving the visions of the Apocalypse, he wanted to kneel before the angel who was speaking to him and he said:

"Do not do it, I am a servant as you and as your brothers are, and of all of them who have the truth that Christ has revealed, worship God" (Revelation 19,10)

Therefore, there is no other way to explain that hatred that Satan has for humanity.

"If this is true, after the revolution that these angels provoked, the planet earth and possibly part of our galaxy was destroyed by the battles that were fought between the heavenly hosts faithful to God and the rebels; this seems to be demonstrated with the so-called "Great Lapse" theory in which it is believed that between Genesis 1 and Genesis 2 a certain time passed; because the only original acts of creation are written by the Hebrew word "Bara", which means bringing something into the existence of nothingness, the same that is only found in Genesis 1-1, 1-21, 1-27 " . (Lindsey Hall). The first refers to the original acts of creation in times impossible to know, in the second case it refers to the creation of all subhuman animals and creatures and finally in Genesis 1-27, the creation of man is described.

Other Hebrew words used in connection with creation do not necessarily imply original acts, but they do mean restoration, repair of a world or galaxy that in Genesis 1,2 is described in a state of chaos. This state of disorder is literally described by the Hebrew words "בוהו וא תוהו" which means "formless"; This expression not only means the above, but rather something that is destroyed as a result of a catastrophe, because as the biblical scholar Barnhouse says to support his theory of the Great Lapse, that God being perfect cannot create an imperfect, chaotic world, destroyed, without form, in darkness and in ruins as described in several passages of Genesis, which would be a violation of the same spiritual principles affirmed by the Holy Spirit.

"A fountain cannot give both fresh and bitter water" (James 3, 11)

Therefore, it is very possible that after the restoration of the land; man was just created, according to the plan that God had planned to do before the rebellion of that angel, who believed himself entitled to contradict his Maker and what is worse, to think and believe that he was equal or more than God.

In the past there was only one will, that of God; there was harmony and holiness, evil was not known, until the pride of an angel, made the universe divide in two and since then evil was a fact.

But what data do we have or how do we know about this unfortunate event? In Ezekiel 28, 12 a mysterious character named the prince of Tire is mentioned. He is described as someone who had the seal of perfection, the chosen one, the leader, the cherub; all the jewels were given to him, indicating that he had the highest rank of all other celestial beings, and was always in the garden of the Lord.

In this passage Ezekiel speaks of the greatest being that God created, one who had no equal in beauty, wisdom, privilege and authority; this is the same as Isaiah describes as the "son of the morning", the same whose name means, "he who shines."

Could these descriptions have been corresponding to some man? No, because first of all men are no longer created; after Adam man is born; second, after Adam no man was perfect (except Jesus Christ); According to Ezekiel's description, this character was perfect from the day it was created.

"Son of man, sing an elegy to the prince of Tire and say: Thus says the Lord, Yahweh: you were the seal of perfection, full of wisdom and finished in beauty; you lived in Eden, in the garden of God, dressed in all preciousness, the ruby, the topaz ... The day you were created they put you next to the cherub, placed on the holy mountain of God ..., you were perfect in your ways from when you were created until the day iniquity was found in you" (Ezekiel 28.12)

Lucifer was created in every perfect sense, he was the one with the highest position in heaven, until evil entered her being, marking his fall and the birth of Satan. It is important to note that Yahweh speaks of Satan indirectly through other characters, as in this case through the prince of Tire. In Genesis 3.14 it is referred to, as the serpent in Eden and in Matthew 16, 23 even through Peter; when Jesus admonishes him.

The prophet Isaiah also tells us about a character he calls: Morning Star.

"How did you fall from the sky, bright star, son of the dawn, cast down the dominator of the nations? And you who said in your heart, I will go up to heaven; On high above the stars of heaven I will raise my throne ... and I will be equal to the Highest" (Isaiah 14, 12-25).

In both cases, a character that was believed to be the greatest and most powerful is mentioned, even compared to Yahweh; but he fell for his arrogance, vanity, and pride, since that time the universe was no longer a center of harmony; there was a second will contrary to the first; that is why God changed the name of Lucifer to Lucifer or Satan, which means the adversary, the one who resists; and demon that means, the accuser. After the judgment of this fallen star, God created hell for him and his followers. And once the rebellion was stifled, possibly the Lord cleansed and restored the earth to continue with his plan to create man.

Now, to understand the "History of Salvation" that God prepared to redeem mankind, and to continue reading this book, it is necessary that at all times we do not forget the existence of these two very powerful forces that for the past Many millennia have been fighting, good and evil. Just look around us to realize that the human being moves and acts based on these two realities. The prophecies of the Bible casually deal with all the events that will occur for good to triumph.

SABOTAGE

We could well say that the first act of sabotage committed in history was done by Lucifer in trying to ruin the works of the Creator.

Yahweh created man and did it in the image and likeness of his own Self (this does not necessarily mean that we are similar by our physique; but rather by the spirit we have, by the will and reasoning to discern what is good and What is bad). Giving them all these attributes characteristic of Him; He has placed them in

Paradise, granting them dominion over all things and crowning them with glory. He entrusts them to grow and multiply.

"And he created them male and female, and God blessed them saying: Procreate and multiply and fill the earth, subdue it and dominate it"(Genesis 1, 27-28)

Certainly, being Adam and Eve the work of God, with powers and dominion over the angels themselves; they were surely the most perfect and complex specimens that ever existed on earth; both physically and spiritually they were the ultimate expression of the work that Yahweh created for the earth, Eva must have been the prettiest woman that this earth knew, quite the opposite of the Darwinian images and concepts that now dominate almost the entire world, thinking that man looked like an ape; in this case we can also apply the aforementioned principle, that from a perfect God, only complete and perfect beings can leave; and no, semi-made beings that are evolving.

Now, God has created a new species of beings and made them perfect, but will they be faithful and loyal to their creator? Previously Yahweh had created other beings with superior characteristics, however the most perfect and beloved was revealed dragging many more with him. That is why God, this time puts a restriction on these new creatures to prove their faithfulness.

"And he gave them this command: Of all the trees of paradise you can eat, but from the tree of the knowledge of good and evil do not eat, for the day you eat of it will surely die" (Genesis 2, 16-17)

It is not exactly known what was the prohibition that God imposed on Adam and Eve; for the previous passage seems to be figuratively like many others; the fact is, Lucifer took advantage of this situation to drag man to infidelity and disobedience, using one of the beasts that were, the snake; sabotaged the last of the works of the Lord.

What would be the main reason that led Satan to commit this criminal act? Would it be the hatred he feels toward God? Or would it be hatred of the man who was perhaps the reason for his fall? Or maybe he just wanted to accuse man and make God see that what he had created had not been faithful; therefore, not only he had been disobedient; Or, perhaps with that he wanted to alleviate his guilt and tried to justify himself; at the same time that with that hatred, again plunged part of the universe into chaos and destruction?

It is amazing how the Bible presents and explains the truths in a simple and comprehensive way, as in the case of the intelligent but criminal attack that Satan undertook against the first parents. The temptations to which they were subjected fall into the main categories that encompass the areas of human existence, as they are, physically, spiritually and emotionally.

Before launching his disastrous attack, Satan observed and studied the situation in Eden and decided to begin the attack on the flank of Eve. Why precisely Eva? - Why didn't you choose Adam? Because women by their nature are more accessible, more open to listen and easy to convince; once persuaded, it would be responsible for dragging the man too; who by the charms and abilities of his partner would also fall into such terrible disobedience.

"The snake... said to the woman: Did God have commanded you not to eat of all the trees of paradise? And the woman replied to the snake: *We eat of the fruit of the trees of paradise, but of the fruit of the one in the middle of paradise God has told us: Do not eat of it, do not even touch it, do not go to die. And the serpent said to the woman: No, you will not die; God knows that the day you eat of it your eyes will open and you will be like God, knowing good and evil. So the woman saw that the tree was good to eat, beautiful to look at and desirable to attain wisdom through it, and took of the fruit and ate, and also gave of it to her husband, who also ate with her." (Genesis 3, 1-6)*

The trick that has given Satan the most success in his evil plans is to contradict the words of the Lord, challenging his commands and sowing the seed of doubt; This worked very well in paradise and has since used it continuously all the time.

From the biblical verses read above it can be deduced that the first trick that the enemy used, was to create the doubt of what God had said, attacked Eve's faith by making her hesitate and instilling suspicion against the Lord.

After having contradicted the commands of God, he resorted to the sensual characteristic of women, to enliven that appetite for the forbidden fruit; Once the respect and fear towards the Creator was lost, Eva let herself be swept away by desire and passion, and finally, the enemy ended up attacking the emotional aspect, making the low feelings of pride and arrogance appear. "So the woman saw that the tree was good to eat (carnal desire), beautiful to look at (appetite and passion that enters through the eyes) and desirable to attain wisdom through it" (disorder of putting confidence in worldly wisdom and science, rather than in the words of God). These were the sins they committed by coming to become followers and confidants of Satan.

DILEMMA

Adam has disobeyed his creator, instead of being faithful he has preferred to follow the vile advice of the devil and has committed not only the sin of disobedience, but also the horrible sin of pride, Satan's own lack of wanting to be like God. From that moment on, all personal relationship with the Creator was broken, nature itself became violent and wild against man and diseases, sufferings and death began.

Many people wonder: If God is almighty, why did he create creatures that would betray him? Actually God created them perfect and even more gave them attributes that He has, such as free will. Yahweh did not want to create robots or programmed dolls, without will, he wanted beings similar to God himself, with intelligence, will, freedom and immortality; However, even with all these qualities, Adam brought his own destruction and that of all mankind.

God told him that his disobedience would bring him death and that was exactly what happened, Adam suffered immediate spiritual separation and subsequently physical death.

In the world there is no way to explain why death exists, outside the existence of evil; there is no medical or scientific reason that explains why man should die. Rather, scientific evidence indicates that man was created to live, to be immortal; but it does not happen, it only reaches a certain point of physical and mental development and begins to deteriorate. The process of cell renewal could continue forever; however, for unknown and illogical reasons the whole rejuvenating process begins to fail until death. Science does not know why our bodies deteriorate; but the Bible gives us the answer and tell us that it is a consequence of sin.

"For one-man sin entered the world, and death for sin, and thus it happened to all men ..." (Romans 5,19)

At this point in human history we find that the Lord is facing a dilemma; Its inherent nature of absolute justice demands the death and destruction of the sinner. God cannot ignore disorder and disobedience, just as he did not overlook the transgression of Lucifer.

At the same time his love for man leads him to have compassion, to forgive him and to think how to restore that creature he loves so much, but who has so ungratefully despised and disobeyed him.

Throughout all the Holy Scriptures, we find passages that tell us how great God's love for man is; Almost all the prophets proclaim the love that God has for him, not only at the beginning when he was perfect, but also through the times of imperfection and disloyalty. The prophet Isaiah gives us a little hint of the purpose Yahweh had in creating this creature that is man.

"I have created them, I have formed them, for my glory" (Isaiah 43.7) Faced with the dilemma of doing justice and condemning the sinner and the love he feels for him, how could the Lord satisfy one demand without violating the other?

The Lord knows that man is guilty, that far from trusting and obeying him he has broken the whole relationship with Him and has preferred to follow the advice of his enemy. God has pronounced his just sentence and that is why man will suffer the consequences of his disorder for generations and generations.

"For you the earth will be cursed, with work you will eat the bread until you return to the earth, for from it you have been taken" (Genesis 3:17)

Yahweh knows that behind this transgression of man, there is the evil being, the true culprit of all the catastrophes that the universe suffers, the true responsible for the misfortune of man, that fallen angel who once enjoyed the presence of the Lord. Therefore, the Lord will not leave man in ruin and misery, he will not leave him at the mercy of the accuser and enemy, but ... Who could satisfy divine justice? What son of man can be perfect and restore humanity? No, there is no one worthy, nor anyone so perfect that it meets the heavenly requirements. Therefore, the only solution is that God himself becomes man through one of the people of his mysterious Trilogy:

The Son, and thus being born as a human creature will achieve perfection and obedience, restoring fallen humanity.

Sin demands punishment and it will be the Lord himself who pays for that fault through the person of the second Adam, the Messiah; Surrendering his own life, he will pay the sin of men and thus the just judgment that demanded punishment and his great love that demanded restoration and friendship for his creation will be satisfied.

Yahweh's attitude toward the man is like that of a father who goes to the rescue of his son who has fallen out of favor, before the son rots in jail for the crime he committed, the father rushes out and pays with his same person the crime of his son, and what is more, he pays with his own life, the sentence pronounced against his disobedient son.

Even before Adam and Eve had been expelled from paradise Yahweh had already devised his plan of attack against the enemy and his plan of redemption for man.

"I put perpetual enmity between you (the devil) and the woman, between your lineage and his, this will crush your head (someone from the woman's lineage) and you will stalk the heel." (Genesis 3. 15)

The redemption plan is clear, someone born of a woman will appear on the human stage and destroy the work of the devil.

The Bible itself is the history of humanity in two parts: the first is the history of evil, which caused man to fall and turn away from God; and the second part, the history of salvation or the path that was opened to man to return to his Creator.

CHAPTER II

HISTORY OF SALVATION

ANNOUNCEMENT OF THE SACRIFICE

Before Adam and Eve were expelled from Eden, God compassionate and gracious, found a way for man to have some kind of relationship with him; and to amend his faults he sacrificed a lamb with whose skin he clothed them.

The efforts of Adam and Eve to cover their nakedness (symbolically their faults) with the fig leaves were not enough; so much so that the Lord himself sacrificed an animal to clothe them with the skin; this was the first sacrifice with bloodshed, because of man's sins; sacrifices that were followed for generations and generations; as an omen of the great sacrifice that the Son of God was going to make to redeem the world.

The Bible tells us that: When Cain made his offerings to God, they were not to the Lord's liking, what were the reasons why they were not well seen? After all, their offerings were not bad, they were the fruit of their labor, the fruit of the earth.

"After a while Cain made an offering to Yahweh of the fruits of the earth ... (The Lord did not like it). Enraged Cain was downcast; and Yahweh said to him Why are you enraged and why are you downcast? Isn't it true that if you worked well you would walk upright? (Genesis 4)

Maybe the offering itself had nothing wrong, but Cain's attitude; because with his offerings, he denied and did not accept that sin had separated God from man. Cain denied the need to reconcile with God through a bloody sacrifice, denied that it was necessary for someone to die for others; He denied that the earth was cursed and insisted that the fruit of the earth and its work should be accepted by God.

On the other hand, Abel, brother of Cain, offered as an offering a lamb with which he confessed and believed that sin was the cause of separation, God-man; as a consequence, death was the deserved punishment. That the sufferings that man experienced were just and finally affirmed that the Lord had provided a way of redemption through the blood of the Lamb.

The blood of the Lamb was the vital difference between these two offerings.

PLAN OF SALVATION - STRATEGIES TO SAVE MAN

The wait of the Savior began practically since our first parents heard the sentences of condemnation and the plan of salvation that Yahweh pronounced in paradise. It is quite possible that Eva had hoped that one of her children was going to be the promised savior; but as we know it was not so. Time passes and the world is in the hands of Satan, mankind lived its worst moments since it was created. Most men live like animals; disorder, chaos, immorality, and evil in general prevail; exactly as the evil one wished. The level of degradation is such that many peoples reached the height of cannibalism and others to human sacrifices said to placate the wrath of the gods. With these filthy and abominable sacrifices, Satan wanted to mimic and insult the Great Sacrifice he knew would have to happen at a time in history. Lord Yahweh, sorry to have created man, wishes to exterminate him completely; but that would please the evil one. Happily, there is a righteous man who has not been spotted like the rest, he will serve to start over.

"Seeing Yahweh how much the wickedness of man on the earth had grown and his heart was not plotting but only raging designs all day ... The Lord repented of having done them and having put them on the earth ... and the Lord said: I will exterminate the man I created from above the earth. But Noah found grace in Yahweh's eyes" (Genesis 6)

Then Noah's offspring repopulated the earth; until after many years, the Lord finds another righteous man, Abraham, and decides to separate him from the rest of mankind and use him to later form a nation that would serve as the basis for his plan of salvation.

"Yahweh said to Abraham: get away from your land, from your family, from your father's house, to the land that I will indicate to you. I will make you a great people, I will bless you and magnify your name and it will be a blessing.

I will bless those who bless you and curse those who curse you. And in you all the families of the earth will be blessed" (Genesis12)

The Lord believes that it is absolutely necessary that the man he has chosen, Abraham and his descendants, remain completely apart from the other peoples and nations, to avoid bad customs, and in general the corruption and darkness that exists in humanity. That is why he orders them to execute several rites, laws and customs that would maintain the union between them and the separation of other people, until the time is right and the Lord can manifest himself to the world.

Then God said to Abraham, "As for you, you must keep my covenant, you and your descendants after you for the generations to come. 10 This is my covenant with you and your descendants after you, the covenant you are to keep: Every male among you shall be circumcised. 11 You are to undergo circumcision, and it will be the sign of the covenant between me and you. (Genesis 17, 9-11)

After Abraham died, his son Isaac continued to enjoy the same graces, promises and advice that his father had from the Lord. ***"I am the God of Abraham, your father, do not be afraid, I am with you, I will bless you and give you many descendants because I promised my servant Abraham." (Genesis 26, 24)***

In the same way it happened with Jacob, son of Isaac; later called Israel.

"Your name is Jacob but from now on you will be Israel. I am your almighty God, you will have many children and nations will descend from you" (Genesis 35, 10)

Thus we see how little by little the offspring of the man that God chose is increasing to reach the 12 children of Israel, who formed 12 tribes, from which they became a nation.

Although Israel was the people of God, it was not free from discord and division. Israel was tough and stubborn; they continually abandoned the Lord, disregarded their commands and went after the corrupt customs of other people. That is why the Lord almost always sended prophet after prophet, punishment after punishment to return them to themselves. For Yahweh it was very important to keep this people apart from others, guiding them and taking care of them so that through the different stages in which they lived, they realize the symbolism that their lives represented; especially for future generations.

Many stages of the life of the Hebrews symbolize the situation that existed in the world; the struggle between good and evil, and the plans that the Lord set out to restore to man.

For example, when the Hebrew people lived mistreated, enslaved and suffering all kinds of humiliations under Egyptian tyranny (symbolically the force of evil that oppresses and enslaves man), God, to get them out of such a miserable state, arouses among themselves. a leader, a deliverer, Moses (symbolically the Messiah, Jesus). Moses, with the power that God gave him, freed his people from the slavery he suffered in Egypt. (Jesus, son of God, freed all mankind from the power of evil). Pharaoh stubbornly refused to let the Hebrews out, not even the plagues God sent through Moses made him change his mind (the enemy clings to enslave man). But one thing forced the pharaoh to free the Hebrews: "The Passover lamb" (one thing forces the devil to free mankind, "the Lamb of God").

"The Lord spoke to Moses saying:

Take each one according to the paternal houses, a lamb for each house, the beef will be without defect, primal male, lamb or kid. The whole Community of Israel will immolate them between two lights, they will take the blood and spread the posts and the lintel of each house of Israel where the lamb is eaten, the blood will serve as a sign in the houses where you are; I will see the blood and pass by and there will be no mortal plague for you when I hurt the land of Egypt." (Exodus 12)

The Lord says that the beef will be without defect. (Jesus was perfect and spotless). With blood they will paint the doors of their homes, so that the exterminating angel will see that there they have eaten the lamb and scattered their blood and not exterminate them, (he who believes in the son of God, as the Lamb who came into the world to atone for sins will not die but will have eternal life). ***"Truly, truly, I say to you, whoever hears my word and believes in Him who sent me has eternal life and is not judged, because he passed from the dead to life." (John 5:24)***

After escaping the Egyptian tyranny, Moses takes them through the desert, where they remain for 40 years, before reaching the Promised Land. Moses could have taken his people along a more direct path; but the journey was a great turn, tortuous and full of fatigue, where they went hungry, thirsty and hard works, (indicating that before being worthy of heaven, it is necessary to suffer in this life and pass the necessary tests to reach the desired goal). The Lord fed the people of Israel with manna, while the desert journey lasted. (Thus Jesus left his church the Eucharist, as spiritual food).

"Jesus took bread, blessed it, broke it and, giving it to his disciples, said: Take and eat, this is my body" (Matthew 26, 26)

As the Hebrew people moved towards their destiny Moses instructed, advised, admonished and punished them; to keep God's people free from evil influences, apart from having taught them the commandments of God's law; as the basis of the new doctrines of love and peace that the Messiah would bring.

You will not have another God but me.
You will not misrepresent the name of Yahweh your God.
You will sanctify the holidays.
Honor your father and mother
You will not kill
You will not commit adultery
You will not steal
You will not testify against your neighbor false testimony.
You will not want your neighbor's wife.
You will not want the assets of others" (Exodus 20)

After Israel settled in the promised land, despite the wonders and miracles that the Lord worked with them, they continually forgot about Him, to go after alien gods invented by the enemy, after customs of pagan peoples and after evils. Of their wayward hearts. That is why the punishments came, to return them to the good way, and the prophets, to admonish them, and, to announce the advent of the son of God; to rescue slave humanity from evil.

PROPHECIES THAT ANNOUNCED THE ADVENT OF MESSIAH

Despite the overwhelming evidence that the Messiah has already been manifesting in the person of Jesus of Nazareth, there are still religions, sects and people who do not believe in such a fact; they present endless arguments without concrete foundations to defend their heresies; Israel itself being one of many in the world who do not believe in Jesus as the Messiah. According to the majority of biblical schoolchildren, there are 333 prophecies concerning the coming of Jesus the Savior. Thus we have that God spoke of this wonderful person from the first moment that man broke the friendship with Him.

"I will put enmity between you and the woman and between your lineage and her lineage, he will step on your head, while you stalk his heel" (Genesis 3, 15) In spite of the transgression of man, he would not be abandoned, but that someone from the lineage of a woman, (Jesus Christ, son of Mary) would crush the enemy's head and defeat him to save humanity.

Genesis 49,10 describes the tribe from which the Messiah would come.

The scepter shall not depart from Judah, nor the ruler's staff from between his feet, until he comes to whom it belongs; and to him shall be the obedience of the peoples.

All the prophets spoke and described the coming of the Savior; It was the main event that humanity had to look forward to and eagerly. The prophet Micah also predicts the place of his birth:

"But you Bethlehem of Ephrata small among the clans of Judah, it will come from you who will rule in Israel, whose origins are old, of days of very remote antiquity." (Micah 5.2)

One of the prophecies that we might consider of vital importance are the stories of Isaiah, who tells us about the human and divine origin of this wonderful Being, prepared as an innocent lamb for sacrifice.

Who has believed our message and to whom has the arm of the Lord been revealed? 2 He grew up before him like a tender shoot, and like a root out of dry ground. He had no beauty or majesty to attract us to him, nothing in his appearance that we should desire him. 3 He was despised and rejected by mankind, a man of suffering, and familiar with pain. Like one from whom people hide their faces he was despised, and we held him in low esteem.

Surely he took up our pain and bore our suffering, yet we considered him punished by God, stricken by him, and afflicted. 5But he was pierced for our transgressions; he was crushed for our iniquities.

The punishment of our peace was upon him, and in his wounds we have been healed. All of us were wandering like sheep, each one following his path and Yahweh bore upon him the iniquity of us all.

Abused, but he submitted, did not open his mouth, like a lamb taken to the slaughterhouse, like a mute sheep before the shearers. He was taken by a wicked trial, without anyone defending his cause, because he was torn from the land of the living and mortally wounded for the crime of his people. Willing was among the wicked his burial, and it was in death matched among the evildoers, despite not having committed evil, or lying in their mouths.

Yahweh wanted to break him with suffering, offering his life in sacrifice for sin ...

The righteous, my servant, will justify many and bear their iniquities. That is why I will give you crowds ..." (Isaiah 53, 1 - 12) Eight centuries before these things happened, a man of God was already asking his people, but did they give themselves time to investigate what that man was talking about? Very likely not, as now, who has time to think that Jesus is soon to return again?

The parallel that exists between the life of Jesus, his acts and words, are incredibly accurate to the stories of the prophets. For example, before his passion, Jesus found himself in Jerusalem riding a donkey, triumphant and acclaimed. Let's see what Zacharias prophet and Matthew disciple says.

"Behold, your king is coming, just and victorious, humble, riding his ass."(Zechariah 9, 9)

"The disciples went and did as Jesus had instructed them. 7 They brought the donkey and the colt and placed their cloaks on them for Jesus to sit on. (Matthew 21, 6)

Also the way how he was going to be betrayed by one of his disciples.

"Although he who had peace with me, he who trusted me and ate my bread, raised his heel against me" (Psalm 41, 10) "The traitor had given them this signal: Who will I kiss that is; turn it on and take it safely.

Instantly he came and approached him, saying: Rabbi, and kissed him, they laid hands on him and seized Him." (Mark 14, 44)

King David in one of his psalms says:

"My God, my God, why have you forsaken me? Why are you so far from saving me, so far from my cries of anguish?" (Psalm 22)

One of Jesus' contemporary men in the narration of his death says:

"And at three in the afternoon Jesus cried out in a loud voice: "Eloi, Eloi, lema sabachthani?" (Which means "My God, my God, why have you forsaken me? (Mark 15, 34)

In the same Psalm 2 mentioned above, David says:

"He trusts in the Lord," they say, "let the Lord rescue him. Let him deliver him, since he delights in him."

Marcos continues to narrate:

"Some of the people who were there heard him and said: Listen, he is calling Elijah ... wait, let's see if Elijah comes to take him down from the cross."

Psalm 22, 15 says: "I am poured out like water, and all my bones are out of joint. My heart has turned to wax; it has melted within me."

Currently, the science of medicine helps confirm that the symptoms described in the prophecies and sufferings of Jesus before he died are exactly what would happen to a person who had been tormented as was the Messiah.

"One of the soldiers pierced his side with his spear, and instantly blood and water came out" (John 19, 34)

Psalm 22, 17 says:

"They have drilled my hands and my feet ... They have distributed my clothes and cast luck on my robe."

John, another witness of the death of Jesus says:

"The soldiers, once they crucified Jesus, took their clothes ... The tunic was seamless ... they said to each other: Let us not tear it, but cast lots on it to see who owns it." (John 19, 23-24)

To alleviate a little the crucifixion pains, the Romans used to give the sentenced some wine with gall.

"They gave him drink wine mixed with gall; but, but after tasting it, he didn't want to drink it. (Matthew 27, 34)

"They gave me to eat poison and in my thirst they gave me to drink vinegar. (Psalm 69, 21)

Traditionally, the legs of all the crucified ones were broken to accelerate their death. According to the Lord's commands, no sacrifice should be with broken bones. (Exodus 12, 46) In the same way it happened with the victimized Lamb of God.

"The soldiers came ... but upon reaching Him (Jesus). They saw that he was already dead and his legs were not broken." (John 19, 32)

The psalmist in his divine inspiration number 34, 20 says:

"Take care of all your bones and not one of them will be broken."

Then the final words before dying:

"Father in your hands I entrust my spirit, saying this expired." (Luke 23, 46)

And in Psalm 31, 6 we read: *"In your hands I entrust my spirit."*

Finally, Jesus Himself predicted his own death, although at that time his disciples did not understand anything.

"That's why the father loves me, because I give my life to take it again. No one takes it from me, it is I who give it to myself. I have the power to give it and the power to take it again. Such is the mandate that I have received from the Father. (John 10, 17)

As you will see the parallels and comparisons in the events that occurred to Jesus with what was predicted by the prophets, they are accurate and there are many others; However, I believe that, with the few described here, it is more than enough to understand that He, (Jesus) is the Perfect Sacrifice sent by God.

MISSION ACCOMPLISHED.

The Messiah has finished his mission on earth, has managed to infiltrate territory occupied by the enemy, like any other inhabitant and has managed to emerge victorious. After three years of public life, where he taught the basic truths of the Gospel, he healed the sick, raised the dead, expelled demons and did many, many other miracles and after having offered his life; He has defeated the enemy and thus to death, giving man again the hope of life and immortality.

He has also achieved that 11 more men believe in the mission entrusted to Him by the Heavenly Father; then as a good instructor in the art of spiritual warfare against the ruler of darkness; He has prepared them to continue the mission of rescuing the rest of the prisoners from evil, freeing those in concentration camps, torture chambers, and freeing slaves. Although for the moment the heavenly armies were not yet going to take the land; before this happens, the Lord needs to have the greatest number of adherents and supporters many of whom will join the fight when Christ returns to take possession of his kingdom.

The Leader and Heavenly Prince prepares to retire for a while until his followers multiply throughout the earth; He retires not before having defeated the enemy and left a channel or network of communication and hope for man installed.

Jesus with his death has paid the transgression of man and with his resurrection he has returned him to immortality and has made known the will of God, his Father.

"I have finished the work you gave me, Father, give me the glory of your presence, the same glory that I have had with you since before the world was done." (John 17, 4-5)

Jesus prepared his followers to continue the work he began; and so that they are not discouraged, he promises that Yahweh will send him someone who will help them spread the truth.

"If you love me, you will obey my commandments and I will ask my father to send you help, a lawyer, to be with you forever and He will be the Spirit to reveal the truth of God." (John 14, 15-17)

Before his death and resurrection, he already announces that he will have to retire to the heavenly house where the Father is.

"Peace I leave you, peace I give you; I do not give it as the world gives it, do not let your heart be troubled or be afraid. You have heard what I said: I am leaving but I will return, if you love me you will be happy because I go with the Father who is greater than me" (John 14, 27-28)

Finally, that morning of his farewell, he told them:

"All power has been given to me in heaven and on earth;

Go and teach all people, baptizing them in the name of the Father and the Son and the Holy Spirit, teaching them to practice everything I have commanded you.

I will be with you always until the consummation of the world." (Matthew 28, 18-20)

INCREDULITY OF THE JEWISH PEOPLE

With all the evidence that Jesus is the Messiah, there are still many who do not believe, among them the same people chosen by God, the Jews; the people who so eagerly awaited the Messiah, when he came he did not receive him. What happened to make this unusual event happen?

Undoubtedly it was the evil influence of Satan that promoted disbelief. It is known that all the things that God does, he (Satan) wants to sabotage and destroy. But Yahweh with his infinite wisdom, for each attack of the enemy has a counterattack, and even uses the same attacks of the devil to carry out his redemption plans. For example, in this same case, Lucifer influenced so that the Jews, his own people, would not believe or receive the Messiah; but in this disbelieved of the Jews; God used it so the rest of the world could believe in him. (Ro.11, 11)

Then at the end near the second coming of Jesus; Yahweh will use other means to realize his mistake and be rescued again.

 The Hebrew people are very stubborn and arrogant, just because they know that they are the people that God chose, makes them conceited, petulant and enclose themselves in the laws that Moses left; without realizing that that is not all; that through the law there can be no salvation, but that salvation comes only through faith in the victimized Lamb, and they fall into the same error as Cain, that of wanting to be pleasing to God on his own merits.

Ironically, the Jews believe in the offerings of immolated lambs, because that was one of the mandates that the Lord gave them through Moses, but they do not realize the symbolism that these immolations represented for the future and for our times with the *"Perpetual Sacrifice"*

On one occasion Yahweh told the prophet Jeremiah:

"Tell the descendants of Jacob, tell the people of Judah; Pay attention you fools and stupid's, who have eyes and do not see, have ears and cannot hear; I am the lord. Why don't you fear me? Why do they not tremble before me?" (Jeremiah 5,20)

With this stubbornness characteristic of the Hebrew people, with their religious hypocrisy, and with their predominantly materialistic mentality, it is easy to imagine why when the Messiah came they did not receive Him. Because of their infidelity they lived continuously subjugated to foreign powers and that is why they dreamed of a Messiah, a leader, a king with great armies, powerful in earthly weapons to free and cast them once and for all to The invaders of Israel.

They believed that the Messiah was going to be a great leader who would banish all his earthly evils; but they never imagined that the Messiah would banish more than physical evils, if not that he would expel the very source of all evils, which is the spiritual evil caused by Satan. But, what a disappointment to them, when they hear that the man they say is the Messiah, is not what they expected; It is quite the opposite, it is not violent, it is meek; He says: If they hit you on one cheek, give them the other! (Luke 6, 29) also says: Love your enemies! (Luke 6.27) They wonder what kind of man is this. Apparently he must be crazy, yes, crazy for the world but not for God. He is neither arrogant nor extravagant, he does not like pomp, instead he is humble, instead of a steed, he rides a donkey, and instead of hate and war he preaches love and peace. What a leader that turned out to the Hebrews! People dominated by hatred

and revenge, were waiting for someone to preach to them about the "eye for an eye and a tooth for a tooth."

Jesus came to preach love and peace, because those are the most effective and contrary weapons to the enemy; only those who love, those who are meek and humble will be those who remain to live on earth when Christ returns again to remain to reign forever.

"I was found of those who did not look for me, I let myself be seen of those who did not ask for me. But to Israel he says: all day I extended my hands towards this incredulous and rebellious people". (Romans 10, 20)

Israel did not believe in the son of God. Will they be discarded by this? Doesn't God love them anymore? Many people think that this is the case and on the basis of this they hate and repudiate them, believe them doomed, evil, greedy and with an endless number of evils; but it is only one more pretext of Satan to destroy man, using ignorance and religious fanaticism.

St. Paul affirms the opposite of those who claim to be Christians and hate their Jewish brothers; besides, we must not forget that Jesus himself and the first Christians were Hebrews.

"Because they sinned, salvation came to other people ... the sin of the Jews brought great blessings to the world and their spiritual poverty, the wealth of the Gentiles.

So how much greater will the blessing be for them! (Romans 11, 11)

CONTINUATION OF THE FIGHT BETWEEN GOOD AND EVIL

Jesus has established his network of indoctrination and militancy; and, although he is not in glorious body here on earth, he has left his real presence as food and spiritual comfort in the Mystery of the Eucharist through which his faithful followers feed, strengthen and comfort.

The enemy knows well that the main battle has lost it (man belongs again to God), but, Satan is stubborn, he will continue the fight to the end. And seeing Christians increase, he unleashed persecutions, torture and death with the most terrible cruelty. But, the seed that God sowed, fell on good ground and quickly grew. After some time, the methods used by the enemy to prevent the spread of Christianity no longer have much effect; That is why he changed tactics and to do as much damage as possible, he will put in practice all the methods used and for having, especially infiltrating the same ranks of Christians to corrupt them and incite fanaticism, disguising him as religious zeal so that they themselves commit crimes and killings. Throughout the world he instigated discords, wars, incited pride and schisms; because dividing is his best weapon, separating Christians is one of his favorite tricks.

"A divided kingdom is a defeated kingdom." (Lk 11.17)

The hatred that Satan feels against humanity is such, that since then he tricked man into moving away from God, he has not stopped inventing methods that make man more miserable, more animal, more willing to hate his own fellow human beings, to destroy each other for the most trivial and silly reasons.

He has made all the bad things you hear about the Catholic Church, all the slander and mistakes made in it, present it in such a way that the weak people are scandalized and desert the true Church.

Apart from corrupting Christians, and inciting hatred against them, it also exerts great influence on heads of state, military and people of great influence in society, it has infiltrated men of science, tilting their knowledge and discoveries towards the wrong; all this with a view to deny the existence of God and human annihilation itself.

It has made almost everyone believe that their existence is only a myth; so that in anonymity he can work better, but at the same time that he denies his existence, he keeps the trickery afloat and how much abomination his followers practice.

However, the devil can never win, even if it seems that evil wins and advances; although in the end everything seems lost, the Lord will save all who believe in Him, pouring out His Holy Spirit on those of good will, the humble and peaceful, so that they may be saved.

"And the power of hell will not prevail over my Church" (Mt. 16,18)

WORLD DIFFUSION OF THE DOCTRINE OF CHRIST

"The Lord says to my Lord, sit on my right, until I put your enemies under your feet." (Mark 12.36)

Christian indoctrination must be worldwide, as long as the Gospel of Christ has not been preached for all the ends of the earth, the Lord will not move on to the next stage of his plan of redemption.

The gospel must be heard by all corners of the earth, by all people, all races, all countries so that everyone has the opportunity to be saved and so that there are no excuses and in the end they want to apologize saying: I did not know! Nobody told me! ... This command of Jesus of:

"Go and preach the Good News all over the world ..." (Mk 16.15)

although with much sacrifice it has been bearing fruit and is one of those fruits of the Church that we are going to talk to teach the goods that have been derived from it, not only in the world of Christianity but throughout the world

Since its inception, the Church did not limit itself to suffering persecutions with patience, nor to theological disputes every time heretics appeared, but also emphasized the conversion and education of the peoples. Work that was done by monks, priests, holy men and holy women, dedicated in body and soul to the doctrine of Christ.

Imagine, what it was, to have converted the doctrine of love, peace, solidarity, brotherhood and understanding to the majority of peoples who lived as animals. Take tribes, villages and entire regions of barbarism, civilization and brotherhood; it is not an easy thing; However, Christianity succeeded.

The new religion soon proved its social importance; being one of the main merits, the abolition of slavery. This important reform was carried out gradually. Christianity improved the conditions of the slaves, preaching the equality of men, instilling the duties of justice and charity towards them. Imposing Sunday rest and sanctifying work, which since then, was still appreciated by the free.

The influence that the Church exerted on the rulers and nations was great and enormous, managing to improve the lives of human beings and the conditions of treatment and work, which was previously unthinkable.

Bossier tells us that it has not been found in any ancient writing, not even in the form of remote hope or utopian hypothesis, the idea that one day may come, to be abolished slavery; However, the Church succeeded in making this idea manifest and becoming consistent in the laws. Constantine removed the right of life and death over slaves from the masters. And, when the German invaders restored it, the Church opened the doors of the temples, to the condemned slaves, from where they could not be removed, with a sworn promise that life would be respected. This is where what is now known as "Asylum Law" was born.

Likewise, the condition of slaves was improved with the abolition of gladiatorial shows. This was achieved in 404, by order of Emperor Honorius as a result of the sacrifice of the monk Telemachus; who having descended to the arena to prevent the fight that was going to take place, he was stoned to death by the people.

The woman began to be treated with greater consideration and respect, always mentioning that she was the image of the Virgin Mary, Mother of God made man. Men had to respect their women as the Gospels recommended; neither could they abandon them; the Church forbade divorce.

By this I do not mean that all women were treated well; but awareness was created to achieve the most humane and equal treatment that has been achieved to date.

Likewise, the bases were laid, so that years later all the Civil Rights that are currently known are achieved, such as: "Declaration of the Rights of Man and Citizen". Approved in France in 1789. The Universal Declaration of Human Rights, adopted at the UN in 1948. The Rights of the Child and Women" In itself, all the reforms that today are enjoyed in this western and eastern civilization, had their fundamental basis in the Christian teachings.

Finally, the Church in this contemporary era, continues to struggle to achieve a better standard of living for the most lagging nations, to avoid wars, violations of Human Rights, to avoid the millions of murders committed with abortion. Fight to avoid debauchery that leads to animal sensuality, crime and drug addiction. The last popes have tried to promote social justice through their Encyclicals and recommendations, which many of them have served as a basis for dictating the legal laws of many countries, for the creation of international organizations that safeguard human rights, for international treaties and even for the disarmament and more humane treatment of political and war prisoners.

Among the most outstanding encyclicals we have the "Rerum Novarum", given on May 15, 1891 by Pope Leo XIII. The one that deals with the fair treatment that workers and the working class must receive. This same Pope, wrote many others of the same social and religious magnitude as: "Diuturnum illud", on the origin of civil power, given on June 29, 1889, "Immortale Dei", on the Christian civil order, November 1, 1885 "Libertas praestantissimun", on human freedom, June 20, 1888, are also important many other writings he made, such as: "Graves de communi", on the Christian democracy that published it on January 18, 1901. Pope Leo XIII was rightly considered as a political pope, but not because he put the political tasks of the pontificate before ecclesiastics and religious, but because in his intention to restore universal pontifical moral sovereignty, he stressed the importance of the Christian doctrine of the State for the order and for peace; preparing the way for a good intelligence and behavior of the States. Pius XI, was the Pope who had to face the political and religious persecution of Christians in Russia, Mexico, Spain and other fascist totalitarian systems that were developed with great strength, which constituted a threat to human freedom; from this a whole series of encyclicals worthy of consideration arose: "Miserentissimus Redemptor", "Quadragesimo anno", "Caritate Christi", "Acerba animi", "Divini Redemptoris", where he outlines an extensive doctrine on natural law. "Non abbiamo bisogno" and "Mit brennender Sorge", treats against the fascism and National Socialism of Mussolini and Hitler respectively.

Then we have: "Pacem in terris" de Juan XXIII, "Peace on Earth"; among the most prominent of this Pope. Then we have: "Laborem Excersem", "Centesimus Annus", "Rei socialis", "Dignitatem Muluebus", all of these from John Paul II. If we were to analyze and describe all these works of the Popes, we would have to do a separate work, which is not our intention and because there are already many works that can be consulted; the important thing is to realize that it is the Church of Christ that, through its people on Earth, is working to improve the ethical, moral, social and political conditions of man; without forgetting the most important of course: man's relationship with his Creator.

Finally, something that nobody can deny, because it is visible in the world, are the social services it provides to humanity. Wherever you go, you will find: schools, hospitals, nursing homes, inns, dining rooms, special services for patients with AIDS, for abandoned or raped women, drug addicts, etc. All of which indicates that the

Church is not embellished or to dominate people or to be served, but has fulfilled, fulfills and will play a very important social role in the moral, social, ethical and religious advancement of humanity.

During the two thousand years of existence of the Church of Christ, there were many times when faith, morals, love of Christ vanished, but God never left her unprotected and hence from time to time holy men appeared. with his example and his teachings, they were prosecuting and guiding the Holy Catholic Mother Church; This is how Saint Augustine, Saint Thomas, Saint Gregory the Great, Saint Francis, Saint Clare, Saint John of the Cross, and many thousands of saints venerated in the Catholic Santoral.

Currently, we could ensure that there is no place in the world where the Good News has not been preached. The missions have extended from its beginnings 2000 years ago to the present; which is another sign to know that the time of the Second Coming of our Lord Jesus is near.

"And this good news of the kingdom will be announced throughout the world, so that all nations may know it; then the end will come" (Mt. 24, 14).

CHAPTER III
SATAN PREPARES THE FINAL ATTACK.

IDEOLOGICAL LIES

Almost all the people of this generation are convinced that we are living in an era where there is much progress, technical and ideological, material and spiritual; but the truth is only about science and technological issues; let us look around to see the wonders of technology.

If a person who lived in the last century returns to current life, he would believe he is in another world, a world of fantasy and fiction. Most of us consider these advances as something natural, something of every day; even more so in industrialized countries where supersonic trips, electronic brains, monitors and personal telephones via satellite, Internet, space travel, robots that do the work of thousands of workers; They are common things. Likewise, the advances in medicine are truly surprising; But even more is the progress that the war industry has achieved, the world has so sophisticated armaments that it seems incredible how they perform and especially the destructive power they have.

As for the sciences of education, psychology and social systems, we boast that we have reached an unprecedented advance. Freud, Jung, Darwin, Marx and many others are talked about as if they were really men who, with their ideas and work, brought immense goods to humanity. But: ***"The wisdom of this world before God is nothing but nonsense" (1 Corinthians 1, 20)*** and the vast majority of people have not noticed.

For two or three centuries ago, some men who have gone down in history as illustrious figures of science and literature have spread ideas that have done much harm to humanity. The pollution that these ideologies have left has been so devastating that it has completely perverted the people of the present century. Many of these illustrious intellectuals laid the groundwork for our current way of conceiving education, religion, society, economics and politics to be radically contrary to Biblical principles. You and I, youth and children and people in general have been ingeniously CONDITIONED to think about the present form we have, without realizing that it goes against the truth of God; many of you will smile at each other thinking that what you just read is the biggest nonsense; well; How are you going to make such serious accusations to those brilliant men known throughout the world and who in many ways made great contributions to humanity? But before we continue laughing, let's read: ***1 Corinthians 1:19.***

"I will destroy the wisdom of the wise, and annul the intelligence of the lawyers; so what will happen to the wise? Where are the experts? And where are the debaters of this age? Hasn't God made foolish the wisdom of this world?

I don't say it, God says it, through the Holy Scriptures.

There is only one being who has much to gain by conditioning the human species in the current way of thinking. Satan is the main genius and the force behind these ideologies, which we will explain to understand the reason for the present hostility towards the point of view that God has on life. The analysis of each of these men and their philosophies will be short and confined to the specific areas in which there is conflict with the Bible. Some excerpts from the topics on these intellectuals were translated and adapted from the book "Satan is alive and well on planet Earth" by Hall Lindsey and C.C. Carlsón

KANT

Emmanuel Kant was a German philosopher who lived from 1724 to 1804, before Kant's philosophy came to influence the intellectual world, classical philosophy was based on the thesis and antithesis process, which means that man thought in terms of cause and effect (If A is true, what is not A cannot also be true), according to this classical philosophy the value was absolute, but, when this man appeared, he began to wonder: How can people accept things that were beyond their five senses? For Kant, external experiences were enough to explain the foundation of the world; in the "Analysis of the Thought Process," he says that nobody can know anything except from experience and believed that individual freedom is in obedience to the moral law that speaks within us. With this kind of thought Kant found no personal basis for accepting absolutes, (that is, God, moral and religious laws) which served to light the fuse for another German to introduce another thought that would go much further.

HEGEL

This philosopher, taking Kant's ideas, believed that a fact or idea (thesis) working against another idea (antithesis) would produce a new idea (synthesis); this thought was the basis for the political-communist ideas of Karl Marx and the nationalist socialism of Adolph Hitler.

Hegel glorified the State, taught that the State did not have to obey any moral law and that the rulers were not obliged under any aspect to maintain agreements or contracts they had concluded. According to Hegelian thought, everything was relative; there were no absolutes, only terms of relativity. With these thoughts, Hegel literally altered the course of the world future, in his relative thoughts, ideas of cause and effect have no place, so there was no need for a beginning or final truth, with the elimination of this first cause, man no longer has any need to believe in a Creator or God.

Now in our times, you can prove that this thought has spread very well in politics; compare the way in which governments around the world act and you will see that they have learned the lesson very well.

KIERKEGAAR

He was a theologian of the Lutheran church in Denmark, is considered the father of existentialism, although he was a theologian, his writings are a denial of the most basic Christian principles.

He believed that man at some stage of his life reached a point where he could find no reason to be, no basis to find the truth or the reason of life, then to find a purpose or excuse of his life, He jumped into the attitude of faith, which was not rational at all.

Soren Kierkegaard introduced the ideas of Kant and Hegel into his theology of the Christian faith, which is diametrically opposed to biblical truths. From Kant comes the idea that there are no rational bases for things beyond the five senses and hence the attitude of taking refuge in a blind faith to find reason for life. From Hegel comes the idea that there is no absolute truth, so we must find relative reasons to explain our existence. And that's how Kierkegaard's existentialist thought began.

DARWIN

Charles Darwin, nineteenth-century English, caused a true intellectual revolution, both in scientific circles and in those that were not. In his theory of the generic development of plants and animals, he presented the idea that low and primitive forms of life advanced to higher and more sophisticated forms because of the struggle between them to survive; then these same ideas also applied to man presenting him as a descendant of primates or monkeys; with which the wick of the confusion and the division of ideas about the origin of the man was lit. And, since these theories continue to be the cause of one of the biggest lies that may have existed in the intellectual circles, it is that we expand a little more to reach the truth.

The wise men of science tell us that the human being is the product of a series of evolutionary changes, carried out in millions of years. We start as tiny cells in the so-called vital broth; until it occurred to one of them to invent a gut and then a stomach and so on until it became the first fish, then the first vertebrate, in reptiles with their greatest exponents the dinosaurs.

Simultaneously to these evolutions the mammals also appeared and with them the primates or monkeys and from there the humans. Being the oldest representative of this evolutionary chain of man, the "Pithecanthropus". They tell us that this primitive being not only walked straight and on two feet like today's men; if not, he had also acquired the faculty of articulated language.

The evidence or remains of this supposed primitive man are: a piece or upper part of a skull, some teeth and a femur; discovered in Java in 1887, by a Dutch anatomist, Dr. Dubois. There is also a skull that goes back as they say a million years ago; found in Mongolia in 1926 which they call: "The Peking Man", which according to the anatomist Grafton Elliot Smith, shows an expansion in the brain surfaces that we associate with the power to emit articulated words.

Then we have the "Neanderthal" man, of whom they found a greater number of bone remains. They lived in the time of the mammoths when Britain, Spain and France were like the current Greenland. They knew fire, made weapons and utensils and believed in a posthumous existence as evidenced by their graves.

Remains of this human have been found in Europe, Palestine, Kenya and southern Africa.

Finally, we have the "Cro-Magnon" man who lived thirty thousand years ago and whose bone characteristics do not differ much from the current man.

Since Darwin published his famous work "The Origin of Species", his theory became the dogma and doctrine of scientific schools, spreading it in all schools, colleges and universities around the world. The vast majority of men of science do not even doubt that the man comes from a chain or species of primates separated from the Sinanthropus or monkeys that we know as the gorilla and the chimpanzee.

However, if we investigate and analyze with an open criterion and with a cold mind without heat and fanaticism; we will find that these theories spread as truth, have a subjective and not scientific origin.

In no way do we doubt that Darwin has contributed much to the advances and knowledge of science; but long before his famous theory of evolution appeared, the atmosphere that dominated the circles of thinkers and men of science was that of a hidden dislike first and then of an open hostility to the institution that had governed the cultural, political destiny, social and religious for several centuries. We refer more specifically to the Catholic and Roman Church, which after having enjoyed religious and earthly power became the victim of fierce attacks.

And, it is here, where this struggle arises to contradict it, and destroy the institution that they considered as an obstacle to the development of science, and thinkers emerge as: Voltaire, Montesquieu, Rosseau, Kant, Engels, Bauer, etc. The men of science align with them and many declare themselves atheists and skeptics. And they launch their famous postulates: "Do not believe if you do not see it" (The same that they use only when it suits them).

Such is the case of the evolutionary theory of man, because until now they cannot prove anything; however, they cling to it and teach it as true. I wonder: How can it be possible that such wise and prepared men have fallen into a sophistry of that nature? - Are a piece of skull, teeth and a femur enough evidence to launch such statements?

We as simple common men, we think with a bit of logic: If man had appeared on earth by evolution, which developed in millions of years: Why do not we find thousands and thousands of bone remains of these beings intermediate between the monkey and the man? Why do these prepared men fall victim to such stupidity?

According to this theory, man as well as other living beings should continue to evolve and we would be presently witnesses of the existence of these intermediate beings between the monkey and the man, between the fish, vertebrates and birds, between the cells and organisms more complex. However, none of that happens; we only see well-defined beings, all belonging to their respective species; without intermediate phases between one and the other. What happened to the logical reasoning of these great sages? - Were those three bones found enough evidence for such great confusion and lies? - Doesn't humanity deserve respect and honesty?

In the magnificent series "NOVA" Adventures of Science, which was published in writing and video, in chapter 70 entitled: "Darwin Revised" informs us that many paleontologists who dedicated their lives to confirm Darwin's theory, ended up completely demoralized and disappointed; because the fossil records they studied did not undergo any major change or transformation in millions of years.

Such is the case of the American paleontologist, Niles Eldredge, of the American Museum of Natural History in New York. Likewise, another famous Darwinian paleontologist and expert Dr. Stephen Jay Gould collaborated with this study. However, these discoveries that contradict Darwinian Theory do not spread and are not taught in colleges or universities, it is worth asking: Why? - Who is behind all this? Satan, to whom it is not convenient for man to believe in his Creator. And as I said before, this proves that men of science act subjectively, out of aversion and fanaticism. I will refer to the case of a great man of science, respected, loved and famous worldwide, author of the series "COSMOS", I refer to Carl Sagan, who in chapter II, entitled: "A Voice in the Cosmic Escape", when talking about evolution and natural selection, he says: "The simplest organism of a cell is much more complex than the finest wristwatch; however, the clocks do not assemble spontaneously or develop in slow periods on their own. A watch was made by a watchmaker. That is why we deduce that there is no way in which atoms and molecules can spontaneously assemble and create organisms of such wonderful complexity." So far the reasoning it gives is the most logical and on which the Church always relied on to explain Creation.

But this famous scientist leaves all his reasoning logically and suddenly changes and says: "But it is not like that... it would be ideal if there was a Great Designer, who provides natural significance and order and of great importance to human beings; but as Darwin and Wallace taught, there is another way of seeing things much more attractive, more human, (and I would add more satanic) and with greater strength to believe that it was. And, this is the "Natural Selection" that Darwin talks about. (Some say that this great intellectual, those who financed the Cosmos series, gave a very good sum of money to affirm such a thing totally contrary to what he was saying).

As you can see, for this great intellectual and man of science, even without the evidence they claim to believe in something, he emphatically says that living beings came to populate the Earth by chance, they evolved because they wanted it to be and they became what they are, including man, in millions of years of evolution.

Therefore, there is no Designer or Creator as we want to call it. - Can you imagine such absurd reasoning on the part of these intellectuals and men of science?

Fortunately, there are some scientists, very brave of course, who dared to release their knowledge acquired by the research they have done, such as: Robert Jastrow, who in his work "God and the Astronomers", explaining the Big Bang theory or Great Explosion, explains: That matter that was compressed at first, exploded, burst, but who caused that great explosion? Scientists call it a great force; theologians call it God.

Just as in the Genesis of the universe there is a Responsible, science currently as more research, more reinforces the idea of "Great Designer"; but the vast majority of these try to downplay or hide the person responsible for creation.

Jastrow himself tells how most scientists, including Einstein, Eddington, Walter Nernst, Philip Morrison, among others, were surprised at the discoveries they were making and felt angry, moody, because this totally changed the cosmological vision that they had been wrongly manufactured.

Now we see how astronomical evidence leads us to the biblical view of the origin of the universe. The details differ, but the essential elements in the biblical account of Genesis are the same.

Dr. Jastrow continues to illustrate: "Science has proven that the universe began with a great explosion. This leads to the question: What caused this explosion? - Who or what put matter and energy in this universe? - Was the universe created from nothing or was it assembled from pre-existing materials? - Science cannot answer these questions, because all research ends at the time of creation.

For scientists who have lived governed by the power of materialism, this story ends as a bad dream. These have climbed the mountain of knowledge based on much study and work; but when they make the final effort of their greatest discovery, just when they reach the highest mountain of knowledge, they find that they are greeted and received by a lot of friars (theologians), who have been sitting there for hundreds of years.

Now, returning again to the issue of the origin of man, which as in the first case in which science itself collaborated to unveil the mystery of the creation of the universe; Science has also indirectly and unwittingly collaborated to unveil the mystery of man's origin.

We have already seen that even though they have searched for the missing link and other phases and tests that lead to corroborate their evolutionary theories, they have not succeeded. The only thing they have found is that each animal species is on Earth as if someone had put it in some given time, with no changes or intermediate phases of the so-called evolution. And, the only certain thing that is seen in any evolutionary theory, both of man and of animals, are gaps and explanations that do not match the scientific evidence they discover.

What is good to clarify to the readers is the lie that the enemies of God are spreading, saying that the Church and Pope John Paul II have already accepted the theory of evolution, which is not true. In this regard, I transcribe a comment by Presbyter Alvaro Rocha, a doctor of medicine and philosophy, to better illustrate this delicate issue:

MARX

Karl Marx, along with his friend Engels created a new political-social thought that also changed the course of modern history. Marxism uses the dialectical principle, which they applied especially in the struggle of social classes.

Marx sees the proletariat (workers) in a state of war and constant conflict with the bourgeoisie (owners and capitalists). The capitalists are the exploiters and the workers are the exploited, so he thought that to create an ideal state the only way would be to eliminate social classes.

In Marxist thought, the influence of Hegel is clearly seen, the three elements of his theory are at stake; the thesis (positive force) the antithesis (opposite force). Facing these two, you get another force different from the previous ones. Marx applied this theory to society, believing that in facing these two forces (proletarians against bourgeoisie) he would create the dynamics to throw society towards a new development.

Marx and Engels believed that this great class struggle would eliminate the cause of all past conflicts of humanity, they thought that the cause of all clashes, wars and discords came from private property; then, if the class that does not have material goods, defeats the class that has them, the result would be that there would be nothing to continue fighting and everyone would live happily.

To rebuild the world and create this classless society, Marxism uses all kinds of weapons, not only is it possible to use tanks, bombs and deadly gases, but it also uses education, indoctrination, religion, commerce and culture to accomplish its tasks. It's supposed objective was to achieve the material improvement of society regardless of the methods used to achieve it; the end justifies the means, he said. The goals set by Marx were: abolish private property; centralize power in the hands of the state; Control or conquer the world to implement the system. Marx justified the violence to achieve his ideal state. For more than a century, we have been seeing what these ideas actually put into practice by the communists, with more than twenty million murdered in Russia alone without counting another sixty million in China and the other countries that fell into claws of communism. Think about the large number of murders that Marxism produced! Is that good?

It would be good to ask: Why was Marxism the cause of so many millions of murders, of so much suffering and death in the concentration camps? Why those fruits so bad for humanity?

But how will he not bear those fruits if his creator, who appeared to be an atheist, was a fervent worshiper of Satan. Didn't you know? Well, find out about this: According to a study by the renowned evangelist: Richard Wurmbrand, there is enough convincing evidence to believe that Marx, Engels, Hess and other characters of those times were very involved in satanic practices.

Many of Marx's biographers have given light on the strange rites, letters and poems he practiced and wrote. For proof of the unbelievers who will want to defend this character that caused the misery and death of millions of people on the planet, there are still his poems and writings that leave no doubt about the true personality and intentions of this fellow. In one of his many poems he writes:

"I wish to take revenge on the One who rules on High."

Then in his poem "Summoning a Desperate," he says:

"Well, one God has taken everything from me.
In the curse and torment of destiny all its worlds gone irrevocably,
only my revenge remains.
I will build my throne in the Heights on an immense and cold summit.
For his bulwark - superstitious horror.
For his sheriff - the blackest agony.

And so it goes on with a series of allegories that recall Lucifer's proud display; as if Marx were the spokesman of the Prince of Darkness.
In another poem titled "The Violinist," he says:

"The infernal vapors rise and fill the mind, until I go crazy and
my heart is totally changed.
Do you see this Sword?
The Prince of Darkness sold it to me ...."

These lines take on special significance if we know that in the rites of superior initiation of satanic worship, an enchanted sword is sold to the candidate; of course, signing a blood pact and alienating his soul.

In another of his drama poems entitled "Culanem," he makes some allegory of what Marxism was when he says:

"I will jump inside, even if I bring the world to its ruin.
The world that expands between me and the abyss,
I will tear it apart with my perennial curses."
"I will narrow my arms around their cruel reality. Hugging me,
(adopting Marxism) the world will succumb stupidly.
And then it will sink into absolute nothingness. "

Like these poems, there is a great deal of material such as letters and comments that his own family, as his daughter Eleanor told, and one of his biographers ends up saying: "There is almost no doubt that these endless stories were autobiographical ... He had a diabolical vision. Sometimes he seemed to be aware of performing the work of the devil. "

Then it is known that Marx met Moses Hess, who made him embrace the socialist ideal, and he himself called him: "Dr. Marx, my idol, who will give the final kick to religion." Another friend of Marx of that time, George Jung, wrote in 1841, that Marx would expel God from his Heaven.

Under this new perspective that few know, it is clear that the expectations Marx and his friends had been not the high social ideals of helping humanity, but of destroying humanity and waging war on God and his Church; As Wurmbrand says: "Socialism was nothing but the bait that would attract proletarians and intellectuals to embrace the diabolical ideal." When the Soviets adopted the saying: "Let's cast the capitalists of the earth and God of Heaven," they were only fulfilling Marx's legacy.

Karl Marx founded the First Socialist International, along with Bakunin, who writes:

"In this revolution we will have to wake up the devil in the people, to provoke the lowest passions."

All these socialist characters, including Proudhom, used long hair and grown beards, as Marx is known, and it is known to be typical of Joanna Southcott's 19th century satanic sect.

It is necessary to clarify that Marx and his comrades, although they were against God, were not atheists as described by the Marxists of the present time. For by openly insulting God, they hated a God in whom they believed. It is not their existence that they objected, but their supremacy.

Once Marxism was established in Russia, China and other parts of the world, the abuse and hatred that they have shown against priests, pastors, nuns and everything related to the Church of Christ is irrational and absurd. Why obscene teasing and torture applied to Christians? Why the diabolical persecutions to which Christians were subjected in the countries of the "Iron Curtain"? What do these vexations have to do with the socialism and welfare of the proletariat? Why this aversion to baptism? just as an example to the thousands of cases that happen: In Albania the priest Esteban Kurti was sentenced to death for having baptized a child; In Communist China and North Korea, baptisms have to be performed in secret. Why this irrational hatred of Christian rites especially of baptism? For atheists as they claim to be the communists; Baptism should mean nothing. Being baptized should not cause harm or benefit; however, they are taught with all those who dare to practice their religion. This is proof that his ideology is not inspired by atheism but in Satanism. The communist persecution against religion could have a human explanation; but the fury and hatred with which they treat the Christian, goes beyond reason.

In the communist newspaper "Vetchernaia Moskva", in one of their editorials they wrote: "Our struggle is not against believers, not even against clerics. We fight against God to tear away believers."

That is the real reason for Marxism. The crimes of communism have no parallel in history. What other political system has killed twenty million human beings as the Soviets have done in half a century? And another sixty-millions were killed in China; For all that, there is no doubt that the origin of this ideology is diabolical, it exceeds the ordinary.

Dear Christian Brothers: There are no possibilities of agreement between Christianity and Marxism. Those who proclaim themselves Christians - Marxists, deceive themselves or try to deceive others. You are either from Christ or from the devil, here there can be no half measures; Jesus came to undo the works of the devil (1 John 3,8).

Communism is not only political, but a philosophy, a psychological conditioning, a doctrinal education, a directed way of life and a religion that promises utopia to its devotees and in which the State is worshiped and revered instead of God.

FREUD

Sigmund Freud, founder of psychoanalysis, was attracted by Darwin's theories; Freud believed that the human race acts primarily for pleasure, said that everything began and ended with sex, according to his theories, man lived constantly repressed by the hypocritical customs of society, who did not let him satisfy his sexual desires freely; This repression made him an unhappy and repressed being because there was a conflict between the search for pleasure and the rules imposed by society.

Therefore, the world was full of neurotics, paranoids and all kinds of mentally ill people. For Freud there was no reason to explain the existence of man; neither was there God, and man himself has no specific goal to accomplish during his existence, consequently everything is allowed. With these theories Freud laid the foundations for the current world to become a permissive society where debauchery is the flag that all fly, and naturally, this found great acceptance among intellectuals, media and all the people in general, those who defend debauchery confusing it with freedom.

DISASTROUS CONSEQUENCES

Before Kant spread his ideas, the world accepted the possibility of the absolute, both in knowledge and in morals; but, after this one, the so-called philosophical dictator Hegel left an inheritance of brutality and violence that invaded the twentieth century. Lenin, Stalin, Mao, Hitler, Mussolini and the other communist dictators, followed these tips perfectly.

Marx laid the groundwork for communist philosophy to believe that everything can be explained and reduced to matter; for them materialism is the beginning and end of reality, all that exists is the result of the ceaseless movement of the forces of nature; for that reason, for them the world is the product of accumulated accidents there are no laws, neither design nor designer (God); In nature there is only matter and strength.

In sum, the ideas that these men introduced caused a truly disastrous impact; since man did not have a special appearance on the planet, he does not have a special destiny either. And this is the kind of thinking that currently reigns throughout the world. Humanity is sunk in despair, disoriented and confused, with a moral behavior on the ground and a behavior worse than that of animals. Millions of human beings live under the bloody dictatorial regimes of some countries such as China, Korea, Cuba and until recently Russia, or what was the Union of Soviet Socialist Republics that had invaded and imprisoned many other countries; where thousands of human beings have been and are killed, massacred, tortured, imprisoned with the most inhuman cruelty; because for these fanatical beings dominated by Satan life is worthless and those who do not commune with their wrong ideas must be exterminated. The same is happening now in Venezuela, where people have to get out of their country in order to survive.

There are also countries that could well say that they are in undeclared civil war, since thousands die every year victims of organized crime, murderers and maniacal thieves; thousands are those who live in such darkness and despair that they prefer to take their lives and thousands who take refuge in drugs, to later become human waste, beings dominated by vice, without will and easy prey to evil.

In the same way the tares that Freud sowed, has grown rapidly and already most of humanity is reaping the fruits. In the entire world, especially in industrialized countries, all kinds of crimes and offenses against the law are committed, however, offenders are consented, excused and defended in the name of modern science of Psychology

Only in the United States of America every 25 minutes there is a homicide, human behavior scientists try to explain and find the causes of this crisis of violence, of unhappiness and despair, of the destruction of man by man. But everything is in vain; and they do not realize that it is a consequence of the social model and thought left by Freud to allow and consent all kind of disrespect in the name of modernism, which is leading to the total disintegration of the family and therefore of society.

Speaking again of the United States (for being the model and expression of the rest of the countries) every week, more than 15,000 minors, flee their homes, schools and institutions; almost all of them to lead a sad and degrading life, because in order to survive they have to prostitute themselves. What leads them to make such decisions? The main reason is the lack of love and understanding of the parents; generally these boys live in houses where parents behave like dogs and cats, all the time fighting and arguing, homes where instead of parents have two automatons or humanoids that do not radiate or offer heat, affection, or love. Many of these parents think that money fixes all their children's problems and where they only have time to work; because his main goal is to have a lot of money, buy cars of the year, dress with the latest shouts of fashion, have fun in dances, drunkenness, drugs and have sex with anyone who shows up, just like the animals themselves. There are many homes, where the father and mother lead a life of alcoholism and drug addiction, houses where living in them is a real hell, because they inhabit, not human beings but depraved and mentally ill who rape their own children and family members

And so with all these tares and misfortunes that humanity suffers, the descendants of Freud, still do not want to distinguish a free society from a society of beasts whose example they take even from the same animals; but see the latest modern dances such as reggaeton, because those who do really behave like dogs. For them, discipline is something that has gone out of style, which is cruel and harmful; But, what a life they spend!

Currently, every 10 marriages 8 end in divorce, no later than 2 years after having married. Sex orgies are practiced on the agenda, by all kinds of people, not only by single couples but by marriages constituted for the purpose of exchanging partners. And all these aberrations are committed by people of all social classes, especially those who at first glance seem to be good, honorable and with respectable professions.

Likewise, there are temples dedicated to sex, masochism and pleasure. There are social, political and religious institutions of lesbians and homosexuals; recreational places where the most depraved sexual scenes between humans and animals are exhibited. Countries, where there are laws that permit have sex with animals.

Seeing all this, one can only ask: What can you expect from Freud's teachings? In man everything begins and ends with sex, pleasure is the goal; and with this we must combat the unhappiness that humanity feels for repressing its erotic desires; for this one, there was no God, therefore everything is allowed. Ironically in our time the ethical influence of Freud, which says that everything is allowed because that must be the natural way of man to achieve happiness and freedom, has grown enormously, leaving a sequel to degradation, despair, dirt, destruction and death.

What a price they pay, to follow the teachings of these wise men, to crawl through the filth of sin, lust and crime! While his psychoanalytic technique, which is supposed to cure mental illnesses, is becoming more and more extinct, however psychopaths, maniacs, madmen and mentally ill people in general, continue to increase, millions of people visit psychiatrist clinics and psychologists throughout the world, incredible sums of money are spent for these mind experts to rid those unhappy of their mental ills. But what irony! the same doctors of the mind, those who know how to return to normal to a lost mind, are those who easily fall into madness and even more, the percentage of suicides among these professionals is one of the highest among all professions. How can this be possible? Could it be that by playing with evil, they themselves fall into the trap? Do they use the wrong means to fight evil? Because what is a mental illness? Are not all evils the product of sin? Those who go to psychiatric clinics do so for months and even years to get some relief, and almost they never get it; but repentance, a confession, a plea of forgiveness or reconciliation, heal and relieve in seconds those enormous weights of remorse and guilt that the men of these times have called mental illness.

To end with this brief theme of the dire consequences that the ideas of these "wise" men have brought, we will say: that humanity and especially youth have come to experience the worst moments of spiritual crisis in their history; due to lack of discipline, lack of morals and ethics, lack of a truly Christian religious education and above all for lack of love for God.

Humanity is lost, without goals and moral and spiritual values, and therefore live empty and desperate, and to fill that void (which only

God can satisfy); they take refuge in drugs, in sexual and material pleasures, in crazy and lustful music, in crime, in esotericism, in abominable satanic cults and in the whole range of filth that the enemy of God has invented for mankind.

The Holy Spirit clearly says that:

"In the last days many people will abandon their faith and obey lying spirits and will follow the teachings and doctrines of demons, doctrines spread by tricksters, hypocrites who have a dead conscience as if it had been burned with burning iron." (1 Timothy 4, 1-2)

But it is also necessary that we realize that we are in the times of great darkness, because the forces of hell have taken possession of the world; John tells us about in Revelation 9, 2.

"And he opened the bottomless pit and smoke rose from the pit like the smoke of a great furnace; and the sun and the air were darkened by the smoke of the well".

Below I transcribe the words of Anne Graham, daughter of the American preacher Billy Graham, which accurately reflect the dire consequences of the teachings of the wise men sent by Satan for the destruction of men:

In the interview with Billy Graham's daughter at the Early Show, Jane Clayson asked him, "How could God allow this to happen?" (He was referring to the attacks of September 11). Anne Graham gave an extremely deep and full of wisdom answer. She said:

"Like us, I believe that God is deeply sad for this event, but for years we have been telling God to get out of our schools, get out of our government and get out of our lives. And being the gentleman who He is, I think he has quietly retired. How can we expect God to give us His blessing and protection when we have demanded that He let us be alone? "

In light of certain recent events ... terrorist attacks, school shootings, etc., I think it all started when Madeleine Murria O'Hare complained that she didn't want her to pray in our schools, and we said it was fine.

Then someone said that the Bible would not be read any more in schools ... the Bible says you will not kill, you will not steal, you will love your neighbor as yourself. And we said it was fine.

Then Dr. Benjamin Spock said that we should not hit our children when they misbehave because their small personalities would be truncated and we could hurt their self-esteem (Dr. Spock's son committed suicide). We said that the experts know what they are saying. And we said it was fine.

Then someone said that teachers and school principals should not discipline our children when they misbehave. School administrators said that it was better for no member of the school faculty to touch any student who misbehaves because we do not want negative publicity and of course we do not want to be sued (there is a big difference between disciplining, touching, hit, slap, humiliate, kick, etc.). And we said it was fine.

Then someone said, let our daughters abort if they want, and they don't even have to tell their parents. And we said it was fine.

Then one of the school administration councilors said, since boys are always going to be boys and they are going to do it anyway, let's give our children all the condoms they want so they can have maximum fun, and not we have to tell their parents that we gave them to them at school. And we said it was fine.

Then some of our top public officials said it doesn't matter what we do privately while we do our job. We agreed with them and said, I don't care what anyone, including the President, does in his private life as long as I have a job and the economy is fine. Then someone said we will print magazines with photographs of naked women and say that this is a healthy and realistic appreciation of the beauty of the female body. And we said it was fine.

And then someone else took further appreciation and published photographs of naked children, taking it even further when he placed them on the Internet. And we said it was good, they have the right to freedom of expression.

Then the entertainment industry said, let's do TV shows and movies that promote profane, violence and illicit sex. Let's record music that stimulates rapes, drugs, suicides and satanic themes. And we said, it's just fun, it has no negative effects; nobody takes it seriously anyway, so go ahead.

Now we ask ourselves: why do our children have no conscience, why do they not know how to distinguish between good and evil, and why they are not worried about killing strangers, their schoolmates, or themselves?

Probably, if we think about it slowly we will find the answer. I think it has a lot to do with: **"what is sown is gathered".**

CHAPTER IV
WARNING SIGNS

THE COUNTDOWN HAS BEGUN

On July 16, 1969, three men, Armstrong, Aldrin and Collins, a little nervous and in their respective seats of the Apollo 11 spacecraft, listened to the countdown transmitted from the Houston control base; each time a number was said they approached zero, at the precise moment when the ship would take off with enormous rumble and speed towards its destination, the moon, where they had to walk, explore and take samples of the terrestrial satellite.

In order to understand the end of this corrupt world, we will give the example of the countdown used for space travel. The earth is making a space travel during which the enemy of God and man is in command of the ship and will raise millions of wild hordes, confusing, corrupting and causing chaos and almost total destruction, of the ship as of all its crew and passengers, in a desperate desire to remain in command of this ship.

Almost near the end of the trip, Christ, commander in chief by right of this ship, will take possession of it, defeating the armies of evil; then at the end, after this spacecraft that is the earth, has passed from the hands of evil that led it to drift and destruction, towards the hands of the good, it will finally and again reach its destination, God, from which it walked away thousands of years ago.

In some countries and on several occasions there have been cases that groups of people have gone to the mountains and depopulated zones because some charlatans alarmed them by telling them that the end of the world would be for this or that day; thought that out of the cities they might be saved. Moreover, these people have no idea how the events of the end will be.

The final count has long since begun ... But, what do we rely on to make such a statement? Because, we cannot, nor should we fall into the same error of the sects.

Well, the signs that the prophets, Christ and the apostles have left written about this event are clear and precise; because they will be developed by stages and events that we have already begun to live and witness; such as: The rebirth of Israel. The armamentism and hatred that is increasing in the Arab countries against Israel and the United States. The unification of Europe. The moral decay of society. The current advancement of science playing gods, manipulating DNA and manipulating human embryos and then disposing of them as unusable material. The emergence of new deadly diseases such as AIDS and now the Covid 19 virus. The millions of helpless human beings killed every day by abortion. The political and moral situation of the United States, Russia and all European countries. The proliferation of satanic sects and religions of all kinds.

The drug problem, the hunger that kills thousands of people in Africa and India. Wars in different countries.

The hate to Catholics and their leader the Pope. The persecution and genocide of Christians across the world is worse today "than at any time in history,"

The study by Aid to the Church in Need, said: the treatment of Christians has worsened substantially in the past two years compared, and has grown more violent than any other period in modern times. The report examined the plight of Christians in China, Egypt, Eritrea, India, Iran, Iraq, Nigeria, North Korea, Pakistan, Saudi Arabia, Sudan, Syria and Turkey over the period lasting from 2015 until 2017. The research showed that in that time, Christians suffered crimes against humanity, and some were hanged or crucified. In Africa, the report focused on countries like Sudan, where the government ordered that churches be destroyed, and Nigeria, where ISIS-affiliated groups like Boko Haram have led a surge in attacks on Christians. In Eritrea, thousands of Christians have been rounded up and imprisoned over the past year because of their faith. The report also documented numerous case studies in which Christians in countries such as India and Nigeria were murdered or beaten for practicing their faith. The scandals that occur within it, (the Church)

The continuing threat of international terrorism either from the Muslim world or from Marxist-Leninist-Maoists. The political, social and commercial phenomenon of globalization. All this clearly indicates that the countdown has already begun.

SIGNS OF THE TIMES.

Yahweh as God and Lord of the universe knows in advance

everything that will happen in the future and what the enemy will try to do to continue making war on him. That is why apart from sending men to announce the advent of the Messiah, he also gave them vision of the future so that through their writings humanity knows in advance what to expect, what they should do and who they should trust. This NOTICE, not only did the prophets give it thousands of years ago, but also Jesus Christ himself and his followers spoke clearly of the things that will happen, emphasizing the horrors that the ruler of darkness will come to realize.

God has long foreseen and put humanity on alert, so that they are prepared for when these things happen

"When you see the clouds coming from the west, they immediately say that it is going to rain, when they feel the blow of the south wind, they say it is going to be hot and that happens. Hypocrites! They can look at heaven and earth and predict the weather conditions.

Why don't you want to understand the meaning of the present situation? (Luke 12, 54)

You cannot ask for clearer signs of the approach of the Second Coming of Christ. Just read in the newspapers or look on the social media to realize that the final tribulation has begun. and who does not want to realize it is simply for foolishness. The facts described below are prophecies that have already been fulfilled or are in full compliance.

WARS

"You will hear about wars and rumors of wars, nation will rise against nation, kingdom against kingdom... but all this is only the beginning of sorrows." (Matthew 24, 6)

The First World War or the Great War was an armed conflict that took place between 1914 and 1918, which resulted in more than 10 million deaths. More than 60 million European soldiers were mobilized from 1914 to 1918. Originated in Europe, it became the first armed conflict to cover more than half of the planet. It was at the time the bloodiest war in history. Before World War II, this war used to be called the Great War or the War of Wars. The hostilities involved 32 countries, 28 of them called «Allies»: France, the United Kingdom, Russia, Serbia, Belgium, Canada, Portugal, Japan, the

United States (since 1917), as well as Italy, which had left the Triple Alliance. This group faced the coalition of the "Central Powers", composed of the Austro-Hungarian, German and Ottoman empires, accompanied by Bulgaria. (http://es.wikipedia.org/wiki/Primera_Guerra_Mundial).

World War II was the largest and bloodiest armed conflict in world history, in which the Allied Powers and Axis Powers clashed between 1939 and 1945. Armed forces from more than seventy countries participated in air, naval and terrestrial as a result of the war, around 2% of the world's population died (about 60 million people), mostly civilians. As a world conflict, it began on September 1, 1939 (although some historians argue that on its Asian front it was declared on July 7, 1937) to officially end on September 2, 1945. (http://en.wikipedia.org / wiki / Second_World_War).

After the two great wars, many others have been raised, here is the relationship of the most important: Indochina War vs. France 1946-1954. Korean War 1950-1953. Vietnam War 1962-1975. Algerian War vs. France 1954-1958. Middle East wars between Israel vs. Arab States 1948-1956-1967-1973. and continue until now. Congo War 1961. Biafra War 1968. Indo Pakistani War 1971. War between the USSR vs. Afghanistan 1979-1989. Iran vs. War Iraq 1980-1988. Kuwait War or Gulf War 1990-1991. US War vs. Afghanistan 2002. Yugoslavian Secessionist War 1991. US War vs. Iran 2003.

Can we ask for more signals? One of the biggest armed conflicts was in Bosnia-Herzegovina, where Medjugorje is located and where more than 60,000 people have died in just 100 days of civil war; Hundreds of thousands have lost their homes, there are thousands of orphaned children and the atrocities in the concentration camps were worse than in World War II. In addition to Bosnia, there is war in Georgia and Ossetia, Armenia and Azerbaijan, in several countries in Africa and Afghanistan. Currently, rumors of a nuclear war that will destroy almost the entire planet are increasingly worrying. North Korea's recent claim that they conducted a test of a hydrogen bomb. Terrorism has claimed thousands of deaths in South Africa, Colombia, Peru, Ireland, Bolivia. Brazil, Palestine and other places.

ISRAEL

The events that happen to the Hebrew people are one of the main clues to affirm that we are near the end; because before Christ returns, the Jewish people have to be a country again, a nation where it once was.

The history of the Jews is full of miracles; their very existence is a true miracle. What people can trace their religious unity up to about 4,000 years? Twice they were destroyed as a nation, they have lived under the most inhuman conditions, always persecuted, always humiliated, mistreated and thrown from everywhere they went. The survival of the Jews is a phenomenon predicted very accurately by the prophets. Moses predicted that by continuing unbelief and contempt for God. Israel would be destroyed twice, in the second the survivors would be dispersed throughout the world, they would be persecuted, they would have no country or place to rest.

"And Yahweh will disperse you, among the peoples from one to the other end of the earth and there you will serve other gods that neither you nor your ancestors knew.

Nor in these villages will you have peace of mind or find a place to lay the soles of your feet. " (Deuteronomy 28.64)

Almost all the prophets, such as Isaiah, Jeremiah, Ezekiel and Amos, predicted this worldwide dispersion of the Hebrew people; including the Messiah who said:

"They will fall by the edge of swords and be taken captive among all nations and Jerusalem will be trampled by the Gentiles, until the times of the nations are fulfilled." (Luke 21,24)

It is important to note that Jesus predicted these facts, emphasizing that the people of his own generation, the same who crucified him, would be fulfilled.

"Truly I tell you that all this will come upon this generation"

(Matthew 23, 36)

History has confirmed these facts, in less than 40 years after the death of Jesus; Titus with his Roman legions destroyed Jerusalem and the entire country, killing hundreds of thousands of Jews and survivors sold as slaves.

For almost two thousand years, Jacob's descendants have roamed the entire world, without a country, persecuted, mistreated and murdered by the imperialist Russia and other European nations until the most recent monstrous act that Hitler's regime committed, killing More than six million Jews.

The history of Israel must be a warning sign for all believers, a sign that among other things must teach us, that what God has said in the Bible is fulfilled.

REBIRTH OF ISRAEL

"The Lord says: The day is coming, when I restored David's kingdom, which is like a fallen and ruined house.

I will return my people to their towns, to their lands, they will rebuild their ruined cities and live there.

I will plant my people in the land I gave them and they will never be taken out of there. The Lord God has spoken"
(Amos 9,11)

Through centuries, many people have not wanted to give credit to the prophecies of the return of the Jews to their homeland, rather they thought it was a figurative return of the Christian world; and they did not realize that, if the first part of the prophecy (the dispersion) was fulfilled. Why would the second part not be fulfilled? (return)

More or less in the year of 1870, some Jews began to found some agricultural colonies in Palestine, hence the idea of the Zionist Movement, of forming an independent Jewish State in Palestine. The idea seemed to be just a dream of some that perhaps would never come true; until an Australian Jew named Theodore Herzl organized the first Zionist movement with effective political force throughout the world. Hitler's crimes stimulated Jewish nationalism and saw in Zionism the solution to the infinite problems they had. The idea of having a homeland again was growing and many Jewish families emigrated to the land of their ancestors; but not everyone thought of that return, for many of them were prosperous in their adoptive lands, until a man who hated Jews came to power in

Germany, declared war on many countries, invading and killing Jews in concentration camps, burning them in ovens, suffocating them with gases and experimenting with them as if they were simple laboratory animals. The world was in turmoil, World War II claimed millions of victims and Hitler, its author, seemed to be going to achieve their purposes, while thousands and thousands of terrified Jews took refuge in the only place they thought would be safe, Palestine; but even to get there they had many problems. The Arabs, who owned these lands, opposed, as did the English, who occupied these territories and did not want to upset the Arabs. During the mandate of the English they only let in 75,000 Jews and many died trying to enter their land; until they finally forced their entry. The British withdrew and on the night of the fourteenth of May 1948, in the midst of endless bureaucratic problems, wars, murders and plots; Jewish leaders proclaimed the creation of the State of Israel, forming a provisional government under David Ben Gurion as Prime Minister. Immediately after and simultaneously the armies of Syria, Lebanon, Egypt, Iraq and Transjordan, began to attack the barely reborn State of Israel.

The new Jewish state lacked the most essential: People prepared for war and weaponry. Just look at the map of the territory that Israel occupies, composed at that time of a few thousand Jews to understand that something miraculous must have happened here, surrounded by enemy countries such as Lebanon, Syria, Jordan, Saudi Arabia and Egypt, more the reinforcement of Iraq, Algeria, Tunisia, Morocco, Iran, represented one hundred million Arabs; but despite that, they emerged victorious in all their campaigns. Israel, against all odds, won its fight, as the prophecies announced.

Days after the existence of the State of Israel had been declared, several Arab countries invaded it, being the most prepared and organized in Egypt, it had seven divisions of well-trained and well-armed men against three divisions of the Israelites, poorly equipped, and without armament Egypt, had over a thousand tanks and Nasser its President, gave the Jews 48 hours to leave the territory, otherwise it would sweep them away.

They also had a strong and disciplined air force, with ships and war frigates. However, the phenomenon cannot be explained with human arguments, but the reality is unquestionable. Israel seized in a few hours seven hundred enemy tanks, swept against the

Egyptian air force, caused more than twenty-five thousand casualties in front of two thousand of its newly constituted army and emerged victorious. How do they say there are no miracles? Why can't they believe the prophecies written in the Bible?

Then came the "Six Day" war in 1967, where Israel occupied almost all the territories that were theirs in ancient times, a war that was also inexplicable, similar to lightning and in which Israel challenged not only Egypt but to all its enemy neighbors that surrounded it. "The explanation cannot be proved right. It is given to us by faith, it is a supernatural force that we condense into an inexplicable phrase for strong spirits: It was written" (Francisco Sánchez Ventura and Pascual) And as **Micah 7, 15-17** said:

"***Work miracles for us Lord, as you did in the days you took us out of Egypt. The nations will see this and become frustrated, despite all their strength.***"

Oh, what wonders the Lord does!

Israel lives surrounded by enemies that do not leave it alone, but despite all the difficulties, it is now a strong, aggressive and prosperous country. Where before it was desert and ruins the cities are reborn and prosper, the desert fields flourish, agriculture advances, the industry in general progresses, the mines that were worked by their ancestors are reopened; in short, they have returned, because God has wanted it that way.

"At that time I will turn Jerusalem into a very heavy stone for all nations. It will hurt any of them that try to lift it" ***(Zechariah 12.3)***

However, Israel exists under three alliances or covenants that the Lord made with this people. The first was the promise of the land that he would give to Abraham's descendants. According to the Bible they would always maintain these lands, if they kept the second covenant obedience to Yahweh, from which the third covenant is derived. The recognition and acceptance of the Lord's envoy, the Messiah.

For more than two thousand years the Jewish people have been living without fulfilling any of these alliances and covenants. Scattered throughout the world without land, or homeland, lost and confused, sometimes wondering why so many misfortunes and sufferings happened to them? And they do not realize that the dispersion caused by the Romans or punishment they have suffered for two thousand years, was for their hardness of heart; not seeing in Jesus, the envoy of God.

The people are hard and stubborn to understand, that's why the Lord allows violence and suffering to return them to their land, the Jews returned to Israel because they experienced a horrific worldwide persecution caused by Hitler; never before had such magnitude and cruelty been reached. Most of them had no desire to return to Palestine, a land full of sand and rocks, was not attractive. The Zionist movement existed but many of them were opposed; That is why it had to happen, something hard and extremely painful for them to be forced to return to Palestine and face the situation with determination and courage.

At that time, Palestine was part of the Ottoman Empire and at that time every comment of the prophecies concerning the return of the Jews, seemed only fantasy, then came the First World War, which resulted in the Jews having the right to live in Palestine (just settle, but not to form a state).

Most of them were not yet interested in going to live there.

Then came World War II where Hitler killed more than six million of them, destroyed all their communities in almost all of Europe. And, the only place where they could take refuge was Palestine; Therefore, it was only there that they realized that their only hope to live, was to form their own State, conquering the lands that used to be theirs.

The Jews have returned to Palestine; they have returned to take possession of almost all their land, but have not yet returned completely to God; because they have not accepted his envoy Jesus. That is why they will still have to experience a crueler, ruthless and inhuman crisis.

So far we are in the present tense; where through the press we learn that they are continually besieged by the Arabs and Palestinian terrorists who are within the same country. The hatred that Palestinians feel against their Jewish brothers is ancestral, irrational and insurmountable. Neither of them will give their arm to twist, because they both believe that they are assisted by law, justice and truth. Both dispute the ownership and right of Jerusalem, the city of David. Yaser Arafat, the Prime Minister and leader of the Palestinians, said that one of the conditions to negotiate was the delivery of Jerusalem to the Palestinian people. For its part Israel says: "Jerusalem is not in negotiation, never will be and is ours." Jerusalem, as the prophets say, will be the fuse that ignites the greatest armed conflict that the Jews will have to face shortly before the second coming of Christ, the Messiah they don't want to see.

HUNGER AND FAMINE

One of the signs of the second coming of Christ is coincidentally the hunger and malnutrition that will be in the whole world. The FAO, a United Nations agency that fights against hunger, says in one of its actual reports that there are over 820 million people suffer from hunger, corresponding to about one in every nine people in the world. The BBC World. com, says: Hunger in India at alarming levels. India has one of the highest rates of child malnutrition in the world. Twelve states in India have "alarming" levels of famine as highlighted by a report prepared by the Institute for Research on International Food Policy (IFPRI). India has more people suffering from hunger than any other country in the world, with about 200 million people. Another report says: Africa is starving. Forty million people in Africa suffer from famine as a result of droughts that affect the continent.

According to the World Food Program (WFP), the countries of the Horn of Africa and the southern continent urgently need assistance.

Hunger could kill thousands of people in Somalia according to the UN.

GENEVA (Reuters) - Hunger could take the lives of 10,000 people a month in Somalia, if the next rainy season is as dry as the weather predicted, United Nations aid agencies said.

In Ethiopia and Eritrea alone, between 10 and 14 million depend on international aid. "This could translate between 10,000 and 12,000 deaths per month," Graham Farmer, an FAO official in charge of Somalia, warned at a press conference.

Hunger in Latin America. The UN food agency launched an alert that shakes: extreme poverty or destitution will increase by three million people in Latin America and the Caribbean. The number of hungry people will reach 71 million. The global economic crisis and the excessive rise in prices in the region erased the advances in this area of the last 20 years at a stroke. The problem is not only regional: more than 1 billion people will suffer global hunger at the end of this year.

"When he opened the third seal, I heard the third living being, saying: Come and see. And I looked, and here is a black horse; and he who mounted it had a balance in his hand. 6 And I heard a voice from among the four living creatures, which said: Two pounds of wheat for a denarius, and six pounds of barley for a denarius; but don't damage the oil or the wine." This indicates hunger and shortage. (Rev. 6, 5)

"For nation will rise against nation, and kingdom against kingdom; and there will be plagues, AND HUNGERS, and earthquakes in different places. And all of this will be the beginning of pains". (Matthew 24: 7,8).

EARTHQUAKES AND DISASTERS.

Since 1990, earthquakes and volcanoes have increased and have had incredible activity in places as unusual as Holland and Cuba; affecting seismic areas in Japan, China, Burma, Peru, Costa Rica, Colombia, Nicaragua, Ecuador, Chile and California in the USA and Alaska. And there will be earthquakes in different places... The dramatic increase in severe earthquakes has led many scientists to conclude that we are entering a new period of great activity and seismic disturbances.

The earthquake in North Pakistan on October 8, 2005, was the most severe in the last 120 years, killing more than 70,000 people. Seismic Monitoring spokesmen say: "It is alarming and we are amazed at the increase in earthquakes in recent years." What is happening? A record from 2000 to 2007 of the telluric movements throughout the world follows:

-2000.- According to the National Earthquake Information Center in 2000, 22,256 earthquakes and 20 major earthquakes all occurred with victims. The epicenters were in order: China, Iran, Indonesia, Argentina, Taiwan, Indonesia, Turkey, Indonesia, Taiwan, Honshu Coast, Nicaragua, Turkey, Afghanistan, China, Ecuador, Algeria, New Ireland, Caucasus, Turkmenistan and Turkey. The total number of victims is estimated at 231.

-2001. - In 2001, 23,265 shocks and 18 major earthquakes were recorded, all with victims. Its intensity varied between 4, 2 degrees to 7, 7 on the Richter scale.

Chronologically they happened in El Salvador, India, El Salvador, China, Japan, China, El Salvador, China, Afghanistan, Germany, near the coast of Peru, Italy, Chile, Peru, China and Peru. The highest concentration of deaths was in India with a total of 20,023, followed by El Salvador with 852 dead in the first shock, 315 in the second, 1 in the third and 1 in the fourth, totaling 1,169. The total balance of victims was 21,357.

-2002. -The year 2002 was of intense seismic activity with 27,453 shivers. 30 earthquakes were recorded between 4, 6 degrees to 7, 6 on the Richter scale. The shocks that left dead, happened in Tajikistan, New Guinea, Republic of the Congo, Turkey, Greece, Turkey, Iran, Afghanistan, Philippines, Afghanistan, Taiwan, New Guinea, Afghanistan, Peru, Balkans, Iran, Caucasus, Taiwan, region from Lake Victoria, Iran, Italy, New Guinea, India, Indonesia, Congo, Italy, Kashmir and China. The total death toll is estimated at 1,635.

-2003.- In the year 2003, a total of 31,419 telluric movements were recorded. The highest intensity record was: Near the coast of Guatemala - 6, 5, Colima Mexico - 7, 6, Turkey - 6, 1, South Xinjiang, China - 5, 3, Flores Region, Indonesia - 6, 5 , Hindu Kush Region, Afghanistan - 5, 9, Eastern Turkey - 6, 4, South Xinjiang, China - 5, 8, Northern Algeria - 6, 8, Halmahera, Indonesia - 7, Northern Algeria - 5, 8 , Western Iran - 4, 6, Yunnan, China - 6, Bangladesh, India - 5, 6, East of Nei Mongolia, China - 5, 4, Dominican Republic - 6, 5, Southwest of Siberia, Russia 7, 3, Yunnan, China - 5, 6, Gansu-Qinghai, China - 5, 8, Gansu, China - 5, 2, Sichuan-Yunnan Region, China - 5, 2, Samar, Philippines - 6, 5, Kazakhstan Border- Xinjiang - 6, Central California - 6, 5, Border between Panama and Costa Rica - 6, 5, Southern Iran - 6, 6. Total dead 33,189. 2004.-In the year 2004 a total of 31,194 movements of the earth's crust of varying intensity took place, the worst were recorded, southeast of the Loyalty Islands - 7, 1, Papua, Indonesia - 7, near the South Coast of Papua, Indonesia - 7, 3, near the south west coast of Honshu, Japan - 7, 2, Sumatra, Indonesia - 7, 3, near the south west coast of Honshu, Japan - 7, 3, near the south west coast of Honshu, Japan - 7, 4, Kepulauan Alor, Indonesia - 7, 2, near the west coast of Colombia - 7, 2, Papua, Indonesia - 7, 1, Hokkaido, Japan - 7, north of Macquarie Island - 8, 1, western coast of North Sumatra - 9, 1, Nicobar Islands in India - 7, 1. Total victims 31,194.

On December 26, **2004,** an earthquake of an intensity of 9 degrees on the Richter scale took place on the north coast of Sumatra in South Asia, this triggered a gigantic tsunami in the coastal areas around the Indian Ocean. It is estimated that 228,802 people lost their lives in a dozen countries, 500,000 were injured and five million were left without basic services. This has been the greatest tragedy that has happened in the 21st century!

-2005.-In the year 2005 there were 30,478 displacements of the earth's crust. The most intense movements occurred in: Mar Celebes - 7, 1, Mar Banda - 7, 1, north of Sumatra, Indonesia - 8, 6, Tarapacá, Chile - 7, 8, north of the California coast - 7, 2 , Nicobar Islands, India - 7, 2, near the east coast of Honshu, Japan - 7, 2, region of New Ireland - 7, 7, northern Peru - 7, 5, Pakistan - 7, 6, near the East coast of Honshu, Japan - 7. Number of victims 82,364.

-2006.-In 2006, 29,568 tremors took place, the great majority of low intensity. The most important were, in the Gulf of Mexico - 6, Bougainville Region, Papua, Guinea - 6, 8, Sea of Scotland - 7, Guerrero Mexico - 6, 1. The total number of victims was 6,605. 2007.-The number of telluric movements between 3 degrees to 7, 9 this year was 29,679. One of the most destructive was the one that took place on the coast of the province of Ica in Peru, which caused the massive destruction of tens of thousands of homes and an estimated 514 dead. The total number of victims this year was 712.

Very recently, powerful and alarming disasters recently occurred in the Americas, such as those in Haiti and Chile, each with the inevitable loss of human life, material losses and damage to the earth's structure; caused by the tectonic or telluric movements of the great terrestrial plates.

The 6 biggest earthquakes in the last five years: -1 Chiapas, Mexico, 2017. An 8.2-magnitude earthquake hit the Mexican state of Chiapas on September 7th, 2017. -2 Ecuador, 2016. -3 Chile, 2015. -4 Nepal, April 2015. -5 China, 2014. -6 Pakistan, 2013 and so on, the earthquakes

This year 2019: -Peru, (2 times) intensity VIII severe, -Papua New Guinea (2) VII very strong, -Ecuador, VII very strong, -New Zealand VII very strong, -Indonesia (2) VII very strong, -United states California IX Violent.

Finally, so that no one doubts it, in December 2004 the worst global disaster occurred that affected several Asian countries with more than 300,000 deaths caused by a tsunami. Tsunami of 2004. The worst and most devastating catastrophe in human memory. More than 300,000 dead said informational newspapers.

Hurricane Katrina: It has been the worst and most expensive of all natural disasters in the US. Hurricane Rita: It affected Louisiana even more. Hurricane Wilma: The most intense there has been in the Atlantic. Time of Hurricanes 2005: The most intense in the history of the USA. A hurricane season for the world record book. There have never been so many hurricanes in a season, in a period of 15 months. 8 of them touched Florida. This was also the first time they had to use the Greek alphabet to name hurricanes. The storms of 2005 cost to the US an estimated $ 150 billion in damages. The Monte Pinatubo Philippine volcano erupted and caused more damage to the ozone layer than all industrial chimneys and automobile leaks together. Floods and storms have been monstrous in Argentina, Uruguay, Chile, Cuba and in several states of the American Union with hundreds of thousands of evacuees.

One of the last hurricanes that hit the year **2019** was in Bahamas. Hurricane Dorian killed at least 50 people in The Bahamas – 42 on Abaco and 8 on Grand Bahamas. Damage was preliminarily estimated at more than US$7 billion. Across the Bahamas, the storm left at least 70,000 people homeless. An estimated 13,000 homes, constituting 45% of the homes on the Abacos and Grand Bahama, suffered severe damage or were completely destroyed. https://en.wikipedia.org/wiki/Effects_of_Hurricane_Dorian_in_The_Baha mas.

CRIMES

All the nations of the world experience an accelerated increase in crimes, the worst atrocities impossible to describe are committed. The daily paper "Las Américas.com" says: It is alarming to read the daily press, as well as listen to radio and televised news, and check how individual or collective murders abound in different cities of the world. And it is alarming because they have no explanation, but a great moral and social decomposition.

Likewise, it happens in all the countries of the world, where ever you live in any country, you are witness of the great insecurity and fear that there is today because of the increase in evil. homicides, rapes, robberies, kidnappings, extortion, it is an everyday thing in every country in the world.

ABORTION.

Never before in the history of mankind have millions of defenseless beings been murdered in the mother's womb. It is inconceivable from the rational, moral and religious point of view that it is the mother herself who kills her own child; However, this savage and satanic practice has extended to unimaginable proportions of hardness, evil and cruelty. An estimated 6 million babies are killed each year, which means that 4,400 unborn children die every day. 1 every 20 seconds. It is also known that 40 children who pass the fifth month of pregnancy are aborted every day. Half of all abortions performed are performed on women who have chosen it as their only method of birth control. Adolescents between 11 and 19 years old account for 26% of all abortions. The 18 and 19-year-old girls have the highest percentage of abortions: 6.3%. Until 1996, abortion was the leading cause of death in the US with a percentage of 46% of the total. The highest abortion rate in the world is recorded in Europe (48 per 1,000 women aged 15-44), which includes the region with the highest rate (Eastern Europe, with a rate of 90 abortions per 1,000 women) and the region with the lowest rate (Western Europe, with a rate of 11 per 1,000). Eastern Europe has the highest percentage of pregnancies that end in abortions (65%). In Europe, few of the abortions performed are illegal. Asia, the most populous region in the world, has the highest global number of abortions (17 million legal and 10 million illegal), followed by Europe, with eight million (mostly in Eastern Europe, Africa (five million), Latin America (four million), North America (1.5 million) and Oceania (0.1 million) In Asia, 59% of abortions in the world are performed, and in North America, only 3%. Little, however, more than 30 million unborn children have been killed in this nation since 1973, the year the Supreme Court legalized abortion, 20 times more than the number of Americans who died in the civil war, the two world wars and the one in Vietnam, combined. Among developed countries, the US has one of the highest average abortions, five times higher than the Netherlands. The US has one of the standards more liberals in the whole world, only communist China compares in its legal support I of abortions at any time during pregnancy and for almost any reason. The increase in the estimated number of illegal or clandestine abortions comes from the new estimates of the WHO, (World Health Organization) which are based on a careful examination of the data corresponding to each region. (International Perspectives on Family Planning, special issue of 1999. The Incidence of Worldwide Induced Abortion. By Stanley K. Henshaw, Susheela Singh and Taylor Haas) http://www.guttmacher.org/pubs/journals/25spa01699.html

The crime of abortion has reached such cruelty and bestiality in humans, that the New York authorities decreed that the child can be killed, at the very moment of his birth. Law given just in this January 2019.

SEXUAL IMMORALITY. -

Immorality spreads everywhere, homosexuals and lesbians increase as a bad ferment; they form social, political and religious organizations and even have the nerve to affirm that Christ was like them; Men and women prostitute themselves as children. Pornography advances like cancer destroying millions of lives; Sex is no longer considered something reserved for marriage, but just like animals, it is practiced wherever, however and with whoever. Adultery is committed equally by men and women. One of the signs that we are at the door of the end is precisely this sexual perversion that reigns throughout the world. Luke 17:28 says: Just as it happened in the days of Lot; they ate, drank, bought, sold, planted, built; 17:29 but the day Lot left Sodom, it rained fire and brimstone from heaven, and destroyed them all. 17:30 This will be the day when the Son of Man manifests.

What else did they do in the days of Lot? Homosexuality was the most serious sin they practiced, so much so that as soon as they saw the two foreigners who entered the city, they wanted to rape them, read: ***Genesis 19: 5: And they called Lot, and said: Where are the men who They came to you tonight? Take them out, so that we know them.***

19: 6 Then Lot went out to them to the door, and closed the door behind him, 19: 7 and said: I beg you, my brothers, that you do not do such evil. 19: 8 Behold now I have two daughters who have not known a man; I will take them out, and do them as you please; only that these men do nothing, for they came to the shadow of my roof. Once Lot and his family left that cursed and perverted city...

Genesis 19:24,

Then the Lord rained on Sodom and on Gomorrah brimstone and fire from the heavens; 19:25 and destroyed the cities, and all that plain, with all the inhabitants of those cities, and the fruit of the earth.

God destroys Sodom and Gomorrah, since the two cities were identical in sexual immorality and all kinds of perversion. The present today is worse than in those times, the only difference is that technology is much more advanced, and used for evil like the Internet used for perverse purposes, such as pornography, and all kinds of sexual aberrations and immoralities. The ease of transporting anywhere in the world has also made many thousands of perverts travel to different countries to seek sexual relations with children, women, homosexuals and men, and they still have the nerve to call it sex tourism. Globalized perversion allows the depraved to choose even countries and cities for their world meetings such as those in San Francisco, California USA, (the city that congregates the most homosexuals in the world), New Orleans in Louisiana also in the USA , Toronto in Canada, Barcelona in Spain, Berlin in Germany, Puerto Vallarta in Mexico, Asian countries are not far behind, Thailand, China, Japan, Bali in Indonesia, Taiwan, Brazil in South America, and we could continue to list many more countries where people from all over the world travel to commit their sexual perversions, without counting on everything that is committed through the Internet.

DESTRUCTION OF THE FAMILY.

The family that is the basis of society and a good established by God, has been practically dismantled, destroyed, discredited, that now few are those who think about getting married and forming a family; most people only come together to have sexual pleasure and hence single mothers and children without fathers abound.

Parents abandon their children and children flee their homes; divorces are more common and frequent than anyone thinks it is a transgression against the law of God. In sum, Satan has managed to destabilize the most important organization and cell of society, the home, where love and worship of God were instilled, where moral and civic values were learned; hence the lack of well-established homes, there are a total chaos in societies around the world.

NARCOTIZATION, ALCOHOL AND DRUG ADDICTION.

drug trafficking with being the lowest, dirty and criminal activity, is the most lucrative and therefore the one that gains more followers every day; Drugs invade almost every home, millions consume it every day. International statistics given by the World Health Organization - United Nations)

The harmful use of alcohol results in 3.3 million deaths each year.

-On average every person in the world aged 15 years or older drinks 6.2 liters of pure alcohol per year.

-Less than half the population (38.3%) actually drinks alcohol, this means that those who do drink consume on average 17 liters of pure alcohol annually.

-Some 31 million persons have drug use disorders.

-Almost 11 million people inject drugs, of which 1.3 million are living with HIV, 5.5 million with hepatitis C, and 1 million with both HIV and hepatitis C.

Worldwide consumption in 2010 was equal to 6.2 liters of pure alcohol consumed per person aged 15 years or older, which translates into 13.5 grams of pure alcohol per day.

-A quarter of this consumption (24.8%) was unrecorded, i.e., homemade alcohol, illegally produced or sold outside normal government controls. Of total recorded alcohol consumed worldwide, 50.1% was consumed in the form of spirits.

-Worldwide 61.7% of the population aged 15 years or older (15+) had not drink alcohol in the past 12 months. In all WHO regions, females are more often lifetime abstainers than males. There is a considerable variation in prevalence of abstention across WHO regions.

-Worldwide about 16.0% of drinkers aged 15 years or older engage in heavy episodic drinking.

-In general, the greater the economic wealth of a country, the more alcohol is consumed and the smaller the number of abstainers. High-income countries have the highest alcohol per capita consumption (APC) and the highest prevalence of heavy episodic drinking among drinkers.

It is estimated that 275 million people used illicit drugs, such as cannabis, amphetamines, opioids, and cocaine, in 2016 which translates into an annual prevalence of illicit drug use of 5.6%. Cannabis is most used with 192 million users. Some 31 million of people who use drugs suffer from drug use disorders.

It is estimated that there are almost 11 million people who inject drugs. World Drug Report 2018

DISEASES AND EPIDEMICS.

And when He opened the fourth seal, I heard the voice that said: Come and see. And I looked, and behold a yellow horse: and he that sat on him was called Death; and Hades followed him: and he was given power over a quarter of the earth, to kill with the sword, with hunger, with death, and with the beasts of the earth. (Rev 6: 7,8).

The worst pests in the world.

Below are the details of some of the outbreaks and threats of the world's most devastating diseases:

*** HIV / AIDS**: - About 33 million people worldwide live with HIV, a condition that destroys the immune system and expands mainly through sexual contact, blood transfusions and the sharing of needles. Almost all those infected with the virus that causes AIDS live in developing countries. - Every year, about 2.5 million people become infected with the virus and 2 million die from AIDS-related causes. Drugs called antiretroviral, which patients once started should take for life, were shown to extend their lifespan. - HIV / AIDS have caused the death of more than25 million people worldwide since its detection in the 1980s. It is the leading cause of death in sub-Saharan Africa.

* **Tuberculosis**: - A third of the world's population, that is, more than 2 billion people, are infected with the bacteria that produces tuberculosis, a disease that fundamentally affects the lungs. - About 9 million people develop the condition every year when their immune systems weaken, usually due to illness or pregnancy. In 2007, there were 1.3 million deaths from tuberculosis among people without HIV and 456 thousand deaths in patients infected with both tuberculosis and HIV. - Normally, tuberculosis can be treated with antibiotics, but drug-resistant disease forms complicate and make therapy much more expensive.

* **Malaria**: - Almost half of the world's population some 3.3 billion people are at risk of developing malaria, a tropical disease that is transmitted between people through mosquitoes. - Annually about 1 million people die as a result of malaria, or malaria, mostly children under 5 years. In turn, between 189 and 327 million cases of the disease that can be prevented with drugs are diagnosed each year. - The most vulnerable groups are children, pregnant women, travelers, refugees and workers who migrate to endemic areas.

* **Influenza**: - Between 3 and 5 million people annually suffer severe cases due to normal seasonal flu worldwide and between 250 thousand and 500 thousand die as a result of it. - The majority of deaths in developed economies occur among the elderly over 65 years. But less is known about the impact of influenza in developing countries, although outbreaks in the tropics would have higher fatality rates than those in temperate regions, where influenza usually appears in the winter. - There have been three pandemic influenza outbreaks in the twentieth century: in 1918, 1957 and 1968 and known, respectively, as Spanish, Asian and Hong Kong influenza. Some 50 million people died during the first outbreak, about 2 million died in the second and between 1 and 3 million died in the third.

* **Cholera**: - Cholera is an acute diarrhea infection that usually spreads mostly in areas with contaminated water and floods and poor hygiene. It can cause the death of healthy adults in hours due to dehydration. The WHO said that millions of people are probably infected with cholera every year, surely a figure 10

times higher than the cases officially reported by the countries. One in two people would die without treatment with rehydration salts or antibiotics. - More than 4,000 people died recently due to a cholera epidemic in Zimbabwe and a smaller amount did in Iraq. Contaminated water sources were responsible in both cases.

* **Hepatitis B and C**: - About 2 million people worldwide have been infected with hepatitis B, a viral infection that attacks the liver. Around 600 thousand people die per year due to its acute or chronic effects. - It expands like HIV, but unlike the hepatitis B virus, it can survive outside the body for at least seven days. It is preventable through vaccination. - Hepatitis C infects between 3 and 4 million people per year, mainly through direct contact with blood. There is no vaccine against this form, which is one of the main causes of acute hepatitis and chronic liver diseases such as cirrhosis and liver cancer.

* **Dengue Fever**: - It is the most widespread tropical disease after malaria and is also transmitted through mosquitoes. In its most severe form, it can lead to bleeding and death. - Some 2.5 billion people, two fifths of the world's population, are at risk for the disease, which is endemic in more than 100 countries. - According to the WHO, 50 million people become infected with dengue every year, mainly in urban areas in tropical and subtropical regions. There is no specific treatment.

* **Yellow fever:** - Named for the jaundice it causes in some patients, yellow fever is a viral condition that causes the death of 30,000 people a year. - Some 33 African countries, with a combined population of 508 million people, are at risk for yellow fever. It is also endemic in nine countries South Americans and several Caribbean islands. Bolivia, Brazil, Colombia, Ecuador and Peru are the states considered in greatest danger, according to WHO.

* **Meningitis** - It is a potentially lethal bacterial infection of the lining that surrounds the brain and spinal cord. Meningitis is more common in sub-Saharan Africa, where an outbreak caused more than 25 thousand deaths in 1996. - There are vaccines to prevent it and several support groups are working to increase its availability in high-risk areas. UNICEF said this month that more

than 2,500 people had died from the disease in Nigeria, Niger, Burkina Faso and Chad since the beginning of 2009. - Up to 20 percent of people who survive meningitis suffer brain damage, hearing loss or learning problems. It can be spread through kisses, sneezing, coughing and sharing kitchen utensils and glasses.
http://www.terra.com.pe/noticias/noticias/act1746041/3/grandes
-epidemias-que-sufrio-mundo.html

* **Cancer.** - Cancer is one of the main causes of mortality worldwide: it is estimated that 7.6 million people died of cancer in 2005, and another 84 million will die in the next 10 years if no action is taken. The World Health Organization (WHO) has proposed the global goal of reducing mortality rates from chronic diseases by 2% annually between 2006 and 2015. Achieving that goal would prevent more than 8 million of the planned 84 million deaths for cancer over the next decade, and WHO is intensifying its response to reach that goal. More than 70% of all deaths from cancer occur in low and middle income countries, whose resources for prevention, diagnosis and treatment of the disease are limited or nonexistent. Tobacco use alone causes approximately 1.5 million deaths from cancer per year.
http://www.who.int/mediacentre/news/releases/2006/pr06/es/in
dex.html

THE SECRET SCIENCES AND MAGIC.

They charge enhancement, never like now anywhere, any city in any country, you will find the enormous proliferation of fortune tellers, mentalists, magicians, healers, sorcerers and sorcerers who "cure all their ills" and "They predict their fate", and even on the same television they make propaganda and invite you to call them to deceive you in the most brazen way. It seems that nobody cares about the prohibitions that God makes through his Church on this moral perversion:

Let's see what the Catechism of the Catholic Church says: # 2116: "All forms of divination must be rejected: recourse to Satan or demons, the evocation of the dead, and other practices that are mistakenly supposed to" reveal "the future. The consultation of horoscopes, astrology, palmistry, the interpretation of omens and luck, the phenomena of vision, the use of "mediums" contain a will to power over time, history and, finally, men, as well as a desire to gain the protection of hidden powers they are in contradiction with honor and respect, mixed with loving fear, that we owe only to God.

2117 All the practices of magic or sorcery by means of which it is intended to tame hidden powers to put them at your service and obtain a supernatural power over the neighbor - even if it is to seek health -, are seriously contrary to the virtue of religion. These practices are even more condemnable when they are accompanied by an intention to harm another, whether or not they resort to the intervention of demons. Wearing charms is also reprehensible. Spiritualism often implies divination or magical practices. That is why the Church warns the faithful to beware of him. The recourse of medicines called traditional, non-legitimate nor the invocation of the evil powers, nor the exploitation of the credulity of the neighbor. So serious and bad is this disorder that Isaiah warns: A misfortune will come upon you that you will not know how to conjure; A disaster will fall upon you that you cannot avoid.

Suddenly devastation will come upon you that you do not suspect. Stay, then, with your spells and your many sorceries with which you get tired from your youth! Can they help you? Will you shake? You have tired of your plans. May those who describe the heavens, those who observe the stars and make known, in each month, what will happen to you be saved.

Look, "They will be like bits of straw, and a fire will burn them up! They will not rid their lives of the power of the flames. They will not be coals for bread or flame to sit on. That will be for you your sorcerers for whom you have grown tired since your youth. Each one will go astray, and there will be no one to save you. (Isaiah 47, 11-15)

THE EARTH, AIR AND SEAS POLLUTED.

The news of all the countries of the earth, cannot be more alarming and worrying, when it comes to the issue of environmental pollution; Just to get an idea, let's see what the different media in different countries say: 1.-Environmental alert in Chile due to air pollution. - In recent days, in Santiago de Chile, vehicle traffic was restricted in order to reduce the high rates of air pollution, which are aggravated by the cut in Argentine gas supply. Yesterday, the 6.2 million inhabitants of Santiago de Chile suffered an "environmental alert", declared by the Intendancy (Governorate) when the levels of polluting particles reach 200 micrograms per cubic meter of air, a situation caused by the high rates of atmospheric pollution.

2.-El blog verde.com/alerta-ambiental "The gases that cause the greenhouse effect in the atmosphere have reached the highest levels recorded so far and do not show signs of stabilization, the UN meteorological agency announced Tuesday."

3.- Madrid again exceeds pollution levels. - The same traffic as always, but with exceptional weather conditions. The combination of the two factors has caused that last night, the second consecutive, has exceeded the threshold of warning to the population for the high pollution in Madrid. Nitrogen dioxide, an irritating gas from the airways generated by the exhaust pipes, has skyrocketed again. www.noticias.com/madrid-supera-de-nuevo-los-niveles-de-contaminacion

4.- Los Angeles suffers serious pollution. - the city suffers from severe air pollution in the form of smog. The air of the Los Angeles Basin and the San Fernando Valley is susceptible to the thermal investment that retains the gases of cars, and diesel engines of trucks, ships and locomotives, as well as industries and other sources. wikipedia.org/wiki/Los_Ángeles.

5.-Pollution levels increase in La Paz. - September 26, 2010, 08:08. La Paz - Bolivia. - Pollution levels in the city of La Paz are increasing and are physically and chemically altering the characteristics of water, land, soil degradation and erosion, among other aspects; In addition to the extinction of the animal or plant species. ww.fmbolivia.com.bo/noticia36663

6.-Environmental pollutions in Venezuela. - triggers respiratory diseases, according to experts. - Environmental pollution in the city, aggravated in recent months by the intense drought, and forest burning, have negative effects on the health of the inhabitants, generating allergies, respiratory conditions and eye irritation. The phenomenon, known as haze (suspension of small dust particles and low smoke atmosphere), also causes the increase in temperatures, because it works as a "plug" that prevents the daytime heat from entering the atmosphere. According to Jacinto Guédez, forecaster of the National Institute of Meteorology and

Hydrology (Inameh). report21.com.

7.-Ozone pollution in Mexico City. Those of us who have lived in the city in recent days have suffered high rates of one of the air pollutants, Ozone. This being the one that for some years has more frequently exceeded the safety limits, and again has remained at concentrations that may jeopardize the integrity of the inhabitants of the metropolitan area of Mexico City. www.mipediatra.com/infantil/ozono.htm.

8.-Thousands of sufferers from water pollution in Pakistan. The humanitarian organizations, focused on curbing the sanitary drama in Pakistan, warned today that diseases related to water pollution are wreaking havoc among hundreds of thousands of people affected and threaten to fire the mortality. "There are already deaths. You can confirm that there are outbreaks of epidemics," UNICEF's emergency coordinator in the South Asian country, Oscar Butragueño, told Efe today. Newsletters

9.- Environmental pollutions in Lima, Peru. Dangerous reality Would it be better to breathe or not to breathe? Lima has become a city where breathing can be harmful and highly dangerous. Pollution has serious consequences for our health. Our respiratory system is one of the most affected but it is not the only one, since our vision, nervous system, among others, are also. In Callao there has been a particular case of contamination, which is lead contamination. This problem, which affects the people who live there, is very worrying, since the damage it causes to health is irreversible ... http://blog.pucp.edu.pe/blog/contaminacionenlima.

Finally, so that readers do not think that only religious preachers are the ones who warn of this problem, let's see what people in the secular world say, such as journalist Manuel Freytas: The destruction and collective suicide of humanity programmed only to consume and vote presidents in the most complete ignorance of the system that governs and orders their lives. For most scientists, these catastrophic phenomena are the natural consequence of pollution and destruction of the planet. For others it is a mystical sign of the "end of the world." It is as if a warning of Apocalypse had erupted: Earthquakes, rains of unusual intensity throughout the southern hemisphere, historical snowfalls in the North American and northern Europe, devastating droughts in the same regions where flooding was devastating entire populations not long ago.

Avalanches, forest fires, floods of rivers and oceans, monumental thaws, massive famines, oil stains spreading like a monstrous murderous of life, like the one already installed in the southern US. The climate explodes in chains on several fronts, the world economy collapses and the financial economic model collapses on a planetary scale, the unemployed, marginalized and hungry already amount to half of the human population, and inter-capitalist conflicts over markets and strategic resources They are generating and raising a climate of global military tension fueled by a nuclear arms race. http://www.ecoportal.net/content/view/full/92851.

"And the nations were angry, and your wrath has come, and the time to judge the dead, and to give the reward to your servants the prophets, the saints, and those who fear your name, the little ones and the great ones, and to destroy those who destroy the earth." Rev 11:18.

FALSE SECTS AND RELIGIONS.

There are thousands of churches that claim to be Christian; but instead of following the teachings of Christ, they follow their own desires and passions; with doctrines that without any scruple or shame separate the teachings and mandates that do not suit them to more easily follow their weaknesses. How can they be considered to be disciples of the Master if they contradict the Master? Many of these churches were created, not because of the mistakes that the Catholic Church had made, but because of human passions, such as pride, ambition and fornication.

In each city of the United States of North America, like in another cities of the whole world there are hundreds and hundreds of temples of all kinds, especially the so-called Christian ones, who, not knowing what name to put them, adopt the names of the streets where they are located, temples whose shepherds are drunk, adulterers, thieves, homosexuals, liars. Churches where blasphemies speak, racist churches that hate anything other than their color or social status, gay and lesbian churches; churches where horrible lies are practiced like miraculous cures; churches that are said to be guided by the Holy Spirit, but that actually seem to be under the influence of the devil, because of the disgusting convulsions they are subject to until they are trance. What monstrous practices, lies and blasphemies dare to say in the name of God! And, those are the ones that go around the world encouraging the foundation of more sects.

Why is there so much proliferation of sects and diverse beliefs? Because Satan, the father of lies is on the loose. John in Revelation tells us that after Christ offered his life and rescued mankind, he chained the serpent, the devil, for a thousand years, after which he will be released for a short time (Rev. 20, 2- 3). We are precisely at that time. Satan has been released, and he knows that he has little time left, so he tries to do as much damage as possible, encouraging the proliferation of sects that divide and separate people from the true Church.

Everything that the prophets and Jesus said is being fulfilled to the letter. As time progresses the moral and spiritual decay is getting worse; especially with the people we believe should be exemplary and religious, but they love money and material things more than the Doctrine of Christ to which they claim to belong; by examining them in detail, we will see that almost all these false ministers perform not for spiritual purposes, but for commercial, material and lucrative purposes, the same ones that live in mansions surrounded by all kinds of comforts; while his ignorant followers give them millions of dollars.

"For times will come when they will not suffer sound doctrine, but having an itchy hearing, teachers will pile up according to their own lusts and turn their ears away from the truth and turn to fables" (2 Tim. 4, 3).

"If anyone teaches anything else, and does not conform to the healthy words of our Lord Jesus Christ, and to the doctrine that is according to godliness, he is puffed up, he knows nothing, and he raves about questions and contests of words, from which they are born envy, lawsuits, blasphemies, bad suspicions, foolish disputes of corrupt men of understanding and deprived of the truth, who take pity as a source of profit" (1 Tim. 6, 3-5).

In short, the one who now commands in any aspect of social, political and religious life is Mr. Money; the majority of pastors are not servant's ministers of God, but of the world and its bubbles. I have seen some of them preach charity and in a few minutes deny an inn to a foreigner; millionaire ministers or pastors who when someone asked for help became violent or sad as if something of their own being were to be taken away; swollen ministers of pride and conceit; Protestant pastors who, after preaching Christ, fled stealing money from their own work centers; Pastors who apart from having their wives, lacking their vows of fidelity, shamelessly live with lovers.

Anyway, in the sects the most scandalous and evil things are seen.

Some years ago one of the most terrible and fatal cases in the history of these sects happened; Reverend Young of the U.S. He moved his church to one of the Guyana's, dared to affirm that he was God and to work miraculous cures (which, by the way, were prepared and fraudulent), then seized all the property and real estate of his parishioners, whom he forced to donate them to his organization, under the pretext that in paradise where he took them they would not need it. When the law took action on the matter and sent people to investigate it, he gave orders to kill them; then he forced all his followers to commit suicide, taking his life too.

This is not the only case, after others have happened like that of the Davidian's in Texas and it happens on a small scale in all places, cities and countries where these seemingly Christian sects operate but whose father is Satan.

However, it is not for us to judge them, but Christ who was the one who said:

"Not everyone who says: Lord, Lord! Will enter the kingdom of heaven, but he who does the will of my Father, who is in heaven. "Many will say to me in that day: Lord, Lord! Do we not prophesy in your name and in your name we cast demons, and in your name we performed many miracles? I will then tell you: I never met you; depart from me, workers of iniquity" (Luke 13, 21)

I have had to write all these previous comments, not with an eagerness to criticize and judge, but to report on these latest events; and above all so that perhaps some of these clergymen and religious who are going astray, realize and amend again, and above all stop deceiving people and cause division in the Church of the Lord.

You now have the way described by Jesus to discern which religion is good and which is not; they know that in these last times the religions driven by the spirits of error will proliferate, dragging millions of unsuspecting and naive individuals.

In the previous theme of the wise men of this world, we saw their ideas and teachings as: Criticism of the Word of God. The philosophy of survival of the strongest. The free expression of debauchery. The individuality or selfishness that is promoted. Marxist theory the theory of evolution that today everyone accepts as true free sex, the confusion of thoughts, mass repression; etc. is in full swing and as a result the world now lives the blackest nightmare of all time. So, whoever lets himself be duped will be for foolishness and not for lack of information.

FALSE ALARMS

Do you remember the story of the liar shepherd? Do not? Well ... I remind you: They say there was a little shepherd who was going to graze his sheep every day on a hill near the village where he lived.

One day, the shepherd shouted: help! - Help! ... The wolf, the wolf, attacks me...! He takes my sheep...! Desperate villagers ran to defend the shepherd boy, but when they arrived with him, he laughed ... telling them it was a joke.

This happened three times, and people came to his aid, because they thought: Suddenly this time is true...! But the fourth time, nobody came, because they thought it was a joke of that liar boy. However, that time it was true, the wolf had attacked the shepherd's flock, but no one believed and nobody went up to defend him.

Exactly the same is happening with the second coming of Christ. Many sects and people influenced by Satan have given this false and liar alarm, in order to create uncertainty, disbelief, doubt and finally disinterest; so that in the end everyone is neglected and when truly Christ comes no one receives it. To make a little history, those who began this series of false predictions contradicting Jesus himself were: Adventists or Millerists, followers of William Miller; who in 1831 predicted that the second coming of Jesus was going to take place in October 1843; As nothing happened, he said it would be for the spring of 1844; later for the autumn of that same year, more precisely for October 22. Seeing that his predictions did not happen, he apologized and retired from public religious life; but the Adventist movement was consolidated under the command of Mrs. Ellen White, under the name of Seventh-day Adventists. She said she had been taken to heaven and had been instructed to keep it on Saturday, hence the name Seventh day and Adventists to remember the idea of its founder.

Then Charles Taze Rusell appeared who also developed the idea of the imminent coming of Jesus. He organized his own Bible classes, published two magazines, one called Watchtower and the other the Herald of the Presence of Christ in 1879 and founded what would later be known as Jehovah's Witnesses. Like his Adventist predecessor, he predicted that by 1914, the end of the world would come; but nothing happened either. Upon his death in 1916, a cunning lawyer Joseph R. Rutherford, took command of the organization and also in 1920, predicted that by1925 Abraham, Isaac and Jacob would arrive in the land and for that they bought a mansion in San Diego, where He lived until his death.

"We want you to tell us, when is this going to happen? What will be the sign of your return and the end of the world? Jesus replied: Be careful that no one deceives you. Because many will come, posing as me. They will say I am the Messiah and will deceive many people ... However, it will not be the end yet (Mt. 24, 4-6)

As you will see, these false teachers and false prophets are already with us for some time; to be more exact since almost 188 years. Let us remember what Jesus said: "However, it will not be the end ..." At present, we are much closer, but people have already become incredulous and no one believes in the second coming because of the false alarm that they unleashed since long ago these envoys of Satan. But those who belong to Christ know and know that they have to be prepared.

THE GREAT APOSTASY

"No one deceives you in any way; because it will not come without apostasy coming before, and the man of sin, the son of perdition, is manifested ..." (2 Thess. 2:3)

One of the strong signs that we are approaching the end of this era full of sin and evil is precisely religious apostasy, which spreads with great strength in different ways in the Catholic Church; the Church that Jesus Christ left (even if it hurts them and hurts the schismatic's, heretics and separated). And it is in this Church that apostasy must occur

But before continuing with this very important topic, let's first see what apostasy is: The word "apostasy" has its origin in two Greek terms: αpo, which means "outside of", and στασις (stasis), which means "to stand ". So, literally the term denotes the idea of departing or excluding yourself from something you were once involved in.

More clearly, it is to deny Christian truths, change your mind or doctrine. This departure from the faith and teachings of Jesus Christ can be done in different ways, either by preaching a new and disguised doctrine or through behavior totally at odds with faith.

And what are we seeing in certain Catholic groups since about 1960? After the Second Vatican Council, to be more exact, they began a series of movements, ideologies and manifestations contrary to the teachings of Christ and his Church. Let us analyze one of the most harmful forms of apostasy: Is it not exactly apostasy, that of Liberation Theology? Those who are partisans of this ideology; Do you feel uncomfortable?

"But the Spirit clearly says that in the end times some will apostatize from the faith, listening to deceiving spirits and doctrines of demons;" (1 Tim. 4: 1)

Let us examine a little more closely the aberrations propagated by this infiltrated current in the Church to realize that it is another sign of the end times; and with the appearance of the Antichrist, this apostasy will reach its maximum evil, with the bleak abomination, the prohibition of Holy Mass or Perpetual Sacrifice and with the persecution and murder of true Christians. The danger represented by this communist ideology disguised as

Christianity is in the fallacious interpretations that make them of the Holy Scriptures, in the distortion of the established terms and concepts, reaching such absurdities, that if it occurs to them that black is white, without No objection would say yes.

Thus, starting with the same elaborate name they have given this movement: "Theology", to deceive and confuse. Theology can be an extensive concept; but, basically it is the Treaty of God, its attributes and perfections that have nothing to do with the political ideologies that these liberationists advocate from the Church.

Scanonne at the meeting of "El Escorial" makes this interesting question: "Can there be a true theology that is so hindered for the language of transcendence? A theology so mortgaged in the language of immanence?" And he also adds: "The theological language must not be emptied of the Theos" (which makes it theological), becoming confused with the socio-analytical-political language (uniquely determined with Marxism).

Our culture has established terms and concepts to designate and explain things and circumstances; for this reason, it is an aberration that completely changes what is established to adjust it to its

political interests. Here is the fallacy, deception, dishonesty.

With their new concepts they advocate a new church with no supernatural dimension. It is not a renewal of the Church as they try to make us believe, but simply to create a distinct institution, with another origin, with other ends and means. In sum, a new sect, which unfortunately has infiltrated and where it is easier for them to manipulate, deceive and even collaborate with groups of extreme left that have nothing of Christians. Let's see some of their insidious treats:

1.-The concept of "People of God", which we would say is formed by all those who do the will of God, whether rich or poor, peasants or city folks, Indians or whites; the liberationists have changed it to replace it with a political concept of "the people", such as mass, proletariat, where only the marginalized, the oppressed, the poor and peasants have a place; completely forgetting that among the poor there are also thieves, selfish, envious, lazy, and that in our Latin American or Third World peoples, the existing state of underdevelopment is, many times, the product of the situation of sin in which they live, putting into practice a foolish selfishness, which translates into the popular saying that says: they live as the dog of the gardener, "who do not eat or let eat."

With regard to violence, Alfonso Lopez in his book **"Theology of Liberation in Latin America"**, referring to this same matter, says: "They come to a tricky use of biblical texts and take out a whole thesis of Christian violence with some texts such as Matthew 11,12, which says: ***"The Kingdom of Heaven suffers violence and the violent conquer it"***, transforming this into a revolutionary harangue, not wanting to understand the true meaning: that we must strive and even sacrifice, to be worthy of the Kingdom of God, armed with theological virtues.

Paul tells us that we must put on the armor that God has given us to stand against the devil's deceptions (Ephesians 6,11) and still, so that we do not doubt that it is a spiritual and non-physical armor, he adds: ***"Because we are not fighting against people of flesh and blood, but against evil spiritual forces "(Eph. 6,12).*** The apostates emphasize two biblical passages that have interpreted them to their liking and manner: The Exodus and the story of Jesus in Matthew 25,31-46. In the Exodus we see how the Israelites had become slaves of the Egyptians, and God pitying

them that he loved them, a leader arouses among them: Moses, who takes them out of the land of Egypt and takes them to the Promised Land. For the Christian faithful to Scripture and God, this biblical and historical passage fulfills two functions:

The first, related to the saving plan that God had drawn for humanity, as it was to have a people free from the evil and superstitious influences of others, separating them so that the Messiah was born there, God made Man.

And second, to illustrate humanity through this historical event, the analogy between the historical Exodus: with its leader Moses and the history of salvation with the prophetic figure of Jesus.

Thus Israel represents humanity lost and sunk in sin under the dominion of Satan. Egypt represents the sinister and dark power with which Satan dominates mankind. God raises among the Israelites a leader, Moses, who manages to get the Jews out of Egyptian rule and exploitation. Jesus is born from among men and by his redemptive work, frees mankind from the power of darkness and eternal death. The time of hardship that Israel suffers when passing the desert to finally reach the Promised Land, is nothing other than this present life that we are living since Jesus came and died and rose again until he finally re-establishes his Kingdom of peace and Justice. On that date we will just be in the Promised Land.

But liberationists or apostates see this passage with a purely political sense; for them God is a God who takes sides for a group, that of the exploited, marginalized, slaves; in short, the proletarians, workers of our times. Then they say that if God takes sides with this group, he has to be against the exploiters, the rich, capitalists and imperialists. Finally, they believe that God agrees with all those leaders out of the proletariat, who do not hesitate to kill to achieve their goals of political liberation, which they claim represent Moses.

This attitude astray from them, is easy to understand, if we read Paul in **Romans 8, 5-8,** where he says:

"Those who live according to the nature of sinful man, only care about the purely human (political) ... Worrying about the purely human, leads to death ... those who care about the purely human are enemies of God, because they neither want nor can submit to His Law. "

This biblical reading gives us great light on the behavior of these poor advanced groups; Priests, bishops, nuns and laity who neither want nor can submit to the Law of God and that is why the testimony of life so disorderly that they project to society, slaves of all the passions and evils of this world.

Ironically, they speak of liberation; however, it is they who need to be freed from their carnal passions, misguided and political fanaticisms and from their naive and silly damages; advocate a purely human and superficial liberation, without delving into the root of evil; in vain they speak and write so sophisticatedly, they philosophize and make dissertations so arranged and, they defend such noble causes as the "option for the poor", but what a pity that they have left aside the "Theos" that is a source of life, truth and justice. The apostle Paul in this regard tells us:

"The wisdom of this world, before God, is nothing more than nonsense." (Corinthians 20)

2.-The Concept of "Freedom"- Without the word freedom, theology of liberation would not exist. But his freedom is human, political, social and economic. They advocate liberation of large foreign capitals, although they know that third world countries do not have the monetary capacity to restore their economies. They advocate a political and ideological freedom and authenticity, although they know that their political ideas are not authentic, but borrowed from Marxism-Leninism and Maoism and naively want to impose it on different realities. The class struggle that advocates the apostate and liberationist sect infiltrated the Church has caused enormous damage among the Catholic people.

In many places in the provinces of Latin America there are no profound economic differences, nor will powerful gamonalists be found, nor poor proletarians; but as they still have to carry out their class struggle, they chose to put the peasant against the people who live in the city's (knowing that many peasants are economically more wealthy than the others), creating hatred and resentment between the two inhabitants. They grant certain religious and economic privileges to the peasant and many restrictions to people of the cities, and, not happy with it, within the town they also encourage division; The fact is that the class struggle must be

carried out as it should. This is not Christian, it is satanic.

They advocate a cultural liberation criticizing negatively and denying all the cultural aspects acquired in the European countries of which America was a colony, encouraging an unhealthy nostalgia for everything that was the native culture.

They advocate a liberation of Catholic dogmas and authority by disregarding and bringing down the tradition of the Church and the authority of the Pope, which they try to ignore by denying the infallibility of the Supreme Pontiff which affects the union of the Church and subordination of the clergy, two aspects that open the doors of division, disobedience and ignorance of the supreme authority of the Church.

The commentator of the Latin American Bible, 94th edition in 1 John, Cap. 4, when explaining on the subject of not trusting any biblical inspiration; He apostately says: **"... but what do you think when it comes to ways of being and acting of the Church? Should we support those responsible in all**

circumstances? This would be to forget that the Gospel forms free people. We cannot blindly follow the opinion of the Pope or the Bishop or the majority ...

As you see, these gentlemen encourage open hostility and ignorance of Christ's own teachings; for with that they do not know what Jesus affirmed when he said to Peter:

"You are Peter and on this stone I will build my Church" (Mt. 16,18).

He also said: ***"Feed my sheep" (Jn. 21)***. Hence the duty that Peter has to supply the food of the doctrine and that which is incumbent upon us to receive it. Now, there is no obligation to embrace the error. - Jesus gave Peter a special security for himself and his successors and a special order:

"I have prayed for you, so that your faith does not faint; and you, once converted, comfort your brothers" (Lc. 22, 32).

That is why it has been said of the Pope: **"He confirms all others, while he is not confirmed by anyone, only by God."** (J.Bonatto).

The authority of the Pope is necessary to reduce controversies and was always recognized since ancient times, so St. Ambrose said on one occasion:

"Where Peter is, there is the Church" and St. Augustine in his sermons 131, 10, 10 said: **"Rome has spoken, the cause is failed"** Moreover, the facts confirm that, despite a long series of pontiffs and an immense variety of issues that have arisen over the centuries, we see that as some bishops diverted, there was never the case that a Pope was wrong as a Doctor of the Church.

The Church has had less good Popes; but never Popes that have taught the error. So, what is this open hostility to the authority of the Supreme Pontiff? Is it because the Vatican and the Church faithful to Christ never accepted the political and disguised teachings of the theology of liberation? His ideas of freedom do not come from a theological and spiritual freedom, but from the Marxist analysis of contemporary problems. Being this movement of atheistic origin, although they do not say it, their writings hint and their actions confirm that they do not believe in the God they preach. For them their God is the people.

3.-The concept of "Sin", as Christ and the saints gave us to understand, they do not comprehend it. For their understanding, sin is plain and simple the economic exploitation and oppression suffered by the proletarians of the world, who must be freed to take away the sin of the world. And then everyone will be saved; consequently, the Kingdom of Heaven is being achieved with the Class Struggle.

4.-The biblical concept of "Poor", according to which it is understood as everyone who is hungry for God; he who puts his heart in the treasure that is not corroded by the urine and the moth; He who suffers morally from living in a world of sin and corruption and who longs for the Kingdom of God. It is understood by these in the Marxist sense. Poor for them is a social class, the proletariat and hence the phrase: "Option for the poor", with which they feel very safe to drive the class struggle, which means taking sides with a certain group. But: "Christ knew the hurtful differences between the one who lacks goods and the rich, between the opulent and the needy.

He knew the domination of the powerful over the homeless. He was fully aware of the claims of the prophets "(Alfonso Lopez, Liberationist Theology). However, Christ being able to do so did not prepare the revolution, much less organize the guerrillas or exclude those who were not poor. On the contrary Christ unites the concept of justice with the mercy in which love overcomes the sin that divides; it never incites violence against the exploiters. As a messenger of peace it invites repentance, reflection; the rich recommends distributing their treasures; does not exterminate them or condemns them.

To his disciples, he forms them as evangelizers of the Kingdom of God, presenting himself with his characteristic greeting: **"PEACE BE WITH YOU"**. It does not make them agitators or revolutionaries. His coming into the world, his life, death and resurrection is only for the love of humanity; having made it very clear that the Kingdom of God can be in us or we can build it if we love God and our neighbor as ourselves. Only when man makes a personal 360 degree turn and out of repentance does he change selfishness for love; Only then will we begin to see a just society, where everyone can see themselves as brothers, children of God, without suspicion, without envy, without hatred or revenge. Only love forgives, unites, changes, builds, builds, creates peace and harmony.

"**The option for the poor**", a phrase that has become their favorite banner and that naively peaks some bishops, priests, religious and laity do not satisfy the spiritual and pastoral demands of the Church; because this option that divides apart is committed to achieving purely material satisfaction. The mission of the Church is to lead man to Christ, through the conscious change from sin to grace which sanctifies, harmonizes and unites man with his creator and with the nature that surrounds him.

Assuming that this option for the poor, material and simplistic will be able to reverse the misery situation of a certain group, people or society; if you have not changed your heart full of selfishness, envy, resentment and prejudice; these new rich will continue, with the same hard and cold heart; ready to continue exploiting and taking advantage of the weakest.

Jesus himself, seeing that unrestrained desire to obtain the material riches of his own disciples, said to them: ***"Worry about the things of the Kingdom of heaven; the rest will come to you in addition "***. Certainly that they lack much Faith, much spirituality!

5.-The concept of Love to your Neighbor. - As incredible as it may seem, they have a cynicism and raving about the love we should have for our fellow men, who have made a whole satanic treaty of Christian union and love.

According to Gustavo Gutierrez, the main liberationist of Peru, he says in his book "Theology of Liberation": "Loving all men does not mean avoiding confrontations", (that is, we can exterminate them and, at the same time, we are loving them, because in this way we will free them from their economic powers and their selfishness). And he goes on to say: "The oppressors are loved, freeing them from their own and inhuman situation as such (rich) and, for that, we must fight them real and effectively ... (That is, eliminate them), that is the new challenge of the Gospel. The new way of loving enemies, truly satanic, don't you think? This satanic infiltrator in the Catholic Church lives as a priest in a Dominican convent and is called "Father", and idolized by his followers and he has received many awards for his struggle for the poor. Here the words of Jesus come to mind when he says:

"And do not call anybody" father "on earth, because one is only your Father, who is in the Heavens ... Matthew 23.9.

J. Girardi in his work: **"Christian Love and Class Struggle"**, says: "The oppressed are loved by freeing them, the oppressors are loved fighting them" ... A whole ideology of violence and death, diametrically opposed to true Christian love of humility and meekness: "If they hit you on the cheek, show them the other" (Lc 6,29). Finally, the devil, through Gutierrez, says: "The communion of Easter joy passes through confrontation and the Cross." Such an abomination to the work and sacrifice of Christ.

Only those who truly belong to Christ will feel outrage at reading and hearing these apostasies and heresies of which Paul, Apostle of Jesus warns us:

"Because these are false apostles, fraudulent workers, transfiguring themselves into Christ's apostles, and it is no wonder, because Satan himself is transfigured into an angel of light. So it is not much, if his ministers become ministers of justice. ". (Corinthians 11,13-15)

As you may have noticed, we are rightly faced with the great apostasy of which Jesus speaks to us and of which Mary, our mother, also warned us.

"You should also know this: that in the last day's dangerous times will come. Because there will be men who love themselves, greedy, boasting, arrogant, blasphemers, disobedient to fathers, ungrateful, impious, without natural affection, relentless, slanderous, intemperate, cruel, loaths of good, traitors, impetuous, infatuated, lovers of the delights more than of God, who will have the appearance of mercy, but will deny her efficacy; avoid them "(2 Tim. 3: 1-5)

As you will see, Pablo points out that in the last days dangerous times will come, characterized by the appearance of these apostates. *2 Ti, 3* shows us the characteristics of these priests, nuns, theologians, bishops, and many lay people close to the Church, many of them hypocrite that stop beating their chest but give a testimony of horrific life.

Undoubtedly, you, reader friend will have seen many of these behaviors in our times, and within your own social circle.

Lovers of themselves: These are egotists, for them the most important thing is themselves, not God. - Avaricious: The love of money in them is very strong, they can have a lot, but they don't conform and want more and more. - Boastful: They seek recognition, like if they were "the best". They don't get off their pedestals of egolatry, proud; although circumstances may be contrary to them, they remain on their arrogance altars. - Unrelenting, cruel, abhorrent of the good: His profile fits with intellectually successful men who have reached important human knowledge, who have led him to think about his own self-sufficiency. They believe that faith does not work, that they do not need God; that's why when somebody talk them about the next coming of Christ, they laugh and get upset, mocking those

who announce it as if they were crazy or ignorant.

Let us pay attention to something very common in our times: "... and out of greed they will make merchandise of you with false words." (2 Pe 2, 3). Does this situation sound familiar? If it doesn't seem close to you, it doesn't take long for it to be. One of the main incentives for these apostates is the economic well-being that they can obtain from their deceptions. The Word speaks of these men discovering new "markets" from which they can extract juicy dividends. They discover that Christians are an excellent source of income, since many can buy education, music, books; attend preaching with the right of admission, etc. We see the existence of "Christian" companies that are dedicated only to get money from Christians.

In most Catholic temples we can see the multiple manifestations of apostasy. We see that the message of the Word of the Lord has lost importance. Music and songs do not fill the spirit or serve to praise God; the manifestations of the Holy Spirit have been displaced by sensuality and emotions and the "Christian" does not commit himself to Christ, attends the temple to "warm up the bench" and when he leaves he continues his worldly life as usual.

http://soloporgracia.wordpress.com/2007/10/23/la-apostasia-falsos-maestros-y-el-anticristo/

Also the Blessed Virgin in her appearance in La Salette, France in 1848, says:

"The Priests, Ministers of my Son, the Priests ..., for their bad life, for their irreverence and impiety in celebrating the holy mysteries, for their love of money, honors and pleasures, have become sewers of impurity. Yes! Priests ask for revenge and revenge hangs from their heads. Woe to the priests and people consecrated to God who, by their infidelities and bad life, crucify My Son again! The sins of the people consecrated to God cry out to Heaven and ask for revenge, and behold, revenge is at the door, for there is no longer anyone who implores mercy and forgiveness for the People. There are no longer generous souls or a person worthy of offering the victim without blemish to the Eternal, in favor of the world." Finally, to end this theme of apostasy, it is necessary to touch one of the most shameful scandals of all time for the Holy Catholic and Apostolic Church of Christ; For precisely because this is the true

Church of Christ, it is that there is an apostasy that is nothing more than Satan's final attack on the Church of God. As the Pope, Benedict XVI said, it is necessary to speak boldly and not try to cover up the sin that many unfortunate priests have tainted the honor and holiness of the Church; I am referring to the last problem raised in different parts of the world, the sexual abuse of priests against defenseless children, which I briefly put them not with the desire to discredit the Church, but rather to realize how Satan works to destroy The Church of Christ.

A journalist from Radio María's news media makes the following comment: "This reality of pedophilia in the church is a painful, shameful reality and is really overwhelming, oppressing, the information that the different media give about it. Many involved, many condemned bishops, and on the accusation of the victims is now weighing another I think so serious, and that is the cover-up, equally complex issue on which you have to work hard too. No one who reads or watches the news is oblivious to the terrible problem of our Holy Church, "The evil suffered by the church today is the infiltration of subjects of bad living, sects, pedophiles, homosexuals and mentally ill, thieves, and adulterers .... Hence the catastrophic consequences that the Church is suffering today because of the attacks that Satan has managed to infiltrate within.

THE GLOBAL ECONOMIC CRISIS.

This sign, together with the one that preceded the Apostasy, is perhaps one of the last to indicate "how close is the coming of our Lord."

"Because there will then, be great tribulation, which has not been since the beginning of the world until now, nor will there be." Matthew 24:21

I think that the real tribulation that there will be, will be when the armed conflicts of the end and the disasters of the natural elements that will ensue are unleashed; but the global crisis that has occurred in recent years, is still a tribulation and suffering never seen before, by the gigantic dimension of how millions of people have lost their jobs in uncertainty and misery. According to the World Bank, the global recession has produced 53 million more poor people and will cause the death of one million children in the next 5 years. According to a report of the International Monetary Fund and

the World Bank.

The economic crisis of 2008-2009 and the rise in prices of food products that preceded it have and will have devastating consequences for the world population.

Nearly one billion people still face serious difficulties in procuring food and often the weakest segments, such as children and pregnant women, are at risk of losing their lives.

According to most experts, the eight Millennium Goals cannot be achieved within the pre-established time limits. In particular, the objective of reducing child mortality in developing countries to 34 children per thousand seems quite unlikely. This rate, according to analysts, will reach 68 children per thousand in 2015.

The IMF report on the economic situation in sub-Saharan Africa was also presented in Washington. Economic growth in the area should be 4.75% in 2010 and then accelerate to 5.75 in 2011 against 2% in 2009.

"The relatively contained economic slowdown in the region - says the analysis - is due to the general health of local economies the year before the crisis and the macroeconomic policies implemented in many countries." In addition, "the governments of about two thirds of the countries in the area have managed to increase public support to sustain economic activity."

The situation of hunger remains, however, at alarming and very serious levels. Nearly ten million people are affected by a serious food crisis that it has hit several countries in the North African region of the Sahel. Especially - say the UN data - in Niger, 7.8 million people are "in a state of food insecurity." (WASHINGTON, Tuesday, April 27, 2010 (ZENIT.org)

A new and more recent analysis of the hunger and poverty in the world, tell us World Vision; who says:

<u>736 million people</u> live in extreme poverty, surviving on less than $1.90 a day. More than half of the world's extreme poor,

<u>413 million people</u>, live in sub-Saharan Africa, an increase of 9 million people from two years earlier. In the Middle East and North Africa, the number of people living in extreme poverty nearly doubled in two years,

<u>from 9.5 million to 18.6 million</u>, mainly due to the crises in Syria and Yemen.

Two regions, East Asia and the Pacific and Europe and Central Asia, have less than 3 percent of their populations living in extreme poverty, already successfully reaching the 2030 target to eradicate global poverty.

1.3 billion people in 104 developing countries, which accounts for 74 percent of the world's population, live in <u>multidimensional poverty</u>, according to <u>a 2018 survey by the U.N. Development Program.</u>

660 million children are experiencing multidimensional poverty, according to the U.N. Development Program.

Sub-Saharan Africa has both <u>the highest rate of children living in extreme poverty at 49 percent</u> and the largest share of the world's extremely poor children at 51 percent.

By 2030, an estimated <u>80 percent of the world's extreme poor will live in fragile contexts</u>.

This crisis cannot be easily controlled, until a charismatic man, a statesman, possibly from the European Union, and he is the one who dictates the most appropriate measures that will lead to the solution of this serious and huge global problem. It is through this action that he will be known and popular throughout the world and will even be considered "the savior" of mankind, and will rule 7 years.

"Seventy weeks have been set upon your people and your Holy City, to end transgression, to seal sin, to atone for iniquity, to establish eternal justice, to seal the vision and the prophet, and to anoint the Holy of the saints " (Daniel 9:24).

THE GOSPEL WILL BE PREACHED THROUGHOUT THE WORLD.

This Good News of the Kingdom (the Gospel) will be proclaimed throughout the world as a testimony before all peoples, and then the end will come. Matthew 24.14

This prophecy said by Christ himself, is one of the requirements we would say to know that the end of this system has come to an end.

Some believe that the gospel has not yet been preached in the whole world; They say that Asia, Africa, Arab countries, etc. they do not know the Gospel and that therefore it would take a great deal for Christ to return, but it is not so; The countdown began since the Gospel was preached by the apostles themselves and if we study history a bit, we will realize that all those countries that now practice the Muslim religion were once Christian and what is happening now is that many who have been good Christians have retired and have been carried away by Satan's deceptions, even Europe has fallen into terrible secularism and has turned away from Christ. Rather it seems that Christianity has already reached every corner of the world and now is when God sees those who have received and maintained it and those who have turned away from it. Just to get an idea of how the evangelization of the world was carried out, let's read some history:

1.-Time of persecutions (1st to 3rd centuries), years where Christianity has no permitted religious character and the Christian option always implies a risk. -

-First century: Christianity reaches a great diffusion, but it is still a minority and urban religion. The main centers of expansion were: Jerusalem, Antioquia, Ephesus, Damascus and Edessa. At the end of the century there are Christian communities in Palestine, Syria, Cyprus, in Asia Minor, Greece and Rome.

-Second century. Consolidates the first nuclei of evangelization and the Christian mission reaches territories that will be fundamental for the early Church: Egypt (Alexandria) and North Africa (Carthage). At the end of the second century, the geographical expansion is impressive: Eastern Syria, Mesopotamia, Egypt, Southern Italy, Gaul, Hispania, and Germania are added to the areas of the first century.

-Third century: Christianity becomes a very significant minority within Empire. Its implementation is greater in the East than in the West and in the cities rather than in the countryside. Preaching begins in the East in the regions of Egypt and Syria, and outside the empire in Armenia. In the West, the mission takes hold in Rome, advances in Italy, reaches a great development in North Africa and arrives in Britain.

2. -Time of tolerance and subsequent acceptance: From the

Edict of Milan (year 313), where the Christian religion is tolerated, supported and finally turned into the official religion of the empire and the number of Christians increases in an extraordinary way. It must be said that none of the contemporary religions that were offered at that time had a history of successes comparable to that of Christianity.

IV century: The Church leaves the status of minority and becomes the majority religion in many areas of the Roman Empire. The Church intensifies its missionary pastoral in two fields that until then had not had priority: the evangelization of the field and the senatorial and intellectual environments. Geographically, the mission is extended outside the empire in the East: Mesopotamia, Georgia Persia, northern India and Ethiopia and in the West it intensifies in the Balkan area, Austria, southern Germany and Hispania. In the middle of the 5th century the Empire is mostly Christian, with a few pagan minorities in rural areas and the Jewish people reluctant to the Christian proposal.

3. - Middle Ages. - V to XV centuries. The area of present day Ireland is evangelized by St. Patrick, who between the years 430-60 creates a church with its own characteristics: around the monastery and the abbot and with a discipline and liturgy of its own. Irish monks evangelize Scotland and create numerous monasteries. England and the central part of Europe will be evangelized from the

Irish and Scottish monasteries: France, Bavaria, Austria, Switzerland, and Northern Italy (V-VII centuries). The area of Western Europe had been occupied by several Germanic peoples, who will follow various processes in their conversion to Catholicism. Visigoths, Ostrogoths (Italy), Burgundies (Southeast of Gaul), Suevos (Galicia) Vandals (North Africa), Lombard's (Italy), Franks (France), Anglos and Saxons (England) gradually accept Christianity during the 5th and 6th centuries.

The conversion of these peoples was via real decision or conversion (that is, when their king, became Christian all the people converted). At this time, the popes who sent religious missionaries to evangelize these lands played a fundamental role. By the middle of the seventh century, the Christian and Roman faith had regained all the former imperial territory: Gaul, Italy and Hispania. It is worth mentioning in this period the outstanding figures of some evangelists of the time: Saint Augustine who evangelized the

territory of present-day England in the fourth century at the request of Pope Saint Gregory the Great; Saint Bonifacio (Wilfrido, apostle of Germany), Wiberto, Wilibrordo, monks of Anglo-Saxon origin who travel the continental lands founding monasteries (cultural centers and new missionaries) and ecclesiastically organizing the territories.

The evangelization of the Scandinavian peoples (Denmark, Sweden, Norway) began in the ninth century and did not end until the eleventh. The mission was carried out by German bishops and missionaries. The way of evangelization was also the conversion of royalty. -The conversion of the Slavic peoples (Eastern Europe), followed two paths: from the East (Constantinople) and from the West (Italy and Germany), and occurs between the 8th and 10th centuries. It is worth noting in this region, the missionary action of the holy monks Cyril and Methodius. These monks strove to inculturate the gospel in Slavic culture. -To the Baltic peoples: Prussians, Lithuanians, Latvians and Estonians came faith from Germanic emigrants and settlers and the force of arms the order of cavalry of the Teutons in the thirteenth and fourteenth centuries. Factors that positively and negatively influenced the expansion of the Church.

4.-Modern Age - XV to XVIII centuries. -Africa: The Portuguese route to Asia opens Christianity in Africa. Portuguese missionaries and then the French, evangelize: Angola, Congo, Mozambique,

Ivory Coast, Senegal ... The missions in Africa do not reach great importance until the late nineteenth and early twentieth century's. - America: Several European countries are involved in the evangelization of this continent: Spain preaches in central and southern America; Portugal evangelizes Brazil, France evangelizes Canada and Great Britain the current territory of the USA. -Asia: The difficult evangelization of the south-east of the Asian continent began with the arrival of the Portuguese in India (1498). From Goa it is missioned by India, from Malacca the Christianity is introduced in Indochina (Vietnam, Cambodia ...) it is arrived at Japan (1549); from Macao (1576) you enter China (1583). The Philippines is evangelized by the Spaniards since 1565 via Mexico. North Asia, Siberia, was evangelized from Russia since the 16th century. He took Christianity to Alaska.

(Http://www.portalmisionero.com/efam/historiadelamision.doc).
San Francisco Javier, was one of those who from 1545, until 1552,

was evangelizing India, Japan and died when he was going to enter China. Currently we could say that there is no place in the world that has not heard the name and the gospel of Christ. Now that they accept it and receive it is one thing, that they reject it does not mean that the Gospel has not reached them.

THE CHURCH WILL BE PERSECUTED AND MARTIRIZED AGAIN.

"But before all that, they will be arrested, persecuted, handed over to synagogues and imprisoned; they will take them before kings and governors because of my Name ... They will be delivered even by their own parents and brothers, by their relatives and friends; and many of you will be killed. They will be hated by all because of my Name." Luke 21: 12.17

From its beginnings the Church of Christ was always persecuted and martyred and in all centuries and ages there have been martyrs;
but this hatred to the Holy Church of Christ, in the twentieth century and in the twenty-first century with the approach of the end of this system has increased even more.
Recently, in the pontificate of John Paul II, a ceremony was held to remember this prophetic event and there it was said:

The Ecumenical Commemoration of the witnesses of the faith of the twentieth century has been one of the most important and expected moments of the Jubilee of the year 2000. In an unprecedented ceremony, John Paul II, accompanied by representatives of the different Christian confessions recalled, in the suggestive framework of the Coliseum, the example of all those men and women who in this century have given their lives for Christ. As he himself acknowledged, this is perhaps the century that has given more martyrs to history in these two thousand years of Christianity. (Witnesses to the faith of the twentieth century. 7.V.2000-VATICAN CITY.)

Now, let's look at some more important cases of the persecution of our church in the last century.

Mexico-1924-1928: 200 laymen and 90 martyr priests in the revolution of the cristeros, 25 of them have already been canonized (making sure that none of them took up arms). They were killed for

being Christians. But the casualties of those who took sides for Christ even with weapons are estimated between 25,000 to 30,000 Mexicans killed by federal government forces.

In the twentieth century, the Masonic generals Carranza, Obregón and Calles, who succeeded the presidency, persecuted the Catholic Church with viciousness and cruelty, a situation that had been cooking since the nineteenth century, with Benito Juárez who decreed the freedom of Cults for all religions except for the Catholic.

One of the characteristics that best stands out in the martyrs is this: when all the circumstances became extremely difficult, they had already chosen to obey God rather than men, knowing that the consequence could be death. They did not believe superheroes but were very aware of their own human weakness, but with the awareness of having to live up to its mission. It was faith and love for Jesus Christ that allowed them to stay strong in the supreme instant of witnessing. **"Long live Christ the King!"** **"Long live the Virgin of Guadalupe!"** Were the words with which they received the enemy's bullets.

Spain -1931-1940: A recently published study on the Spanish civil war written by Catalan philologist Jordi Albertí, who defines himself as Catalan and believer, has published an analytical chronicle of the first months of the Civil War in Catalonia, focusing on persecution Against Catholics, it is titled "**The Silence of the Bells**", *the religious persecution during the civil war*, and has been published by Proa.

According to Albertí, **the 1936 massacres were planned**: they were planned by the libertarian communists, that is, the anarchist party (the FAI) and its union, the CNT. Other groups on the left were complicit in different measure. The killing of Catholics of 36 was planned, not spontaneous. The Silence of the Bells, dismantles the myth of the Uncontrolled and gives us light on the martyrdom and persecution of the Church in Spain.

Data of clergy killed in Catalonia:

(it was the most punished, with the exception of Valencia): 4 assassinated bishops: Irurita (Barcelona), Huix (Lérida), Borrás (auxiliary of Tarragona), Polanco (of Teruel, executed in Gerona in 1939). Diocese of Lleida: 270 clergymen killed, 65% of those there

were. [Only Barbastro lost a higher percentage of clergy: 88%].

Diocese of Tortosa: 316 murdered, 62% of the clergy. Diocese of Vic: 177 murdered, 27% of the clergy. Diocese of Barcelona: 279 clergymen killed, 22%. Diocese of Girona: 194 murdered, 20% of the clergy. Diocese of Urgell: 109 murdered, 20%. Diocese of Solsona: 60 murdered, 13% of the clergy. [data from Vicente Cárcel Ortí in **"The Great Persecution, Spain 1931-1939"**, Testimony Planet, 2000]

Hatred and death, by dates in Spain. -Year 1931: May; assaults, looting and burning of almost 100 churches and religious buildings in Madrid, Valencia, Alicante, Murcia, Seville and Cadiz. The Civil Guard and firefighters do not intervene.

Year 1932: Expulsion of the Jesuits (more than 3,000). Burns and assaults of ecclesiastical buildings in Zaragoza, Córdoba, Cadiz (January); Seville (April); Granada (July), Cadiz, Seville and Granada (October). Feeling of impunity Year 1934: Revolution of Asturias, 33 priests and religious killed in Mieres, Turón, Oviedo. Year 1936, before July 18, day of the military rebellion: 17 priests and religious killed. From July 18 to August 1: 861 clerics killed. August 1936: 2,077 murders (more than 70 a day), including 10 bishops. Accumulated murders as of September 14: 3,400 priests and religious killed (we do not count lay people) in less than 2 months. The rest of the victims will be distributed during the following years of the war.

Spain 36-39: The greatest anti-Catholic persecution in world history. Spain, 1936-1939: about 7,000 ecclesiastics and about 3,000 laymen martyred for being Catholics, that is, about 10,000 martyrs. Antonio Montero, in his book **The religious persecution in Spain,** published in the BAC in 1961, speaks of 4,184 diocesan priests (including 12 bishops and many seminarians), 2,365 religious and 283 nuns. But as the investigations have progressed, there are greater figures: Montero counted 334 priests killed in Madrid, while the postulation of the cause has later seen that they were at least 491. http://www.forumlibertas.com/frontend/forumlibertas /noticia.php? id_noticia=7896. At present, some very faint news about the persecution of the Church says: The Church is again the Church of the martyrs. In the**20th century alone, about 45 million Christians were killed** in the world for religious reasons.

More than **160,000 Christians died in 2001 worldwide** for reasons related to their faith. For the reader to have more information on this topic, I transcribe a recently published story:

"In some countries, professing the Christian faith, both in the private and public spheres, is a high-risk activity, since those who practice it run the risk of being killed with impunity. Last Sunday, in Baghdad, Al Qaeda perpetrated an attack against the Syrian Catholic Church that resulted in the tragic balance of 52 dead, including 45 hostages. It is not the first time that Christians suffer the wrath of radical Islamists in Iraq.

Since the war began in that country more than two hundred Christians have died in violent episodes in hundreds of attacks. The persecution reaches such a degree of virulence that the exodus is continuous. The Pope, as he has done on numerous occasions, condemned the attack with words that cannot be more accurate: **"An absurd violence that has ended the life of defenseless people."** Indeed, it is an absurd violence that, unfortunately, is spreading throughout the world until it becomes an undeclared and global conflict. The report on religious freedom published by the Commission of European Episcopal Conferences (COMECE) denounces that at least **one hundred million Christians are persecuted in the world**. Last March, clashes between Muslims and Christians resulted in a massacre in Nigeria, a fact that previously happened in Pakistan and Afghanistan. In China, Catholics are imprisoned and sometimes executed, as is the case in North Korea. They are also repressed in other parts of the globe such as Saudi Arabia, Sudan and Yemen to name a few examples.

It is difficult to stop these massacres because of the complexity of the political, social and religious context in which they occur. The murders of Christians are perpetrated in countries with a very serious democracy deficit and an absolute disregard for human rights and religious freedom. Christians are also helpless in states where a majority confession tries to bend the rest, as in Muslim countries, or in countries where the right to be Catholic is legally recognized but its exercise is hindered by the State.

The seriousness of the situation demands from the international community a firm and unequivocal pronouncement that, so far, has not occurred with the exception of the Vatican. It is hardly understandable that the publication of some Muhammad cartoons

cause diplomatic clashes between the West and Muslim countries and that the killing of Christians is only answered with an indifferent silence, as if they were stigmatized. It is becoming increasingly palpable that we live in a world where religious intolerance is cornering the faithful until they are taken to ostracism, something that fortunately does not happen, not because of the protection they can obtain from the public powers that must ensure their safety, but by individual attitudes of a commendable vital and spiritual integrity and coherence.

It should be remembered that the Church proposes the truth of Christ, does not impose it. It would be desirable that this exercise of freedom proposed by the Church be reciprocated by those who are now trying to cut it off."

Cases of persecution in Pakistan: - (1) The situation of Christians in Pakistan is extreme. In recent months, various violent acts against the local Christians have taken place, resulting in 7 deaths, 18 wounded and more than fifty houses of burned Christians (cf. Laicostrinitarios.org, August 2, 2009). Unfortunately, this situation of violence has continued to stir. Below we transcribe a recent news article on www.minutodigital.com on September 16, 2009. The news is as follows:

On Friday, September 11, a group of Muslim extremists set fire to a Catholic church in the town of Jethki, located in the Punjab province, in Pakistan, in the same region where a group of Christians were burned alive last month. According to the international organization Aid to the Church in Need (AIN), Islamic fundamentalists sprayed the church with kerosene and set it on fire, after which they went to the nearby houses and threatened their Christian residents with death. (2) Pakistan: Last August five Christians were shot to death in the center of the city of Quetta (Baluchistan), in Pakistan.

Pakistan: Two elderly Christians, James and Buta Masih. The two innocents spent more than two years in prison. From 1986 until today it is estimated that the accusation has fallen on 982 Christians. Of them, 25 have been killed by Muslim fans. (3) Pakistan: The Catholic church had suffered damage, also as a result of the suicide bombing on May 27 in Lahore. The building was completely destroyed, with 35 dead. But four adjacent buildings also collapsed: the bookstore of the Daughters of St. Paul and three upper Catholic middle schools.

(4) In March 2008, Lahore Cathedral had also been damaged, due to a bomb against a neighboring building belonging to the government. In a telegram sent on August 3 to the Bishop of Faisalabad, Joseph Coutts, signed by the Vatican Secretary of State, Benedict XVI has expressed his pain "for the foolish attack on the Christian community of Gorjan", with the "tragic murder of children, innocent women and men. " And he has called on Christians in Pakistan not to give up the effort to "build a society that, with a deep sense of trust in human and religious values, is characterized by mutual respect among all its members." (5) Persecution in Pakistan to Christians. The Salesian order has decided to significantly reduce its presence in Pakistan after the attack of a Taliban command to its facilities in the south of the country. Pakistan - the second Muslim nation in the world, and the only one with the nuclear weapon - has a significant Christian minority in regions such as Lahore and Quetta. The attack against the Salesians occurred recently. The two Salesians who were currently taking care of the house - an Argentine priest and another Pakistani were dragged out of their bedrooms, and remained on their knees for an hour with the kalashnikov stuck to their heads, while the

command devastated the facilities and accused them of being agents of the United States. They were not killed, but the final threat was blunt: We will return in a few days, and if there is any foreigner we will cut it into pieces.

Cases in Morocco: -A Franciscan religious of Egyptian nationality is among the dozens of Christians expelled from Morocco recently. The bishop of Tangier, Monsignor Santiago Agrelo, requested the reasons for this expulsion from the Moroccan authorities, but has not yet received any response. In this diocese there are between 2,000 and 2,500 Catholics, among its more than four million inhabitants.

Cases in Iraq: (1) Archbishop denounces a new wave of anti-Christian violence in Iraq, after the murder of five Christians in recent days. The archbishop of Mosul, Monsignor Emil Shimoun Nona, warned that the new wave of violence and intimidation by Muslim extremists threatens to erase the Christian presence in this city of Iraq. Monsignor Paulos Faraj Rahho, was kidnapped and murdered, describes how the recent murders generate Christian

emigration, which worries the millenary local Church present in the region since apostolic times. (2) Iraq: Four Christians were killed in cold blood in four days in Mosul; The situation is tragic, warned Patriarch Vicar Chaldean, Monsignor Shleimun Warduni. (3) Iraq: 58 Catholic skilled and more than 70 wounded in the armed assault on the church of Sayida an-Naya (Our Lady of Help), in the center of Baghdad. Faced with this new terrorist attack in Iraq on October 31, 2010, on the eve of All Saints, the attack was perpetrated by the terrorist group al Qaeda.

(4) Iraq: In just four days, between January 6 and 9, up to nine car bombs exploded against Catholic churches in Iraq. Aid to the Church in Need (AIN) denounces a strategy of "religious cleansing" launched by Muslim extremists that seeks to "eradicate Christianity from key areas of Iraq," such as the cities of Baghdad, Mosul and Kirkuk.

Algeria: 50,000 Algerian Christians live their faith from hiding out of fear; Some 50,000 Algerians converted to Christianity practice their new religion almost in hiding according to information from El Periodic. Samir, a young man converted to Christianity, affirms that the social pressure in his country "is much stronger than that of the authorities, and not everyone supports it" while explaining that with two religious texts the crime is already committed of proselytizing, for which religious have been expelled in recent years.

North Korea: A 2008 Report on freedom of religion in North Korea indicated that 99.7% of North Korean citizens cannot freely profess and practice their religious creed. The 2008 Report published by the Commission for the Reconciliation of the Korean People belonging to the South Korean Episcopal Conference was carried out in collaboration with the Data Collection Center for Human Rights in North Korea. The report is based on the testimony of 2,047 North Korean citizens who managed to escape from the country by taking refuge in South Korea. The interviewed also narrated cases of religious persecution against people who have tried to live their Catholic faith. Religious persecutions have increased in the Asian country after the 1990s and those who oppose established norms or perform unauthorized religious activities are systematically imprisoned.

India: In the Indian province of Orissa, 300 villages were attacked and people fled in horror with scenes in their eyes of murders, premeditated fires and rapes. At the apex of violence, 54,000 men, women and children hid in these forests. Among these 54,000 families were also relatives of about 40 Catholic priests, the families of about 25 religious, and about 25 priests who were hiding and waiting for the moment when the police would return to restore order. For some of them, the police arrived too late. Nearly one hundred people died there, including three Protestant pastors and a Catholic priest.

Vietnam: Catholics flee to Thailand. Some Catholics in Vietnam are seeing terrified as the police themselves push them to flee to Thailand because of the pressures and threats received. Forty faithful from the parish of Côn Dâu have fled to the border to ask for asylum in Thailand, Eglises d'Asie (EDA), the agency of the foreign Missions of Paris, reported Wednesday. Radio Free Asia journalists contacted a group of Catholics from the Côn Dâu parish in the Vietnamese diocese of Da Nang who could no longer withstand the climate of terror installed in their parishes. According to information collected by journalists, the group of Catholics clandestinely left the parish during the month of May to take refuge in Thailand. Among these people who have requested asylum there are men, women and children. The oldest is 70 years old and the youngest is of age to go to daycare. Some have arrived accompanied by family members; others alone. For fear of the police, the refugees of Côn Dâu live for the moment almost clandestinely, in rented rooms. Due to lack of means and their lack of knowledge of the language, they live in a very precarious way at the moment because of their condition as Christians.

Cyprus: a church sacked and humiliated. The situation is dramatic: more than 500 churches and monasteries - the most obvious proof of the island's true identity - have been looted or destroyed since then; More than 15,000 icons, countless liturgical objects, gospels and other valuable pieces have been reduced to ashes. A small number of churches have been "saved" to be converted into mosques, museums, entertainment venues, hotels (such as Saint Anastasia, Lapithos) or even warehouses, such as San Antonio, in the Famagusta district and three monasteries The Maronite monastery of the prophet Elijah was wildly bombarded by Turkish

aviation, burned and turned into a stable. But the worst part is that the wonderful Byzantine frescoes and mosaics have been torn from the walls by antique dealers and have been illegally sold to foreign collectors.

China: The Chinese regime especially persecutes Catholics, making its preferred target of Church leaders, especially those who are especially esteemed. China tried to annul the Vatican by creating in 1957 the patriotic Catholic church, which expressly disregards Rome. The Catholic Church, faithful to the Pope, goes underground. Catholics are always persecuted, while patriots are recognized by the Chinese government. He appoints bishops without recognition of the Vatican, who are automatically excommunicated. On the part of the last Popes there have been attempts to approach and, to the surprise of Beijing, many of their bishops seek communion with the Pope. In recent years, among the prelates of both churches and among the faithful there grows a climate of sympathy and desires for unity, after long decades of mutual contempt. A good part of the 138 dioceses of China together with Rome have no bishop and all are obstacles to the practice of faith and liturgy, while the patriotic church has its pastors and has open cathedrals and churches. Sometimes, bishops faithful to Rome secretly ordain new bishops, in order to ensure the ministry of priests and the life of communities.

Benedict XVI on December 24 expressed his deep disgust at the situation, and denounced that "grave violation of religious freedom", warning that "he now considers it necessary to give voice to the suffering of the Catholic community in China", which suffers the most cruel persecution from Stalin's against the Catholic Church of Ukraine.

THE DISAPPEARED. - According to the official website of the Association of Fraternities of the Trinitarian Laity of Spain-South, the data is chilling. While President Hu Jintao and Prime Minister Wen Jiabao go around the world proclaiming their "social progress," the Catholics of the Boading diocese do not know if Bishop Zu Shimin, imprisoned in 1997, is alive or dead. They do not know what prison he was sent to, nor have they had any news of him in the last eight years. The same goes for An Shuxin, auxiliary bishop of Boading, arrested in 1996, who has only been seen once since. Neither his family nor the faithful of the diocese know if he is still alive or has died in jail, as happened in January 2009 to the bishopof Jantai, Gao Kexian. There are about 46 "clandestine" bishops, who have spent their entire lives in jail, in labor camps, under house arrest or under close surveillance. Among the 7 bishops currently imprisoned are octogenarians such as Xiwanzi, Yao Liang, and seriously ill such as Wenzhou, Lin Xili. Among the ten prelates under house arrest is a paralytic, Lin Guandong, bishop of Jisian, and one banished on a mountain, the bishop of Tianjin, Li Side. At the moment, at least 20 priests and 3 seminarians are in jail, while many others are in fields of "reeducation for work", the fearsome "laogai", to which any police commissioner can send a person without Need for trial up to a maximum of four years. If he does not consider him sufficiently "re-educated" on his return, he sends it again for another two or three, with the same absolute arbitrariness.

In recent years, since the emergence of the self-styled, Islamic State, persecution and murder of Christians has intensified and spread in most Muslim countries, killing Christians with incredible methods of cruelty and demonic insanity, slaughtering them, burning them alive or drowning them in the sea.

In short, persecuted Christians, especially Catholics, increase in the world. It is not news that appears in the media, but it is a daily reality that missionaries, religious, priests and lay Christians from all over the world have to deal with.

This has been just a sample of the persecutions and martyrdom of the Church of Christ, as the Lord himself said; but this persecution and murder of Catholics will be much heartless and intense when the government of the Antichrist is underway, when he has forbidden Holy Mass and he has proclaimed himself as god.

CHAPTER V.

POSSIBLE POLITICAL AND PROPHETIC EVENTS.

THREE POLITICAL ALLIANCES

Before continuing and explaining in detail one by one what will happen to the United States of America, The Catholic Church, Israel, and the last battle known as Armageddon, we will try to give a brief description of how nations will be formed in the last times

Everything seems to indicate that in the last days three blocks of nations will be formed that will be the protagonists of the last wars and insidies against the United States of North America, against the Church, against Israel and against Christ himself.

-The first block of nations corresponds to the vision of Daniel 2, 7-8 and the Revelation of John 12, 17-18. In which he explains how the Roman Empire is reborn with the union of the European nations. Now, in Revelation 17, 16 we see how the Antichrist and his kingdom are made up of countries around the world; but they hate the prostitute or Babylon (USA). reason why it is deduced that the USA will not be part of the kingdom of the Antichrist. Why do they hate him? The reasons are above all commercial, political, military interests and above all a question of survival strategies.

For several decades ago, Freemasons have been promoting the idea of establishing a "New World Order", in which all the nations of the earth will be subject to a single globalized government, with a series of laws equally for everybody with one president who directs the destinies of the Earth. - For this future event they have been preparing all the governments of the main countries of the world to accept this idea. For a long time almost all the presidents of the world have referred to that like the New World Order. They proclaim that would be the solution to all the problems that plague the world, among which are, of course, environmental pollution, poverty, hunger, epidemics, lack of water, overpopulation, etc.

If we look for the archives of the different presidents of the United States, as of Europe, we will find that in their speeches they already speak of the New World Order, Reagan, Ford, Bush, Clinton, Obama, all of them speak on the same subject; so do the presidents of Europe. They have been working on this idea for a long time and have an agenda that they are complying with step by step. - Freemasonry since it began with the English monarchy (1717) has moved in the highest spheres of economic and political power, which is why among those who promote the new world order are the richest great families on earth, such as the Rockefeller, the Rothschild's, the Du Pont, Morgan, Bush, and many others and individuals who have become wealthy lately such as Bill Gates, (father) George Soros and others. There are also the majority of statesmen from the governments of Europe and other countries in America.

Everything seems to indicate that the forces of evil each with their different nuances have come together to make a single block and promote the government that will lead the Antichrist. Communists, Freemasons, Muslims, LGBT groups or collectives, Gender Ideologies, feminists, animalists, abortionists, atheists, agnostics, Satanists, witches, shamans, fortune tellers.

In North America, a country where communism was unthinkable, it suddenly turns out that the Democratic party has become communist; Hillary Clinton, Nancy Pellosi, Obama, and many others are staunch advocates of the new world order.

But how have the Freemasons managed to concentrate power and unite the most powerful people on the planet? - Besides that in their different Masonic lodges worldwide they assimilate the majority of the wealthy and influential people from all over the world, to attract others who are not Freemasons, but who have a lot of political or economic power, have used the famous **"Bilderberg Club"**. Since 1954, Bilderberg Club members represent the elite of all Western nations. Industrials, bankers, politicians, multinational corporation leaders, presidents, prime ministers, finance ministers, representative of the World Bank, the WTO. and the IMF, media executives and military leaders and kings, have formed a shadow government that meets in secret to debate and reach consensus on the global strategy.

Any change of regime in the world, any intervention on the flow of capital, any change in the welfare state is plausible if in one of these meetings its participants include it on their agenda. According to Denis Healy, a former British Defense Minister:

"What happens in the world does not happen by accident: there are those who make it happen. Most national or trade-related issues are closely managed by those with the money. "

Club Bilderberg members decide when wars should start; how long should they last (Nixon and Ford were taken out for ending the Vietnam War too soon); and when they should end and who should participate. Subsequent border changes are up to them and also who should benefit from the reconstruction.

Bilderberg members "own" central banks and are therefore in a position to determine interest rates, the availability of money, the price of gold and which countries should receive loans. Simply by moving money, Bilderberg members earn billions of dollars. His only ideology is that of the dollar and his greatest passion is power!

All American Presidents since Eisenhower have belonged to the Club. Also, Tony Blair, as well as most of the leading members of the English governments; Lionel Jospin; Romano Prodi, former President of the European Commission; Mario Monti, European Commissioner for Competition; Pasca Lamy, Commissioner for Trade; José Durao Barroso; Alan Greenspan, head of the Federal Reserve; Hillary Clinton; Jolm Kerry; the assassinated Swedish Foreign Minister Anna Lindh; Melinda and Bill Gates; Henry Kissinger; the Rothschild dynasty; Jean Claude Trichet, the visible head of the European Central Bank; James Wolfenson, President of the World Bank; Javier Solana, Secretary General of the Council of the European Community; the financier George Soros, a speculator capable of making national currencies fall to his advantage; and all the royal families in Europe. Next to them sit the owners of the mainstream media.
https://www.bibliotecapleyades.net/sociopolitica/historia_bilderberg/historia_bilderberg01.htm

But this does not end here, entire world organizations are also committed to the new thinking, among which are: The United Nations (UN), the World Health Organization (WHO), the World Bank (WB), the Fund International Monetary (IMF), the United Nations Educational, Scientific and Cultural Organization (UNESCO), and the United Nations Children's Fund (UNICEF) And it is because the heads of these organizations are also Freemasons or belong to the Bilderberg Club.

On the other hand, there are the communists who initially defended their ideology of class struggle in order to seize power by making an armed confrontation between proletarians and bourgeoisie, with which the only thing they achieved was the genocide of millions and millions of people in Russia, China, North Korea, Cuba and other places where this satanic ideology was implanted, are still in force in all countries, lurking to seize the power of their respective governments as soon as circumstances allow, no matter that it has been a complete failure, he always finds followers who are willing to continue and repeat the same failed methods that they always carried out.

Although at first glance it seems that communists and freemasons have nothing in common, incredibly now they are working together in pursuit of a common objective that they both agree on... waging war on God. Thus, in the late 20th century a series of Non-Governmental Organizations (NGOs) began to be created of the most different nuances, at first it was said it was for social, charitable and humanitarian purposes, etc., this is how all the human rights NGOs appeared, which only defend the murderous communists, but never if the victims are of another political or religious, LGBT groups appeared, with all their tints and shapes. The largest promoter of abortion worldwide is Planned Parenthood; whose owner is the father of Bill Gates. The feminist collectives, the animalistic collectives, those of gender ideology. Finally, as the mother of all these NGOs, because it is this that finances all the others described above; There is the greatest of all: the "Open Society Foundation" whose owner is George Soros, a somber, Jewish and Freemason character, born in Hungary, a billionaire who has only recently become known worldwide, but who in fact, it has been many years, working so that the plan that all the subjects and organizations mentioned above become a reality, the implementation of the New World Order.

All these characters, institutions, organizations, countries, they are all very committed to forming a single global government and something that could seem unusual even Pope Francis is seems to be committed to this idea of the New World Order, recently in September 2019, he called to a world meeting to the main leaders to a meeting to discuss the world education to be implemented. It seems that the pieces of the puzzle have just been completed.

HOW THE NEW WORLD ORDER WILL GET STARTED

For the objectives of the New World Order to be achieved, they have long been putting into practice a series of changes in the way people think and behave. They call it "Social Reengineering."

Actually they have managed to divide humanity by different and varied ways of thinking and behaving, most of them so stupid but they have succeeded and their influence is increasing towards their final objective that would be to achieve a government with a global president. We have already seen that the majority of the most influential people in world politics agree, all the heads of world organisms have already implemented many of the plans of this new world order, for example; for this elite group of members of the Bilderberg Club, for them overpopulation is a serious economic problem and that is why for about 60 years ago they began to destroy the institutionality of the family, marriage, and having children... result: Europe has grown old and there are no young people, men and women instead of raising children or grandchildren are raising dogs ... Another of the measures they put in place is the promotion of homosexuality, all very well designed so that no one dares to question morally if this sexual orientation is good or bad and they have implanted it throughout the world through the ministries of education, that is why it is seen in the curriculum of the schools, aberrant immoral subjects where they teach children to become homosexuals, apart from teaching them the satanic invention of gender ideology, in which children are told that if they want to be male or female, they can be, no matter if their physical bodies are male or female.

They have also established laws in most countries whereby anyone who protests against homosexuals is immediately prosecuted and convicted. They also promote the group of lesbians, gays, bisexuals and transgender people (LGBT), and the others that are accompanied ... The idea is, if homosexuals are the majority of the world, there will be no more human births ... Those that are needed to workers will be planned in advance and produced in laboratories. - They have promoted the misnamed "Feminism", which is nothing more than hatred to the male gender and to a life to be born. With this they would also achieve the same goal as with homosexuality. hatred between men and women, no conception of new human beings... - "Animalism", apparently they are people who love animals but in an abnormal, exaggerated way and believe that an animal has the same rights as a human, and even if they have that choosing the life of a human being or that of an animal, they choose the animal, is a more disguised way of hating man. These gentlemen who make up this famous Bilderberg Club, among which is the famous billionaire George Soros who finances all these groups, is the same one who supports all abortion clinics, apart from the main one, Planned Parenthood, owned by the father of Bill Gates where millions of abortions are performed every year and apart they sell the organs of the children they kill ... more abortions, less human beings. They call all this "human re-engineering"

All their plans are aimed to extinguish the human race and that malicious attitude only comes from a reprobate mind, full of hatred to the humanity, so much hate that all their efforts are to destroy it completely. Hence he invents this whole range of ways and means to make humanity disappear. He had already tried it with the communism that invaded the world and in the places where he settled and wanted to settle, millions of human beings died, but his ultimate plan did not work for him, he thought that by creating two enemy camps to death, capitalism and communism at some point a nuclear war would be unleashed and that between both powers they would destroy themselves and with it the entire planet, but it did not work for him, so his plan B is this new form described above.

In order to establish the New World Order, it is necessary to destroy the identity of nations, we are seeing this especially with Spain and other countries in Europe. As long as countries have a history, a religion, customs that unite them, this world government would not have much power, that is why they have tried to destroy and go against all Catholic religious' customs and rites in Europe, preventing them from praying in the schools, they removed the crucifixes and images from schools and other institutions. Carrying any religious object was prohibited. The product of all this anti-Catholicism is the burning and destruction of churches throughout Europe, the murder of priests and nuns.

The identity of nations has also been attacked, ridiculing and mocking history, denying that this or that glorious and noteworthy historical fact is true ... In this sense, the communists who are part of the conspirators for this world order to exist have in charge of creating a new story, discarding the real one. Dividing a nation into small states is another way of destroying the unity and identity of a country, they have done the same with Spain, which is the nation most attacked in Europe, they have invested millions of Euros for separatist groups to emerge in all communities such as Catalonia, the Basque Country, the Canary Islands, Navarra and Galicia, the Valencian Community, the Balearic Islands, Aragon, Andalusia, Asturias, practically everyone wants to separate from Spain in this way, this nation that was the mother of 20 American nations and the broadcaster of its culture, language and religion, which was the most holy to the world; it would be destroyed forever. The hatred that Satan has for this country is understandable, because he was a light to the world and rightly so, Pope John Paul II, on one of the times he visited Spain; He said: *«I am attracted by an admirable story of fidelity and service to the Church, written in apostolic companies and in so many great figures who renewed the Church, strengthened her faith, defended her in difficult times and gave her new children across entire continents. Indeed, thanks above all to this unequaled evangelizing activity, the largest portion of the Church of Christ speaks today and prays to God in Spanish. After my trips, especially through the lands of Latin America and the Philippines, I want to say at this singular moment: **Thank you, Spain; Thank you, Church in Spain**, for your fidelity to the Gospel and to the Bride of Christ! »*. Indeed, thanks to Spain, the majority of the 1,313 million Catholics in the world are due to the apostolate of Spain that not only came to America, but went to every known place on earth, it is also due to it. Catholic fervor from the Philippines, Equatorial Guinea and other nations.

Another of the plans that the new world order has put into practice in Europe to destroy the Judeo-Christian culture or western civilization; has been to allow Muslins to invade all Europe as refugees. Those laws that the organisms of the European Union gave, that each country must receive and take care of all the Muslim immigrants that arrive are express orders of the followers of the New World Order ... with the millions of Muslims who have a high number of births, and the very low reproduction of Europeans, in a few years, Europe would be Muslim, with its culture, language and religion totally different. Christian Europe, it would not exist anymore...- See how, everything they are implanting is to destroy the Christian culture and religion ...If you are good observers, you will realize, how this people express irrational hatred towards Christianity, all these groups of gays, lesbians, feminists, transsexuals, animalists, communists; all of them obey orders from their father, the evil one.

After having caused the destruction of the family and society as we knew it only 50 to 70 years ago, the next step is to spread a virus or bacteria that causes many millions of deaths, (This pandemic we are experiencing with the Covid 19, it is only a trial, which they have done, to see the results, how the people had reacted, what they have done, how governments had behaved, how many people died and how many recovered, how many were immunized etc. The next pandemic will be much more destructive so much so that the whole humanity, with so much suffering, will gladly embrace any help that comes, even from hell itself. And God will allow it, because in the face of such a terrible situation He will also know who are his people and who are not.

But whoever endures to the end will be saved. Matthew 24, 13

Now, these people who believe they own the world and the lives of the people may change their minds and not use the biological weapon, but could use conventional weapons creating wars between different countries that in some way or another they have conflicts ... USA versus China. Arabs versus Israel, etc.

OFFICIAL IMPLEMENTATION OF THE NEW WORLD ORDER

With the family destroyed, people confused as to whether they are men or women, with a large number of homosexuals, lesbians, transsexuals, with a high rate of drug users, with countries destroyed in chaos by the misrule of the communists, with a church distorted and confused, persecuted and closed in many places, with a very high suicide rate for all these ideologies, with a lack of work for most people, with economic recessions and diseases and a pandemic that kills millions of people throughout the world; In the midst of a desperate crisis for all of humanity, a savior appears, a man who is introduced by a highly respected religious leader, (Possibly the Pope). This man presents himself as the one who has the solution to all the problems that humanity has, especially for the plague that has terrified people. This savior has the vaccine that will save millions of people, and it will be distributed free of charge, it brings many more ideas to get humanity out of chaos, out of work, etc. but he asks everyone to accept him as the president of the only world government there should be on earth.

Almost all governments accept it, because previously they have already been convinced with huge amounts of money, all that remains is for all the world's inhabitants to accept it. Humanity desperate for disease and hunger and faced with the promise of salvation through the vaccine, accept. They also agree to receive the card or credential of the New World Government, which will be implanted in the hand or on the forehead, so that everyone no longer needs to be using IDs or credit cards, everything is on the implanted chip. The new era of the New World Order has begun.

GOVERNMENT OF THE NEW WORLD ORDER

By the time the NOM leader manifests, the world population should have declined greatly (according to these people's plans), especially in the poor countries of Hispanic America, Africa, and Asia, it could be said that half of the population has disappeared, the pandemic has killed millions, those of the new world order are happy because coincidentally they were looking for that, to get rid of people from third world countries whom they consider a human waste and hindrance and the less people better control those who survive .

The vaccine that the new world president has provided to the world has paid off, the pandemic has disappeared, people once again regain their spirits and confidence, economic activities begin to normalize, jobs are created, but only those who have the chip that identifies them can get to work. Through this tiny electronic device, people are recognized as citizens of the new government, they also pay their taxes to the government, get their payments, have access to health service, social activities, anything they want to buy or sell, travel or go to vacations can only do it through the new ID (chip)

In most countries, which have accepted to be part of the new world order, they are doing great, the help of the new government reaches everyone, hospitals are built, people have very efficient health insurance, most people in the Underdeveloped countries in America as in Africa, they continue to be vaccinated against all diseases, they are very happy, but they can no longer have children, they have been sterilized. the idea is that more and more the races that are not white disappear, they are the undesirable ones, although they do not know it ... for them the President is their god. They do not lack to eat, since agricultural production of transgender food in general is abundant, but also harmful to human health and reproduction.

Among the countries that have not agreed to be part of this New Government are Russia, China, the United States, Israel, the United Arab Emirates, Qatar, Saudi Arabia, Kuwait with whom the Leader of the "New Ordo Seclorum" has friendly conversations with the aim of passing to be their allies and eventually become part of the new world government.

The new president travels all over the world and with him the Pope introducing the New lider and encouraging people who must trust him and thank him for all he is doing.

The dictatorship of the absurd, has been installed, the immoral, the unnatural, lesbian collectives, homosexuals, transgender, feminists, animalists, have the unconditional support of the government. Boys who want to be women immediately change their sexes, just like girls who want to be men... abortions also have the support of the government, a woman who gets pregnant immediately goes to an abortion clinic and ready, it is not necessary for the parents of the minors to know or give their consent. In schools from the first year of kindergarten they teach them to masturbate and learn that there are different forms of sexual pleasure, they teach them that pedophilia is one more option to have sex. In schools there are designated environments to practice sex with whoever they want and however they want. Parents cannot have an opinion or authority over the education or sexual preferences of children, the government decides what it teaches them in schools and what it does with them. Father who opposes immediately goes to jail.

Prisons are occupied by Catholic priests, lays and religious doctors and teachers who opposes to the new teachings, accused of attacking public tranquility. Although Holy Mass is still celebrated in churches, very few go, for they are seen with bad eyes by society, they are seen as foolish, superstitious and retrograde people.

Many cathedrals and churches have been transformed into museums, and centers of commerce and even entertainment.

As for countries such as Spain, Poland, Hungary, they have been excluded from many financial aid because they continue to struggle with their Catholic religiosity. The United States also resists being ruled by a single world leader, and is viewed with great suspicion by the ruler of the New World Order.

MANIFESTATION OF THE ANTICHRIST

Three and a half years have passed of a wonderful relationship of the President of the New World Order with all the countries that are affiliated, the popularity and acceptance of this great leader could not be better; but someone doesn't want him, they've attacked his life and practically killed him, but astonishingly this great leader is resurrected. The Pope, his great friend, reverences him and presents him as the Savior, to whom all nations must pay tribute to him.

The great world leader, after the attack very much opposed to what happened, goes to St. Peter's Basilica, and in a ceremony broadcast to the whole world, he is crowned king of the world and God of the universe... He also commands that it is no longer necessary any cult or worship any saint of the Catholic Church and therefore from that moment cease all religious ceremonies and especially perpetual sacrifice (Holy Mass). (Rev. 13:5-7) the last bloody persecution begins for all Christians, priests, bishops and catholic faithful who resist this order, will be cruelly murdered or placed in concentration camps.

And there was given unto him a mouth speaking great things and blasphemies; and power was given unto him to continue forty and two months. And he opened his mouth in blasphemy against God, to blaspheme his name, and his tabernacle, and them that dwell in heaven. And it was given unto him to make war with the saints, and to overcome them: and power was given him over all kindred's, and tongues, and nations. Revelation 13, 5-7

The United States is a country that is giving a lot of headache to the president of the New World Order. In the past all of its presidents had supported the installation of a globalized government, but this the last president has refused to be part of this global plan, has not wanted to align with them, and remains a major obstacle to total globalization.

Then, the world leader comes to an agreement with the Chinese and Muslims, to attack America with treason. After a prepared meeting of these countries, partnership and peace treaties with the

United States; it is attacked simultaneously and several of its major cities have been completely destroyed, although the US has also managed to send missiles to its enemies has not been able to get away from the destruction. The Great Babylon, has been destroyed... traders all over the world lament... now who will buy our goods from us? (Revelation 18, 11-17).

The Muslims' deal with the World Leader to attack the US has also been to let them wipe out Israel, their arch-enemy to death, and the Antichrist who also hates Israel agrees. Now without the United States to balance the military might of the world, all muslin countries make one bloc. Egypt (South King), Iran (Persia), North Africa (Cus), Libya (Fut), Turkey (Togorma), Petra and Jordan (Edom and Moab), Ethiopia, Syria and Iraq. (See: Genesis 10. Ezequiel. 38, 8-12). All these staunch enemies of Israel will unite with Russia (King of the North, Gog and Magog, Mesec and Tubal, (Cossacks, and nations that constituted the former USSR). More Germany (Gomer) (Ezekiel 38, 5-6).

Once such an alliance is made, these nations will attack Israel; Jerusalem will be hollowed out by the gentiles and it is at this time that the great tribulation for God's people will really be. (They go back on a greater scale and degree of suffering and violence, which had already happened in the first destruction of Jerusalem in the 70th AD)

The war is fierce, Israel has managed to neutralize Muslims, but then, various European countries sent by the Antichrist, go to aid Muslims. Germany, Turkey, Ukraine and many others who hate Israel... Israel can no longer continue with this war, it is totally destroyed, it has no more weapons. His best friend and ally the United States, has been destroyed too and there is no one who can help them. They are on the verge of total annihilation... Then they turn their eyes to heaven, plead to God to help them. At this time will appear the Sign of the Son of Man in heaven, a great Cross in the firmament, visible from the four cardinal points of the earth. It is only at that moment that Israel understands who the Messiah is, realize his mistake, the deicide they committed, and crying for forgiveness; repent (Matthew 24:29)

It is in those days that Heavenly Jerusalem will appear in heaven and before it surrounded by his angels and his innumerable armies, Jesus and every eye will see him, even those who pierced him.

"Look, it comes in the clouds; All will see him, even those who wounded him, and will weep for his death all the nations of the earth. Yes, it will be." (Revelation 1,7)

Seeing the arrival of the Celestial Jerusalem astonished, the few Jews who have survived have gone to Mount Zion, where Christ is. Attacks by Israel's enemies have stopped; but immediately, the - third bloc of nations has been formed, this time made up of the entire world, including the east or nations of the rising Sun, China, Japan and others; all will march to make war on the Son of Man, gathering for the final battle, for Armageddon, (Revelation 16, 13).

The great world leader, the Antichrist, travels all over the earth urging all countries, to go to Jerusalem to attack the intruder who has arrived and who is settled on Mount Zion ...

And he will go out to deceive the nations at the four ends of the earth, Gog and Magog, in order to gather them for battle; their number is like the sand of the sea. (Revelation 20: 8)

All nations have prepared and soon reach the area of Israel, by sea, land and air hundreds of armies ready to fight with the alien who has arrived ...

Then I saw the beast, the kings of the earth, and their armies gathered together to wage war against the one on the horse and against his army. Revelation 19:19

The Antichrist commanding his armies gives the order to attack, but as they get closer their minds get so confused that they destroy themselves. It is a bloody and cruel war full of darkness like themselves, until there is nothing left but the Antichrist with his closest collaborators who are captured by the angels of the Lord ... to be judged and destroyed forever.

"And the beast was caught, and with it the false prophet who made signs in his presence, with which he deceived

those who had received the mark of the beast and those who worshiped his image; the two were thrown alive into the lake of fire that burns with sulfur." Revelation 19:20

The fact is that after this, the Antichrist will be destroyed, and Satan, the false prophet, along with his followers taken prisoner forever. (Rev 19, 20). Does it sound like a horror or science fiction tale? However, the same will happen so that man can only live in peace and rebuild the earth under the command of Christ our Lord.

The earth has been a disaster, but the angels of God with their saints and the good people who survived begin the task of rebuilding and there will be no more wars, evils, diseases or death, God has brought his dwelling for the earth.

And I John saw the holy city, the New Jerusalem, come down from heaven, from God, arranged as a bride dressed for her husband. And I heard a great voice from heaven saying: Behold the tabernacle of God with men, and he will dwell with them; and they will be his people, and God himself will be with them as their God. God will wipe away every tear from their eyes; and there will be no more death, no more crying, no crying, no pain; because the first things happened. Revelation 21, 3-4)

So far what I have described is a brief sequence of events that would take place in the very near future; but it is necessary to broaden the subject about the characters that acted or that are already acting, the places or countries involved, and the explanations of the biblical quotations that are difficult to understand with the naked eye.

THE ANTICHRIST AND HIS GOVERNMENT.

As we have just seen in the previous topic of "Three Political Alliances"; shortly before the end of these times, the Roman Empire will be reborn, not exactly as it was before but in the form of several confederate nations that will be a direct product of Roman civilization, because in reality this empire never disappeared, basically all the Western culture carries in all aspects of its life, the Roman heritage. Some men who have gone down in history tried to revive this empire, Carlo Magnum, Napoleon, Hitler and others, however, none of them was successful, three or four decades ago no one would have believed that this rebirth would be possible.

The power group mentioned above, the Bidelberg Club, has long started to design in a trial plan how it could make a union of countries in Europe, different in all its forms and to the surprise of many, managed to form the most important and complex institution of all the times: The European Union. First they started making efforts to create: The European Common Market with the idea of unifying and strengthening their economies, facilitating trade, abolishing border taxes and creating an international currency; in synthesis create the European United States. Which is already fully operational with many united nations. Many years ago the prophet Daniel interpreted a rather strange dream that Nebuchadnezzar, king of Babylon, had:

"His head was made of gold, his chest and arms were silver, his waist and hip were bronze, his legs were iron and his feet were part of iron and part of clay; while looking at the statue, a stone came off without anyone touching it and hitting the feet of mud and iron on the statue and collapsing it into dust and the wind took it away without any trace of it; while the stone that wounded the statue became a great mountain that filled the whole earth" (Daniel 2)

Daniel reminded Nebuchadnezzar of the dream and at the same time gave him the interpretation that the Lord had revealed to him:

"You are the head of gold (Babylonian kingdom) after you will emerge another kingdom smaller than yours (Medo – Persian) and then a third that will dominate the entire earth (Greek); there will be a fourth strong empire like iron (Roman Empire) that breaks everything and destroys ... what you saw from the feet part of clay and iron is that this kingdom will be divided but it will have some of the strength of iron. In the time of those kings (the present time) the God of heaven will raise a kingdom that will never be destroyed and will not pass to the power of another people and will crumble all those kingdoms, but He will remain forever." (Daniel 2)

History itself confirmed us of the existence of those four kingdoms beginning with Babylon under the command of Nebuchadnezzar to whom the dream was revealed more or less in 530 BC. Darius conquered Babylon by conforming the Medo-Persian kingdom

Then the Greeks grew in power and in 331 BC. Alexander the Great defeated the Medo-Persian Empire, establishing this third kingdom until in the year 68 BC the Romans became absolute world power. Since then, although its political power has been eclipsed and apparently disappeared, the culture that developed this empire never disappeared, "The Western Culture" that is made up of many countries. Part of this empire will be reborn, those feet of mud and iron means its extension and division, the feet have ten fingers and mean the ten countries that will make it up; the stone that collapsed the statue is Christ whose kingdom will grow and be eternal.

The prophet Daniel not only interpreted this mysterious dream but also had a vision of four beasts, which gives us more light to understand part of the future of the world.

"Four big beasts came out of the ocean, different from each other. The first beast was like a lion with an eagle's wings ... behold, the second was like a bear ... I kept looking after this, here is another third similar to a leopard with four bird wings on its back and with four heads ... and I saw the fourth terrible beast, dreadful, exceedingly strong, with great iron teeth, devoured and crushed and the leftovers crushed them with the feet, was very different from the previous beasts and had ten horns; when I saw the horns I saw that another smaller horn was coming out and it took three of the ten horn; this horn had eyes like a man and a mouth that spoke with great arrogance. " (Daniel 7)

The vision is easy to explain because it is Daniel himself, who asked one of God's assistants in the vision to explain:

"Those beasts are four kingdoms that will rise on earth ... the fourth beast is a kingdom that will be distinguished from others, will devour the whole earth and crush it (it will encompass the whole earth and enslave it) the ten horns are ten kings that at that time they will rise and after them another one will rise that will be different from the others and will overthrow three of these kings, will speak arrogant words against the Most High will pretend to change the times of the law". (Daniel 7, 23)

This fourth beast or kingdom has the same meaning as the feet of the statue. In our time the ten kings will be ten presidents who have joined for different reasons to form a great confederation, a great kingdom (The European Union); but then another great leader will emerge with new ideas, with the power of conviction, that in the face of the critical situation that will exist in those times, he will seem to be the only solution; That is why seven of these statesmen will voluntarily submit to this man, but not three of them, who will be overthrown by this charismatic and charming leader, for the eyes of the world and those who do not have their hearts on the Lord. God of armies. What nations will be subjected to force? It is possible that they are Portugal or Spain, Poland, Hungary, for its deep Catholic roots.

"This horn had the eyes of a man and a mouth that spoke arrogantly ... he spoke arrogant words against the Most High and oppressed the people of God ..." (Daniel 7)

This man will be proud and arrogant will believe that he is the best in the world, will come to believe that he is God, will blaspheme and insult the Lord, will have anger and hatred against especially Catholics and will persecute, oppress and try to exterminate the Jews as well.

Between the prophecies of Daniel and the Apocalypse written by Saint John, there is a similarity so great that it undoubtedly demonstrates that it is the same case. Let's see:

"Then I saw, a beast that came out of the sea and had 10 horns and seven heads ... in each of the heads there were names insulting God ... the dragon gave the beast its own power, its throne and its authority; one of the beast's heads seemed to be seriously injured, but the wound was healed and the whole earth marveled by this left behind her.

They all worshiped the dragon because it gave authority to the beast and said: Who as the beast? Who can fight him?"

(Revelation 13)

The little horn that had the eyes of a man and that blasphemed, is the same character that John describes as the beast; the Antichrist, who will come to power thanks to the powers that the dragon gives him, but who is the dragon? ***Revelation 12, 9*** tells us: ***"And the dragon was cast out, the snake that is called a demon or Satan."***

So it will be the same demon acting on earth.

The Antichrist will be well known in the world; but he will increase his popularity when he suddenly receives a head injury (someone will want to kill him). For medical science, perhaps this man has no hope of returning to normal life; but mysteriously it will be completely healthy. It is at this moment, when the devil will give him his powers and become incarnate in this man. Of course, the world will not realize this transformation but its full recovery so they will marvel and be dominated and deceived.

The kingdom of this man will be full of terror, abuse, murder, who dares to contradict him will have the worst of deaths, and as the prophet says he will have dominion over different races, peoples, nations, and almost all the entire earth will have to obey him." What ***terrible times those will be!***

John also tells us that in addition to the first beast that came out of the sea, he saw another beast that came out of the earth and had two ram-like horns (power) and spoke like the dragon (demon), used the authority of the first beast and He forced the inhabitants of the earth to worship the first beast (Antichrist) and had the power to work miracles and deceive the people of the earth.

Perhaps it will be easier to understand what the prophet has just told us, if we speak in current terms: The first beast will be a well-known and popular man who will become a dictator. He will have someone who endorses and supports him (second beast, who we will talk about in more detail later). This character will also be someone very important and that by the ram's horns he has indicates that he will falsely represent religion, spreading the great ideas and works that this dictator performs. - According to them for the best distribution of economic wealth, education and health in the world. This representative of this dictator will use all kinds of tricks, witchcraft and dark powers and he will be the one who orders everyone to make a statue of the dictator and to worship him as God. And although this may seem incredible, many will (remember the respect and veneration that Hitler received) and as Juan says; people will say who is like him? Who can against him? So that no one escapes the influences of the dictator, his representative will order that all people who want to work, buy, sell or make any kind of transaction will have to bear the mark or sign of the dictator (the apostle mentions the number 666. The 6 represents to man but repeated three times, symbolizes that this man think he is God; for being three the number that represents the divinity).

Who has not been in a highly developed country, could be skeptical about these tales of the mark of the beast; but currently with the electronic era and with the wonders that computers perform, it is possible to register millions of people, have all their data archived and get that information in a matter of seconds. This will be the way the future dictator would control the inhabitants of the earth.

John in the Apocalypse says that the mark that put the inhabitants of the earth was on the right hand or on the forehead. Currently, many people use credit cards, with which they can buy whatever they want in any commercial establishment without touching a penny, or they can also withdraw money from banks and financial institutions anywhere in the world. Something very practical to carry out and easy to carry.

But with the advancement of technology there is now something else that will surprise you. According to the Canadian magazine "San Miguel Archangel", in one of its numbers of the year 2001, they published a report that said that, precisely the most powerful financial entities in the world, which of course are in the USA. They had entrusted the men of science to make a credit card the size of a grain of rice, which is a microchip where not only the information of how much money the person has is stored but also an identification card, there they are all your personal data, date and place of birth, how much money you have, how much you earn, where you live, where you work, profession, nationality, etc.

The experiment has given excellent results and has even been inserted in the back of the hand and in the forehead of many people, and for being so small it is not noticeable. Nothing more and nothing less than what John says in the Apocalypse!

Do you see how the pieces of the puzzle come together as time goes by? Finally, there are many thousands of people who are already using this microchip today, such as identification or personal data card, blood types, medicines that the person uses, etc. If you want to have more information about this product and even send this brand (which of course we do not recommend), you can go to the Web: www.verychip.com and you will have all the information you need.

This is the method and the way in which this world leader of the future will control humanity.

Recently, the country whose people are using it massively is Sweden, Thousands of Swedes are Inserting Microchips Under Their Skin. Jowan Osterlund holds a microchip implant in Stockholm in 2017.... They also can be used to store emergency contact details, social media profiles or e-tickets for events and rail journeys within Sweden.

Jhon also tells us that the Antichrist will resemble a leopard indicating how quickly this subject will move to invade and conquer the mind of the people all over the world. It will be like a bear, indicating the strength and power it will have wherever it goes. It will be like a lion indicating his vanity, arrogance and pride, with whose mouth he will insult God and his Saints. Living in those times will not be pleasant, since his government will be bloodthirsty and horrifying, he will make the regimes of Stalin, Hitler, Mao and the great murderous dictators, as insignificant. But the strangest thing is that humanity will take this character (Antichrist) and these facts as normal.

WHEN WILL THE ANTICHRIST'S GOVERNMENT BEGIN?

In fact, the kingdom of Antichrist is already present throughout the European Union and from there it is also spreading to the other nations of the world. The Parliament of the European Union, which is like the central government and other related organizations such as the European Court of Human Rights, United Nations, has already begun to dictate certain norms and laws that go directly against Christ and his people.

Recently, the latter organization ordered the removal of all crucifixes from Italian classrooms (as it has done in other countries as well). Fortunately, the Italians stood up in defense of the symbol of Christianity and for the moment they have not let this anti-Christian law come true; but there are already countries like Belgium, England, Germany, France that are complying with these anti-Christian norms.

Another of the norms, for example, is the prohibition of praying in schools, the prohibition of Christian or Catholic religion classes; but they do let Muslims, or other non-Christian religions, have their religious signs or make their daily prayers and have classes and courses in their religious philosophies. Do you see how clearly the influence of the Antichrist is already?

In 2009, the European Parliament, gave a law according to them "anti-discrimination", with which they want to force Catholics, for example to give Holy Communion to anyone who asks for it, even if it is not Catholic, but would process it by discrimination.

A doctor who refused to perform an abortion was prosecuted for discrimination and bad practices. A judge, who refused to marry two homosexuals, was also prosecuted and dismissed from his job, for continuing his Christian conscience of not being part of that perversion condemned by God.

In Argentina just this year 2019, a medic Leandro Rodriguez, was put in prison for having save the life of the mother and his son who were in danger of dead, after the woman took an abortion pill.

Catholic schools that want to teach their Christian doctrine cannot, because they undermine the beliefs of other students who are not Catholic, these laws not only threaten confessional schools, hospitals, adoption agencies or the like; but to the whole Catholic Christian culture that for hundreds of years has been the basis of European culture.

The Antichrist is already laying all the foundations for a great Catholic persecution that will culminate in the taking of the Vatican and the prohibition of the Holy Mass and every symbol and practice of Christian life.

THE CATHOLIC EUROPE ABANDON HIS RELIGION AND TRADITION

The devil as we said in previous issues, has been preparing the ground for a long time, with the ideologies we saw earlier, all of them contrary to Christ, what they now call secularism, Marxism, socialism, evolutionism, Darwinism, Freudianism, New Era, Gnosticism, liberalism; relativism, all this has been making Europeans especially those who have come to take on political power, most of them communists are contrary to the norms of the Church, it is this spirit contrary to Christ, who has allowed the Muslim emigration invade all Europe and be benevolent in every way with them, (Muslims) even if they break European rules and laws and be hostile to the Catholic religion and every Christian principle.

Currently, Muslims in Europe are controlling local and national governments of most European countries and in a few years, they will take all political and religious power. It is more than certain that the Antichrist in person could be one of them.

With the latest events of the civil war in Syria, and the establishment, of the self-styled Islamic State, has triggered a massive migration of Muslims to Europe, reaching it, millions of them to European soil. What the Muslims could not through wars of expansion since the sixth century that began as a sect full of hatred to all who did not share their principles; He has achieved it peacefully by invading Europe, through deception and political circumstances that Europeans themselves and the United States of America themselves have created.

With this opening of Europe to Muslim migration, which now adds many millions without knowing it, they have put the rope around their neck.

The hatred of Christianity, does not allow them to see the reality of their actions, they are so foolish, that wanting to be very humanitarian, open and tolerant to other cultures, they have closed and betrayed their Christian roots to open themselves unconditionally to the religion and culture that wants to exterminate them.

The Koran has more than 100 verses inciting hatred, discrimination and death and for them, (followers of Muhammad), that is law and has to be fulfilled; However, most Europeans and especially their political leaders, including Obama, the ex-president of the United States of America, say that Islam is a religion of love ... There is no doubt that they have to be blind! They do not see the reality. Driven by the spirit of the Antichrist, they glorify and embrace the religion of violence and death and despise and persecute the religion of life and love. -See: (The Koran, a hate book. Https://jaime48.wordpress.com/tag/coran/).

With Europe already taken by the Muslims, governments will soon take over and attack their only and main ideological and religious enemy, "The Catholic Church." The Church that in past times, despite preaching total and unconditional love, out of necessity of defending the truth and freedom had to lead the wars of just defense against the Muslim enemy following a satanic religion of destruction and death.

The fiction stories taken to the cinema of The Lord of the Rings and others like Narnia, etc. They are nothing far from reality. Given this planned invasion and seizure of the religious, political and military power of Muslims in Europe; open reactions of Christians forming make shift armies to defend their faith and freedom, as there were in the past and as there was in Mexico at the beginning of the twentieth century, when the Catholic population especially the peasants joined together to defeat the government forces of Plutarch Elias Calles, Mason and declared enemy of the Catholic Church. In the end, in the midst of this worldwide conflagration of a whole series of moral, religious, political, military, social disorders of extreme evil, of the invasion and near extermination of Israel, as we have mentioned before, the great sign of the Son of the Man (Jesus) will appear announcing his glorious coming, to end the beast, the Antichrist and his infernal hosts.

Only with this piece of the puzzle, (Europe taken by the Muslims) can be understood, why the hatred that this character and this union of countries (the Antichrist and the beast) have against the "Great Babylon" (United States of North America), for them (Muslims) the US represents their 2nd most hated enemy after Israel.

THE DESTRUCTION OF BABYLON

When I started writing this book and reached the point where I had to choose, what would be the current nation that meets the requirements to be the Great Babylon of the last days, I was reluctant to accept that it could be the USA. I said in myself: No, it can't be … if you feel so good, so understanding, so friendly! But, when I began to enumerate his faults and sins, there was no time to finish, (and I have yet to touch many more). And, when I read the biblical quotation concerning the fall of Babylon, there was no doubt that it is this country and no other to which the prophecies refer.

John, the apostle, in his book of Revelation, tells us about the fall of Babylon. We know from history and from the archaeological remains that Babylon was destroyed hundreds of years before the Apostle wrote the Apocalypse, so which country of these times represents the Babylon of John?

"The great Babylon fell. All nations drank the wine of their immorality, the kings of the earth with it fornicated, and merchants from all over the world with the power of their luxury became rich. (Revelation 18)

Undoubtedly, by these sentences we are faced with a country with an overwhelming moral corruption that many rulers of different nations involve in their immoralities; his sumptuousness and luxuries are indescribable, he runs a lot of money and a lot of businessmen from all over the earth become rich because of his extravagances. It is a superb nation, swollen with pride, has a lot of material wealth, and she says:

"As queen I am sitting, I am not a widow, nor will I ever see grief." (Revelation 18, 7)

Isaiah also tells us that this great Babylon said:

"Me and no one but me, I will not widow or know the orphan hood"

(Isaiah 47, 8)

So far there is only one nation in the world that fills most of these particularities that the prophets say, especially **Isaiah in chapter 47** and by the **Apostle John in Revelation 17 and 18.** This nation is very powerful to make itself be called **"queen of the nations"**. **The United States of America** is the only nation today whose power encompasses most of these aspects. In the material or economic it is the one that enjoys the greatest prestige and stability worldwide, all other nations are subordinated to the ups and downs of their economy, the dollar is the currency that is worth anywhere in the world; its material power is such that many countries sink or rise.

Militarily it is the nation best equipped with sophisticated war material, in its arsenal they include: airplanes that can easily be confused with spacecraft, satellites, lasers, divisions of men with anti-radioactive equipment and capable of flying individually, it has rockets and missiles capable of destroying the world, not only once but many times; missiles that guided by electronic brains can hit the exact target even though the launching bases are thousands of kilometers away. Rockets that fly flush with the earth so as not to be detected by opposites, weapons capable of destroying living beings, but not cities; airplanes and submarines that travel at great speeds with unsuspected characteristics to make war; features that still seem like science fiction stories.

As for the technical advancement in civil matters they also take the lead to others, they have ships that come and go from space, men on the moon, factories operated entirely by robots, computers and electronic brains that simplify the work of millions of people; Telling the progress this country has would take another book.

Actually it is a great nation, the country of opportunities, people from all over the world want to go there and it is that wonders of this country are told; in truth it is another world full of material advancement.

But, something very serious has; its morale is found on the ground. How much sexual degradation exists in this country! Crowds of sexual deviants of both sexes. How many mentally ill! How much crime and homicides! The people are cold and calculating, what matters is business, money, no matter how you get it; for there is no ethics, there is no moral, there is no love or human warmth; Only love of wealth and much selfishness. Sorcerers and astrologers, witches and worshipers of evil increase every day to such an extent that influential people from the same government and executives of large companies are involved in such abominations.

"You said:

I will always be a queen forever, and you did not reflect or think about your end.

Listen to this lover of pleasure, you who think that you are saved and safe, that you say that there is no one else like you ... you who are confident in your evil, and said nobody sees me.

Your wisdom and your science deceived you ... an evil will fall upon you that you will not know how to counteract, and the ruin that you will not be able to erase will come upon you, the devastation will come suddenly without you

knowing it ... those who save you They divide the heavens and watch the stars, those who tell you month by month what is to come upon you."

(Isaiah 47)

Astrology gains followers every day, almost all of them in some way or another have practiced witchcraft, spiritualism or some kind of extrasensory phenomena, sometimes using different kinds of drugs. Currently to give a more scientific image, sorcerers and fortune tellers have changed their names, now you can find them with the name of "Psychic".

As things go, by the time of their destruction, these abominations will have spread not only in this country, but in all others who are under their influence; as is the case with the proliferation of violence, terror and pornography films; corrupt, unnatural and immoral sexual magazines and literature; like its detestable customs that reach the most remote and unsuspected places in the world.

That evil influence that projects everyone is one of his most serious sins, author and responsible for scandals and global corruption. A small example is the celebration of Halloween. Every October 31 is celebrated in the USA. the satanic feast of witches' night; now in many western countries alienated from the culture of the USA, they have also begun to celebrate that silly pagan custom of present-day Babylon.

There is yet another very significant similarity of ancient and modern Babylon. The word Babylon, in itself, is a word that was derived from Babel, that city that, in the midst of its vanity and pride, built a tower so high that it wanted to reach God and where the confusion of languages and races happened. The United States is currently called "The melting pot", which means something like the "common pot" where they have thrown everything; today, you can find there all the races and languages of the world as it was Babel or ancient Babylon. Don't you think it's too much coincidence?

But the day will come, says the Lord and then:

"Behold, like pieces of straw, consumed by fire will not be able to save their lives from the power of the flames, they will not even be able to save themselves (astrologers, and sorcerers), the flames will be very hot". (Isaiah 47)

The destruction of this country will be through fire, which means that they may be nuclear explosions.

"One day there will come plagues, diseases, pain and famines, it will be consumed by fire, for the Lord God who has judged it is mighty." (Revelation 18)

This description of the apostle John is exactly equal to the dire consequences of a nuclear war, those that were not destroyed by fire, heat and radiation near the point of the explosion will be killed by the plagues that will be unleashed causing great mortality, diseases radiation product; terrible pains, without drugs to relieve them, hungry for lack of the most necessary to survive. What can be saved in a nuclear explosion?

Other similar parallels between the US and Babylon, it is that of merchants; Actually this country is the one that buys everything and everyone. Let's go to a mall in this country and we will see that most of the things they sell come from different places in the world. Wherever we go, we will find traces of the commercial and cultural influence of the United States of North America; That is why when this nation cease to exist, the merchants of the world will be terribly sorry that there will no longer be anyone who buys their merchandise.

"The rulers of the land who had a deal with it and gave themselves up to luxury will cry and lament that there will be no one who buys their merchandise ... Every pilot and navigator, like sailors and those who sail in the sea stopped at away and they cried out when they contemplated the smoke of their fire and said: Who was like the big city? (Revelation 18)

How will its destruction ensue if it is the first world power? We just said that it has the best war arsenal, how can it be possible that it is surprised and destroyed?

When a country falls victim of immorality, when its rulers and the people in general have fallen into spiritual and moral degradation, nothing can save even their sophisticated armaments, their armies will sleep very calm and confident, the lookouts will be drunk, drugged and busy in their immoralities and sexual promiscuity.

"The objective reality of a nation is composed of principles," beacons "that govern human development and happiness;

natural laws, interwoven in the plot of all civilized societies throughout history, and that include the roots of every family and institution that has endured and prospered. These principles emerge to the surface again and again, and the degree to which members of a society recognize them and live in harmony with them determines that they move towards survival and stability or towards disintegration and destruction" Stephen R. Covey

I have allowed myself to quote this thought from Stephen R. Covey, author of many books on leadership and personal effectiveness; so that they see that not only a religious man agrees with these ideas, but many other thinkers who, although they do not have God in mind; they know that if moral and natural principles are violated, unfailingly, men, institutions and societies disintegrate, self-destruct, disappear, what is happening with America.

Who will be responsible for the destruction of this modern Babylon? Although for the moment it seems impossible, it will come from several European and Muslim countries led and promoted by the Antichrist.

"Listen to the noise of the mountains, noise of many people, sounds of nations and kingdoms gathering ... They come from far away countries. In his anger the Lord comes to rough the whole country" (Isaiah 13)

Possibly these countries plan to destroy Babylon because it interferes with their plans and does not allow them to act at their free will. It is known that the United States has a lot of political and economic power over almost every country on earth and will continue to have it until the end of its days.

"And all the arms (of the Babylonians) will faint and the hearts of men will freeze, they will be filled with terror and anguish, they will look at each other with stupor and their faces will light up." (Isaiah 13)

Knowing that they are being attacked by surprise and betrayal, all people including armies will be confused, desperate and terrified that they will not know what to do.

"The land will be made a desert and I will exterminate sinners. The stars of the sky and their stars will not give light, the sun will not shine in the morning, the moon will

not give its light; and the earth will tremble in its place."
(Isaiah 13)

Again the description is consistent with the disasters caused by the explosion of nuclear bombs; the earth as desert, the sun, the moon and the stars are not seen by the radioactive dust that the explosions have raised, the sunlight will only be seen in a very diffuse way as a cloudy day and only when the day is already advanced.

"As the unchained hurricane that comes from the desert, disaster comes, from the dreadful land. I have seen a vision of cruel events, vision of betrayal and destruction ... In the vision a banquet is prepared, the carpets are arranged so that the guests feel, they are eating and drinking, suddenly the alarm voice. Officers prepare your shields!"

(Isaiah 21,1-5)

A conventional war using all kinds of rocket planes and bombs would be like a true hurricane unleashed. Much more so will be a nuclear war. The prophet says he has seen preparations for a banquet and then betrayal and destruction. As happened in the time of Hitler who spoke of peace and soon unleashed his dreadful war; In the same way it will be at the end of time. This Babylon will be told about peace and she will fall into the trap. It is very possible that the same President of the United States of America, is in Europe having dinner and celebrating some important agreement with their European and Arab hosts and will be just at that moment when they are surprisingly and treacherously attacked.

"Babylon the great, mother of all the prostitutes and perverts of the world. And I saw that the woman was drunk with the blood of the people of God and those who were killed because they were loyal to Christ" *(Revelation 17, 5)*

This country, among other things, will be punished for being the source of sexual corruption worldwide. For being the main focus of the harlots and perverts. Let's go to any city in the United States and we could well imagine that maybe we are in the old and missing Biblical cities of Sodom and Gomorrah, because in those streets and even entire cities like San Francisco, Los Angeles, New York, Chicago, Miami and other more, evil and promiscuity has spread everywhere. Of every 10 people living in San Francisco, eight are gay or lesbian; On the other hand, witches, sorcerers, fortune tellers, psychic and churches of Satan have invaded almost every home in these perverted cities.

Shortly before its destruction, hostilities, crimes and murders will be committed here in against all those who are loyal to Christ, possibly many Christians especially if they are Catholics will be persecuted and killed, for their faithfulness to the teachings of the church.

For several years, they have begun to attack and vandalize some Catholic temples for their position against abortion, contraceptives, homosexuality and their ideas of prevention against AIDS.

It is no secret to anyone that in countries that are called defenders of democracy, there is hatred against Catholics; One of the main obstacles that John F. Kennedy had to face to become president was that of belonging to a Catholic family and that was what led to his death; because they could not bear to be governed by a Catholic. Did you know that Nagasaki and Hiroshima were the only cities with a Catholic majority in Japan and precisely these 2 cities were chosen to be destroyed with the atomic bombs dropped in World War II? - When Pope John Paul II announced his intentions to visit England and the USA, many protests arose from religious fanatics and atheists who threatened to kill him. The same has happened lately with the visit of Benedict XVI, when he visited England, they even threatened to imprison him. When the Catholic bishops of the USA declared that the manufacture of nuclear weapons went against all moral and ethical principles, for endangering all humanity, many Protestant pastors rose up in outrage raising accusations of treason, cowardice and countless insults; so in those days hatred and fanaticism will be greater against true Christians.

"The ten horns you saw (ten presidents of ten nations) and the beast (Antichrist) will hate the prostitute (Babylon) they will snatch everything she has and leave her naked, eat her flesh and destroy her with fire. (Rev 17, 16)

The destruction of this Babylonian country will be when the Antichrist has already made his appearance on earth; and be the President of the ten Confederate States of the European Union, which the Bible makes mention of (and which by the way does not necessarily have to be exactly ten nations, the number can be symbolic), This character with the evil power he has will come to be a great leader in the eyes of the world, they will consider him as the savior of the world, his power of persuasion will be such that humanity will be mesmerized before his charisma; but this same man with his allies will be those who destroy Babylon. All this will happen almost halfway through his reign.

WHY GOD WOULD PERMIT THE DESTRUCTION OF AMERICA?

I always listen the expression **"God bless America!** ... that would be my wish too, because I admire its positive aspects, order, work, cleanliness, solidarity and because I live at and I have many close friends and family living in there. But, analyzing things well, getting rid of all sentimental inclination; it is very difficult for God to bless America, that is, the United States, for the many sins this nation has committed and is committing.

Every time I know her more, every time I think about it more, every time I search the Holy Scriptures more, I realize that America is running towards its own destruction. In fact, without resorting to the Bible and faith, only by reasoning logically, we know that one day America will cease to exist as a power, because it is a kind of universal law, nations grow, develop, become corrupted and fall.

But, if we turn to the Bible, we will realize more clearly that this great country, which has developed so much, is condemned for the innumerable sins it has committed throughout its history.

When we read the terrible stories of how the Chaldeans and some ancient civilizations sacrificed their own children in honor of Moloch their god, we were terrified and surprised by such savagery; however, in the country that is considered the most civilized in the world, the US It is estimated that more than 28 million children are killed annually for the most cruel and barbaric practice of abortion. This is more than all the natural disasters and wars that have occurred in the world. Why do Americans pay such a high price for murdering their children? ... Because they worship their god, dollar, their god gold, their god selfishness, their god sex and pleasure. One of the capital sins, most abhorred and rebuked by God, is homosexuality, and America carries on its shoulders and on its conscience having become a great Sodom and Gomorrah, a great harlot. Millions of Americans and why not say it almost everybody think that being homosexual is normal and still dare to think that God approves it.

Sodomites struggle day and night to assert their rights and have managed to infiltrate all areas of society that currently dominate all media, influence politics, influence the education of children and youth, influence Protestant churches, and other denominations and finally, drastically deny that the Bible condemns them; although very clearly God speaks of the curses they will receive.

Now they get married, they can adopt and raise children, they are ordained as pastors and they have launched an entire advertising campaign around the world to be accepted as normal. They make use of elaborate arguments but without scientific or religious foundation and much less moral; but there are people who because of their ignorance believe them and even manage to inspire affection. Poor people! they say ... it's their hormones, they have born like that! Something completely ridiculous and wrong, any biologist, or honest medical doctor can check and say that it is false. Otherwise they would not have to inject female hormones to appear more at the opposite sex.

Finally, to strengthen their sin and mental deviation, they have created the day of the "Gay Pride", which is celebrated on a certain day by all the countries where they are allowed. That day is practically what Sodom was, its perversion is such that there is no doubt that the demons have taken the body of these poor people to do what they do, to express hatred and insult God. All public and private institutions, all companies and businesses endorse and support them, all show in those days the flag that has been made of 7 colors of the rainbow to identify themselves ... City squares, airlines, public buildings all they adorn their places with lights in the colors of their flag ... they truly feel proud of their evil ...

"No man will have sex with another man; God hates that ... Do not make yourself impure by committing these acts ... Obey the commandments I give you ... I am the Lord your God. " (Leviticus 18,22-30)

In these last years, they have come with the invention of the different kinds of genders, the most stupidity of modern man, here the definition of this aberration:

Gender identity is how a person feels and who they know them self to be when it comes to their gender. There are more than two genders, even though in our society the genders that are most recognized are male and female (called the gender binary) and usually is based on someone's anatomy (the genitals they were born with). This is gender assignment and it is based on an assumption that someone's genitals match their gender. However, gender isn't about someone's anatomy, it is about who they know them self to be. There are many different gender identities, including male, female, transgender, gender neutral, non-binary, agender, pangender, genderqueer, two-spirit, third gender, and all, none or a combination of these.

There are many more gender identities then we've listed. Gender can be complex and people are defining themselves in new and different ways as we gain a deeper understanding of identities. Some terms may mean different things to different people. There are certain terms some folks may not like to use or call themselves and some terms that they may like to use or call themselves. If you're not sure what to call a person, it's best to ask the person what they would like to be called. It is always up to us to decide how we identify, and how we express our gender. However, you decide or identify deserves to be respected and supported.
http://teentalk.ca/learn-about/gender-identity/

Completely out of their mind, out of the minimum rezoning, completely out of the will of God.

Like Babylon, America is also the most religious country in the world, from it have come the majority of aberrant, radical and liar's sects that now swarm around the world sowing confusion and division, there you can find churches of white's racists, resentful blacks, gays and lesbians, dreamers and fraudulent miracles, occult and satanic sciences; Eastern religions churches. All revolve around the lie and the lord money, all claim to be the true Church and all without exception attack the Catholic Church. You realize now! Who is the real one?

America ... poor America! As if everything we have said was little; It is infested with satanic musical groups, whose purpose is to lead people through their music to demon worship, drug use, pornography, crime and finally suicide. The most modern, most practical and technical country, the most materialistic country on earth that has become skeptical of what is not seen, discarding even many religious beliefs; It has become the number one in following the enemy of God, satanic churches proliferate with their abominable rites, where animals and even human beings sacrifice. Witches, sorceresses and fortune tellers have multiplied by thousands and thousands. All media, such as TV channels, radio stations, newspapers and magazines have a liar or astrologer who keeps fooled millions of naive and fools; all of which constitutes an abomination to the eyes of God. However, for America it is only a matter of freedom and even pride.

Finally, America has become a great biogenetic laboratory, where they play with human genes, cells and embryos, as if developing human beings were simply parts of a machine where they take out the parts they need and the rest they throw it away.

As you can see, the sins of America are enormous. Unfortunately, most people who live there don't realize it; because they live in a permissive society that envelops them and hypnotizes them with consumerism, material abundance and pleasure. Everyone is conditioned from childhood by those ideological lies we had seen before; therefore, even if the moral disorders and chaos increase and live in spiritual misery, they do not realize and believe that it is normal.

There are many more faults, such as lack of honesty, something that they hypocritically boast of being an honest nation; but most of all private companies, especially those dedicated to selling services, all state agencies, local or municipal entities, steal and exploit people, imposing a series of arbitration, taxes, and fines, fatally oppressing the people conditioned to pay all that they are asked for and the only thing they say resigned is: "We cannot go against the System" The Americans also boast of living in the country of freedom; but they do not realize that they live as slaves of money, slaves of the government that oppresses them with high taxes, fines and sanctions, slaves of debauchery and the whole series of sins and evils such as crime, pornography, drug addiction, racism and discrimination.

Babylon as we all know from history, was the main religious center of the past, so this new Babylon is the main promoter of the sects and it is from here that they spread the error, division, hatred, and lies everywhere in the world, accusing and slandering the Catholic Church. Many of them know how bad they are, who they are and what awaits them; But they don't say it.

"It has already fallen; the great Babylon has already fallen! ... For all the nations got drunk with the wine of their immoral passion; the kings of the world committed sexual immoralities with her and the merchants of the world became rich with their exaggerated waste ...

For their sins have piled up to heaven, and God knows their evil minds. Give her the same thing she has given to others; pay him twice what he has done ... give him torment and suffering as he gave himself to pride and waste" *(Revelation 18)*

WHAT CAN AMERICAN CHRISTIANS DO TO BE SAVED?

For God there is nothing impossible, there is a possibility that the Lord will forgive this great nation if they repent. There have been cases before, such as the case of Nineveh.

And the men of Nineveh believed God, and proclaimed a fast, and put on sackcloth from the greatest to the least of them. (And the repentant King also ordered): cover yourselves with sackcloth men and animals, and cry out to God loudly; and turn each one from his evil way, from the prey that is in his hands. 9 Who knows if God will turn and repent, and turn away from the heat of his anger, and we will not perish? 10 And God saw what they did, that they turned from their evil way; and he repented of the evil that he had said he would do to them, and he did not do it. (Jonah 3)

Repent, repent, **many cities on the past has been saved for repentance,** maybe God, change the fate of this country if He sees their repentance.

Humbling themselves before God, confessing their sins with prayer, and turning from sin, are means of escaping wrath and obtaining mercy. It happens with people of Nineveh, the people followed the example of the king. It became a national act, and it was necessary it should be so, when it was to prevent a national ruin.

The Ninevites hoped that God would turn from his fierce anger; and that thus their ruin would be prevented. They could not be so confident of finding mercy upon their repentance, as we may be, who have the death and merits of Christ, to which we may trust for pardon upon repentance. They dared not presume, but they did not despair. Hope of mercy is the great encouragement to repentance and reformation. Let us repent sincerely, and God will look upon us with compassion. God sees who turn from their evil ways, and who do not. Thus he spared Nineveh. We read of no sacrifices offered to God to make atonement for sin; but a broken and a contrite heart, such as the Ninevites then had, he will not despise.

Undoubtedly, not all Americans are contaminated, despite living under this system; there must be many who maintain their faith and are faithful to God; I hope it was...! And others who, although they are sinners, want to change and repent; if so, they will be touched by the Holy Spirit, by these and many other warnings and will worry about their fate.

Finally, another thing I can say in my humble sinful condition is simply what Jesus recommends and what God says through the Bible:

Be faithful, resist until the end! - Be alert, do not be fooled! - Seek advice from the prudent! - Don't be foolish! Don't be naive! Examine and analyze which of all the churches that claim to be of Jesus have given better results! Which one stays true to its principles! And finally if they can do what Revelation 18 says:

"I heard another voice from heaven saying":

"Come out of that city, you who are my people, so that you do not participate in their sins, nor reach their calamities"
(Revelation 18)

Of course, although not all the righteous can leave, God will provide a way to save them.

"A thousand will fall to your left, and ten thousand to your right; but it will not reach you. Just open your eyes and you will see the wages of the wicked, because you made the Lord your refuge, you took the Most High for defense ...
(Psalm 91)

THE GREAT TRIBULATION

In fact, in all this time, beginning with the destruction of Babylon, the world will know the punishment. The sacred books describe this inevitable catastrophe with all kinds of details; but without all the righteous suffering their extreme consequences. **Isaiah in chapter 24** says:

"The land will be plundered and totally devastated... Because the Lord will ravage it and its inhabitants will be swept away. Because of so many sins his curse weighs on them ... There will be no one who transits through it ... Everything will be deserted and no commotion will be heard anywhere. The earth will wobble like a drunk ... The men who are in it will be like the sporadic clusters that remain in the vineyard once the harvest is finished or as one of those olives that are in the olive trees after the harvest".

Ezekiel 32, 15 It says:

"Uninhabited and desolate I will leave the earth in all its roundness, because I will scourge all its inhabitants."

Later in **Ezekiel 32,** himself he explains what is likely to happen in Israel:

"Here is what will happen on the day of the arrival of Gog (the Antichrist) on the earth, The Lord says: My indignation will rise, so that in those days there will be a great stir and commotion over all the land of Israel, and the fish of the sea and the birds of the sky and the beasts of the forest will stir before Me and how much reptile moves on the earth. The mountains will sink, the buildings will collapse and every wall will collapse. Brothers will fight brothers and I will attack them with pestilence, blood and fire and with desolate storms falling on my village huge stony, fire and brimstone. And I will be glorified, sanctified and recognized in the eyes of the nations. And they will know that I am the Lord and against Me there is no one who can"

Daniel, in Cap. 8, 10-12, speaks what will happen to the Church of Christ (the Catholic Church): *"And the Beast was emboldened, threatening the sky, from where he brought down not a few stars and trampled on them, pretending* *to attack even the omnipotent Prince, trying to abolish the Holy Sacrifice, and striving to tear down his holy place ... And because of the sins of men were given power to attack the holy Sacrifice, violating and trampling the truth on earth."*

Money and immorality will prevail more than justice, reaching its peak in the time of Antichrist, for whom there will be no more law than brute force and damn material interest. And the bewildered humanity and victim of its natural appetites will rush into the most frightful catastrophe the centuries have seen. This prophecy of Daniel is complemented by the Apocalypse of John 13, 17 which says:

"... And they worshiped the beast, saying: Who like the beast, and who can fight it? ... And, it was given authority to act forty-two months. And he opened his mouth in blasphemy against God, to blaspheme his name, his tabernacle (Tabernacle and Eucharist) and those who dwell in heaven, (the saints).

And he was allowed to make war against the saints (Church on earth) and defeat them. He was also given authority over every tribe, people, language and nation."

The prophet **Hosea in Chapter 4, verse 1-3** says:

"Listen to the Word of God, because I am going to make a judgment on the inhabitants of the earth. I don't see the truth anywhere. If there is no truth, there is no mercy and there is no fear of God on earth. Instead the curse, fraud, lies, homicide, robbery and adultery have flooded the world. Because of these crimes, the earth will suffer and everything that inhabits it will become ill."

The Prophet **Zechariah 13, 8-9** says:

"On the day of great punishment and universal purification, two-thirds of humanity will perish ... Here is what will happen on earth: two parts of them will be dispersed and ruined. Only one third will be saved. But even this will have to go through the crucible of suffering to purify itself as silver or gold. And the people that remain will call on my name and I will listen and say: you are my people, while he will say to me: You are my God."

This third part of humanity will be the one that is part of the glorious people of God, people purified like gold and silver.

The prophet **Zephaniah 1, 2, 14, 18** also says:

"The great day of the Lord is very close, it is near and it is fast. Oh, the bitter and terrible voice of God! Even the strongest and bravest will tremble with horror and terror because it will be a day of anger, tribulation and anguish; day of great calamity and misery, of fog and torment; day in which I will afflict men, who will walk like blind people, because they will sin against God and shed their blood like water. And their bodies will be thrown away as garbage. In great strides the end and consummation of all things will come, because I am going to throw men from the face of the earth that will be covered with the corpses of the wicked."

The prophet **Amos 5, 18-20** says:

"Terrible day of the Lord, this day of darkness and not of light. It will be like the one who runs away from a lion with a bear; or like the one who, leaning on a wall so as not to fall, his hand is bitten by an asp"

But, as we have said before, this is not the end of the world, but the end of a dark and iniquitous era, where all those who have not been faithful to God or wanted to repent, or comply with the Lord's commandments will die, nor have they listened to the prophecies of their saints and have also rejected the warnings of their Mother the Virgin, who with so much request and love seeks the salvation of her children.

THE DESOLATING ABOMINATION

The apostasy that has emerged in Latin America and other countries with the theology of liberation, has a direct correlation with other forms of apostasy that exist in Europe, such as the horizontalism of many prelates and priests and of freemasonry that has also infiltrated the Church. This path prepared in advance will be the one that facilitates the worst of his aberrations to Antichrist and culminates this apostasy with the desolate abomination, which itself also refers to himself (Antichrist).

"Let no one deceive you that the day of the Lord is near, but first the apostasy must come, and the man of iniquity, the son of perdition, must manifest itself; the rebel who has to rise against everything that bears the name of God, or deserves respect; he will go and sit in the temple of God proclaiming himself God." (2 Thess. 2, 3)

Halfway through the reign of this charismatic leader, (3 and a half years) he will be acclaimed for the progress he has made under his mandate. He has done an excellent job, has brought peace and prosperity to the entire world. By this time, someone will try to kill him (will it be the Intelligence service of the United States?) By shooting him in the head; but as the prophecy says, he will not die, because the devil will give him life and become incarnate in him.

"One of the monster's heads seemed to have a deadly wound; but the wound was healed, and the whole world was filled with amazement and followed the monster" (Revelation 13.3)

And it is there, when everyone in the world, admired by this fact, will go after him, lose his mind for him, and make him his idol. Possibly, the Church, raise his voice for these idolatrous events and will protest the abuses and iniquities that he will begin to commit. Then it will be when the Antichrist manifests the greatest hatred of the one who already has the Church and when he is acclaimed, applauded, idolized and revered by the world, the fumes will rise and he will go to the temple of God, and sitting on it will proclaim God, but not before having martyred the Pope and the faithful followers of Christ; among which there will be some bishops, priests, religious and laity. But many other infiltrated or liberalist and Masonic prelates will be very happy with these events.

"At his command troops will be presented and will desecrate the sanctuary and the fortress and will cease the Perpetual Sacrifice and raise the desolate abomination." (Daniel 11.31)

In which temple will this apostasy be performed? Almost everyone who writes on this subject; because they are Protestants, they speak of a third Jewish temple in Jerusalem, which has not yet been built. But, the temple into which the Antichrist will enter is one of the Christian world, then, is it not the religion left by Christ that belongs to God? The Jewish religion is for the moment apart from God, for not accepting the Messiah and for the deicide they committed; therefore, it is outside the prophetic events concerning the temple. If so, what will be the Christian temple that will be desecrated? Although badly despite the detractors of the Catholic religion; it will be the Basilica of San Pedro, in Rome, the main temple of the Christian and Catholic world; the entire Vatican or fortress of which the prophecy speaks is invaded. As soon as the Antichrist commits this abomination, he will cease every ceremony of the Holy Mass, the only true rite of the Perpetual Sacrifice.

To understand this of Perpetual Sacrifice, it is necessary that we go back to the times where Moses, by the command of God, orders them to sacrifice a lamb or a beef as an atonement for the sins of man (a rite that of course was already done since the time of Adam). This meant that in order for man to be able to reconcile with God a bloody sacrifice was necessary. But that would have been millions of lambs and cattle; they were not enough to bring man back to God. This sacrifice was rather a symbolism of the real and definitive Sacrifice that God would offer as a ransom in the person of his own son Jesus Christ, who comes into the world to offer himself as a victim for the salvation and forgiveness of humanity's sins. When Jesus is crucified and dead, the prophecy of the sacrificed Lamb of God is fulfilled. God himself made man, offers himself as a victim to rescue humanity and take it along the path of good until it finally returns after a time to end once and for all with evil.

Before going back to heaven, he recommended that the Holy Eucharist or Holy Mass be perpetuated, which is nothing more than the bloodless Sacrifice of Jesus, which he had already established before his passion at the Last Supper. So, in it, taking bread tells them:

"Take and eat, this is my body, and drinking wine says to them: Take and drink this is my blood; Do this in remembrance of me" (Matthew 26.26-27)

From there, it has been celebrated for two thousand years, this wonder port that Jesus left, as **"Perpetual Sacrifice".** Jesus changed the cruel sacrifices of animals, which the Jews made, for the species of wine and bread that are transformed into his body and blood; He is the Perfect Victim who rescued us.

Who believes in Him and in his sacrifice, even if he dies he will live and be saved. But until he returns, he left this sacrifice of bread as his body and wine as his blood, for the spiritual nourishment of his Church.

Knowing the demon that has little time left, the Antichrist will do everything he can to destroy the Church of Jesus, (Catholic Church) destroy the people of God (Israel), and destroy humanity in general by raising wars, persecutions against Jews and Christians and against anyone who opposes him and does not worship his image.

"He was also allowed to make war against those who belong to the people of God, until he defeated them; and he was given authority over every race, people, language and nation. That monster will be worshiped by all the inhabitants of the earth whose names are not written, since the creation of the world, in the Lamb's book of life that was sacrificed.

If anyone has ears, hear: those who must be taken prisoner will be taken prisoner; and those who must die by the edge of the sword will be killed by the edge of the sword. Therefore, those who belong to the people of God need strength and faith. " (Revelation 13.7)

In this same chapter John tells us about the second beast that we said before, we would explain better:

"Then I saw another beast that rose from the earth; and he had two horns similar to those of a lamb, but he spoke like a dragon.

And he exercises all the authority of the first beast in her presence, and causes the earth and its inhabitants to worship the first beast, whose mortal wound was healed" *(Rev 13,11-12)*

Here, you have to pause to analyze this character in more detail. The prophet says, that he had horns like lamb. The lamb itself represents Christ, the Church. Which indicates that possibly this character of the second beast is a religious (cardinal or bishop). Notice well that he says: "He had horns similar to those of a lamb," he does not say horns of a lamb, which indicates that he is someone who is not a true Christian. He must be a cleric of the many infiltrators who are identified as liberals or members of

Freemasonry. And he also tells us: "but he spoke like a dragon." This tells us that he will have the appearance of a religious, perhaps he will wear clerical robes; but he speaks like the devil, blaspheming God and defending the Antichrist, of course in a superlative degree; because this is already happening with the phenomenon that we explained before about the theology of liberation.

I recently heard a pretty young priest say at Sunday Mass that he did not confess because he was bored, and that people should not go to confession because to be told they did not go to Mass on Sunday, what a great thing! What a sin! He later said that Jesus had come for the poor and that the poor should unite and fight for their rights and if they have to run blood to run, because Christ shed his blood for the poor. That true Christianity is to watch over and fight for the social and economic interests of the most relegated, the rest (prayers, masses, devotions) is garbage.

If you are someone educated in Catholic doctrine, you will realize the very serious and terrible heresies and apostasies that this poor man says; but if not, you will believe that the bullshit that this priest says is phenomenal, he is very good and he is a hero, a leader.

However, it attempts against the sacraments of the Church, (confession and penance) and against the commandments of God, (sanctify the holidays and not kill). This example priest is "in small" what will be the second beast. (Dressed in priestly robes but speaks like the devil).

How will this beast come to ecclesial power? It is no secret to anyone that the freemasons and liberalists are infiltrating the highest hierarchy of the Church and have long been struggling to reach the papacy, even everything seems to indicate that they have committed several murders with the previous popes, John XIII, Paulo VI, of which it was so well planned that nobody noticed; but of John Paul I, there is much evidence of his murder. First, because he was a relatively young, healthy Pope, he did not take medicine, he had regular checkups, he died just the day before the audit they were going to do to the Ambrosian Bank, in totally mysterious circumstances and they did not let them do the autopsy.

Then in the subsequent two years of his death, many other prelates who were implicated for better or worse in the Ambrosian case, died mysteriously, (they cleaned up all kinds of witnesses).

The different investigators who have followed this case, say that those responsible for this murder were the freemasons of the P2 lodge. (It is possible to clarify that the Ambrosian Bank was created by Pope Pius XII to cover the expenses of social good that the Church was doing throughout the world; eventually the enemies of the Church entered it, and turned it into a real cave of thieves, where money was washed badly). Let's see what Jesús López Sáenz, one of the investigators of the Albino Luciani case says:

"John Paul I did not die naturally. This message, completed in turn by subsequent data, has been received not by chance, on December 29, 1984, the feast of Saint Thomas Becket, that "nosy priest" with whom John Paul I is compared. In a certain sense, in this whole affair "the Archangel Michael fights with the devil" disputing the body of John Paul I who died precisely on September 29, feast of St. Michael. In no way can we bury his testimony; On the contrary, we have to proclaim joyfully before the world that there are still envoys capable of launching the frontal challenge to the powers of evil: Who as God? Able to act in the name of God until the last breath".

Subsequently, Pope John Paul II has been subjected to several attacks and currently; How much they would have killed him! if God were not involved, the Blessed Virgin and her Angels to remember the life of this penultimate Pontiff. Pedro Miguel Lamet in his presentation to the research article by Jesús López, entitled: "La Incógnita, Juan Pablo I". (New Life, No. 1,497 5-10-85) says:

"… On the occasion of the aforementioned ephemeris (7 years of death), we publish in this issue a report by Jesús López, whose conclusions, supported by data, compiled by him and others, are chilling. Before these data there are two attitudes; that of the ostrich, claiming that the Church should not be analyzed with secular criteria and that we must flee all research because it is a Pope. And that of the light, which does not fear the search for truth, so that it may shine in all its splendor.

Those who are scandalized at the possible murder of a Pope, ignore the history of the Church and even want to hide the reality of things that are occurring. Pope John Paul II who had been subjected of several attacks, one of which reached his physical integrity, lately as it is known, it has been publicly threatened by the Italian Red Brigades.

Whether the evidence adduced by Jesús López in his report, the figure of the brief Pope Luciani, grows over time, is inconclusive. It seems obvious that he wanted to undertake serious reforms and an unclear drama fluttered behind his smile. Isn't it time for an official investigation to be taken to clear all the unknowns? It would be the best tribute to that "evangelical fragility" that - I remember - when looking out at the balcony of the basilica, made us cry to not a few believers that we were that day in St. Peter's Square.

Well, now you have an idea of the physical and spiritual struggle that exists for the power of the Church and that many who do not know misunderstand things. It is a true struggle between the forces of Good and the forces of evil. But the interesting and relevant thing is that although apparently the Church loses and its faithful members are killed; She has never been defeated so far, nor has evil taken full possession of her.

As you have seen, on several occasions they have not hesitated to assassinate the Pope himself. So it will be at the end of time, one of these infiltrators, liberal or Mason put there by Satan, will be the one who fulfills the role of the second beast. After the Antichrist assassinates the last Pope, he will put him as a replacement for this son of Satan and will be his right hand in his government of violence and terror.

ATTACK AND INVASION TO THE STATE OF ISRAEL.

"Esau conceived a deep hatred against his brother Jacob because of the blessing his father had given him, and it was said in his heart: the days of mourning for my father are near, then I will kill Jacob my brother" (Genesis 27, 41)

After reading this biblical quotation we find ourselves in a better position to understand this ancestral hatred that these two relative peoples have so close; For through her we know that the Arabs descend from Jacob's brother, Esau, who married a daughter of the descendants of Ishmael, his father's brother Isaac. The Bible when referring to the Arabs always speaks and mentions the house of Esau, since it was from those times that Esau hated his brother Jacob for having taken his birthright.

"When my people Israel live in peace, you will set in motion (Gog, one of the names of the Antichrist)***, from your land in the farthest north, accompanied by strong and numerous***

armies, and cavalry troops, and you will attack me Israel people ..." Ezequiel 38, 14

The Antichrist with his allies, among which are the European Union, (Antichrist's own kingdom) the Arab countries and Russia; they will invade Israel, for three powerful reasons: **-The Jerusalem dispute**. **-The riches that exist in Israel**, who have made the deserts flourish. And, **-the immense hatred** that in these times will be increased against them, not only by the Arabs, declared enemies of the people of God, but also throughout the Confederate kingdom of the Antichrist, plus Russia and its previous satellites, who will feel an aversion so great against Israel that its goal will be to throw all the Jews into the sea, the Hebrew race disappear just as Hitler wanted to do. What the Arabs did in the continuous wars they have had with Israel, they will do on a larger scale and with more hatred and cruelty. All the writings of the prophet Obadiah are concerning this chapter of the future Jewish and Arab situation.

Do not enjoy the day of the perdition of Judah, do not utter arrogances with your mouth on the day of his tribulation, do not enter through the doors of my people on the day of his ruin, nor are you contemplating his misfortune on the day of his disaster. Do not store your hands on their wealth on the day of their ruin. Do not put yourself at the crossroads to exterminate the fugitives, do not give up escapes on the day of their tribulation. (Obadiah 10)

Then, foreigners will be the ones who will invade and throw out the house of Israel (Armies of the European Union, Russia, Egypt, and all Arab countries, commanded by the Antichrist). The Arabs will be glad of the Jewish misfortune. These days will be of great calamity, great mortality, great pain, great despair for the Israelite people; the land they have worked hard; their country, which was his only hope of peace, is destroyed and about to pass into the hands of their worst enemies; many will fall prisoners and keep them in the desert, in concentration camps; the conditions in which they find themselves will be so subhuman that it will appear that Israel has lost all hope of recovery; all that will remain of Israel will be like a valley of dry bones as Ezekiel says.

"Son of man, those bones are the entire house of Israel. They are saying our bones have dried up, our hope has failed, we are lost.

This is how the Lord Yahweh speaks: come, O spirit! Come from the four winds and blow these dead bones and they will live" (Ezekiel 37)

That time of calamity will also be for Jews who are still in different parts of the world; from all the countries where they are, they will be expelled and killed, on the orders of the Antichrist.

But, when it seems that it is the end of Israel, the banner or sign of the Messiah will appear in heaven. Only at that moment, the surviving Jews will recognize in Jesus the Messiah whom they crucified and rejected.

"Then the banner of the son of man will appear in heaven and all the tribes of the earth will mourn, and they will see the son of man come upon the clouds of heaven with power and great majesty" (Matthew 24,29).

This sign (A great Cross) that will be seen in the sky and visible throughout the roundness of the planet will indicate that Christ is about to arrive. And all the peoples of the earth, that is, the people who are still alive, will mourn. Some because they will recognize that Jesus is the Messiah, that Jesus is the Son of God and they did not want to believe in Him, nor in His Church. And others will mourn because they know that they have very little time left to continue serving Satan, because they see their political interests, and material wealth threatened, because the corrupt system in which they have lived ends.

"Then they will look at the one they pierced, and then they will grieve and cry for him as for the death of the only child or the eldest son. There will be such a great duel in Jerusalem..." (Zechariah 12,10)

Immediately afterwards Jesus will be manifested on Jerusalem who will come as the prophet John said, in the Celestial Jerusalem, a resplendent, huge and wonderful city.

"... And he showed me the great holy city of Jerusalem, which came down from heaven, from the presence of God. The city shone with the radiance of God; its brightness was like that of a precious stone, like a jasper stone, transparent like glass. (Revelation 21, 10)

The Antichrist personification of the devil, knows very well who has arrived and that his time is over; but still, he will send his emissaries all over the world so that all countries meet in the biblical place called Armageddon to make war on God and his Christ.

And so it will be, all the countries of the world, some of which had not yet been involved in these last wars, will send their armies, air forces and maritime forces to fight against the intruder who has arrived on earth and is in Israel. Even the countries of the East, such as China, will come to the call of the Antichrist.

THE BATTLE OF ARMAGEDÓN

As we are seeing at the end of time, when the world has entered into complete chaos and destruction, caused by the Antichrist, after it has destroyed Great Babylon, it has invaded the Vatican, sitting on the throne of Peter, declaring himself god, has commanded the cessation of Perpetual Sacrifice or Holy Mass and has invaded Israel; there will still be one last battle, better known as "Armageddon"; which will be the battle in which the Confederate kingdom of the Antichrist and most countries of the world allied with him will be found, against the Heavenly Hosts of Christ.

The enemy of God, personified in a man, seeing the banner or sign of Jesus in heaven and the presence of the Heavenly Jerusalem, where Christ is located, will immediately send his emissaries throughout the world; so that all countries send their armed forces to make war on the intruder who has invaded the Earth.

"And I saw that from the mouth of the dragon, and from the mouth of the beast, and from the mouth of the false prophet came three unclean spirits, like frogs that are the spirits of demons, who make signs, which are directed towards kings of the earth to bring them together to the battle of the great day of God All Mighty ... and put them together on the site that in Hebrew is called Armageddon. (Ap. 16,13)

"The sixth (angel) poured out his cup on the great river Euphrates, and its waters dried up, so that the way was ready for the kings of the rising sun" (Rev. 16, 12)

The rising sun was the designation from time immemorial for the races and eastern nations. Could it be that in the area of The

Euphrates River the innumerable army of the Chinese will camp to face Christ? ***"The number of the cavalry armies was two myriads of myriads. " (Rev. 9, 14)*** - He is describing the enormous amount of the Chinese army. Together with all nations of the earth surrounding Mount Zion. But something mysterious will happen that it will be the same enemies of God that fit their own grave and destruction.

"Release the four angels that are bound over the great river Euphrates, the four angels were released ... so that they would kill a third part of men ... The number of the armies of the cavalry was two myriad of myriads." (Rev. 9, 14)

Then those will be the days of which Jesus said:

"Because then there will be a great tribulation which did not exist from the beginning of the world until now, nor will there be and if it were not shortened those days' no one would be saved; but for love of the elect those days will be shortened. (Matthew 24, 21)

According to Zechariah, horrific fights will center around Jerusalem.

Isaiah also says that it will be in the vicinity of the Dead Sea and ancient Edón.

And, the apostle John says that so many people will be dead that blood will rise to the brakes of horses for distances of up to 200 miles.

This conflict will not be limited only to the Middle East, but all the earth will be struck by waves of atomic bombing. John says that all the important cities of the world will be destroyed; The consequences of these bombings will be so horrifying that many men will blaspheme and curse God for the torments they will suffer. The bombs will produce earthquakes, air and water will not support life, epidemics, pests, freezing will occur; people will die burned by both atomic radiation and the sun; The ozone layer will have been destroyed.

... the foundations of the earth are shaken.19 <u>The earth is utterly broken apart, the earth is split open, the earth is shaken violently.</u> 20The earth staggers like a drunkard and sways like a shack. ... " (Isaiah 24)

The curse devours the earth and its inhabitants are guilty, that is why the inhabitants of the earth who are victims of their own armaments will burn.

"Then immediately, after the tribulation of those days the sun will be darkened and the moon will not give its light, and the stars will fall from the sky and the powers of the sky will be moved" (Matthew 24,29)

Understand that these stars that fall from the sky are not the ones we commonly known in astronomy, but the stars to which the sacred books refer from ancient times, are beings that were once good angels and now because of their evil they are enemies of God.

He also says that the sun will darken and the moon will not give its light, hence the idea of **the three days of darkness** that will be in the whole world, perhaps caused by these infernal hosts that have arrived on earth and where it is said that they will end up with hundreds of thousands of human beings unprotected from the grace of God for not having had a life according to their will. It is a struggle not only spiritual but physical in which all the powers of hell unleashed, try to end life on earth. It is Satan himself within the Antichrist and all his legions of demons that are millions in the war declared against God, to exterminate man and the planet. And on the other hand: Christ Jesus, the Blessed Virgin, her Saints and her Angels, fighting to save humanity. It is a very unequal struggle, because God apart from protecting his children tries to save and rescue the vast majority of humanity who foolishly went after the beast.

THE FUTURE OF ESAÚ'S HOUSE

The Muslim Arabs who are the descendants of Esau and Ishmael, those who irrationally hate Israel and all of humanity, are currently ruled countries by the Mohammedan religion which has caused much harm and suffering to humanity, they are responsible for all the wars that the West had to fight to defend Christianity and western civilization. Spain have had to fight almost eight hundred years to be able to get rid of this religion that enslaves everybody, that does not listen to reasons, nor there been treaties or agreements. They don't accept anything other than their own book, the Koran and according to their holy book; their prophet orders them to killed everybody who doesn't convert to their religion... In the Koran, there are more than 150 citations where they are urged to kill all those considered for them unfaithful. Islam is the antithesis of Christianity, while the God of Christians is Love, freedom and liberty of decision; the god of the Muslims is hatred, destruction, and oppression.

They are two antagonistic forces in which there cannot be agreements or the slightest friendship, from which it clearly follows that they cannot come from the same source, they are from two very different forces. These are the ones who still today have their women enslaved and humiliated, practice pedophilia and abuse with girls, practice polygamy, are the promoters of the bloodiest terrorist groups and factions and have never stopped dreaming of conquering all the planet. They have very cleverly invaded all of Europe and practically settled in it, they live according to its laws and nobody messes with them, because if not, they kill ... Feminists don't say anything about how women are slaves for Islam ... gays and transsexuals don't either say nothing, because they will throw them from an upper floor to be crushed, animalists also do not say anything despite the fact that in their religious festival of Ramadan, they kill millions of rams...

European governments are afraid of them ... The police of the different European countries in where they live does not enter Muslim neighborhoods, it is a state within another state ... Pope Francis is the only one who has held several talks and treaties of peace and brotherhood with the main leader of Islam.

But, knowing them well how they think and how they act, they will never change one iota of their scriptures because for them it is their holy book and mandate of their prophet ... it is impossible that they could respect mutual agreements, although apparently these were carried out, because If they would have to choose between one agreements or the mandate of one of their fundamentalist imams, they without hesitation will obey their leaders. With which we deduce that as long as Islamism and communism exist there will be no peace on earth ...

That is why the Lord of Christians, also refers to them in the sacred scriptures and it is that at the end of these times when the great sign of the Son of Man appears in the firmament, those who do not repent and convert to Christianity, those who do not recognize that

Jesus is the Lord and the Messiah ... they will unfailingly be against the God of Hosts and unfortunately they will be eliminated...

"Then the banner of the Son of Man will appear in heaven and all the tribes of the earth will mourn, and they will see the Son of Man coming on the clouds of heaven with power and great majesty" (Matthew 24:29).

This is the time when all the tribes of the earth, including Muslims, recognize Christ as the Messiah to convert and be saved ... The Jews who have repented and converted, who are a few, are now saved on Mount Zion.

"But on Mount Zion there will be a portion saved and it will be holy and the house of Jacob will plunder those who plundered it ..." (Obadiah 1: 17-21)

"The remnant of the house of Judah that is saved will again take root below and bear fruit above." (Isaiah 31, 37 32)

But to Muslims who by their own nature and fanaticism did not want to take the opportunity God gives them to save themselves, he says:

"For the mortality, for the violence inflicted against your brother Jacob, shame will cover you and <u>you will be extirpated forever.</u>" - "Because the day of Yahweh is approaching for the peoples; as you did so they will do to you ... and <u>there will be no survivor of the house of Esau</u>, because Yahweh has spoken. " (Obadiah 10)

CHRIST ON EARTH

"I saw, the open sky, and here is a white horse, and the one who rode it is called faithful, true and with justice judges and makes war and wears a mantle soaked in blood, and is called the verb of God. He is followed by the heavenly armies on white horses, dressed in pure white linen ... he has his name on his mantle and on his thigh written: KING OF KINGS AND LORD OF LORDS" (Revelation 19, 11)

The Lord will be accompanied by his angels and his saints; John also tells us that the Church was granted the privilege of dressing in pure bright linen, because it means the righteous works of the saints.

"Then I saw. To the beast with the kings of the earth and their armies; They were gathered to fight the one who was riding a white horse and those of his army. But the beast was captured and also the false prophet ... then the devil, the seducer, was thrown into the lake of sulfur fire, where the beast and the false prophet were already" (Revelation 19, 20)

The two armies are front to front, the host of the Lord, with him in first file and armies of the devil commanded by the rear by Satan in the body of the Antichrist and all his followers the false prophet and most of the kings of the world.

Numberless are the armies of the devil engaged in battle with the celestial hosts; but the power of God almighty will defeat the armies of evil.

This biblical quote above gives us the vision of God's triumph over evil, with the capture of the beast, the false prophet and the final imprisonment of Satan.

THE FINAL JUDGEMENT

"Then the King will say to those on his right:

Come, blessed of my Father, take possession of the kingdom prepared for you since the creation of the world. Because I was hungry and you fed me; I was thirsty and you gave me a drink ... And the righteous will answer him: Lord, when did we see you hungry and feed you, thirsty and give you a drink? ...

and the King will tell you: in truth I tell you how many times you did that to one of my younger brothers, you did it to me.

And he will say to those on the left: Turn away from me, cursed, to the eternal fire, prepared for the devil and his angels. Because I was hungry and you didn't feed me; I was thirsty, and you didn't give me anything to drink; I was a pilgrim and you didn't lodge me; I was naked and you didn't dress me; sick and in jail and you didn't visit me.

Then they will respond by saying: Lord, when did we see you hungry, or thirsty, or pilgrim, or sick, or in prison and did not help you?

He will answer them by saying: in truth I tell you that when you stopped doing that with one of my little ones, with me you did it.

And they will go to the eternal torment, and the righteous to eternal life" (Matthew 25, 34)

As we see from these sentences of Jesus, it is the charity manifested in concrete works that will save Christians on the day of the final judgment. Because:

"Let us not love in word and mouth (as the sects who say they evangelize and think that they are already saved only by believing) **but with facts and truth" (1Jn 3,18).** Well, it is, based on love, how we will be judged.

It is worth mentioning here that after the punishment and purification of humanity; The mercy of the Lord is also clearly predicted by the prophet when he says:

"Who is similar to You, Lord? Only You are able to liquidate iniquity and cancel the sins of the righteous of your inheritance! You will not get carried away with your fury, because you prefer mercy! You will have mercy on us, you will free us from our iniquities that you will enclose in the abyss of the sea. You will shine the truth about Jacob manifesting the promised mercy to Abraham and to our parents from time immemorial." (Micah 7, 18-20)

Christian, rejoice, and bless your Lord who comes with great love and glory to rescue us from evil and to love and care for us like the apple of His eye.

CHAPTER VI

ERRORS OF THE END OF TIMES
AND
OTHER EXTRA-BIBLE PROPHECIES

ERRORS ABOUT THE END OF TIMES

There are two ideological currents or tendencies of thought on this subject. On one hand, there are those who proclaim in a loud voice that the end of the world is approaching with all its apocalyptic and catastrophic consequences for humanity, among which the majority of modern sects such as Jehovah's Witnesses, Mormons, and Adventists are the main exponents. And on the other hand, those who deny and affirm that all this is a lie, that they are nothing more than pessimistic predictions and bad agorers, that those supposed prophecies will never come true, they have been announcing it for more than two thousand years and nothing has ever happened.

Both trends use in most cases biblical quotes, separated from the general context to reinforce their thoughts, both defend their positions to fanaticism, taking everything to the letter or denying everything and even changing the same meaning of the words established by the languages current.

Both trends are harmful to God's work and plans. Being apparently contrary, they come from the same source of evil; to cause division, confusion and fear in some and total unconcern and indifference in others.

But the most worrying thing is that people close to the Church as theologians, priests, religious and bishops are the first to have taken the leadership of indifference and disbelief.

For 2,000 years, from the same apostles, saints and popes have lived with the hope that the day of the Second Coming of Christ will happen in their time and now that the time is closer than ever, those who should be full of enthusiasm and preparing to the flock of the Lord to receive it; They are the first to deny God's own promise.

It seems that Satan's strategy, to send many liars first (sects and charlatans) to alarm the population by giving exact dates of the apocalyptic event, openly contradicting the teachings of Jesus; about the day and time of his Second Coming; in which he said that not even he himself knew it, but only the Father, has given the results that he (enemy) expected.

One could say that 90% of Christian believers are now indifferent to the Second Coming of the Lord. The rest is made up of lying, apparently religious apocalyptic; but instruments of the devil and only 2% are those who, without denying or affirming, wait calmly and faithfully for the Coming of the Lord with the hope of positive and good changes that will result from it.

It is important to note that many of the sects that now swarm and divide Christians, proclaim and teach certain truths, with which they attract people, but immediately drag hate and fanaticism into the division. Many things that they say are no longer good and from that we can deduct that they are not of God. For example: They teach that when Jesus comes everything will be happiness, and that the earth will not be destroyed but restored, both are true; but in giving dates of the Coming of Jesus, in speaking against the Church of Jesus and his representative the Pope, in discrediting the Mother of our Lord, we see that they are not of God. But an instrument of the devil, people disguised as lambs with an apparent mercy; but that in the end they bring out their lowest passions, with what we see that they are children of Satan.

THE OPINION OF MANY CATHOLIC CLERGY ABOUT THE SECOND COMING OF CHRIST.

The idea and attitude that the majority of the Catholic clergy currently has about the Second Coming of Christ is very varied, wrong in some respects, carefree and even annoying.

It is varied because some believe that at the end of time, or end of the world; The whole earth will be destroyed and nothing will be left. That scares them and they prefer to think that all these predictions are not true and doubt the Word of the Lord and reason by saying: How the stars are going to fall, science says that our solar system will last several million years yet...

Others think that the kingdom of God of which Jesus speaks, is already here, who receives Christ and lives according to his doctrine is already living in the kingdom of God. And, that this kingdom of God, with the passing of the years that can be 100, 1,000, 1,000,000, who knows?

This kingdom will improve and until all have changed the kingdom of God will have reached its goal.

Others think that Jesus may never come again. He already came they say ... the earth will continue to exist forever ... The judgment to which the Bible refers, is a personal judgment that is made at the time of the death of each individual. Jesus already came once and does not have to come again. The second coming refers to when each individual receives it in their conversion...

Do you realize the damage that the liberal ideas of apostasy have produced? Years ago everyone believed in blind faith what the Bible said, without questioning it, because it is the Word of God.

As you will see, all these ideas, although they may have some truth, are in themselves wrong and lead to indifference. Well, if the priests themselves do not agree ... And, although everyone has their own theory. Yes, everyone agrees that: No need to worry!   But:

How can I not worry if I know that my Lord returns? How can I not worry if I have to make preparations to receive it as best I can? How can I not worry, if I have to tell the rest of my brothers to get ready too? And, don't you think it's better to be ready and prepared than not to be? Do not you think it is better to start work and make merits in the building of the kingdom to wait until the last when there is no time?

"Blessed are those servants to whom their Lord, when he comes, is watching; Truly, I say to you, he will gird himself and make them sit at the table, and he will come to serve them" (Lk. 12:37)

For all these people, the notices of the Virgin Mary, the prophecies already fulfilled at the end of time, what Jesus himself said, have no validity and have set up a whole system of teachings to discredit the Holy Scriptures. Giving themselves a halo of legality and scholarship, because all these are "doctors in Bible and Theology." How intelligent and crafty is Satan! -But how stupid these doctors!

The few Catholics of the clergy and lay faithful who believe in the imminent coming of the Lord must keep their distance from the rest; They are discriminated against and seen as retrograde or weirdoes. What are you going to be thinking about those things...! That is what the sects do, the ignorant ... They tell you and laugh at the concern you feel for preparing the coming of the Lord.

It is truly a shame that this happens in the same members of the Church; but it is another sign of the "Signs of the Times". That is why the Scriptures say: Only a few will be saved, because most will suffer the consequences of their disbelief, of their lust, of their vanities, of their pride, of their estrangement from God.

ANSWER TO DOCTORS OF THEOLOGY AND OTHER INTELLECTUAL EMINENCES.

Recently, a book entitled "Bible and End of the World" by Eduardo Arens, doctor of Biblical Theology, principal professor of Sacred Scripture at the Higher Institute of Theological Studies in Lima, Peru, fell into my hands. Author of many religious books, related to the theme of Revelation, a very intelligent man and prepared for his studies in the US, Switzerland and Israel; In addition to many other virtues.

As soon as I started reading that book, I realized that Dr. Arens had a concern and a message to give, very similar to the one I just described in the previous topic: "Don't worry, nothing will happen." "The final judgment will never happen, as they paint it in the Bible." "The end of the world will never come; scientists assure us that our planet will last many millions of years." "The judgment of which the gospels speak to us is a personal judgment of each Christian with God at the time of death."

Well, of all your statements, I support that which says that the Earth will not be totally destroyed; because the Bible says it very clearly. But there is much to disagree, because like all those involved in the issue, whether credulous or unbelieving, use the biblical quotes literally or metaphorically according to their interests and, moreover, fall into complete contradiction with the very teachings of Jesus. as we will see next.

Without wishing to argue with him (Dr. Arens) or with any other that has different points of view, (of which I believe no one will take them out, unless they break their pride and become like children, perhaps God would grant them the truth), I think it is important to compare and analyze these different points of view; so that those who have not yet been fanaticized, discern and have the freeway to know the truth.

For starters, most exponents who do not believe that the time of the "Second Coming of Christ" is near, are contrary to the real meaning of the word "Prophecy." This is more understandable when we realize that all these intellectuals think so because of the influence they have received from the so-called theology of liberation; apostasy, which as you know is Marxism disguised as

Christianity.

This political movement is very interested in discrediting, denying and changing fundamental truths of the Christian tradition; and they do not hesitate to affirm that certain concepts, for hundreds of years taken as truth, are no longer. Therefore, for them, prophecies such as predictions of the future do not exist, and only limit themselves to saying that the so-called prophets, were only people who were dedicated to denouncing the injustices of their times or were the voice of the Poor and dispossessed.

According to Dr. Arens, the prophecies that speak of the destruction and end of the peoples and civilizations that are often found in the Bible, are nothing more than threats of these denouncers of injustices, to frighten the Jewish people and thus achieve to become or behave. But that in the real sense of the word, they knew that those threats of destruction were never going to happen. And, the times that were fulfilled, as for example: some invasions, destruction of temples and exiles of Israel; It was because they either wrote it just before the fact occurred, when everyone knew what was going to happen or after it had already happened.

Conclusion: for Dr. Arens, these prophets who were chosen by God to be their spokesmen, were liars, dishonest and exploitative of the circumstances. (Of course they don't say it with these same words, but in a very subtle and diplomatic way; but the message is the same).

The modern doctors of the Holy Scriptures also tell us that the Old Testament prophets wrote for the public of their time, not for us, much less for people who would live thousands of years in the future.

That many prophecies where they threatened the destruction of Babylon and Tire (just to name two examples), have not been fulfilled; because according to these wise men, Babylon is currently Iraq and Tire is a port city of Lebanon. (Contradicting the science of archeology, that has discovered the place and ruins of ancient Babylon).

That the promise to Jerusalem, the holy city, where it is said that uncircumcised or impure will not enter it again (Is. 40-55), nor fear terror, because if someone attacks it will crash ... and that no forged weapon will succeed against it ... (Is.54, 11-17).

Like the previous announcements this prophecy was not fulfilled either, because they say that the year 70 AD, the Romans entered and razed Jerusalem.

It says so:

"Non-compliance with ads is understood at the moment when the purpose of those ads is understood. In some cases, the prophet in question was not making an announcement so much about a fact to be taken literally, that it would inevitably happen and as he presented it, but that he described a future in metaphorical, figurative language and as a good often exaggerated Semite ... other cases the prophet was simply wrong because his announcement was risky..." (Eduardo Arens - Bible and End of the World. p. 30)

As you can clearly see, for Dr. Arens, these men chosen by God to be their prophets were simply people who ventured to speak things that made no sense, who said it figuratively and metaphorically; they exaggerated the facts and whose prophecies were never fulfilled.

In short, we have a Bible with a God who, although he is the author of history, sent men that He himself called them, chose them to be his prophets and guides of his people; But they were a mess. Nothing they said was true and only served to instill fear in the Israelites.

If you are a good son of God, if you are a good Christian, you can hardly believe in this string of hoaxes, in this defamation very well concealed, because you never say it openly, but very hypocritically and gently sow doubt and the denial of the powers of God; of the mystery that exists in his designs and of the plan of redemption that he has for humanity.

As others have also done with the explanations of the Latin American Bible itself, where they deny even that Jesus has performed miracles. Thus, in the comments corresponding to the Gospel of Mark 6, the biblical commentator of one of the many editions says:

"Jesus laid hands on the sick and healed them. But he did not do any true miracle, nothing that exceeds the abilities of a good healer ..."

And in a newer edition instead of the above they have put:

"If the miracle is due only to people's faith, where is the difference? Between the one who asks with faith to God and the one who goes to any healer? It would be enough in this case for one to suggest oneself and the person he trusts would not matter most."

Do you see how they confuse and diminish the power of Christ? Truly, we are faced with an apostasy of the worst kind, written by commentators in the Bible itself.

Therefore: Do not be surprised that the devil has entered the Church and with the same Bible!

For a greater understanding of this tangled trick of confusion very well designed to sow doubt, divide and finally not believe in God as the Being who has a plan of salvation for humanity; We will once again transcribe part of Dr. Arens' book, Bible and End of the World. Page 35 where it says:

"In certain circles today (and for some time, to tell the truth), the highlighted texts are usually quoted without respect for their literary and thematic context, to affirm that the end of the world is announced there. However, respecting their contexts we observe that it is, on the one hand, not forecasts or information about what will happen, but invitations to conversion by a known mechanism that can be described as a threat, close to emotional blackmail. On the other hand, we observe that it refers to the dreamed future of Israel, which goes hand in hand with satisfying the thirst for punishment for those who mistreated them: It is the so-called <Yahweh Day>. Those features and themes are also found in other works, including John's Apocalypse."

In this quotation, they tell us again that prophecy is not prophecy, but a threat, blackmail. And the Day of Yahweh that is supposed to be the day when God will judge the nations; It is simply a story, a product of the Israelites' thirst for revenge against their enemies who mistreated them.

Elsewhere, after quoting Zechariah and John in the Apocalypse, about the plagues and seals that the prophets saw of which an angel explained to them what they meant; Arens says that nothing has to do with events of the future, but that: "These and other visions that follow, concern the reconstruction of Jerusalem as the city of God, particularly as its center." And then place a series of numbers or biblical quotes that invite you to read, but do not put who these quotes are, if the book of Revelation or Zechariah, who says that John was copied.

As for Daniel's prophecies, they explain that they are a consequence of the situation of hostility that the Jewish people lived under King Antiochus IV Epiphanes, successor of Alexander the Great, of the Greek empire and that it has nothing to do with the Roman Empire. This vision of Daniel was taken again by John in his work of the Apocalypse by applying it to the tyrant of that time Emperor Domitian. That is, in itself; John with his Apocalypse is a poor man who copied himself from Zechariah, Isaiah, Daniel and so have the other prophets who plagiarized each other, hence, says the similarity of many prophecies.

We could continue listing more and more anti-biblical arguments of these gentlemen "doctors of the law"; but I think that with the already explained vast to realize how wrong they are for the following reasons:

1.-If the Jewish and Christian people have the Bible and the prophets, Jesus and apostles as envoys, chosen by God as sacred and by God's Word; Doubting and belittling their works constitutes a true aberration especially if they come from people who say they are Christian and much worse if they are priests. This is what the same Holy Scriptures call: "Apostasies of the end times."

"First of all you must know that no prophecy of Scripture is of private interpretation; for it was never uttered by human will, but, led by the Holy Spirit, men spoke from God" (2 Pe 1, 19-20)

2.-In his eagerness to minimize the mysteries and designs of God; These "little doctors of the law", try to give human explanations and without logical sense to what is really true but not everyone will understand.

"... Those things are closed and sealed until the time of the end. The wicked will not understand but those who have understanding will understand" (Dan. 12, 8)

3.-The prophecies written by the prophets of the Old Testament are mainly related to two important events in the history of salvation.

The first is the coming of the Messiah as a meek and humble lamb and the second is the return of the Messiah himself, as king, followed by his armies and saints.

"What God had said for the prophets, that his Messiah had to suffer, has accomplished." (1 Pe 2, 21-24)

4.-If the prophecies concerning his first coming were fulfilled just as it happened; Why are not going to meet the references to his second coming? Thus, for example, from the place where he was to be born:

"But you Bethlehem of Ephrata small among the clans of Judah, it will come from you who will rule in Israel, whose origins are old, of days of very remote antiquity." (Micah 5, 2)

Of His suffering:

"He was pierced for our iniquities and ground for our sins ..." (Isaiah 53, 1, 12)

5.-Currently the prophecies concerning the second coming, some have already been fulfilled, others are in full compliance and others are still missing. One of the prophecies already fulfilled is the one referring to the Jewish people. Before when people talked about the people or tribes of Israel, they thought they were referring to the Christian people; For the people of Israel did not exist as such. For two thousand years it was scattered throughout the world; but in 1947, with all the forecasts and conditions against it, it became a nation again.

"I will return my people to their lands, they will rebuild their ruined cities and live there" (Amos 9, 11)

6.-If some prophecies seem to have not been fulfilled, it is because their time has not come. It is not good to pass trials and say that for example the prophecy against Babylon was never fulfilled, or that Israel's immunity did not happen either; as both are missing.

7.-It must be taken into account that some names of cities, countries, objects and descriptions of events; the prophet took them according to the mentality and environment of those times and although they are perfectly related to it (the prophet) he was not given the power to say the exact name of the city that would later be destroyed, because if he says so already there would be no mystery, nor is it in God's plans to reveal it that way. Any modern city of today could have resembled the Babylon that the prophet knew and therefore took that name.

8.-The prophecies are written in a way to some extent hidden, mysterious and in which God repeatedly told the prophets to keep the message because it was not for their times, but for later times.

"I saw but not understanding I asked: My lord, what will be the end of these things? And he replied: Go Daniel that these things are closed and sealed until the time of the end. " (Dan 12, 8)

9.-Part of the hidden message, it can be understood if we realize that the prophets received the message through visions and images of which they understood little or nothing, and as I said in point 7, they tried to adapt their limited knowledge and vocabulary to the terrible as wonderful things that they saw as much of what was going to happen on earth as in heaven.

Hence many prophecies, especially of recent times; they talk about things that most readers don't understand. But as I also mentioned earlier, the progress of the science of our times and the fulfillment of some previously predicted facts; they allow us to uncover the curtain that concealed the prophetic language.

"The sun turned black, like mourning clothes; the whole moon turned red like blood ... The third part of the earth was burned, along with the third part of the trees and all green grass ..." (Ap. 6.12.8.7)

The same is the report of current science with different language when describing nuclear winter.

"Their meat will be corrupted while standing. His eyes will be consumed in his basins and his tongue will melt in his mouth" (Zechariah 14, 12)

The consequence of a war with nuclear weapons is that the bodies before they fall to the ground are already dead by the heat wave generated by these weapons; hence the meat, eyes and tongue consumed.

10.-While it is true that in many prophecies they end up saying that: "the time is near", this is no reason to doubt that one-day God's prophecies and promises will be fulfilled. Let us not forget that in the visions the prophets received except for Daniel, (who asked, when will that happen?) The Lord did not set the time.

What could be for a very important reason, that the people of God always remain alert thinking that any day and time could happen?

"Blessed the servants whom his master finds awake". (Luke 12.37).

The apostles themselves thought that Jesus would return when they were still alive; however, that was not the case, since the fullness of time had not yet come. The thoughts and desires of man are not the thoughts or plans of God.

11. -Finally, since there is a will contrary to God, there will always be people influenced by this negative force, who carried by disbelief, pride and foolishness will not let them see the truth or reality. No matter how many tests you may have, they would never believe. Unfortunately, not only atheists are in this group, but many so-called Christians, including priests, nuns and theologians who, swollen from their human sciences, influenced by consumerism and communism and Marxism, do not want to give their arm to twist and it costs them believe that soon very soon they can end their lives so comfortable and selfish they lead.

The coming of Christ is for them as a threat to their earthly interests hence the resistance they place and the blindness with which they behave. It seems that humans live very happy in the midst of their miseries, sorrows, filth and suffering.

"There is no worse blind than he who does not want to see" The popular saying goes, which would not matter much if it were not a matter of life or death, of salvation or eternal damnation; For those who have fallen into the game of Satan, work hard from their strategic positions to hide the truth. To negatively influence humanity and the members of the Church, to stop worrying and neglect the events that announce the Second Coming of Christ.

The aforementioned saying is corroborated by the quotation from Luke 10, 21; where Jesus says:

"I praise you Father, Lord of heaven and earth because you hid these things from the wise and intelligent and have revealed them to the little ones."

Marxists with their misnamed theories of materialism or scientific socialism, (which as a scientist have nothing); and liberation theologians deny the coming apocalyptic events; they speak in such a way that many will be those who fall into their sophistry. They explain in a seemingly honest and sincere way that many will believe them. If not, read what Dr. Arens says:

"A moral of the above is that every extrapolation of these texts, as of any biblical text, is an abuse of them and every literal projection into modern times is a betrayal of the message and the intention of the inspired author. It is a matter of honesty to respect the literary and historical contexts of the texts". (Bible and End of the World. P. 47).

What honesty can someone talk about who has changed the same sense of word and context? How can this man speak of treason to the prophet's message, if he himself is the one who completely changes the message and the intention? How can he speak of treason if he himself has called the prophets, blackmailers, liars, exaggerated?

John, at the beginning of the Revelation says:

"The revelation of Jesus Christ, which God gave him to manifest to his servants the things that must happen soon ... Blessed is he who reads and those who hear the words of this prophecy and keep the things in them written because time is near (Ap. 1.3).

It is illogical for a Christian to think that the message that Jesus himself gives to John, is something that he came up with to write, as a copy of other prophets, such as harangue, threat, secret message, or encouragement to the Christian community of those time; if Jesus himself later tells him:

"Write the things you have seen and what they are and what they should be after them." (Ap. 1,19)

It cannot be clearer ... ***"And those that have to be after these ..."*** indicates events that will occur in the future.

Modern theologians claim that John to write the Apocalypse was copied from Daniel and other prophets; Without realizing that making such a statement is reckless, dishonest, and nothing respectful to the apostle John, Jesus' intimate friend. He is indirectly accused of being a plagiarist, a liar, of naming the name of God and Jesus in vain; And they don't accept that it was God himself through Jesus who sent the message.

"The revelation of Jesus Christ that God gave him to manifest to his servants the things that must happen" (Rev. 1, 1).

This, as you will see, has only one explanation: The enemy of God not only attacks the Church from the outside, but has entered the same ranks; but let's not be alarmed, this was planned, and it is another sign to know that we are really close to the Second Coming of Jesus Christ.

THE ERRORS OF THE APOCALYPTIC SECTS

On the other hand, there are the apocalyptic sects who make their start since the nineteenth century, being the first to take advantage of this matter religiously and economically the Adventists, whose founder was William Miller, who said that in October 1843, would be the coming of Christ; when this failed he said it was for the spring of 1844, then he again affirmed that it was for the fall of that same year, to be precise by October 22.

Then took the reins of the sect a self-styled lady prophetess Ellen G. White, who consolidated the Adventist movement by adding the doctrine of the seventh day, hence their name as "Seventh-day Adventists."

Then the Jehovah's Witnesses continued, (who have nothing as witnesses), the Church of Latter-day Saints or Mormons, who have no saints either; and many others who have continued with the same lies. The Jehovah's Witnesses also made completely reckless and unbiblical statements; for they set exact dates when the second coming of Christ would take place.

It should be clarified that this sect has been changing many of its anti-biblical statements and practices and hiding the historical truth of its mistakes; So the new followers of this sect, when these issues are touched, think that we are slandering them. The Russellites, (as they are also called as followers of Charles Taze Russell), said that the end of the world was going to be in the year of 1874, then they changed it to 1914, then they said that in 1925 Abraham and Isaac would return and Jacob, for this they bought a mansion in San

Diego, California; so that when these biblical characters arrived they were staying there, but apparently the only one who stayed there until he died in 1942, was his second boss Mr. Rutherford. Then they said that the year 1975 was without a doubt the battle of Armageddon; and thus they have been lying and deceiving for a long time, openly contradicting the teachings of Jesus:

"As for the day and the hour nobody knows it, not even the angels of heaven, nor the Son. Only the Father knows" *(Mark 13.32).*

Currently, as we explained before, the Russelites or witnesses have stopped predicting the date of the Parousia because these lies brought them many defections. New members of this sect are no longer taught that, but their doctrinal errors undermine the same teachings of Jesus, and their lies and hatreds against the true Church multiply and enlarge. This also constitutes another sign of the last times, which was predicted by Jesus himself:

"Be careful that no one deceives you... And false Christ's and false prophets will appear who will make signs and wonders in order to deceive even the elect, if possible. Well, be prepared; I have warned you beforehand. " (Mark 13, 5-21)

Do you remember the story of the liar shepherd? It agrees exactly with these and other doctrines that have appeared lately. Be prepared, I have warned you beforehand, says Jesus. Do not be fooled please...!

Likewise, the apostle Peter tells us:

"But the day of the Lord will come as a thief in the night... Almost in all his epistles (of Peter), of these things; among which there are some difficult to understand, which the undocumented and unstable twist, as well as the other writings for their own downfall. (Note well that these who speak and preach will be condemned.) So you, O beloved, knowing it beforehand, beware, lest you be dragged by the error of the wicked, fall from your steadfastness." (2 Peter 3, 10-17)

DISCOVERING HOW GOD'S ENEMY WORKS

Seeing how the sectarians have put all their efforts into propagating exact dates of the second coming of Christ, as well as attacking the Catholic Church, along with the Virgin Mary, Mother of our Savior and our Mother, and the successor of Peter and Chief of the earthly Church set by Christ; And, seeing how on the other hand, certain Catholics put all their effort into denying and discrediting this second coming of Jesus, creating confusion and above all carelessness to these very important events that are happening and about to happen; there is no doubt that this situation is the work of Satan, who both factions are following the game and are serving, without perhaps knowing. That is why it is necessary to realize and analyze a bit the work, the intention and the way in which this evil being, enemy of God and of man works.

We must never forget that this fallen angel is one of the most intelligent beings in the universe and, all his intelligence has overturned it to destroy the work of God. In destroying man with man, the Church with the same Bible, making men interprets the Holy Scriptures in many different ways. Making them not believe in the existence of himself (demon), making the Church of Jesus divide more and more with seemingly good new doctrines, making the prophecies of his soon return discredited, In short, he has used and uses hundreds in different ways to end the Church and humanity and make it the most unhappy race that has ever existed in the universe.

Then, considering the very high degree of intelligence that this evil being possesses, we see that it has established throughout history, the body of intelligence and the largest logistics in the universe; to boycott, infiltrate, seduce, deceive, fanaticize, mesmerize, instigate, plot, conspire. And, many are the men of science, intellectuals, doctors, theologians, politicians, sociologists, philosophers, kings, military and even charlatans, preachers, priests and nuns who have fallen into their networks. And, the worst part is that these poor people who have fallen into their lies, they think they are wise, they think they are enlightened, they think they are chosen, they think they are doctors, they think they are theologians; while Satan laughs out loud watching how these fools, full of pride and vanity go in their footsteps, preaching their liberal and atheistic theories or their opposite and fanatic extremes.

Thus, for example, insufflating a great dose of arrogance, arrogance and vanity, it was enough for one Karl Marx with an Engels (who already belonged to a satanic sect) to spread his work "The Capital", from which it was derived Marxism, Leninism, Maoism, and Stalinism. All of these served the evil interests of the enemy. All these butchers in history and others killed millions and millions of human beings in their own countries. And even more he was about to get what he most yearns for, (demon) destroy the entire planet along with man (missile crisis, 1961)

How did he accomplish such an evil feat? (We are talking about Satan) - Easy, with a little political strategy. First he studied, analyzed and identified certain human problems: inequality, poverty, economic difference from one another; the injustice; (evils that he has implanted). Then he sows in the minds of these men that he has also chosen them to be his instruments, the apparent solution to the problems of humanity: to create a "new political-social order." But with this solution, he launches his fury, resentment and poison, so that humanity destroys itself: class struggle, terrorism, war, selective and massive murder, concentration camps and torture. Likewise, he has managed to infiltrate the same Church of Christ, through certain bishops, priests and nuns who believe they are modern, advanced, saviors of the world, who intend to change injustice with their only Marxist ideology, hypocritically using the much beaten phrase: "Option for the poor" How Satan laughs at these fools! that they have elaborated a whole doctrine and a philosophy for themselves to deceive themselves, and they do not realize that they are following Satan their boss.

How do we know that Marxism comes from the devil? It is very clear, **"By their fruits you will know them,"** attack with blind and irrational fury all that represents God on earth. Hence the persecution of the Church, the murder, imprisonment and torture of thousands of priests and religious faithful to Christ. The tremendous phobia and inhuman punishment inflicted on those who baptized or were baptized, the terrible hatred of the Holy Eucharist and the other Sacraments and the most pathetic fruit of Marxism, are the millions of deaths they caused; that is exactly what Satan wants, that man destroy himself; so that God cannot save his creature and there is no reason to restore the Earth.

Recently a series of sexual aberrations was discovered that many bad priests from different parts of the world had committed with children; Such was and is the scandal that many people now see the Catholic Church with very bad eyes, many have ceased to be Catholics, others no longer believe in Christian doctrine, others have gone to swell the ranks of sects and every time hatred of the holy Church of Christ becomes more evident.

Let's think, if the Catholic Church is the true Church; why are there priests so bad? The Holy Scripture tells us (Matthew 13, 3-9) that within the good wheat seed there is also tares and it was not put by God, but by the enemy; and it is the enemy who has placed and infiltrated many, many bad elements that now function as priests, bishops and cardinals, coincidentally they are doing the work of their father Satan to discredit the Holy Church of Christ.

Currently Satan is doing everything possible to distract humanity from these very important events that announce his second coming; through music, television, shows, sex, pornography, drugs, science, the arts; everything, absolutely everything is being used to discredit the Church and so that man does not realize what is happening and what is about to happen. Will you be surprised by this evil strategist, having been put on notice?

Also resort to Saint Michael the Archangel and your Guardian Angel to help you be awake and alert about everything that can take you away from God and to defend you from the attacks and insidies of the evil one.

OTHER SIGNS OF THE SECOND COMING OF CHRIST

"When you see that the cloud leaves the west, you say: it will rain and so it happens. And when the south wind blows, you say: it will be hot; and does it" (Luke 12,54)

Apart from the prophecies found in the Old and New Testaments, about the time of the end of this corrupt system; there are other signs that help us understand that time is really near; as for example:

-The apparitions and messages of the Virgin Mary.

-Certain prophecies or predictions of holy men such as: Saint Malachi, Pius X and others. -The internal crisis of the Catholic

Church. -The crisis and systematic destruction of the family. -Acceptance and total complacency of aberrant homosexuality. -The advance of science and technology especially that used for war, genetics and communication. -The terrorism spread almost everywhere. -The hatred to death of the Arab or Muslim countries against Christianity. -The political and economic state of Europe. -The unsustainable progress of evil in all its aspects. -The US military and economic power and its influence in the world. -The permanent state of conflict that Israel lives with their Muslims neighbors. -The appearance of countless sects and strange religions. -The emergence of incurable diseases such as AIDS, and others.

-the appearance of stupid ideas imposed like truth for the governments, like the gender ideologies.

-the upsurge and imposition of aberrant and stupid laws contrary to God's law, such as abortion, euthanasia, homosexuality and others.

-the control of the leftist governments worldwide.

-The careless attitude of the people about this important signs of the second coming of Christ.

They are some of the most visible signs so far to deduce that we are at the doors of the "big change". The Second coming of our Lord Jesus.

MESSAGES AND APPARITIONS OF THE BLESSED VIRGIN MARY.

God, from the beginning of the History of Salvation he used men and women to fulfill his plans and projects. Thus he used Abraham to form his people, Moses to free them and give them their laws, the prophets to correct them and warn humanity about the future, he used a Woman, the Virgin Mary to come into this world incarnating as a human being. He used his disciples to establish his Church and many holy men to continue his work. Today, it seems that God wants to use Mary again, as a precursor to the Second Coming of his Son Jesus; Hence, some supernatural cases are happening, whose prominence is attributed to the Mother of Christ.

Francisco Sanchez Ventura y Pascual, Spanish writer specializing in the themes of the apparitions of the Virgin, the parousia and other issues related to supernatural phenomena of mysticism, in his book: **"Mary Precursor of Christ in his Second Coming to Earth" says:**

"Around us there is a world apart from the natural and visible that influences our lives, monitors our behavior and providentially governs our daily occurrence. In that world invisible beings live and act. In certain circumstances some people manage to see them and hold surprising dialogues. These are the seers, souls chosen by heaven, humble, simple, ignorant, without culture or preparation on most occasions so that they are docile instruments to act unconsciously in the service of God.

Today we live in the middle of Marian activity. The Virgin, the Mother of God, is trying with her intervention to help her children to rectify the path taken by humanity. In tireless apostolate it appears through different points of our geography".

These messages of the Virgin through her instruments, generally children, have special coincidence with the manifestations that appear in the sacred books in both the Old and New Testaments, in relation to this time of the end of time.

There are some people who doubt that God wants to use the Mother of his Son, they cannot conceive the idea that God with all his power and his familiarity with the Blessed Virgin Mary entrusts her with the task of warning and reminding men that the time of the end is near; after all, Jesus Himself constituted her as the Mother of men and she feels the need to warn and try to save most of her children. Well, at least of those who consider themselves their children, for there are many who do not want to be, such as Protestants and sectarians; but these poor do not realize that God himself since he pronounced the sentence of punishment to our first parents; He gave the Virgin, (sum of human humility) the task of defeating the devil, (sum of angelic pride)

"I put perpetual enmity between you and the woman, between your seed and her seed, she will step on your head and you will stalk her heel" (Genesis 3,15).

This is a mystery and one of the worst punishments for Satan; being defeated by a woman who gave the "Fiat" to God to be the mother of her son, who with her sacrifice would restore the humanity that believes in Him.

The truth is that the Virgin has had, has and will have a leading role in the History of Salvation and is fulfilling her role as Mother, warning humanity that time is coming to an end, and that they repent and change their attitude to save yourself.

In Genesis 3.15; enmity is announced between the spirit of evil and the Woman, Mother of God; It is said that such enmity will lead to fierce struggles. And, in Revelation 12,1-18, the development of this unique struggle is mentioned. From these texts it follows:

1º That if the man managed to be knocked down by the devil because of a woman - the first Eve; for another woman - the second Eve,

the Woman par excellence - that we are promised here, God wants to avenge the man and rehabilitate him.

2º Hence the eternal enmity with which the evil spirit will look at the woman or new Eve, (Mary); from the first moment, and the constant struggle against her and her children, she will sustain with growing rage.

3º This fight started in the same paradise will intensify and find its way through the centuries, acquiring its virulence at the end of the centuries. That is why evil is represented as a simple snake at the beginning in the Genesis account and as an infernal dragon in the Apocalypse story. (Francisco S.V. and P.)

Saint Louis Maria Grignon of Monfort comments:

"God has never made or formed more than a single irreconcilable enmity, which is the enmity between Mary and the devil; between the children and followers of the Blessed Virgin and the spiritual children and followers of Lucifer".

Thus the most terrible of the enemies that God has created against the devil is Mary; for Satan, because of his pride, suffers much more when he is defeated and punished by a small and humble slave of God; and His humility hurts and humbles him more than all divine power. Hence also, that lately there has been intensified a great hatred and a great campaign of discrediting the Blessed Virgin, especially for the sects that appear to be Christian but that are not, because they act as instruments of the devil".

Let's not forget the cause for which the devil revealed himself against God, as we explain almost at the beginning of this book. Lucifer is revealed because God was going to create man by giving him power over the same angels, that is, over Lucifer himself.

He does not comply with the wishes of the Creator and separates; because he considers man an insignificant and unworthy being to have dominion over him. Before the rebellion of this spiritual being that was the right hand of the Creator, God, as we have already seen, prepares an all Pure Woman; so that He himself being God becomes man; giving Lucifer a terrible lesson of humility and at the same time an enormous punishment; because although the enemy of God, did not want to be under the dominion of man and did the impossible to prevent man from being more than him; He has not been able to achieve it. For God becoming man in the person of the Son. He beat him and humiliated him forever. Jesus, the Son, has power over everything:

"And in the name of Jesus, every knee will bend, in heaven, on earth and in hell." (Philippians 2, 10 - 2.31)

In 1917, the Virgin Mary appeared in Fatima, to warn that communism threatened to spread from Russia to the whole world and that it was necessary to pray and consecrate that nation to God so that those calamities are not unleashed, but nobody paid attention to it and the error, cruelty and death spread throughout the world until today that there are still terrorist groups of communist tendencies that believe that with their wild and animal methods they will be able to change the world. Likewise, he warned that the Church of Christ, the true one, would have to suffer a lot, for the apostasy that would enter the same bosom of the Church, something that also occurred, as we saw earlier, priests, nuns, bishops and cardinals, Marxists, with an apparently Christian doctrine, but in disguise, with which they have managed to cool the faith of parishioners throughout the world.

Father Stefano Gobbi, who wrote the book: **"To the Priests, favorite children of the Blessed Virgin"** And which are locutions he receives from the Virgin Mary, he repeatedly says:

"*The times have come for the general confusion and the greater disturbance of the spirits. The confusion has penetrated the souls and the lives of many of my children. This great apostasy is spreading more and more, even, inside the Catholic Church itself. Errors are taught and disseminated, while the fundamental truths of the faith are denied with all facility, which the authentic Magisterium of the Church has always taught and vigorously defended against any heretical deviation. The bishops maintain a strange silence and no longer react ... Victims of the great apostasy are my children who, often, unconsciously, are carried away by this wave of errors and evil. Victims of the great apostasy are many bishops, priests, religious and faithful."*

Elsewhere it says:

"Know how to read the signs that God sends you through the events that happen to you, and accept his serious warnings to change your life and return to the path that leads to Him... If you saw with my own eyes (of the Virgin) how extended There is this spiritual epidemic, which has hurt the whole Church. It immobilizes her in her apostolic action, hurts her and leads her to paralysis in her vitality, often making her evangelization effort even empty and ineffective."

-You live under my worry so painful to see you still victims of the sin that spreads; observing how everywhere, through social media, life experiences are proposed contrary to what the holy law of God prescribes. Every day you are nourished by bread poisoned with evil, and you are given a drink at the contaminated source of impurity. Evil is proposed to you as a good; sin as a value; the transgression of the law of God as a way of exercising your autonomy and your personal freedom.

In this way it is possible to lose consciousness of sin as an evil, and injustice, hatred and impiety cover the earth and make it an immense wasteland deprived of life and love. The stubborn rejection of God and of returning to Him; the loss of true faith; the iniquity that spreads and leads to the spread of evil and sin: Here are the signs of the perverse time in which you live!

See, however, with how many signs I intervene to lead you along the path of conversion, good and faith. With extraordinary signs that I make in all parts of the world, with my messages, with my frequent appearances, I indicate to everyone that:

"The great day of the Lord is approaching."

The Blessed Virgin Mary has appeared in various parts of the world and on different dates, like this: In 1858, She appeared in Lourdes, France. In 1917, at Fatima, Portugal. In 1961, Garabandal, Spain. And in all the appearances the message is almost always the same: he asks for prayer and repentance and made known what we mentioned earlier, that many cardinals, bishops and priests were on the path of perdition. Preventing Christians, we walk very carefully and doubt the new social and political doctrines that entered the Church, precisely in the sixties.

In 1976 She appeared in Bethany, Venezuela; where even now the faithful continue to affirm that they continue to see her and many miraculous cures happen.

In 1981, Virgin Mary appeared to several young Yugoslavs in Medujorge. That same year, she also appeared in Kibecho, Rwanda. In 1987 in Ukraine.

In All these apparitions the messages of the Virgin have only one purpose: **"Repentance and preparation for the Second Coming of Jesus Christ."**

We must prepare, while there is time; As the night progresses, the day is near; But humanity, it seems blind, does not want to understand, does not want to realize the signs of the times and as the Gospel says:

"As it happened in the time of Noah, so it will also happen when the Son of Man returns. In those times before the flood, and until the day Noah entered the boat, people ate and drank and married. But when they least expected it, the flood came and took them all. This will also happen when the Son of man returns ... Stay awake because you do not know what time your Lord will come. *(Matthew 24, 37-39)*

OTHER PROPHECIES

THE PROPHECY OF SAINT MALACHY.

Apart from the Old Testament prophets, Jesus and the Apostles in the New Testament, and the messages of the Blessed Virgin; there are other holy and visionary men who have somehow left written messages and visions they have had about this last age; being one of the main, **Saint Malachy**, a religious who lived in the 1100s. He is the author of **"El Lignum Vitae"**. Better known as **"The Prophecies of the Popes"** It was published by Friar Arnaldo de Wion, in the year of 1595; after four centuries from the date the Saint of Armagh wrote it. It consists of 111 currencies or legends that identify the Popes of the Church from the year 1143; but it ends with a name that he calls: "Peter the Roman" and that in total would be 112.

What gives value to these predictions, are the coincidences of the most outstanding characteristics or legends of each Pope, which allows to define and recognize it since 1143, the year in which the list begins, until the last as Paul VI who defines as: **"Flower of the Flowers"**. Title that he found very successful, for the moral suffering that this Pope suffered during his teaching, for the enormous problems he had to face, because with him the crisis of the Church (that is the apostasy) manifested, and, the flower is Symbol of martyrdom or suffering. The next Pope, John Paul I, who only lasted a few months, bore the title: **"Of the mediation of the moon"** According to scholars, this father was elected in a 1978 crescent moon and found dead 33 days later, on the next half moon. John Paul II, according to Saint Malachi's, bears the title: **"De Labore Solis"** or **"The Work of the Sun"**. That some interpret the busy work he did from sun to sun. Others believe it was because he was born in an eclipse of the sun and 84 years later he died with another eclipse of the sun. His successor who is supposed to be the last Pope, bears the title of **"De Gloria Olivae"**, **"The Glory of the Olive Tree"**. This would correspond to Benedict XVI; supposedly "The Glory of the Olive Tree" refers to a pope who will be martyred, the pope who in the revelation of the Virgin of Fatima is taken from the Vatican, and killed in a mound. but Benedict XVI has not been martyred, (yet) but has resigned and in his place Pope Francis has been appointed; having, as never before in the history of the Church, two popes, elected alive. In any case, having abdicated Benedict XVI, his name or title would have been erased and the Glory of the Olive Tree would be Francisco; who if he would be the martyr Pope, as he has announced several times, saying that he would not last long the Muslims have already threatened him with death.

However, there is another version in which Benedict XVI would continue been the Pope, because he never gave up his papacy. When the dark forces that have infiltrated the Vatican, force him to resign; He writes a document in which he says he renounces all administrative positions of the Church, but ***"The position of pope I received on April 19, 2005, I'll take it until I die, because that cannot be resigned"***. So he is still the Pope, and Francisco would then be an antipope.

Returning to the prophecy, everything said above, makes us

assume that if there are no more popes, after the latter (Benedict XVI) means that the story of the Popes on Earth comes to an end. Saint Malachi ends with "Petrus Romanus", or "Peter the Roman" and explains that:

"In the last persecution of the Holy Roman Church, he will occupy the chair Peter the Roman ", who would feed his sheep suffering many tribulations. which the City of the Seven Hills (Rome) will be destroyed and the tremendous Judge will come to judge his people".

Then, until the moment in which Pope Benedict XVI still lives that the currency "Of the Glory of the Olive tree" would correspond to him, then "Peter the Roman" will come, which in fact does not correspond to any currency or motto. Therefore, he will take over the Church in an irregular and improvised way, but legitimately; without proper protocol choice as in the current conclaves. Why? Because this Pope, when the Church is headless and outlawed, would assume the command of the Catholic Church. Here it is possible to make two very important speculations with what we saw earlier on the theme of the Antichrist and his kingdom, on the second beast that John saw. - The first and most likely speculation is that:

According to the indications given by John, the Virgin Mary, Saint Malachy, and the vision of two pontiffs; the Antichrist, to disavow the leadership of the Pope Benedict XVI has chosen an antipope, which will be that second beast with lamb horns. That in this case although is painful to tell it would be Pope Francis...

Then **"The Glory of the Olive"**, the legitimately elected Pope which is Benedict XVI, that has been obligated to resign but is still a big problem for then, even when he is apart and quiet would be killed by the Antichrist. And then is when "Peter the Roman" takes command of the Church in an almost improvised way, all in the midst of the "great tribulation" and prior to the beginning of the Kingdom of God.

I stress again that the most likely thing is that the pope with the currency: "The Glory of the Olive Tree" is killed or imprisoned or **forced to resign**. The symbolism that surrounds the olive tree is of glory to the passage and triumphant entrance of Jesus as it is related in the Scriptures. The olive branches commemorate the entry of Jesus into Jerusalem, when his followers tore branches from the trees and spread a carpet on which Jesus passed; to enter the Holy City. Likewise, this last Pope will practically be in the anteroom of Jesus' second triumphant entrance into Jerusalem. The olive tree also symbolizes wisdom, it is the tree of the promises of God and the tremendous need to be clear about the Doctrine of the Church; The olive tree has to do with privilege and responsibility on earth with the profession of faith.

We are already entering the reign of the Antichrist very soon, who, in the middle of his period, will try to completely destroy the Church, the Pope and all the bishops, clergy and laity faithful to God; thus fulfilling the prophecies predicted by Jesus about the general apostasy of those days (Lk. 18,8), by St. Paul in (2 Thess. 3,3). And, Daniel the prophet, who tells us:

"And the Beast was emboldened, threatening the sky, from where he brought down not a few stars (the apostate angels) and trampled on them, pretending to attack even the omnipotent prince, trying to abolish the Holy Sacrifice, and striving to tear down his holy place ..." (Daniel 8,10-12).

This makes us understand that in this very near age, God will allow Satan and his agent the Antichrist to display all his power against Him (Jesus), and against his Church because of the many and grave sins of men. It is at this time that we already have it around the corner that Daniel continues:

"And because of the sins of men, he was given power to attack the Holy Sacrifice, violating and trampling the truth on earth. Money and immorality will prevail more than justice, reaching its peak in the time of Antichrist, for whom there will be no more law than brute force and damn material interest. And the deviated humanity and victim of its natural appetites will rush into the most appalling catastrophe the centuries have seen." (Daniel 8, 10-12).

VISIONS OF TWO PONTIFFS

Francisco Sánchez Ventura, in his aforementioned book of: **"Mary Precursor of Christ in his Second Coming to Earth"** Say that: Don Bosco, Catholic saint and founder of the Salesian Congregation; He had a dream in which he saw a pontiff flee the Vatican followed by a long procession. The dream coincided with the visions that Pius X and León XIII subsequently had.

Pius X, who had previously prophesied the war of 1914, had a vision, during a General Chapter of the Franciscans, in the year 1909, where after being ecstatic, he exclaimed "It is horrible what I have seen! Will I be or will be my successor? I ignore it, but the fact is that I have seen the Pope flee the Vatican, walking on the bodies of his priests. Don't tell anyone while I'm alive."

Leo XIII, on an autumn afternoon of the year 1889 saw legions of satanic angels that were launched against the Church of Rome. The vision was immediately told to his secretary, Monsignor Tarozzi, and, impressed by what he had seen, made the following prayer and commanded to be prayed at the end of the holy sacrifice of the Mass:

*"**St. Michael the Archangel, defend us in battle. Be our defense against the wickedness and snares of the Devil. May God rebuke him, we humbly pray, and do thou, O Prince of the heavenly hosts, by the power of God, thrust into hell Satan, and all the evil spirits, who prowl about the world seeking the ruin of souls. Amen"***

These visions do nothing more than confirm the prophecy of Daniel, of Jesus and Paul that mention the desolate abomination at the end of time, when the Antichrist is present and functions will happen:

"At his command, troops will be presented that will desecrate the Shrine and the fortress and will cease the Perpetual Sacrifice and raise the desolate abomination." (Daniel 11, 31)

THE THIRD SECRET OF FATIMA

As we well know the first and second Secrets of Fatima, they were long ago disclosed, but the third secret had long remained unknown; practically as his name says it in secret by order of the high ecclesiastical hierarchy, because they possibly thought that it could frighten the faithful for the terrible thing that this revealed; it is known that John XXIII read it and returned it to the Holy See and did not make it public, just as it happened with Paulo VI, who kept it again. However, Pope John Paul II, long after his attack in which he almost lost his life, finally decided to disseminate it for everyone's knowledge and says:

The Third Secret of Fatima revealed. Taken from the Vatican, June 26, 2000. Official translation of Lucia's manuscript. WYD

Third part of the Secret revealed on July 13, 1917 in the Cave of Iría - Fatima.

"I write in obedience to you, my God, that you ordain it through His Most Reverend Excellency the Lord Bishop of Leiria and the Blessed Mother of yours and mine.

After the two parts that I have already exposed, we have seen on the left side of our Lady a little higher an Angel with a sword of fire in her left hand; blinking, it emitted flames that seemed to burn the world; but they extinguished the contact with the splendor that Our Lady radiated with her right hand directed towards him; the Angel pointing the earth with his right hand said in a loud voice: Penance, penance, penance! And we saw in an immense light that is God: "something similar to how people look in a mirror when they pass before him" to a Bishop dressed in White "we have had the feeling that he was the Holy Father." Also to other bishops, priests, and religious climb a steep mountain, on whose summit there was a large cross of rough timbers as if they were cork oak, with the bark; the Holy Father, before reaching it, crossed a large city half in ruins and half trembling with a hesitant step, sorry for pain and sorrow, praying for the souls of the bodies he found along the way; reaching the top of the mountain, prostrated on his knees at the foot of the great cross he was killed by a group of soldiers who fired several shots of firearms and arrows; and in the same way the bishops, priests, religious and diverse lay people, men and women of various classes and positions died one after another. Under the two arms of the Cross were two Angels each with a glass jug in his hand, in which they collected the blood of the Martyrs and gave with them the souls that approached God".

As you can see, the Third Secret, surprisingly coincides with the other visions. But the reason why he finally decided to make this secret known seems to be due to the attack that Pope John Paul II suffered on May 13, 1981; thinking that the vision referred to him.

But it is not so, this event as we said before, comes to corroborate and support the other prophecies of the end of the times, when the man of iniquity rises, the Antichrist, will surround the Holy City (the

Vatican) will take out the Pope who is ruling at that time, (according to the prophecies of St. Malachy, would be Benedict XVI), and together with his bishops, priests and lay faithful will be eliminated and that is where he will **suspend the Perpetual Sacrifice or the Holy Mass**; without the Perpetual Sacrifice, it will also abolish the priesthood, the altars and temples not only of Italy, but of all of Europe and possibly its evil influences reach the whole world. There will be many corrupt and rotten governments that imitate their example in various countries; where the Catholic Church is a stone in their shoes and a voice of alarm that does not leave their consciences calm. Then it will be installed in the sacred place, in the Temple of God, this will be in the Basilica of St. Peter, the most important and representative temple of God and the Church

He will proclaim himself god thus fulfilling the prophecy of the installation of the desolate abomination, of which Daniel, Jesus, and John speaks to us, and that will last for approximately three and a half years.

All this things will do the Antichrist, with the help of the second beast, the one with horns of a sheep.

WHO COULD BE THE SECOND BEAST?

"And I saw another beast coming up out of the earth; and he had two horns like unto a lamb, and he spoke as a dragon". Apocalypses 13, 11

There are some journalists, priests, and organizations like Tradition in Action, who claim that the third secret of Fatima was not the last of the prophecy, that there is a fourth secret, that the Roman curia will never tell, because it casually refers to them (the Freemasons in the power of the Church) And according to history, Sister Lucia writes:

"We saw a false pope who was cheered by the crowd but who led the Church to hell." In itself, the spirit of the Antichrist has been present and acting for several decades, the infiltration of communism, Freemasonry and homosexuality within the church, all the anti-Christian laws that take place in the different countries of the world come from him (Antichrist) laws promoting the murder of unborn children, gay marriage, gender ideology, the prohibition to talk about men and women so as not to hurt homosexuals, openly anti-Catholic leftist governments, laws that make schools teach children all kinds of sexual aberrations, the laws of the European Union and other countries that host millions of Muslims to the detriment of the European population itself, the attack on Catholic churches around the world, the feminist and animalist protests, the persecution and the extermination of Christians throughout the world; All this and much more is a product of the spirit of the antichrist that his followers are fulfilling on foot.

The people of Satan have long worked to bring chaos and extermination of man to the world, but it is necessary for a charismatic figure, a figure of respect throughout the world, a man of much moral and religious influence to endorse all this. filth proposed and ordered by Satan and this is where the second beast of the apocalypse enters, which says that it rises from the earth, indicating that it is a human who has two ram's horns, meaning that he is a religious figure ... Who Whatever it is, he has already made himself known for his charisma and apparently very successful, pious, very fraternal teachings with the poor and dispossessed, but at the same time he says and does things totally contrary to Catholic faith and dogma; more than religious, he seems a politician who practices diplomacy in the detriment of his people and his institution. - The visions of many saints point out that he would be a personage of very high ecclesiastical office of the Church. Now it is up to you to guess or imagine who he is ...

* What are the chances that a religious leader of the Catholic Church will be the one to help the Antichrist? The same Catechism of the Catholic Church contemplates it when it says:

"***Before the final day, the Church must pass a test that will shake the faith of many believers. The "Mystery of iniquity" will be revealed in the form of a religious imposture that will be that of the Antichrist, that is, there will be a pseudo-messianism in which man will glorify himself by putting himself in the place of God.***

OTHER MESSAGES FROM THE END OF THE TIMES AND MANIFESTATIONS OF THE APOSTASY.

Throughout the world, certain people have appeared who, because of their holiness and religiosity, are serving as messengers of the warnings of Jesus and his Mother the Virgin Mary, (of course that next to them are also a series of charlatans sent by the devil;

Therefore, it is necessary to ask God for much discernment to know who is of God and who of the enemy). Among the best known are Father Stephano Gobbi, of whom we had already mentioned above; but I think it is necessary to delve a little deeper into some of his messages received from the Virgin Mary as phrases; Thus, in one of the first messages the Blessed Virgin says:

"I have come from Heaven to reveal to you my design in this struggle that involves everyone, enrolled at the orders of two opposing leaders: The Woman clothed with the Sun and the Red Dragon. I have indicated the way to go: that of prayer and that of penance. I have invited you to the inner conversion of your life. I have also prepared a shelter for you to be collected, protected and strengthened during this storm, which will still increase. The refuge is my Immaculate Heart."

Jesus is the only Redeemer, because He is the only Mediator between God and men. However, He has wanted to associate to his redemptive work all those who have been redeemed by Him so that He can shine the most merciful work of His love in a grander and wonderful way. Thus you who have been redeemed, can cooperate with Him in his redemptive work. He in you, who are so intimately united with Him to form his own Mystical Body, can gather in your time the fruit of what he has accomplished only once on Calvary.

I am for you the perfect model of your cooperation to the redemptive work done by my Son. Indeed, because I am the Mother of Jesus, I have been intimately associated by Him with his redemption.

My presence under the Cross tells you how my Son wanted to perfectly unite the Mother to all her great pain at the moment of her passion and her death for you.

If the Cross has been his gallows, the pain of my Immaculate Heart has been like the altar on which my Son has offered the Father the Sacrifice of the new and eternal covenant.

Because I am Mother of the Church, I have also been intimately associated by Jesus to the work of his redemption, which acts in the course of history to offer all men the possibility of receiving that salvation that He obtained at the time of his bloody immolation. Thus, the more numerous are the men who achieve salvation, the more the masterpiece of their divine love is realized.

My maternal mission is to help, in every possible way, my children to achieve salvation; also today is to cooperate in a very special way to the redemption carried out by my Son.

Reason for my crying, for the crying of the Mother, are these children of mine, who in great numbers, live forgotten of God, submerged in the pleasures of the flesh, and run without remedy to their downfall. For many of them my tears have fallen into indifference and emptiness. Above all, the priests my favorite children, the pupil of my eyes, all these my consecrated children are the cause of my cries. See how they don't love me anymore? How do they no longer love me? Do you see how they don't listen to the words of my Son? How often do you betray him? How Jesus, present in the Eucharist is ignored by many of them, left alone in the Tabernacle, often offended by them with sacrileges...?

-All these priests, my children, who have betrayed the Gospel to support the great diabolical error of Marxism...

-Then it will be these poor children of mine who will begin the great apostasy ... -The moments of great and unspeakable tribulations are prepared: if men knew, perhaps they would repent. But who has heard my messages? Who has captured the meaning of my tears, of my maternal invitations? Almost none, few and unknown souls for whose merits the punishment has been removed for the moment ...

-How many thorns afflict to my Heart the souls that move away from my Son ... The most painful thorns are provided to me by my most beloved and beloved children: The priests. Those who betray every day, like Judas my Son Jesus and his Church, how many are already the hesitant, the insecure, the infidels! They celebrate Holy Mass, administer the Sacraments and no longer have faith ...

-Today also speak the false prophets, those who announce the Gospel betraying him, and these are heard and followed! And they carry confusion and confusion among the most faithful children of my Church ...-The time has also come when some of my priestly children prepare to publicly manifest themselves against my Son, against me, against the Pope and my Church. Then I can no longer recognize them as my children; I myself will come down from heaven to put myself at the head of my favorite children and destroy their machinations. After a great revolution and the

purification of the earth, my Immaculate Heart will sing victory in the greatest triumph of God ... It is no longer a time of doubt and uncertainty; It is the time of battle! ...

- This true division in my Church, this true apostasy, on the part of many my priests, will be accentuated, until it becomes a violent and open rebellion.

- This world is increasingly moving away from God and no longer hears the word of my Son Jesus. Thus it falls in the darkness of the denial of God, in the deceptive mirage of thinking that one can do without Him. You have almost managed to build a civilization only human, stubbornly closed to any divine influence.

God in his infinite Majesty cannot help but laugh at this Humanity that has gathered to rise against Him. In this way the ice of selfishness and arrogance is constantly increasing. Hatred prevails over love and every day causes innumerable victims ... known and unknown victims; violence to inerrant and innocent creatures, who at all times cry out for terrible revenge before the throne of God.

-And sin penetrates more and more in all environments. Where is a sinless place today? Even the houses consecrated to the worship of God are desecrated by the sins committed there: It is the consecrated persons, it is the priests and religious themselves who sometimes lose the sense of sin ... Some of them in thought, in words and in life, sacrilegiously let themselves be led by Satan. Never as much as now the devil has managed to seduce you so much. It seduces you with pride and so you even justify and legitimize moral disorder. And after the falls he manages to quench in you the voices of remorse, which are a true gift of the Holy Spirit, which urge you to conversion.

How numerous are my poor children today who spend years without confessing! They rot in sin and are consumed in impurity, they are dominated by excessive attachment to money and pride.

This is how Satan is now camping among the ministers of the Shrine and has brought the abomination of desolation into the Holy Temple of God.

It is therefore necessary that the Mother speak to you and take you by the hand. His mission is, first and foremost, to guide you in the fight against the infernal dragon. That is why I tell you: these are the times of purification, they are the times when God's justice will punish this world, rebellious and perverted, for its salvation.

Purification has already begun in my Church, invaded by error, obscured by Satan, covered by sin, betrayed and violated by some of his own pastors. Satan shakes you as is done with wheat. How much straw will be scattered soon by the wind of persecution! From now on my presence among you will become more continuous and clearer.

The Hour of Darkness. - This is the hour of Satan and his great power. This is the hour of darkness! Darkness has spread throughout the world and men, while boasting of having reached the peak of progress, walk in the densest darkness. Everything is blackened by the shadow of death that takes away your life, from the sin that imprisons you, from the hate that destroys you.

Darkness has also invaded the Church. They spread more and more and every day they reap victims among their same favorite children.

How many of them seduced by Satan have lost the light to walk the straight path; the path of truth, of fidelity, of the life of grace, of love, of prayer, of good example, of holiness!

How many of these poor children of mine still leave the Church today, criticize it, answer it or, openly, betray it and hand it over to their adversary! "Judas, with a kiss do you deliver to the Son of Man?" You too, with a kiss, betray the Church today, daughter of your Celestial Mother! ... You are still a part of it and through it you live; you exercise his ministry and often you are his pastors. You renew the Eucharistic Sacrifice every day, administer the sacraments, spread its announcement of salvation ... And yet some of you sell it to your enemy and hurt her in her very heart because they corrupt truth with error, justify sin and live from according to the spirit of the world that, in that way, penetrates through you into the Church, endangering your very life.

In the Spirit of Wisdom know, therefore, read the signs of the present moment that you live. The Lord is at the doors of this generation ... Go back to your God, who wants to save you and leads you to peace. Go back to your Redeemer. Open your hearts to Christ who is coming. Never as today the world in which you live has become a desert, which produces such poisonous and perverse fruits. Never as today my adversary tries in all ways to hinder you, seduce you, hit you. Never like today, Satan, exercising the great power that has been granted to him, tries everything to ruin my plan and to destroy my Work of love, which I myself am carrying out in these last times.

What today obfuscates the beauty and splendor of the Church? It is the smoke of the mistakes that Satan has introduced into it. It spreads more and more and leads many souls to the loss of faith.

Cause of such a vast diffusion of errors and of the great apostasy are the unfaithful shepherds. They shut up when they should speak boldly to condemn the error and defend the truth. They do not intervene when they should unmask the raptors, who have entered the flock of Christ disguised in sheep's clothing. They are mute dogs that let the flock tear apart.

When the Son of Man returns. - You read in the Gospel: -When the Son of Man returns, will he still find faith on earth? - Today I want to invite you to meditate on these words spoken by my Son Jesus. These are serious words that make you think and make you understand the times in which you live. You may ask, first of all, why Jesus pronounced them. To prepare you for your second coming and to describe a circumstance that will indicate the proximity of your glorious return. This circumstance is the loss of faith.

Also in another passage of Divine Scripture, in St. Paul's letter to the Thessalonians, it is clearly announced that, before the glorious return of Christ, a great apostasy will take place.

The loss of faith is a true apostasy. The spread of apostasy is, therefore, the sign that indicates that the second coming of Christ is already near.

I have predicted in Fatima that the time would come when true faith would be lost. These are the times. The causes of the loss of faith are: 1) the dissemination of the errors that are propagated, often taught by theology professors in seminars and in Catholic schools; in this way they acquire a certain character of authenticity and legitimacy. 2) The open and public rebellion against the authentic Magisterium of the Church, especially the Magisterium of the Pope, who has received from Christ the mission of preserving the whole Church in the truth of the Catholic faith. 3) The bad example set by those pastors who have allowed the spirit of the world to take over them completely and have become propagators of political and social ideologies instead of being announcers of Christ and his Gospel, forgetting the mandate itself received from Him: -Go to the whole world and preach the Gospel to every creature.

As Mother I am with this poor humanity, sick and oppressed under the weight of her stubborn rejection of God and her Law of Love. How she has turned away from the Lord! He has wanted to build an atheistic and materialistic civilization; new values have been proposed, based on the satisfaction of all passions, in the search for all pleasures, in the legitimization of all moral disorder. In this way selfishness and hate have replaced love; pride and disbelief, to faith; greed and lust, to hope; fraud and deception, to honesty; the evil and the hardness of hearts, to goodness. Satan has sung victory because he has brought sin to souls, division to families, to society, and to nations in and among themselves. Thus, peace has never been so threatened as in your days ... And in addition, the evils that threaten the moral integrity of the peoples are increasingly spread: such as impurity, pornography, drugs, divorces, recourse to all means to prevent life and those cursed abortions that claim revenge to God.

Also the Church in this (American) Continent lives and suffers, is threatened by an interior division, caused by the separation of the Pope and the opposition to his Magisterium by some bishops, theologians, priests and faithful. Above all, my adversary wanted to strike her (the Church), with the deceptive insidiousness of liberation theology that is a true betrayal of Christ and his Gospel.

The huge red Dragon. -It is the atheistic communism that has spread everywhere the error of denial and stubborn rejection of God. The huge red dragon in these years has managed to conquer humanity with the error of practical theoretical atheism. That has already seduced all the nations of the earth. In this way it has been possible to build a civilization without God, materialistic, selfish, hedonistic, arid, cold, which carries in itself the germs of corruption and death.

The beast Similar to a panther. -If the huge red Dragon is Marxist atheism, the black beast is Masonry. The Dragon manifests itself in the vigor of his power; the black beast, on the other hand, works in the shadow, hides, hides, to be introduced hereby everywhere.

The aim of the black beast, that is to say of Freemasonry, is to fight in a sneaky, but tenacious way, to prevent souls from traveling this path, indicated by the Father and the Son and illuminated by the gifts of the Spirit. Indeed, if the Red Dragon works to lead all mankind to dispense with God, to the denial of God and for this he disseminates the error of atheism, the goal of Freemasonry is not to deny God, but to blaspheme him. The beast opens its mouth to utter blasphemies against God, to blaspheme his Name and his abode, against all those who dwell in Heaven. The greatest blasphemy is to deny the cult due only to God to give it to the creatures and to Satan himself ... Here is why in these times, after the perverse action of Freemasonry, black masses are spread everywhere and the satanic worship.

The beast similar to a lamb. -Above all as Mother, I wanted to warn you of the great dangers that threaten the Church today, because of the many and diabolical attacks that are carried out against Her to destroy her. To achieve this end, the black beast that rises from the sea, comes to the aid of the earth, a beast that has two horns similar to those of a lamb.

The beast with two horns, similar to a lamb, indicates the ecclesiastical masonry infiltrated within the Church and that has spread mainly among the members of the hierarchy. This Masonic infiltration into the Church has already been predicted by Me in Fatima, when I announced that Satan would be introduced to the apex of the Church.

If the goal of Freemasonry is to lead souls to perdition, leading them to the cult of false divinities, the end of ecclesiastical Freemasonry, on the other hand, is to destroy Christ and his Church, building a new idol, it is say a false Christ and a false Church.

Ecclesiastical Freemasonry acts in a cunning and diabolical way, to lead everyone to apostasy. It also has the purpose of justifying sin, presenting it not only as an evil, but as a value and a good.

Ecclesiastical Freemasonry favors exegesis that give Jesus rationalist and natural interpretations, through the application of the various literary genres, so that it is lacerated in all its parts. In the end, the historical reality of miracles and His resurrection is denied and the very divinity of Jesus and his saving mission are questioned.

The Church will know the time of her greatest apostasy, the man of iniquity will enter into her interior and sit in the same Temple of God, while the small remainder that remains faithful will be subjected to the greatest trials and persecutions. Humanity will live the moment of its great punishment, thus be prepared to receive the Lord Jesus, who will return to you in glory.

Just as he tells us about the apostasy he is going through and what the Church will go through; He also gives us his message of hope:

-The Angels of Light of my Immaculate Heart are now gathering the elect from everywhere, called to be part of my victorious army. They mark you with my seal, they cover you with a strong armor for battle, they cover you with my shield, they give you the crucifix and the Rosary, as weapons to use for the great victory. The time for the final fight has arrived.

-Don't be afraid! I cover you with my immaculate mantle and protect you.

-The Priests of my Movement must restore purity in souls and must firmly fight the demon of lust in all its manifestations. They must fight against fashion, increasingly inconvenient and provocative; they must fight against the press that propagates evil and against the shows that are the ruin of customs (good). They must fight against the current mentality that legitimizes and justifies everything, the moral situation that allows everything. Above all my priests must be pure, very pure!

-What should you do, priests of my Movement, for the salvation of all these priests who are sick and in need of my maternal help? Help them, without ever judging them. Do not condemn them; it's not up to you to do this. Love them with your suffering, with your testimony, with your good example. Be an example to them in defense, even outwardly of your dignity: Never abandon the ecclesiastical habit, obeying in this the will often manifested by the Vicar of my Son, the Pope.

-Forming an incessant chain of prayer and love to ask for their salvation and for my Immaculate Heart to be, especially for them, their safest refuge, with the Pope, with the Bishops, with the faithful priests...

-This is really the time of the great falls for my favorite children, for my priests. To some, Satan will stalk them with pride, others with

the passion of the flesh, others with doubt, others with disbelief, and others with discouragement and loneliness. How many will doubt my Son and Me, and believe that this will be the end of my Church! Priests consecrated to my Immaculate Heart, beloved Children, which I am gathering for this great battle: **THE FIRST WEAPON YOU SHOULD USE IS TRUST IN ME,** in your most complete abandonment. Beat the temptation of fear, discouragement, and sadness. Distrust paralyzes your activity and it helps my opponent a lot. Stay happy, be calm! This is not the end of my Church; the principle of its total and wonderful renovation is prepared.

Even if you had been injured, even if you had fallen frequently, even if you had doubted, even if at one time you had been unfaithful, do not be discouraged, because I love you.

The hour of my great Light, that Light that I give you in an extraordinary way so that all of you can go to meet my son Jesus, King of Love and Peace, who is about to arrive.

In these dark times of the great tribulation, if you do not get carried away in my arms with filial abandonment and great docility, you will hardly manage to escape the insidious overlaps that my adversary tends you.

His seductions have become so dangerous and subtle that he can hardly escape them. You will run the great danger of falling into the seductions that my adversary tends you, to get away from Jesus and Me. everyone can fall for their deception. Priests and bishops fall into it. They fall faithful and also consecrated. The simple ones and also the learned ones fall. The disciples and the teachers fall. Never fall into it, those who - like little children - devote themselves to my Immaculate Heart and let themselves be carried between my maternal arms.

- In the hope of his glorious return do not fear: He guides the events of human history to the realization of the Will of the Father and his great plan of salvation.

All things are subject to Him. All their enemies will be humiliated and defeated under the footstool of their feet. The risen Christ will return to you over the clouds of heaven in full brightness of his glory. - Live today awaiting your glorious return.

Do not be discouraged by the momentary triumph of evil and sin. Do not let even doubt or distrust assail you when you see the Church so hurt and beaten, insidious and betrayed.

-I invite you to walk the path of fasting, mortification and penance.

I ask the children to grow in the virtue of purity and in this difficult way be helped by parents and educators.

I ask the young people to form in the domain of the passions with prayer and the life of union with Me, and to give up going to the cinemas and discos where the serious and continuous danger of offending this virtue so pleasing to my Immaculate Heart.

I ask the bride and groom to refrain from any relationship before marriage.

I ask Christian families to be trained in the exercise of conjugal chastity and never use artificial means to prevent life.

How much desire of the priests the scrupulous observance of celibacy and of the religious the faithful and austere practice of their vow of chastity!

-Live in the contempt of the world and of yourselves. May faith be the only light that illuminates you, in these times of great darkness. May only jealousy for the glory of God consume you, in these days of so much aridity.

-Pray to ask for the salvation of this world, which has already touched the bottom of impiety and impurity, injustice and selfishness, hate and violence, sin and evil.

-Now come out as brave apostles of these last times and go all over the earth to bring the Light of Christ, in these times of darkness, and the dew of his divine love, in these days of great aridity.

In this way you will prepare hearts and souls to receive with joy the coming Christ. With all your loved ones, with the souls that have been entrusted to you, I bless you with the joy of a Mother who has been so comforted by you.

-Evangelize all men, preaching that the Kingdom of God is near. The moment of the second coming of Jesus is coming, of the return of Christ in glory, to establish among you his Kingdom of grace, holiness, justice, love and peace.

Announce to all this his glorious return, so that hope may flourish in the world and the hearts of men open to receive it.

"Open wide the doors to Christ who is coming." Therefore, preach the need for prayer and penance; the brave practice of all virtues; from the return to the perfect cult of love; of adoration and reparation to Jesus present in the Eucharist. Spread all the Cenacles of Prayer that I have asked you, among the children, the young priests and the faithful. Above all, spread the Family Cenacles everywhere that I ask as a powerful means to save the Christian family from the great evils that threaten it.

Come out of these Cenacles as the Apostles of this second Evangelization. Do not fear.

I am always with you and I lead you along this luminous path.

With your loved ones, and with the souls that have been entrusted to you, I bless you all in the name of the Father, the Son and the Holy Spirit.

Only when Jesus has established his Kingdom among you, can all mankind enjoy, finally, the great gift of Peace.

So far part of the phrases of the Virgin Mary to Father Estephano Gobi

*There are also messages supposedly given by Jesus, the Virgin Mary and the saints, to a very pious woman named **Veronica Lueken** of Bayside, New York. Messages he received from 1968, when the visions began, until 1995, the year he died.*

She transmits a series of warnings, to defend the faith and the Church that is going through a terrible crisis as it never was. Crisis that began according to these messages as well as according to some ecclesiastical scholars and analysts with the Second Vatican Council. It is said that in this Council, although it was convened by Pope John XXIII, those who took the reins of this event were theologians, bishops and cardinals of the so-called liberals or progressives; most of them communist agents infiltrated the Church to try to systematically destroy from within the Catholic Church, who was the only one who tenaciously faced the diabolical ideologies of communism.

Many are the sources that confirm these facts, among them the same messages of the Virgin of Fatima given in 1917, messages that nobody took into account. "Russia will spread its mistakes" "The Holy Father will have to suffer a lot" etc.

But there are also other secular testimonies such as that of one of the same communist agents published in a book called: AA 1025 - **"Memories of an Anti-Apostle."** Which is the diary of one of the many communists infiltrated into the Church. They all have a purpose, to destroy Catholic faith and dogmas; Little by little, without people noticing. Thus they began, for example, to cancel many of the rites where the great respect for the "Most Holy" was expressed. Older people who had a reason before the year 1963, will remember how to kneel when passing in front of the Tabernacle; now they just do a bow badly done. Holy Communion was received kneeling, now it is stopped. The "Most Holy" could not be touched with the hand because it is extremely sacred, now whoever can receive it in his hand. The faithful were aware that it could only be communicated by being confessed, duly prepared, now 80% of Catholics commune in grave sin, without being prepared or having confessed (the same ones digging their own condemnation). Kneeling communion had a very powerful reason; For the Holy Eucharist is the Real and Present Body of Jesus, your King and Savior and as such you have to kneel before Him. Kneeling does not only mean receiving it with humility but it is also a way of expressing. How much we love and respect him!

In this regard, St. Michael the Archangel in the messages to the visionary of Bayside says:

"As in the past, can you not recognize the Mystery of Heaven on earth? Didn't Moses' staff become a snake by the power of God? Didn't the river of Egypt become blood by the power of God? And, by the Power of God, could he not turn bread and wine into his Body and Blood? In your Real Presence? (San Miguel, February 1, 1977).

The fruit of this Council is that the faithful Catholics no longer kneel before their King and Lord and therefore receive Holy Communion only standing, and even oneself can grab it with their hands and bring it to their mouths; something that could not be done before because it is the most sacred thing on earth. (Pope John Paul II often indicated that Holy Communion should be received in the mouth, directly from the hands of the priest). Now, many are the bishops who in disguised form have suppressed the good habit of *kneeling for consecration. Many are the temples where they have only put comfortable seats and nowhere to kneel.*

Fray Regis Scanion says: From the perspective of the Catholic Doctrine, discouraging Catholics from kneeling at the time of Consecration is extremely bad, St. Augustine said: "It was in the flesh that Christ walked among us and it is His flesh that we Give as food for our salvation. No one eats his Meat without first worshiping it." (St. Augustine, Psalm 98.9 of Paul VI. Mystery Fidei Book, No. 55. P. 323)

Pope Pius XII in his Encyclical Mediator Dei, on the sacred liturgy, says: *"External acts of religion serve to foster piety, ignite the flame of charity, increase faith and deepen our devotion. This also leads us to distinguish genuine Christians from false ones or heretics".* And then the Holy Father Pius XII emphasizes: *"It is therefore the desire of the Church that all the faithful kneel at the feet of the Redeemer, to tell and express: How much we venerate and love him!"*

Dietrich Von Hildebrand, whom Pope Pius XII called him the Doctor of the Church of the 20th Century, asks: *"Since when does contempt for kneeling come? Why should the Holy Eucharist be received standing still? Isn't the classic expression of worship and reverence kneeling?* (The Charitable Anathema, P. 42). And, we would add: Are not the Angels all the time prostrated in praise and worship to God? Why we weak and sinful creatures, no?

Cardinal, Ratzinger, writes about the importance of kneeling during the liturgy: *"Here the gesture of the body (kneeling) takes the form of a confession of faith in Christ; Words cannot replace such a confession"* (Cardinal Joseph Ratzinger, The Feast of the Faith. San Francisco, Ignacious Press 1986. P. 74.75).

Bishop John Keating of Arlington, Virginia in his Pastoral Letter to the Eucharistic Reverence, says: *"There is no clearer body posture that expresses the disposition of a soul in its reverence to God, like the act of kneeling. Conversely, the kneeling posture reinforces and deepens the attitude of reverence of souls"* (A Pastoral Letter. December 4, 1988).

Finally, to end this emphasis on kneeling in front of the Holy Eucharist, **Fray Robert Skuria,** on April 4, 1982 at St. Peter's Cathedral in Scranton, Pennsylvania; he urged all the faithful to kneel to communion; we say: *"In the name of Jesus, everyone should bow down,"* then: *Why do we stand and stand for Holy Communion, if we are facing the very Person of Jesus? The Scripture says: "For every knee will bow before Me"* (Isaiah 45, 24).

And, returning to before the Council, the priests used cassock or habit, like the religious and were treated with much respect, now the priests do not wear cassock (those who do are very rare) are confused with anyone and He has lost their respect; because of course they are seen as "any other of the bunch". (And, in that they have become the vast majority). Holy Mass was a rite where God had the priest's preference and attention; because he did not turn his back on the Blessed Sacrament but on the faithful, now the sword is turned on the Blessed Sacrament and the faithful are preferred. Religious songs had to have a sacred letter and music, with appropriate instruments, now subversive songs can be sung, and other songs that can no longer be called sacred because they imitate worldly songs or sect songs. The language with which God was praised was Latin, with which he predisposed the faithful to strive and learn this religious language and thus it gave him an even more sacred sense to communicate with God. A Catholic from Europe, Asia, or America had no difficulty understanding Mass and rites anywhere in the world. The most ignorant people and even those who could not read prayed in Latin. This language was also abolished thinking maybe that people would learn their prayers better, which as you will see did not work, now people pray less and know less prayers than in the past. In many churches today, the "Most Holy" is no longer in the Main Tabernacle, but next to the altar; (they have set it aside) as if God should not be in the most principal place of the temple. And so we could continue listing many more aspects that were changed.

But returning to the above-mentioned book of the infiltrated communist agent, he says: "**To weaken the notion of the Real Presence of Christ, all respect and decorum must be set aside. No more expensive and elaborate ornaments or tablecloths to dress the altars. No more music called sacra; especially no more signs of the Cross. No more genuflections, only passive attitudes and especially the faithful should leave the habit of kneeling and this should be absolutely prohibited when they receive communion"** (p 90)

What you just read, written by one of the many infiltrated communist agents is what they have already achieved.

There are many things that most people do not know and therefore do not realize; but it is good that the "Signs of the Times" are now revealed so that their eyes are opened and they see how immediate the Glorious return of Our Lord Jesus Christ is.

Returning to the specific theme of the Second Vatican Council, so that they realize what happened and how the devil works; According to **Anne Muggeridge**, political daughter of the famous Catholic journalist converted, **Malcolm Muggeridge**, in his work: **"Desolated City"**, tells that Cardinal John Heenan of Westminster, reported: During the first session of the Council, Pope John XXIII realized that there was Lost control of the process. He tried to reorganize the event with a group of faithful bishops; but before the second session of the Council opened, John XXIII died. His last words on his bed of agonizing (according to Jean Guitton, the only lay Catholic who served as an expert in the Council), were: "Stop the Council, stop the Council"

It was in this Council where the word "Revolution" was used numerous times to describe the same event and so much so that during the debate on the constitution of the Liturgy, Cardinal Ottaviani asked: *Are these parents planning a revolution?*

And so it was, the Satanic-Marxist power that had been preparing to infiltrate the Church for several decades, had succeeded. Those who took control and dictated the new rules of the new Council were the liberal advisors or experts. Priests who at the time of Pope Pius XII were blacklisted by suspicious heretics, including the Germans: Hans Kung, Edward Schillebeeckx and others.

These priests and liberal bishops of the Council avoided by all means that the majority of conservative bishops and cardinals let their claims be heard that were certainly numerous; but all those documents were lost and nobody knew about them. The liberal bishops also avoided condemning communism and modern errors; but above all they deliberately imposed many ambiguities in the conciliar texts which were intended to exploit them after the Council; as the same expert, Father Edward Schillebeeckx, will declare saying: *"We have used ambiguous phrases, but we know how we will interpret them later"*.

The great confusion, the great apostasy and the modern changes were already underway and neither the Council of Trent nor any other Council would impede their advance. Yves Congar, one of the reformers, declared very proud: *"The Church has had its Peaceful October Revolution"*, referring to the Bolshevik (communist) revolution. And, Cardinal Suenens, another of the liberals, said: *"The Second Vatican Council is the French Revolution of the Church"*.

Fray Paul Kramer, in his book: **"The Final Battle of the Devil"** says: *On October 13, 1962, a day after two Russian communist observers were at the Council and just on the anniversary of the Miracle of Fatima, the History of the Church and the world underwent a profound change in one of the best planned events in history by the communist power of Russia. (The Second Vatican Council).*

Some will still wonder, but what's wrong with the Second Vatican Council? Why is this Council criticized?

Because through it many changes were introduced in the liturgy and in the very life of the Church, which has then led to a series of disorders, such as the Theology of Liberation itself, coincidentally because of those ambiguities left by the infiltrated Marxist planners in the church.

Soon the faithful bishops of the Church were relieved by the communists, such as Cardinal Mindszenty by Cardinal Lekai. Cardinal Berán of Czechoslovakia by Cardinal Tomsee. The same happened in Lithuania. In the book: **"Moscow and the Vatican"** you can read how the Lithuanian priests wrote to their respective bishops: *"We do not understand what is happening. Before our bishops supported us in our fight against atheistic and satanic communism and they themselves died martyrs and many of them are still in prison; And, now are you (bishops) who condemn us, who do not let us fulfill our apostolate and tell us that we have no right to resist, because it is contrary to the laws of communist governments?*

There were many bishops who came out terribly unhappy of this Council; because the changes made were not from everyone's consensus, but from a minority who took command and did what they wanted. Fray Paul Kramer wrote in his aforementioned book that hundreds of bishops tried to condemn communism and ignored them. The bishop who asked for that was invited to sit down and shut up. This was confirmed by the French Archbishop Marcel Lefebvre (who was later separated from the Church for not accepting or abiding by the new changes of this Council). At a press conference in Long Island, New York in 1983, he said: *"I delivered 450 signatures of bishops to the council secretary, condemning communism, but we were silenced and ignored our request; however, when only one of them (liberals) spoke, their requests were immediately heard and approved..."*

The great Council, the Council that brought the discord, disunity and destruction of many souls, according to visionary Veronica Lueken, said that Saint Michael the Archangel told her that this happened due to lack of prayer and that Satan himself was sitting inside it. Council playing a game of chess where the pieces were red and purple hats, moving them to their liking and watching them with great pleasure as the evil progressed rapidly.

This Council also brought as a novelty, "Ecumenism", where they did not proclaim Jesus desire to work because the separated churches return to the fold where they came from; but through their ambiguities they encouraged a kind of coalition of churches, creating an immense and new church made by men, contrary to the Doctrine of Jesus and his only Church.

Fray Frank Poncelot writes: *"Ecumenism is a modern movement that aims at the union of religions"*. This false ecumenism is one of the problems facing the Church; because the modernist elements infiltrated the Church and many unauthorized theologians are trying to dismantle the Church of Christ ... especially with its far-fetched word: "Option" And, as true Catholics know, **"There can be no salvation outside the Church left personally by Christ and there can be no alliances with evil" (Catechism, 846)**

One of the most serious changes suffered was that of the liturgy. Cardinal John Heenan, of Westminster, participant of the Council, in his book: **"A Crown of Thorns"** explains: *"The seemingly most debated issues were the reform of the liturgy. It would be more accurate to say that the bishops had the impression that the liturgy had been sufficiently discussed. In retrospect, it is clear that they were given the opportunity to discuss only general principles. In sum, subsequent changes in the liturgy were more radical than*

Pope John and his bishops thought".

The liturgy expert, Monsignor Klaus Gamber, says the same thing in his book: **"The Reform of the Roman Liturgy",** that the new liturgy was not agreed at the Council. *"One statement that we can say with great certainty is that the Novo Ordo of the Mass that has now emerged, did not have the approval of the majority of the conciliar fathers".*

This situation described on the Second Vatican Council has resulted in a series of practices (which we mentioned earlier) that instead of improving and approaching God take us away, and make faith go extinct.

Only 30% of Catholics in the US believe in the doctrine of the Real Presence of Christ and this is almost the same in other countries. Who can now doubt that the elaborate and systematic plan of the modernist changes promoted by the Second Vatican Council has not worked? And, moreover, forbidding the faithful to kneel before Christ Himself (Holy Eucharist), is already an open rebellion against God and a denial of the Sacrament of the Altar.

These changes apparently small and unimportant, will eventually lead to great sin; that of the rebellion against God and the appearance of the abomination of desolation, as the culmination of apostasy.

Hence the messages of Jesus and the Virgin received by Victoria Lueken make sense and become credible; when she says:

-Stop Changes. - Pastors, you who have our sheep under your care, must stop making changes based on modern developments, because they are destroying young souls and dispersing the rest. "I repeat my children: The great Council of Rome of Vatican II, the intentions were good; but Satan sat among you and played with you as you play with chess."

"You were given the fundamentals of faith based on the tradition and knowledge of the prophets. You cannot start this new religion; because it would lead you to a religion that is not of my Son, which does not carry the true foundation and in it (New church) you took the Body of my Son to defame it, so as not to give it more recognition of its divinity ..." (Our Madam, August 5, 1976).

-Rebellion against the Pope. - Many clergies have become slaves to

the pleasure of the flesh, many others have fallen into the sin of heresy and have despised the truth of their vocation. Many have rebelled against their leader, the leader God gave them, their Vicar. In matters of faith and morals, man cannot change the laws given by God from the throne of Peter and established in the world through the tradition of the true Church of my Son. (Our Lady, October 6, 1979).

-Corrupted Life Testimonies. - Religious and priestly vocations are very f few, why? Because the testimonies of life are corrupt and rotten. True religion has been set aside by modernism and humanism. (Jesus, December, 31 1977).

-Derision of the Past of the Church. -Recognize the signs of the times, get out of their darkness. You are sleeping my shepherds. I have sent many notices to humanity. I have allowed Satan to tempt the earth as a measure to separate the sheep from the goats. You (shepherds) have given themselves over to Satan and quickly fall into hell. "The plan of salvation given to them was a simple plan of faith. Faith in what was delivered in the past, in tradition! And they have begun to build a new church; but you know: **"the gates of hell will not prevail against my Church." (Jesus, May 15 1976).**

-The Great Apostasy. -Don't accept the fallacy that a man can be God. There is only one God and no man can rise above his maker. OH, my children: Can't you recognize the signs of the times? The great apostasy is upon you! (Our Lady, December 7 1976)

-The Sword. -As a lost and wandering generation, given to sin and the abomination of the flesh, they will be brought to trial. (San Miguel, July 15 1975).

-Traitors. - Oh, you men of little faith, full of pride and arrogance in your worldly knowledge. That they have closed the doors to my sheep and dispersed them. You traitors of Peter's chair, you (cardinals, bishops and priests) with all your worldly wisdom and your pride cannot understand the designs of the Eternal Father. They will receive the just punishment for their arrogance, their apostasy and the bane of souls. (Jesus, October 6 1978).

-Stay Faithful and Fight. -My children, you recognize the facets of evil. Satan has entered the highest strata of my Church. Pray a lot for priests, for bishops, cardinals and other clergy. A lot of prayer is necessary, because many are those who are on the path of perdition, dragging many others with them. My children, do not put aside the sacraments, they are like armor for the coming days. Do not leave the Church. Do not ignore it because of the man who will seize it in ignorance and pride by changing it until it appears unrecognizable. With you I am my children, do not leave her, you must stay and fight. In this way the sheep will be separated from the goats, it will be a form of purification. (Jesus, July 15 1977).

-The Battle rages. -The True Church of Jesus in Rome is being attacked by the forces of 666 which is a worldwide diabolical movement ... The struggle now grows, and all those who have gone after the world, will not understand why they are from the world. And many have now adopted and accepted a new father. Not to the Eternal Father of Heaven; but to the father of lies, to Satan. "All who do not recognize Jesus as the Christ are the antichrists, learn from this!" The clerics who have given themselves the error are carrying with great determination the destruction of the Church of my Son. Why? Because they have lost faith. Pray, pray a lot for your clergy, my children; without their prayers many miter will fall into hell. (Our Lady, April 17 1976).

We could continue to write many more messages; but I think they are enough to realize that they agree with the truth, especially of these times; especially when he describes the chaotic and moral situation in which our humanity lives, in the loss of faith and in the rot and abomination of many clerics who, very proud, still believe they are right. Poor, truly poor, they run in a hurry and blindfolded themselves to hell and eternal punishment.

The current situation of the world and of the Church is being assembled as a puzzle, in which we already glimpse and see how the forces of evil take possession of everything, absolutely everything; of the same Church (apostasy), of customs, fashions, radio, television, Internet, magazines, books, cinemas, videos, music, politics, economics, arts, arms; Each and every aspect of man's life seems to have united and conspired against God. And, they are reaching the highest point in the history of mankind in an effort to destroy it completely; But we know that the forces of good with Jesus in command will intervene before the earth and humanity are destroyed; then:

"You will see the Son of Man come with great majesty and glory." (Mark 13, 26).

To end on this painful issue of communist infiltration in the Church, we will only say that those who tear their clothes, are scandalized and do not accept this truth, they should only remember the history and words of Lenin, who said: **"We must destroy The Church from within. You have to penetrate Catholic seminars"**. The Church is currently divided, because within the hierarchy they have managed to climb the minions of Lenin to the top. That is why in the famous secret of Fatima it was said: **"Satan will reach the highest peaks in the hierarchy and bishops will face against bishops and cardinals against cardinals."** That will be the beginning of the end" (Francisco Sánchez Ventura and Pascual. The Great Apostasy. From the book: Mary Precursor of Christ in his Second Coming to Earth).

SOME OF THE FRUITS OF THE II VATICAN COUNCIL

Although most of the hierarchy of the Church does not want to accept that this Council had its great mistakes; and they always try to disguise things to give the impression that everything is going great and it was the best thing that could have happened to the Church. Jesus gave us that infallible rule to know if something is good or bad: **"By their fruits you will know them"**. Let's think a little: What are the fruits of this Council? Pope Paul VI himself, shortly after the Council said: **"I don't know why the smoke of Satan has leaked into the Church"**. Regarding this same subject, Father Frank Poncelot, ecclesiastical analyst writes:

"That there are ambiguities in the XVI documents of the Council, nobody can deny it. You can check it in your numerous sentences to approve or disapprove many ideas. This was done deliberately and frequently to support their previously deviated schemes" (Of the liberals).

Cardinal Ratzinger (Prefect of the Congregation for the Doctrine of the Faith) observed that many documents of Vatican II, such as Gaudium et Spes, compromised Catholic truths, the same that were necessary to correct them. These documents, he says, are an irreconcilable attack on the position of the Church adopted in 1789 under Pius IX and Pius X. And, it is because of these ambiguities that this Council is currently full of; there is a divided Church, with the majority of priests disobeying the Pope, in open rebellion to God, and has his vows of chastity; a Church made by men without prayer and without God. A Church that is divided among the communists who proclaim themselves "advanced" (they really advance but to hell) who are the vast majority and those who are faithful to Christ and the Pope who are the minority, among those who imitate the sects in their healing rites (some of which are pure business, quackery and witchcraft). And the faithful and true Church that silently suffers or asks for God's intervention but without scandals. A church made to mundane and modernist tastes that wants to be secular and horizontal, a wild church, a church that doesn't go anywhere, because it does nothing.

Once a religious woman told me: I don't know what happens ... but we (Catholics), we don't hit ... we preach, we take the gospel to different communities and nothing. While the sects build temples and form groups immediately. And, it is true; I would like to ask the majority of priests, nuns and catechists: How many people have they converted the last year of their apostolate? The last 2, 3, 5, 10 years ago? They remain silent, they say nothing ... They have not converted anyone. So what are they for? What have they done about their ministry? And that means that they are not with God, in their lives there is no prayer and that is why they do not bear fruit: The Lord says:

"I am the vine; you are the branches; who remains in Me, that bears much fruit" (John 15, 5).

And now, we have a church designed by men that allows everything among its members, especially among those of the clergy. We now have priests who openly give their opinions and teachings contrary to God's law and let them know as if they were true.

Priests and religious who live in sin; but that thanks to the ambiguities of Vatican II and the liberality of many priests, they make the faithful believe that this is fine and that they must be accepted; because the Church has to change, they say ... according to modern times; as if we did not know that Christ is immutable: **"Christ is yesterday, today and forever".** We cannot create a church and a Christ according to our conveniences, tastes and ways.

And, those are the fruits of these ambiguities of the Council. Now we have long been priests, terrorists, guerrillas, homosexuals, adulterers, schismatic's, apostates, heretics, pedophiles, bishops who love power, pleasure and money; Bishops who fight for power and wealth and have completely forgotten the reason for their mission. Priests who have made the Church a cave of thieves, and an easy church. To be being a Christian is not easy, it requires sacrifice, discipline, morality, honor and total surrender to Christ.

You are shocked huh...! Are you outraged by what you just read? You will say: How is it possible to speak so hostile of priests and bishops, especially if you are one of them? If you are hypocritical like the Pharisees you will surely be very scandalized and outraged, and you may be one of these bad children of God. If you are honest, you will be saddened by your bad actions or your brothers who behave like that. This may serve to reconsider and convert. If at least one returns to the fold, we will have fulfilled our purpose.

Recently I had the unfortunate opportunity to see how a priest turned the Holy Temple into a theater, where they took shows of very young women, some girls, in miniskirts, crazy music and other totally mundane themes that have nothing to do with the Church and less with God; however, all that was very good; they gave voices that even the bishop had given permission and nobody said anything, no one brought out his face for Christ, knowing that the only time He was so angered was when they turned his Father's temple into a market, and this priest that He had done because they charged for his theater show.

All this is a product of modernism that our priests live. They have built a modern, but blasphemous church, where Satan is very happy; For it is he who is in the hearts of these poor priests and not God. A cheerful, prostituted life church. This was also warned by our Lord Jesus Christ when he said: that even the elect will be deceived (Mt 24:24). And, with all this: Do you still not want to realize that apostasy is already here?

Many faithful ask: If the devil is still in the same Church, what can we do?

Many first think they are going to be part of a Protestant church or any other sect; but that would be a serious mistake, because there you will not find Christ, for these are the false teachers and prophets disguised as lambskin that Jesus also speaks to us, who will deceive many. (Mt 24, 11). Others will choose to become indifferent, not to believe in anything, to think that everything is a farce.

Neither one nor the other; For that is exactly what Satan expects us to do, leave the Church and move on to a sect or simply stay out. In any of the two things he would be very happy and he would win.

More, what does Jesus tell us? ***"And many false prophets will rise and deceive many ..."*** (Religions and sects separated from the Holy Catholic Church). ***"See that no one deceives you ..."*** (This includes the same priests some infiltrators and others who do not know that what they do and teach is wrong, because the devil has blinded them and makes them believe that this is fine, as the followers of liberation theology, ecumenists, modernists, horizontalists, relativists, certain charismatic's and others). ***"And, because the evil has multiplied, the love of many will be cooled..."*** (So many scandalized people have turned away from the Church) ***"But he who endures to the end will be saved"*** (MT. 24, 11-13) With this Jesus tells us that although we see the misrepresentation of the Gospel and the corruption of clergy (Apostasy), we must persevere until the end. Nor do we mean by this that it is necessary to make deaf ears and blind eyes to the evils and abominations that are committed, no; if not that: as the Virgin says in one of her messages to the visionary Victoria Lueken:

"I ask you not to remain silent when you encounter badly done things or with heresies and abominations. But speak and denounce to correct these situations that are offensive to God and that lead to the destruction of souls". (Our Lady, November 20, 1979).

Even so, the majority of Catholics are poorly prepared, they are adrift, without adequate nor trusted guides to whom to turn. What to do? Also here Jesus tells us, the Blessed Virgin, the saints, the Pope, "Pray, pray, pray, incessantly"; so that the Lord will assist us in these last times and also of his grace to the priests and we have holy priests that in fact there are them; but you have to look for them with magnifying glass and with great care, especially if we want to have them as confessors or counselors.

Well-formed Catholics must collaborate with Christ, taking the Gospel to Catholics who do not know, as well as to those who are not Catholics, forming Houses or Cenacles of Prayer, as the Virgin advises. Spread the Prayer and the Holy Rosary. That each Catholic home becomes a Center for Prayer and the propagation of the Faith. Always seeking for oneself and for others the true conversion and salvation of our own souls such as that of our relatives, friends and neighbors, (otherwise we would fall into selfishness in seeking only our own salvation and that is not right; for Christ died for all, not only for me.) Pray, pray and ask the Lord for his guidance, his protection and his blessing, until he is again with us.

Depart from the world; For we know that everything in the world is dominated and corrupted by Satan. ***"We are in the world, but we are not of the world"*** (Jn 15:19). Therefore, there can be no concessions, if we want to save ourselves and be from God, we cannot live according to the world, what is now called society, the true Christian has to depart from the fashion that arouses sensual appetites, from discos, drinks and bad companions, movies and novels, bad music, music videos; because in all that is the devil; even from the same media, radio, television, Internet, etc. Some will think that what I just said is an exaggeration, however to those I ask: Can you mention any commercial TV channel in the world that sent good programs to your viewers? There is none, all honest people in all countries complain about the garbage and immoralities that these TV channels turned into instruments of Satan send to the public to scandalize and corrupt children, youth and adults.

"These things I have spoken to you so that in Me you may have peace. In the world you will have affliction, but trust. I have defeated the world" *(JN. 16, 33)*

To conclude on the delicate and serious situation of our Holy Church; Brothers: Understand! it is not the Church of God, which is failing, what happens is that the hosts of Satan have taken over the minds and hearts of many priests, nuns, bishops and cardinals; and, they are using the same temple of God (our Catholic temples) to do the greatest damage to Jesus and his Church. Understand! that this, (the apostasy) had to happen in the true Church of God, therefore do not be scandalized and run to the sects, because these are of the devil. The Lord wants us to remain faithful to Him and his Church and continue to pray much and frequent the Sacraments until the end, even though many of his ministers do not work for Him, we must respect them and pray for their conversion. How difficult does it not? What a crossroads of the Holy Church! But it is also to test and purify it. True Christians will realize and remain faithful until the end, which certainly is not long enough. The Christian of these times must remain close to God, praying much and frequenting the sacraments. But away from the religious and priests of doubtful behavior, so as not to be scandalized and if possible help Christ our Lord to convert as many people as possible. Ask God to give you the grace to be his instrument of salvation and He will put in your mouth the words you have to say. Do not be afraid!

CONCLUSIONS ON THE II VATICAN COUNCIL

We, as Catholics, would like to say that this Council was one of the greatest and best in history, which brought many benefits to the Church of Christ, (as most cardinals, bishops and priests think, or want to make us believe, especially those from Latin America).

In fact, there are many good things about this Council that, thanks to God's intervention, have been inspired and shaped for the government of his Church; For this Council is how Pedro's boat is currently guided. The important thing here is to realize that ***"God writes straight even in crooked lines"***, and although many sacred things have become less and confusion, corruption, division and disobedience to God and the authority of the Pope have increased; It is also true that through this Council greater participation has been given to the faithful lay Catholics, who at present and by inspiration of the Holy Spirit, are working in various forms and places, in many cases if not in the great majority, filling the gaps and voids due to the lack of priestly and religious vocations; as are also the lay faithful who are keeping the Church afloat and drawing their faces for Christ.

It seems that the shot that the liberals intended to take with the new and modern rules of Vatican II, came to them by the butt, because now there are many lay organizations that preach the Gospel faithful to Christ and to the Magisterium of the Church; and its influence is so great that now many of the liberal and acting prelates try to diminish, endure or not give the respective permits for the laity to work. See how God still takes advantage of the enemy's malice?

IS SATAN INTO THE CHURCH?

It is more than certain that the members of the sects whatever their denominations, when reading this article, them will say: You see? If Satan is within the Catholic Church, what will the true Church be like? Impossible! - We were right, the Catholic Church is the great Babylon, the Pope, is the Antichrist, the beast, etc. etc. However, they are so blind that they do not realize that because it is certainly the true Church of Christ, it (the Catholic Church) is attacked inside and out, day and night, month after month, year after year, without rest, by all the flanks and with many and diverse strategies to make it fall and destroy it completely.

Pope Paul VI once said: ***"The tail of the devil is functioning in the disintegration of the Catholic world. The darkness of Satan has entered and spread throughout the Catholic Church, even to its peak. The apostasy, the loss of faith, is spreading throughout the world and even at the highest levels within the Church"*** - Pope Paul VI, October 13, 1977.

In an interview they did to the priest Gabriel Amorth, the exorcist of Rome, in the next question asked, he replied: - Journalist: *Are you saying, then, that in this, as in all wars, Satan wants to conquer the high command, to take the generals of the adversary prisoners?*

Amorth: It's a victorious strategy. You always try to put it into practice. Especially when the adversary's defenses are weak. Satan also tries. But, thanks to Heaven, it is the Holy Spirit who directs the Church: ***"The gates of hell will not prevail".*** Despite the defections, and despite the betrayals, they should not cause astonishment. The first traitor was one of the closest apostles to Jesus: Judas Iscariot.

The Virgin Mary appeared in La Sallete, France (1846) to two shepherds, Melanie and Maximino, to whom she revealed many things, including the terrible degradation to which many priests would come referring to these times: - *"The priests, ministers of my Son, for his bad life, for his irreverence's and his impiety in celebrating the holy mysteries, for his love of money, honors and pleasures, have become sewers of impurity. Yes, priests ask for revenge, and revenge hangs from their heads. Woe to the priests and people consecrated to God, who by their infidelities and bad life crucify my Son again!"* No wonder so many pedophilia scandals and other aberrations they commit without any impudence.

In the convents, the flowers of the Church will be corrupted and the devil will become like the king of hearts. Let those who are in charge of the religious communities' watch over the people they are to receive, because the devil will use all his malice to introduce people committed to sin into religious orders, because the disorders and love of carnal pleasures will be They will spread throughout the earth.

In fact, Satan is within the Church and for a long time, the death of Pope John Paul I, is attributed to the freemasonry infiltrated within the Vatican, there is also talk of a possible death caused by these together with the communists of the Death of Pope John XXIII, so that they can control the Council that was developing and of which we have already talked about how it greatly affected the Church.

The struggle is intestine, within the Vatican a war between good and evil takes place, a struggle in which it seems that evil is winning because it controls almost all strata of the Catholic hierarchy; it is known that there are cardinals, bishops, priests and infiltrated nuns who work to win a papacy with which they can dictate their norms not as God commands but as Satan wants.

But, despite this, the Church continues on its way. The Holy Spirit maintains it, and therefore, Satan's attacks can only be partially successful. Naturally, the demon can win battles, even important battles. But he will never win the war.

IS FREEMASONRY INSIDE THE CHURCH?

REVELATION 13 It seems important to me to talk about Revelation 13, because it will shed light on what is happening today and that most of us do not realize. Revelation 13, tells us of a beast that arises from the sea, it has seven heads and ten horns, both on the horns and on the heads it has blasphemous names against God, it says that the dragon has given authority to the beast to make war to the saints and defeat them. It also says that one of the heads looked like a wound, but that the dragon healed it and all the people marveled. This head has a man's name and its number is 666, that is, the Antichrist. The other heads are diabolical forces that have seized political power through institutions and ideologies that are dragging people to perdition and hell.

As things are going, most Christians who are waiting for the events of the parousia expect to see the figure of the Antichrist, but since it is not yet revealed, it seems that nothing happened; however, the beast has long ago made a presence on earth with its heads active and present exerting all the evil pressure to turn humanity away from God and lead them to the destruction of all the good that the Church had already managed to implant.

-The first head of the beast and the oldest is **"Freemasonry"**, which it always sought and was created with the sole purpose of destroying the Catholic Church and Spain as a country. Freemasonry was created in England, a staunch enemy of Spain and the Catholic Church, in 1717. Freemasonry acts as a secret institution whose members in the last degrees are brought to deny Christ, trampling on a crucifix or consecrated hosts stolen from the temples. Their great architect that they mention and that they say is the one referring to God, is Satan. The Church has excommunicated them through three papal bulls and three different popes. Freemasonry for its way of working slyly, as a cunning and evil serpent has been gradually achieving its objectives, the first were to destroy Spain as an Empire making all the territories that had them as viceroyalties be taken from them. Then she was immersed in the Cristera war 1926-1929, when the Mason Plutarco Elias Calles, President of Mexico, ordered the killing of thousands of lay and religious Catholics, simply for being Catholics.

It was also immersed together with the communists in the Spanish civil war, 1936, where as in Mexico, 13 bishops, 4,184 secular priests, 2,365 friars and 283 nuns were assassinated. To these data we should add the 8,000-odd (impossible to establish exactly) of so many Spanish Catholics who died victims of hatred against religion, in a persecution that resembled that of the first Christians, the hatred felt by the devil towards Catholics is great. Seeing that with arms he has not been able to destroy the Church, he has long schemed to infiltrate the Church, recruiting people to enter the church as priests and then influencing them to become bishops, cardinals and finally have a Freemason as supreme head of the church ... the Pope, who knows exactly what he has to do: destroy it inside and out and apparently they have already achieved it... -The second head of the beast is **"Communism"**, call it Marxism, Leninism, Maoism, Socialism, Left, all aim to destroy the Catholic

Church. - Like the Masons, already in Stalin's time they created a special school of secret agents to infiltrate the Church. Years later by the time the Second Vatican Council was held, the communists already had many bishops, cardinals and priests within, and they were the ones who wrote the new order for the church... together with the freemasons who already had people inside.

-The third head of the beast is the **"Abortionists"**, who have killed millions of human beings at the beginning of their defenseless lives. The life that was created by God for his glory and love of humanity is thrown away without the least compassion by the followers of Satan. It is necessary to make it known that for those who incur abortion there is also an ipso facto excommunication for murdering their own children.

-The fourth head is **"Homosexuality"** in all its forms and names, lesbianism, LGBT groups, feminists, animalists, all these groups feel enormous hatred towards God, his Church, commandments and traditions.

-The fifth head, the **"Satanists and False Religions"**. Judge them how they have done so much damage to the Church of the Lord through divisions, confusions, hatred and slander.

-The sixth head: **"Islam"**. This religion is the antithesis of Christianity, since its creation by Muhammad in 622, they wanted to conquer the whole world and establish their religion as the only truth, thanks to the Catholics who faced them, they did not succeed in establishing themselves in Europe; however, what they could not do with arms, they are about to achieve it with the massive immigration of millions of Muslims who are now living in Europe and the entire Christian western world.

-The seventh head, is the same **"Antichrist"**, who will appear as a great charismatic leader and good for the eyes of the world.

Then we have the 10 horns that are presidents of the nations that make laws to destroy and enslave the human being with their ideologies that impose them under penalty of imprisonment for the moment, then they will also apply death sentences, if they are left.

As we have already explained before in another paragraph, the three horns that were removed will be three presidents of three nations who will give them a coup, for not agreeing with the beast and the dragon.

Conclusion on the title of this article, there is not only Freemasonry within the Church but the entire beast, with all its hatreds and mistakes.

THE THREE DAYS OF DARKNESS.

We have thought it convenient to address the theme of the three days of darkness, because many are the seers who talk about this phenomenon that will supposedly occur when this corrupt life system is destroyed. When will it happen? nobody knows, they just say that there will be a telluric movement so violent that it will transform the earth by moving it 23 grades to later returning it to its normal position. Then there will come absolute and total darkness that will cover the entire earth. In those days every evil spirit will go loose doing evil and killing all souls who did not want to hear the Word of God and those who did not want to repent. As they say the Blessed Virgin also prevents:

In order for you to prepare and remain alive, as my children, I will give you these signs:

"*The night will be very cold, strong winds will blow, there will be anguish, and in a short time the earthquake will begin, the earth will tremble. In the house close doors and windows and do not talk to anyone who is not in your house. Do not look out, do not be curious, because this is the wrath of the Lord. Light your blessed candles, since there will be no light for three days. Kneel down and ask God for forgiveness. Do not go outside and do not let anyone strange enter your home. Only the good will not be in the power of evil and will survive the catastrophe*".

The main seers who have predicted this phenomenon are: -Ana Maria Taigi godly woman who lived from 1769 to 1837. She predicted many historical events of his time. –Saint Gaspar of Buffalo (1786-1836), Founder of the "Missionaries of the Most Precious Blood." He announced: "*He who survives after three days of darkness and horror will also be seen as alone on earth, because in fact the world will be covered with corpses, nothing similar has been seen since the flood, with great slaughter also of priests*". – Sister Mary of Jesus (1878) Carmelite religious, founder of the Bethlehem Monastery. She announced: "*For three days of darkness, people delivered to their depraved roads will perish, so that only a quarter of humanity will survive.*" - The Venerable Father Bernardo

Mary Claus (1849), religious of the order of the Minima. - Sister. Mary Adalfune (1814 Religious of Saint Augustine. –Appearance of the Virgin of La Salette, France, September 19, 1846, says among other things: *The sun will be dark. Many large cities will be swallowed by earthquakes. The entire universe will tremble in horror. All persecutors of the Church, all men abandoned to sin, will perish and the earth will seem like a desert.* "- Mary Julia Jahenny (1850-1941), French stigmatized, wrote: *"These three days of great darkness will come; Only the blessed candles will illuminate during this horrific darkness. A candle will last three days, but in the houses of the wicked they will not burn. During these three days, the demons will appear in horrible and abominable forms and will make the air resonate with dreadful blasphemies. Three-fourths of the human race will perish"*

–Venerable Isabel Canori Mora (1774-1825), Franciscan Tertiary, deceased in smell of holiness in one of his visions, she saw the wretched that every day with more pride and carelessness, they trample the holy religion and the divine law. They use the words of the Holy Scripture and the Gospel, corrupting their true meaning to support their perverse intentions and twisted principles. (Given this, how not to think of certain "theologians and theologies" and very fashionable sects within a "popular church", who pervert the divine words in a political-social or fanatic-religious sense and preach that Christ has come to liberate to the poor from the oppression of the rich, forgetting that He said: ***"My kingdom is not of this world"*** - Sister Catalina Emmerich (1774-1824) This famous German stigmatized received the wounds of the Lord's passion. She says: "*Fifty or sixty years before 2000, Satan will be unleashed for some time. There will be violent fighting with the heavenly militias under the command of St. Michael the Archangel...*" (This can easily be seen by seeing evil as it progresses and has been imposed on all institutions and ways of life of today's society).

We could continue to enumerate many other seers even contemporary, but for sample it is enough. Rather, I transcribe the words of the priest who wrote this book: ***"Heaven Warns Us Very Next Three Days of Darkness"*** and from which I have drawn this data, and says: "I am a Catholic priest and I just spent a few weeks of great inner anguish. Talk or shut up? if I speak, many will make fun of me ... if I keep quiet, my conscience will shout at me Coward!

And the Word of God will remorse me:

"When I tell the wicked - you are going to die - and you do not admonish him, if you do not speak to prevent the wicked from abandoning their misconduct, I will ask your blood for accounts" (Ezekiel 3, 18).

Better to look good with God than with men ... Due to a series of privileged circumstances, I had access to virtually unknown documents in our environment; prophecies from the most varied times, from very distant countries and languages and from people who are absolutely unknown to each other. Now, the really amazing and inexplicable thing is the UNANIMITY and the INSISTENCE with which all these saints privileged souls and ordinary people have received at this time **"WARNINGS FROM HEAVEN"** indicating that in a very short time, three quarters of humanity will perish for three days of darkness.

I know this seems like the biggest nonsense ever heard. It seemed absurd and crazy to me too. Totally incompatible with goodness and divine mercy. But reading, meditating, reflecting, I convinced myself. So it should be and so it will be. It is not possible that so many people of courage in the eyes of God, authentic stigmatized, canonized saints, founders of religious orders, mystics, apparitions of Mary, all approved by the Church, are so unanimously mistaken. It would be even greater nonsense not to believe this. I had to surrender to this evidence. God will punish the world very soon in such a terrible way as it has not been since the flood, nor will there ever be. And, if so, I have to warn my brothers and shout at them this terrible reality.

Believe or not believe these terrible prophecies? Each one must take them in the context in which they are presented and analyze them with discernment. I want to finish with these two tips. The first is from St. Paul: *"Do not despise the prophecies. Examine everything and keep the good"* - The second is from Saint Peter Canisio: *"There is less danger of believing and receiving what, with some probability, people of faith refer to us and who serve the building of others, who reject everything with spirit reckless and contempt"-*, as pitifully many and not few priests do. The world has always mocked the prophecies, until they are fulfilled. Then the strongest scoffers are the first to fall, crying on their knees, if they repent. This time will not be different.

Now, where do these three days of darkness fit into the chronological events of the end times? It is very possible that it is when all the nations of the earth have met with their armies against the Son of God, who is in the Celestial Jerusalem in the last battle of Armageddon. According to the prophet Joel, on the theme of: ***"The Last Combat and Salvation"*** in Chapter 4, verse 15, it says:

"The sun and the moon darkened and the stars withdrew their radiance" later also says: ***"The sun will be changed in darkness and the moon in blood, when the day of Yahweh approaches, a great and terrible day. And, all who call on the name of Yahweh will be saved..."*** (Joel 3, 4-5)

Days of darkness and shadows, day of clouds and thick fog! (Joel 2, 2).

Finally, we are now living in a time of darkness, never before has there been such ignorance and stupidity scattered throughout the world, with so many evildoers and evil conformers of Satan's hosts spreading their mistakes as if they were true and forcing them with force. laws that criminalize those who do good and glorify evil and error.

IS THERE A TRUE AND FAITHFUL CHURCH OF CHRIST?

Of course there has to be a true and faithful Church of Christ, otherwise Jesus would have failed. If this Church did not exist, then we would be talking about the fact that the power and wisdom of the Holy Spirit stopped influencing the people of God (Church). And it is not so, for some reason Jesus said:

"And the powers of hell will not prevail against it" (Matthew 16, 18)

That means that there is a church that is alive and working as Jesus commissioned.

It is not my intention to hurt the susceptibility of the separated brothers of the Catholic Church, but I think it is necessary that this very embarrassing issue is also discussed, because it also falls on our consciences if we do not, despite all the arguments they may have in against her, (The Church) I believe that many will reconsider and return to the Mother where they came from.

Although it is not the best time to return to it, because of the crisis unleashed within it by Satan; It is good to remember the words of Christ when he said:

"He who endures to the end will be saved." (Mt. 24, 13)

"False prophets and false Messiahs will rise and will make signs and wonders to mislead, if possible even the elect, but be on notice, I have told you all these things beforehand so that you will be prepared" (Mark 12,22)

Once in North America, a cosmopolitan country, being gathered at the time of rest in a working center where there were workers of different nationalities, touching on the subject of religions, an Iranian worker of Muslim religion made the following comment: You the Christians only live fighting, arguing, criticizing and dividing, while with us such a phenomenon does not happen, to which the other workers of different religions reaffirmed that this was true; they did not experience such divisions as occurs with Christians who have countless churches, creeds and sects. At present it exceeds the incredible amount of thirty-three thousand sects that are called Christian throughout the world and each of them claims to be the true.

Thinking about such comments, the Christian religion is the only one that since its origin lived under innumerable attacks, persecutions, schisms and divisions; some were overshadowed and others charged enhancement. Iranian words were very right, especially the last one: "dividing." This word to divide has enough meanings if we analyze what a warrior or strategist would do if he has to fight a numerous and powerful enemy, the first thing would be to create confusion and then try to divide, so the combat is easier and more successful. This is precisely what the enemy of Christ has been doing; confusing Christians, using the fallen nature of man, instigating greed, pride, lust, material desires, etc. Why don't followers of other non-Christian religions experience as many divisions and disputes as Christians? Easy to see this situation. If we take into account, the words of Jesus:

"Every kingdom divided against itself will be devastated, and house to house will fall. If Satan were divided against himself. How would his kingdom be maintained? (Luke 11.17)

Well, why will he divide or attack the other religions if they are already part of his legions? On the contrary they are instruments to expand error and falsehood throughout the world.

Satan attacks in the same ranks of Christianity, from the beginning of the Church; we know all the disorders that were in the Church, starting with heresies, struggles for power, contradictions, meddling in politics, promiscuity and immorality, the error and fanaticism that led to schisms, so-called holy wars, to the Inquisition; inciting hatred among those who call themselves Christians. Situation that still persists today in some places like Northern Ireland where Catholics and Anglicans hate each other to death. How can anyone say that he is a Christian and hate his brothers? If they are in breach of Jesus' main mandate that he repeatedly recommended:

"And now I leave a new commandment: Love one another as I have loved you, if you really love each other, you will know that you are my disciples." (John 13.34)

Then he also tells us:

"Brothers do not criticize each other. He who speaks against a brother misjudges him, speaks against the law or judges against it. And if you judge the law, you no longer comply with it, but you become superior to it. But one only made the law and at the same time can judge. He who is able to save or condemn, but who are you to judge your neighbor?" (James 4.11-12)

At the moment the antagonism and rivalry between the churches and sects that call themselves Christian, remains a serious problem, because it causes discord and resentment among Christians, which should be treated as brothers. I do not believe that any religious sect is the only and true one where their parishioners are guaranteed their salvation, as their leaders try to imply. Salvation is not found in the sect or church to which people belongs, but in the **faith and behavior of each individual,** because in the end there will be many saints who in life attended different churches, whether Protestant, Orthodox or Catholic. But, there are sects that think they are the only ones privileged with the truth and that have the entrance pass to the kingdom of heaven; but these poor people, only hurt Christianity, arouse a feeling of pity and sorrow, because they are not following Christ as they say, but rather to the enemy of God.

Instead of teaching to practice what the Master said, of still loving enemies, they teach to hate their own brothers, simply because they do not belong to their sect. Sadly I have seen how some Protestant sects have fallen so low and dirty to instigate a deep hatred against the Pope and the Catholic Church, they call him the Antichrist, the demon in person, prostitute of the Apocalypse, the great Babylon, etc. and not happy with this they also invent a number of ridiculous lies, such as; that the Pope is the head of the CIA. That the Pope controls the banks around the world, that the Pope controls politics and the US rulers. and other countries of the world, that the Pope has deals and agreements with important Jewish organizations to control the world, that the Pope owns a contraceptive factory. Before all these manifestations of hatred and hostility against the Catholic Church and its spiritual leader, I wondered:

Why is the Catholic Church the most besieged, hated and attacked? No one attacks Muslims, or Buddhists, or Hinduists, or Mormons or other pseudo-Christian denominations. No one attacks Anglicans, or Baptists, or Episcopalians, or Lutherans. Why this inexplicable hatred against the Blessed Virgin Mary, against the Pope and the Catholic Church? Who is behind this hatred, isn't it that this is the faithful Church of Christ? And, that is why this desire to discredit her, however it is? - Of course it is! The Catholic Church, with all its deficiencies that it may have (because it is carried by men), is the only and true Church left by Jesus; hence the hatred and systematic attack on her, by Satan through his henchmen disguised as Christian sects, intellectuals, Gnostics, politicians, and now, with the so called collectives of lesbians, homosexuals, LGBT, feminists, animalists, etc.

We know very well that hate and violence are low, dark and negative passions that come from the devil; so ... Isn't it the same Satan who speaks through these false shepherds? It is very rare that many of these sects are stubborn and angry with so much hatred, knowing that the others left the Catholic Church and that despite all its defects and errors it may have, it is the most faithful guardian of the teaching of the Master Jesus Christ. Isn't it the Catholic Church that opposes the criminal practice of abortion? To the pagan custom of divorce, to aberrant homosexuality and to all kinds of filthy sorceries and immoralities?

There is no doubt that these stubborn attacks on the Catholic Church come from the enemy of God, because it is the true Church of God. Therefore, even Marxism-Leninism of the Union of Soviet Socialist Republics, (also a satanic force disguised as social policy), seeing that this was a spiritual strength and the main intellectual impediment to spreading its erroneous communist doctrines, launched one of the most devastating attacks against her. He infiltrated into the Church hundreds of agents trained by the KGB throughout the world, who were ordered like Catholic priests. A few years later, within the Church, doctrines of demons disguised as humanitarian, charitable and socialist ideologies came out. Among them and the most widespread throughout the world, the famous Theology of Liberation, which is nothing other than Marxism disguised as Christianity. Soon the Church was wobbly, within it not only were the infiltrators, but now they already had hundreds of adherents who had taken out of the new seminars where they took the reins, some of these agents reaching important hierarchical positions as bishops and I imagine that even cardinals must be there. The new priests who took a new pseudo-Christian approach did not hesitate to be an active part of politics and even participated in subversive, guerrilla and terrorist activities.

The crisis of the Catholic Church is serious, the devil has hurt her on the side of politics by dragging thousands with the story of: ***"The Option for the Poor"***, and as if this were not enough, he has also wallowed them with sexual passions of all forms; forces inherent in man and that Satan knows how to take advantage of it. As a consequence, there is a very extensive cooling within it, worsened by the immoral and dishonest behavior of many of these priests who were educated with the Marxist approach.

"And because evil has multiplied, the love of many will cool down. But he who endures to the end will be saved". (Mt. 24, 12)

In 1914, this attack was put on notice by the Virgin Mary herself, when three shepherds appeared in Fatima and warned about all these mistakes that Russia was going to spread and therefore recommended that the Catholic world should approach God wholeheartedly, that prayer be practiced more, that Russia be devoted to her Sacred Heart. However, it seems that her recommendations were not given more credit and that is why everything we are seeing now happened.

In these times of the end, the Church will continue to suffer a great emptiness and cooling due to the lack of faith and love for Christ and others on the part of its leaders, clergy and parishioners.

"But the Spirit clearly says that in the end times, some will apostatize from the faith, listening to deceiving spirits and doctrines of demons; for the hypocrisy of liars who have conscience cauterized". (1 Tim. 4, 1)

The attack that directs the devil in these times is frontal and fierce, especially against the Church, because he knows well that knocking down a priest or a nun, he loses thousands of souls scandalized by the behavior of these poor who have fallen out of favor.

"For we have no fight against blood and flesh, but against principalities, against powers, against the rulers of darkness of this age, against spiritual hosts of evil in the heavenly regions" (Eph. 6, 12)

However, we must not lose hope, Jesus himself told us:

"The gates of hell will not prevail over my Church"

(Matthew. 16, 18)

And that has happened throughout the two thousand years that the Catholic Church is in operation, there have been many crises that have happened but all of them have come out well fought and that is another sign to realize that she is the true Church, many have been the times that it has been threatened with schisms, struggles and internal intrigues, for the power, fanaticism and infiltrations of unscrupulous and evil people who did not hesitate to infiltrate as cures to get their illicit means. Now it is clear that all these attacks have been devised and put into practice by that evil power of the enemy of God with the sole purpose of destroying it.

But, God never left her helpless, if on the one hand the demon infiltrated corruption; on the other hand, God raised, innumerable good men to repair the destroyed and continue with his work; This is how the so-called saints appeared, such as: Ignatius Bishop, Augustine of Hippo, Gregory the great, Elizabeth of Hungary, Francis of Assisi, Clare of Assisi, Anthony of Padua, Teresa of Avila, John Bosco, and the hundreds and hundreds of saints, true friends of Jesus, listed in the Catholic Holy.

Likewise, as I had mentioned before; the Virgin Mary, in her apparition warned that the Pope and the Church will have to suffer a lot, but that in the end, their Sacred Heart will triumph.

This topic, of the Church of Christ, I am sure that it has not been liked by many readers, because it is very possible that they do not commune with the Catholic Church for different reasons, either because they belong to another denomination or because of the scandal and bad behavior of some of its members, (which we have already explained the main reason); but it is not me who perhaps by fanaticism tries to defend it in detriment of the other denominations, but it is Jesus himself who gives us the clue to know what the true Church is.

On one occasion when Jesus was telling them to be careful because near the end there will come many who will impersonate prophets and even the Messiah himself to confuse and divide the parishioners, the apostles ask him:

"Lord, how will we know who is true and who is false?" Jesus answers: "By their fruits you will know them". (Matthew 12.34)

And He also tells them:

"By this you will know that you are my disciples, that you love one another" (John 3,11)

With such responses, it is easy to analyze and see who the sects that have appeared lately are. Could it be that those that appeared for 500 years and that continue to multiply in abundance are the real ones as they cry out loud? If so ... So, what happened to the Church that Jesus Christ himself left? Did Jesus change his mind and said: I am founding other churches because I didn't like the first one I left? Let's see ... just a blind man, like those who don't want to see or realize they would hold these arguments without any foundation!

Finally, the strongest test to know if a church is true or false, are its fruits, and the main fruit is the love of neighbor and charity that the Christian demonstrates in his personal life or the Church as an institution. It is not enough to say to someone: I love you and then do nothing to prove it, as many do by preaching the Word of God to the sick or the hungry, telling them: God loves you, become! And they offer no relief for your needs. Imagine a poor homeless person dying of hunger or a poor patient dying of pain and being told that God loves him, without giving him bread to satisfy his hunger or medicine to relieve his pain, and worse, some scoundrels still tell them: give me your tithes and the Lord will give you one hundred fold. They are seeing that they do not have and yet they insist on taking away what they do not have ... Do you think they could be Christians? And, it is coincidentally where it comes to confirm that: ***"By their fruits you will know them."***

Thank God, Catholics have many examples of Christian charity and holiness, the most recent and contemporary being that of Mother Teresa of Calcutta, who although she has passed away, her work of charity and holiness has spread throughout many countries of the world for good of many children, poor and sick of all kinds.

Now, what Church apart from the Catholic, has been concerned with the welfare of the poorest, the dispossessed, the sick, the prisoners, the uneducated, the orphans and many other problems that Do they affect society in general?

How many hospitals, how many nursing homes, how many schools, colleges and technology, how many orphanages, how many homes for youth and how many dining rooms for the destitute, do the other churches claim to be the real ones?

I once said that, to a brother of the so-called Jehovah's Witnesses, ah ...! He told me: is that our apostolate is limited to carrying the Word of God, so that everyone knows it, that Jesus commanded and that we are doing, but what this man did not realize is that Jesus never preached without doing good first. Everywhere he went, he healed the sick, raised the dead, fed the people, forgave sins, taught to pray and did endless miracles. This man also forgot the main Rule of Christianity that of ***"Loving one another as if we were brothers".*** Preaching is easy, anyone with a regular knowledge of the Holy Scriptures comes out and preaches. The difficult thing is: Clean the filthy, purulent bodies of incurable sores and pestilent excrements of nursing home elders and sick people in hospitals served by Catholic nuns or brothers! Attend to the crazy, mentally ill, drug addicts and AIDS sufferers! In other words, the brothers who the world considers as the scum of society. That is Christianity! If in your Church, there is no such love and dedication to the poorest, then rest assured that you are not in the right church.

Another sister separated from one of the thousands of sects there, told me: It is that we have no money like Catholics to put hospitals, nursing homes or dining rooms. Mother Teresa of Calcutta began her work with zero cents in her account; she only carried a great love for Jesus Christ and her brothers in need. And just as she almost all the works that exist in the world have been born with zero cents in the accounts of these true fruits of the Holy Spirit

"Not everyone who says Lord, Lord, will enter the kingdom of heaven, but he who does the will of my Father" *(Matthew 7, 21)*

By last:

"The children of God and those of the devil are recognized in this: He who does not do justice is not from God, and neither does he who does not love his brother." (1 John 3.10)

If you are not yet convinced of this, I suggest you read the Gospel of Matthew 31, referring to the Last Judgment and you will see based on what behavior Jesus will judge.

CHAPTER VII.

THE GLORIOUS KINGDOM OF GOD ON EARTH.

THE KINGDOM OF GOD ON EARTH

Many of the Old Testament prophets speak about this time of grace that will reign on earth, it will be a time of happiness, love and universal peace; caused by the great imperative of then: **"LOVE"**, as opposed to current selfishness. Isaiah 11.9. (F.S. Maria Precursor ...)

Zephaniah says that in this era of restoration and the beginning of a new era:

"All the people of all the remaining nations will form something like a single heart and a single tongue that will invoke and glorify the Lord in unison and will serve and love him with one heart and one soul". (Zephaniah 3, 9)

This is repeated later when he says:

"That those who remain after the great tribulation will no longer embrace evil or act deceptively, but will serve the Lord all at one"

Isaiah 9,6-7 states that: *"Jesus will be the Prince of Peace, the" Pacific. " It will grow and multiply its empire and peace will be unalterable and will have no end"*

Hosea 2.18. He says: *"I will agree with them on a unique alliance, banishing the bow, the sword and all war instruments from the earth, for I will abolish the war of the earth, so that everyone can sleep peacefully and without any fright of any kind".*

Isaiah 11,6-9 and 65-25, says: *"The wolf will live with the lamb, and the leopard will lie with the kid and they will eat the calf together with the lion, and a little boy will graze them ... there will be no more damage or destruction in all my holy mountain because the earth will be filled with the knowledge of Yahweh"*

Psalm 45,9-10 says: *"Come all and see why the Lord filled the earth with wonders, forever fighting away from all its confines and enmities, breaking spears and throwing weapons, shields and rounds into fire".*

We could continue mentioning many more texts of the prophets, but I think that they are enough for the show. All these wonders will happen when Jesus is here again.

When Christ returns and reigns on earth there will be the true peace and happiness that everyone craves, justice and equity will reign, there will be neither poor nor rich, there will be no difference in social classes; neither will there be those of blue blood or commoners; or whites and Indians, blacks or Chinese; For all these things were invented by the enemy to divide and annihilate man.

This empire of the Messiah-God and consequently of the Church will be Catholic, that is to say universal, comprising all peoples and nations until the last ends of the world. The psalmist says:

"I will give you as an inheritance to the nations and peoples and your possessions will encompass the very ends of the earth". Later he adds: ***"All the ends of the earth will return to the Lord and all the peoples and tribes of the earth will bow down before their observance. Gentility". (Ps. 21, 28) -***

Psalm 66, 4, 6, 8 says:

"May the people praise you, Lord, all; May all nations bless you, and so the earth will finally give its fruit, that long-awaited fruit"

Let us not forget, to understand the significance of the promise, that all these announcements and texts taken from the sacred books are words of God.

LAST CONCLUSIONS

The Lord, God the Father, has wanted to keep secret the moment when the second coming of Jesus Christ will take place; However, it gives us the necessary signals and reveals the circumstances that allow us to know that this great event is closer than we think:

"From the fig tree learn the parable. When its branches become tender and the leaves sprout, you know that summer is near. So, you too, when you see all these things know that it is near the doors. Because heaven and earth will pass but my words will not pass". (Matthew 24.32)

From these circumstances and signs we conclude that:

1.-We are in full compliance with the last moments of this wicked system. And as it is popularly said we are just around the corner. (Mat. 24, 32)

2.-Israel after 2000 years of dispersion, miraculously was reintegrated again as a nation. (Amos 9, 11)

3.-The Gospel is being preached in every corner of the world. ***"And this Gospel, of the Kingdom throughout the world, will be preached for a witness to all nations; and then the end will come" (Mt. 24, 14)***

4.-The false messiahs, prophets and teachers, swarm everywhere. If you have not noticed are the countless sects that are apparently good.

"For many will come in my name, saying I am the Christ and many will deceive" (Mt. 24, 5).

"And many false prophets will rise and deceive many" (Mt. 24,11).

5.-The Church of God is constantly attacked and accused of being false, to the confusion of the weak in faith.

"But whoever is constant until the end will be saved" (Mt 24:13).

6.-The apostasy of the nations, is a fact that is also in full compliance, given the form imposed on human thought, moral and religious values have been neglected, today's humanity lives completely away from the laws of God, and behaves worse than animals.

"But when the Son of man comes, will he still find faith on earth?".   (Lk. 18, 8)

But, the worst of the apostasies predicted even by the Virgin Mary herself, is already within the true Church, the Catholic Church, which is in full compliance with the development of the so prestigious (in the eyes of the world) and mentioned Theology of Liberation, which since the sixties has been causing many confusions and errors, within clergy and religious, completely changing the Gospel of Christ for that of Marx, (spokesman and son of Satan).

"When you see that these things take place, widen your breasts and lift your heads, for your full and perfect redemption is coming" (Lk. 21, 58)

We only need to wait for:

A.- The public appearance of the Antichrist, which must already be somewhere as a harmless political or religious man or maybe like a good philanthropic fellow. "He will come with the help of Satan; It will come with a lot of power and with false signs and miracles. (2 Thess. 1,12)

B.-The apparent peace and material progress in the world, under the globalized government of the Antichrist. (Rev 17:17)

C.-The destruction to treason of the Great Babylon by the Antichrist. (Isaiah 21, 1-5; Rev. 17. 18.).

D.-The abomination of desolation and the suspension of Perpetual Sacrifice. That is the Holy Eucharist. (Rev. 13, 7). And, the persecution of the Catholic Church.

E.-The coming of the two witnesses of heaven, Elijah and Moses. (Rev. 11,3-13).

F.-The almost total annihilation of Israel, by the Antichrist and the Arabs. (Ezekiel 38, 12)

G.-The great sign of the Son of man in heaven. (Mat. 24,30; Is.11,10-12)

H.-The conversion of the Jews to Christianity, acknowledging their mistake. (Rom. 11, 23-27).

I.-The return of Christ to earth. (Mat. 24, 30)

J.-The gathering of nations under the leadership of the Antichrist to fight against Christ. (Rev. 16, 13)

K.-The Battle of Armageddon. (Rev. 16, 13)

L.- Definitive defeat of Satan, destruction of the wicked and imprisonment of the devil with all his minions. (Rev. 20, 7-10).

M.-Fair Trial. (Mt. 7.1-5; Rom. 2, 1; 1 Cor. 4, 5)

N.-Land restoration. (Isaiah 11.6)

O.-Victory of God and establishment of his glorious kingdom on earth. (Mt. 25, 31; Lc. 1.32).

RECOMMENDATIONS: WHAT TO DO WHILE THING ARE FULFILLED?

There are many people who, after reading this book, will change course and try to amend themselves to be prepared to receive the Lord; but there are others who don't really know what to do; Our recommendation is:

DO NOT BE AFRAID, READ THE SINGS

Within this world, invaded by the darkness of evil, full of poverty by the prevailing selfishness, little illuminated by the reigning apostasy, sore by terrorism and conflict. The Gospel, the good news of salvation, must be transmitted. Who better to do this, than those who carry the love of Christ within themselves, Christian Catholics of all nations, cultures and languages. The Mystical Body of Christ, the Church. Reading the signs of the times is a constant and urgent need in our fast and changing world.

It is within this Church that God Inspires and spills the power of the Holy Spirit. And it is in this inner solitude and silence, where we can enhance our awareness of what God wants for his Church, and how he should behave at the end of time.

That Holy Spirit is a soft, gentle and tiny voice, a gentle breeze, whispering in our joy or screaming in our pain.

The Holy Spirit tells us, don't be afraid!

With this advice of the Holy Spirit, we dare to give the following recommendations:

1.-Renew your baptismal promises, your faith in Jesus; He is your Redeemer and Lord, that is: Become, change your life, I know it costs, but think: it is better to enter the kingdom of heaven one-eyed or lame or lame as Jesus said, than to enter hell completely.

"Do therefore fruits worthy of repentance" (Mt. 3, 8)

2.-Work to spread the Gospel and the kingdom of Christ. Do not be content to be a mere spectator, remember that Christ said:

"Go therefore to the nations of all nations and make them my disciples". (Mt. 28, 19)

But do it according to the guidelines of the Holy Mother Catholic, Apostolic and Roman Church.

3.-Frequent the sacraments, which are a source of repentance and life in Christ Jesus.

"For it is not the hearers of the law that are righteous before God, but the doers of the law will be justified" (Ro.2, 13)

4.-Do not forget to give your time and your assets to the poor. Remember that we will be judged by the love we have shown to our neighbor.

"Little children, let us not love in word or language, but indeed and in truth". (1 John 3:18)

It will not help you to accumulate so much wealth, because you will not take it and worse, they are riches that are corroded or you can lose them from one moment to another, Treasure goods in heaven! Do not be hard on the poor who need your help or the faithful Church that needs for their missionary works.

5.-Do not believe or go after any new gospel, church, or ideology; however good you see them they seem to be. Be wary of everyone. Remember what Paul warned:

"Thus we came or an angel from heaven with another gospel, do not believe it, be cursed!" (Galatians 1, 8)

6.-Change your character, banish the old man, be better and better, do not let yourself be enveloped by the attractions of the world; so you will be awake and in expectation of the next coming of the Lord.

"Make die, for the earthly in you; fornication, impurity, disorderly passions, bad desires and greed that is idolatry. Things for which the wrath of God comes upon the children of disobedience". (Col. 3, 5-6).

This means that you must stop frequenting any place that endangers your spiritual and physical life, that is: No discos, no dances, no bean feast, no drunkenness, no modern music, no immoral movies, no bad television, no videos; because with all these things you jeopardize your salvation and what is more important, your eternal life for a little time of pleasure? Remember again:

"We are in the world; but we are not of the world"

7.-Exercise in prayer, and in penance, that this pleases God and helps you not to fall into evil.

"Persevere in prayer, watching over it with thanksgiving" (Col. 4, 2).

8.-Trust and give yourself totally to God, to Christ, to the Blessed Virgin your mother, **pray the Holy Rosary every day**, it is a true weapon against the enemy. And make your life a continuous Yes to the Divine Will.

9.-Seek to congregate in some group of your parish where you can participate in your Christian life.

10.-Pass the message of salvation and collaborate with Jesus so that others may also be saved. It bears fruit so that you may be saved and not be rejected.

11.-Start evangelizing around your house, talk to your family first, then your neighbors, friends and other people with whom you get to interact. Pass this book to others so that they also reconsider and be saved.

12.-Never stop talking about God and sound doctrine, once you do not can be the difference between life and death for someone. But don't just talk, act as a child of God, remember that the example convinces more than a thousand words.

May God enlighten, bless and defend you in these last events of planet earth. And may God allow us to be counted among his elect.

And, do not be afraid, the Lord is with us.

Amen.

Bibliography

1.-Arens, Eduardo - "Bible and End of the World". 1998 Pauline Editions. Lima Peru.

2.-Bartra Martial - "With the Bible in Hand". Christian Projection Center. 1993 Lima, Peru

3.- "Latin American Bible." Artes Gráficas Carasa S. A. 1994, Madrid Spain.

4.-Bloomfield, Arthur. "Armageddon." Bantam Books. 1980. N.Y. USES.

5.-Bonato, Julio. "Course of Religion and Moral". Editorial Liturgia Española S.A. 1962, Barcelona, Spain.

6.-Bullock, William H. Bishop, "A Message of Faith" Some Words on Pentecost. Internet message. 2002

7.-Ediciones Nueva Lente S.A. "Great Prophecies" Nº 15 - 1986 Madrid, Spain.

8.-Gutierrez, Gustavo. "Liberation Theology, Perspectives." Alfa Publishing. Lima Peru.

9.-Hal, Lindsey & C.C. Carlson "Satan is Alive and Well on Planet Earth." Bantam Books, 1980. N.Y. USES.

10.-Mendel, P. Arthur. "Essential Works of Marxim." Bantam Books- 1986. N.Y. USES.

11.-Mesters, Carlos. "The Apocalypse, The Hope of a People." Lima Peru.

12.-Rumble & Carty Fathers. "The seven Day Adventists" Radio Replan Press society 1980. St. Paul, Minn. USES.

13.-Sánchez, Francisco. "Mary Precursor of Christ in her Second Coming to Earth." Librería Studium S.A. 1970, Lima Peru.

14.-Sánchez, Cobaleda José. S.J. "The Catholic Dogma." Editorial Salt Terrea. 1964 - Santander, Spain.

15.-Tarcisio Bertone Archbishop- "The Message of Fatima" (Secretary of the Congregation for the Doctrine of the Faith). Vatican 2000.

16.-Whalem, William J. "Jehovah's Witnesses." Claretian Publications. 1979 - N.Y. USES.

17.-Whalem, William J. "Armageddon Around the Corner". A Report on Jehovah's Witnesses. Claretian Publications. 1952 - N. Y. USA.

18.-Vision Magazine. Vol 64 No. 1 "The Nuclear Winter" 1985 - N.Y. USES.

www.ingramcontent.com/pod-product-compliance
Lightning Source LLC
Chambersburg PA
CBHW070000180726
48002CB00019B/1773